TIME TRIAL

A MOUNTAIN TIME MYSTERY

Library of Congress Catalog Card Number: 99-61617

ISBN: 1-890437-27-1

Western Reflections, Inc.
P.O. Box 710, Ouray, Colorado 81427

Book Jacket design by SJS Design (Susan Smilanic)

TIME TRIAL

A MOUNTAIN TIME MYSTERY

R. E. DEROUIN

WESTERN
REFLECTIONS, INC.

To Lois, who has been there, for years and years.

INTRODUCTION

Parkside, Pennsylvania police detective, David Dean, recuperating from a gun shot wound, is offered temporary residence in beautiful Ouray County, Colorado. But Dean's peaceful convalescence is abruptly disturbed when five eccentric house guests elbow their way into his tranquillity. A two-year-old homicide seems somehow tied to their mysterious interest in the San Juan Mountains' history from the last century. It becomes Dean's reluctant chore, together with his feisty stepfather Fred O'Connor, to prove that in spite of compelling evidence to the contrary, *history didn't happen*!

CHAPTER 1

Day fifty-two of David Dean's sabbatical from reality had dawned with a similar look to most of the fifty-one days preceding it. It was a Colorado picture-postcard kind of day, with puffy white clouds and an autumn sky so clear you could almost reach out and touch the mountain tops that circled like a mother's arms. Van Cliburn was doing his Chopin magic on the stereo. It was quite a change from the jazz Dean had spent so many years listening to, but the music came with the house and he was developing a taste. The restful sound and the pine-scented air was enough to put you to sleep. Not a care in the world, or so it should have been.

Dean put aside his book, closed his eyes, and with a push from his size tens against the railing of the deck, started his rocker in motion. Late September on the western slope of the Rocky Mountains was as close to heaven as he ever expected to get and he relished every minute of his time here alone. But now, those minutes were rapidly drawing to a close. Finally, with a deep sigh, he pulled his six-foot frame to standing position, reluctantly turned his back on the scene before him and entered the house.

When Marian Anderson, the wife of his lieutenant on the Parkside, Pennsylvania police department, had mentioned a need for a house sitter for a Colorado home she had recently inherited, Dean had given it about ten seconds thought before jumping up and volunteering. Just four days after a vacation in Colorado, a low-life had shot him, badly enough for a three-week hospital stay with a prescribed eight weeks of R and R. He couldn't think of a nicer place to recuperate. And there was a second incentive. He had promised to give Cynthia Byrne, a lady with whom he was very serious, the year she had requested to clear her head after the recent loss of her husband. But a snub-nosed thirty-eight in the hands of a panic-stricken kid followed by the hospital bit had brought Cynthia Byrne and David Dean back to close daily contact. So, much as he wanted to continue with her Florence Nightingale ministrations, he bit the bullet and went west, leaving his stepfather/roommate Fred O'Connor back in Pennsylvania, baby-sitting Mrs. Lincoln, their resident cat, and allowing Cynthia Byrne the balance of her year of reflection.

Weeks earlier Dean had ceased wearing a watch or even paying attention to the time. However, the mantle clock remained in place, pointing out that he had less than an hour to make it to the Montrose airport to meet the damn plane.

The phone call had come two days earlier. Marian Anderson was apologetic to her house-sitter about intruding on his privacy but a family friend had begged her to use the place, just for a night or two. No, he wouldn't have to move out; just give up a spare bedroom for a couple of days. Normally, Dean wouldn't have minded, but he knew the friend. It was Neil Archer. Kiss solitude bye-bye and welcome an overgrown playboy college professor who is best served in extremely small doses, like a couple of lines annually on a Christmas card.

Dean had known Archer for twenty-five years, since they were both know-it-all freshmen attending Spinnersville College, a state school in southeastern Pennsylvania. They were roommates and a pair of record breaking hell raisers as freshman, never missing a party – at least for the few months it took until Dean outgrew that scene. Archer was a history major, of sorts, while Dean concentrated on criminal justice with a far higher level of seriousness than his roomy. During the summer before their junior year, Dean finally gave up the financial struggle of college and dropped out. That action ended any further thoughts of an academic future and any direct contact with Archer. While David Dean sloshed through the backwaters of the world for the U.S. Army, and later, the back streets of Parkside, Pennsylvania, Neil Archer continued to chase underclass cuties and methodically plod on to one academic degree after another. He wasn't overly intelligent; he was simply too lazy to join the real world. Archer had climbed the ladder of scholastic instruction a rung at a time, under one government program or another until he, finally, settled in at Spinnersville as a professor, teaching winsome undergrads the gory deeds of their Civil War ancestors.

It wasn't that Dean didn't like Neil; he had simply grown up while his old roommate had leveled out as a twenty-year-old and stayed there.

Dean bounced his rusty Honda up the dirt drive and down the dusty road to the state highway. It had been a half-dozen years since he'd seen Archer at some social event he couldn't remember and, for the life of him, he couldn't figure out why the professor would choose to visit 2,000 miles across the country, probably with the teenage squeeze of the month. It didn't make a whole lot of sense but it was Marian Anderson's house and Dean was obliged to be sociable, much as it riled him.

8

The thirty-five mile stretch of Colorado highway from Ouray to Montrose slides down the Uncompahgre Valley from the San Juan Mountains at the south, following a river of the same name, in the general direction of Grand Junction, Colorado, and to Utah beyond. The road seems nearly level but drops over 2,000 feet as it passes scattered houses and small ranches and a newly-created reservoir that reflects the surrounding mountains and mesas like a deep blue mirror. The more spectacular view was in the rearview mirror as the land flattens to the north and west. Infrequent trips to Montrose, mostly for shopping, were always a letdown for Dean, as if reminding him his mountain retreat was temporary and soon he'd be leaving it for good. But it was an easy trip, with no towns after the crossroads hamlet of Ridgway, and after forty minutes he pulled into the parking lot of the small airport.

The modern facility provided service to and from Denver several times a day but Dean was surprised to find no flights were scheduled to arrive for the next two hours. He ran down the list of possibilities in his mind. No, he was sure he had heard the correct time and the right day. And this was the only airport that made sense. The ticket agents for both the represented airlines confirmed what the announcement board had listed, nothing due. Dean was about to give up in disgust when a little redhead behind one of the counters smiled at the sound of an approaching plane.

"Maybe that's your friends," she said.

Dean crossed to the door in time to see the wheels of a private plane touch the ground. It was a jet, a silver cigar that fairly oozed dollar signs, as it hummed its way up to the passenger gate.

"Unless Neil Archer won the lottery, this can't be it," thought Dean but a door magically appeared in the side of the plane, converted itself to a short flight of stairs, and out popped Professor Neil Archer. He had a grin the size of Alice's cat's as he shaded his eyes against the western sun and searched both left and right as if looking for a bevy of rose-tossing worshipers.

Archer looked every bit the eastern college professor, bedecked in an out-of-season sweater and tweeds that hung on his Ichabod Crane frame like clothes tossed over a chair. He clutched a small aluminum suitcase as if it contained the family jewels. As soon as Archer spotted Dean through the terminal window, he made a bee-line down the steps and in two leaps and a bound was enthusiastically pumping the hand of his reluctant host.

"Great to see you! Great to see you, pal!" He was as nervous as a kitty in a canine kennel.

"What number did you play?" asked Dean, glumly nodding toward the aircraft.

"Oh, the plane? That's my friend's."

"She must be a banker's daughter," Dean answered. "You don't buy jet airplanes on student aid."

"No, no. It's not a 'she,' it's a 'he.' Wait a sec, I'll get them." Archer turned and was out of the terminal as quickly as he'd arrived, leaving Dean repeating the pronoun 'them' with a puzzled but unhappy look on his face.

'They' began emerging from the plane, five in all, like clowns from a circus funny-car, one after the other. The group marched down the runway and into the terminal, following Archer, the Pied Piper of Academia, until the group circled Dean who awaited introductions.

"This is Dorrie Briscoe," Archer squeaked, patting the back of a pretty brunette in her thirties who held out her hand. She was the only one in the group who smiled and didn't look as if she wanted to be 2,000 miles back in Pennsylvania.

"And this is Mrs. Brown," Archer continued, indicating a dour woman, the type ads describe as full-figured, somewhere between the ages of fifty and seventy. She looked like a Victorian schoolmarm who would slap you silly the instant you stepped out of line. "I'm sorry, I don't know your first name," Archer said.

"'Mrs.' will do," she said caustically, turning away leaving Dean's hand dangling.

"I'm Henry Whitcomb," the third traveler announced impatiently, grabbing Dean's hand in a knuckle-breaker. He was silver-haired, at least six-foot-three, and moved with the confidence of a five-star general who had just kicked the butts of an entire regiment.

"And Hays Crawford," Archer continued, pointing out a pony-tailed young man in his mid-twenties, dressed like a panhandler, who stood back from the others and gave a half salute.

"See, see. What did I tell you?" Archer said to his friends as he put his arm around Dean's shoulders. "A bullet in the ass didn't even slow down my good buddy, Davey Dean! This guy's a real, one-hundred-percent hero!"

Dean cringed. "What class," he thought to himself.

"Let's get this show on the road," Whitcomb said, with the same impatience he'd displayed since they landed. "Crawford, you get the bags. And tell that stupid pilot to shut off the engine. He's wasting my fuel." Hays Crawford gave the older man the look of a surly teenager but reluctantly left to comply, giving a one-fingered salute to Whitcomb's back as he exited the terminal.

Dean took a deep breath. "Neil, we have a bit of a problem here," he said, trying to control his rising temper. "There are six people, Lord knows how much luggage, and I'm driving a Honda."

Archer began to perspire. "Is it far? A couple of us could walk..."

"It's thirty-five miles, Neil," Dean answered in a measured tone, but before Archer could answer, Mrs. Brown thrust her pointed jaw in Dean's face.

"For heaven's sake! Why didn't you make arrangements in advance? Mr. Whitcomb isn't used to..."

Archer interrupted. "I guess it's my fault. I didn't explain in detail to Marian Anderson..."

"For Gods' sake," Whitcomb burst. "Just rent a limo and let's get the hell out of here. I've got a headache that's killing me."

Crawford, who was just coming in with an armload of luggage, looked at Whitcomb with a peculiar smile. "We've got a cure for that, haven't we?" His friends responded as if they could kill him on sight but no one commented.

At Kennedy, Newark, O'Hare and other major airports, legions of little men in black uniforms hold up handwritten signs for arriving passengers announcing the waiting stretch limos. In Montrose, Colorado, the situation is considerably different. Finally, after thirty minutes of worn tempers and frenzied negotiation, they found a taxi willing to make the trip south. A mountain of luggage was strapped onto and into the two vehicles and the group finally was on their way. Archer, Whitcomb, and the ever-pleasant Mrs. Brown rode in the cab which followed Dean, Dorrie Briscoe, and Crawford, who slouched down in the back seat of the Honda, reading *Taking the Mystery Out of Wild Mushrooms*.

As they rolled through town to the open highway, Dean seethed in silence, wishing for an opportunity to beat Neil Archer into a pile of jelly. He was certain Archer hadn't told Marian Anderson the size of the crowd or she would surely have warned Dean.

Dorrie Briscoe seemed to find the entire situation amusing.

"Dr. Archer didn't tell you we were all coming, did he?" she asked.

"Dr. Archer didn't tell me a damned thing."

"Like who we are, and why we're here?" she asked questioningly, in a disarming way that made it difficult to stay pissed off.

"For starts," he answered.

"I'll bet you were expecting Dr. Archer and the bimbo-of-the-month," she said, smiling.

"I see his reputation remains intact."

Crawford piped up from the back seat, "We're just your run-of-the-mill tourists, out here in God's country, seeing how the hicks live." The others ignored him.

"I'm an American literature professor and Hays, in spite of his efforts to dispel the rumor, is a very intelligent young man who just finished grad school in electrical engineering."

"Any small wiring job you need...outlets, lamps, VCR's...I can do 'em all."

"So who are Whitcomb and Miss Personality?"

"He's a...business man. He's very private. There's nothing sinister about it...he just doesn't want everyone to know who he is or that he's out here," Dorrie answered.

"Just call him, 'Henry the First,'" quipped the backseat passenger. "First in everything he touches."

"Mrs. Brown is his...."

"Resident slave," added Crawford.

"None of which tells me why Neil hauled you all out to Colorado."

She answered in a perky fashion. "The fall semester's always a little quiet. Perhaps we could all use a couple of restful months in the mountains." Dean looked over at her with a scowl and saw her biting back a smile. She laughed; a not unpleasant sound. "No, I'm sure we won't be staying until Christmas."

"So why did you come in the first place?"

"Big mystery," said Crawford, dragging the words out in a low and sinister voice.

Dorrie Briscoe quickly became serious. "I think I'd best let Neil or Henry explain that. It's no big deal." She changed the subject. "Did you really get shot?"

"Yes."

"In the ass?" asked Crawford. Dean could see him in the rear view mirror, combing his long hair with his fingers and smiling.

"Yes," he answered. "But I wasn't running away." There was an edge to his voice, but it didn't stop Crawford from pushing the subject.

"Kind of sensitive on that point, aren't we?" he quipped.

"It can't be any fun getting shot, regardless of where it is." Dorrie said quickly. "How did it happen?"

"We were on a drug bust and someone tipped off the bad guys. All hell broke loose."

"So you're out on disability?"

"Yes. But the vacation has pretty well run the route. Maybe a couple more weeks at best."

"Then you'll be going back to Pennsylvania?"

"Unfortunately." No one spoke for a few moments until Dean felt a need to explain his feelings. "It's not that I really dislike the job. I like the detecting part. I just don't take kindly to people trying to kill me. Mixed emotions, I guess. Besides, I'm becoming attached to this part of the country. I'll miss it."

"It's so exciting," Crawford muttered sarcastically, closing his eyes and burrowing his head in the corner of the back seat. "The opera, major league sports, the night life...." Like a bratty kid looking for attention, Dean thought.

They were rolling through low hills, amber in the September season, a windshield filled with the splendor of an incredible number of mountains, each silhouetted against the gold of a setting sun. Some of the tree tips were just beginning to color and the yellow fields held neatly stacked blocks of hay, a dozen bales high and as wide as a house. The afternoon sang with a sharpness that defied description.

"I can't blame you for loving it. It's really beautiful out here."

"Maybe my emotions aren't so mixed after all. I'm just plain comfortable here. I don't miss Parkside, Pennsylvania, a hoot." She looked over at him as he continued. "It's peaceful in addition to being beautiful. The people are friendly and they don't seem to want to kill each other. It makes you feel alive, more healthy. I'm eating better and I've even lost fourteen pounds."

"Sounds like heaven," she said with a laugh.

"The only hook is that I have a life back east and I don't have an income that lets me rent jet airplanes." He sighed. "So, I guess I have to go back to work."

"Do you own your place out here?"

"No such luck. My boss's wife inherited it and she was willing for me to house sit. She's the one who agreed to let Neil and the rest of you visit. Apparently she knows Neil or his family."

"I don't suppose there's room for all six of us in the house any more than there was room for us in the car." The funny little smile was still there, as if the whole escapade was a Broadway comedy, and she was sitting back, enjoying herself, waiting for act three.

"Put Brownie in the bathtub," Crawford muttered without opening his eyes.

"I only have a stall shower," Dean answered.

"All the better!"

"Is your wife there as well?" Fishing without a license, Dean thought.

"No." He paused, considering how candid he should be. "I've never been married, but I'm seeing a woman back in Pennsylvania."

"Sounds like a strike-out, Dorrie. You may end up with me after all!" Crawford had a grin as wide as the valley before them.

She waved a hand back to swat the young man. "Don't blame him," she said to Dean, looking slightly embarrassed. "He's just a boy with a warped mind."

She waited, as if to see if Dean was going to explain further, but he changed the subject.

"About the bunking, there are three bedrooms so I suppose we can squeeze in everyone, depending on the sleeping arrangements."

"Hey, Dorrie! Here's our chance," piped up Crawford.

"I'd rather sleep in the shower, with the water running!" she answered, laughing, and then turned back to Dean. "So, what did that creep Dr. Archer do, invite himself?" She squirmed around to face him, drawing her legs up under her.

"Apparently. Marian Anderson didn't explain to me but I'm sure Neil didn't let her know any details or she would have passed them along."

"Like an ant to a picnic," she said. "I'm sorry." She sounded as if she really meant it.

"Why are you sorry?" he asked quickly. "It wasn't your fault."

"Or my picnic. I just work with the ant...or, perhaps, 'leech' is a better description. I don't know why I'm surprised. It's just like Neil Archer. How are you fixed for food?"

He shrugged. "I laid in a few burgers and some beer. Not enough for a half dozen people."

"What?" asked Crawford. "No 'Rothschild 1847' for the king?"

"We could eat out," Dean suggested but Dorrie vetoed the idea.

"I'm afraid not. Once Henry gets one of his headaches, the only thing he can do is lie down."

Crawford coughed, and Dean could see him smiling in the mirror, a secret to which he was not a party. Dorrie said nothing but Dean could tell she was peeved in a first class way.

"Henry gets rather nasty when his headaches start up," Dorrie said, almost as an apology.

"Just nastier than normal," piped up Crawford.

"If it's a medical problem, he should be able to do something about it," Dean said.

"He lost his wife and son two years ago and I don't think he's ever gotten over it." Dorrie spoke in a funeral home voice, as if the incident had just happened.

"They were murdered," Crawford said in a bitter tone, "and the cops aren't sure King Henry himself didn't blow them away."

"That's nonsense!" Dorrie said sharply. "It was horrible!" She explained to Dean. "Someone broke into the house in broad daylight and shot them both. They never caught the killers. Henry thought the sun rose and set on his son Michael and he was devastated. He still is."

"Michael was his only child?"

"No. There's Jeremy. But Jeremy has always been...how shall I say it...on the outside. He and Henry never got along for some reason, at least not like Michael and Henry."

Surprisingly, Crawford had no further comment and the four lapsed into silence for the next few miles. They hadn't passed a town in the twenty-five miles since Montrose but rounding a curve, the early evening lights of a settlement came into view.

"That's Ridgway up ahead," Dean said. "It's only about five miles from the house. I'll drop everyone off and come back and pick up a few groceries."

Dorrie nodded in agreement and nothing more was said until they pulled off the highway and began the short climb up the dirt road to the two-story house on the escarpment.

Marian Anderson's Colorado "cabin" was no camp in the woods. The building was a full-size, well-built, modern house less than twenty years old with all the amenities of city living; running water and a toilet indoors, not out back with a half moon on the door. It was furnished tastefully, more with comfort in mind than impressing anyone. There were two large bedrooms upstairs and another on the first floor sharing space with a den, kitchen with eating area, and a large combination living room-family room that opened to an outside deck. All rooms were well-windowed, taking advantage of the spectacular 360-degree view beyond. The place had been home to Marian's elderly cousin. He had built the place after retiring from thirty-five years of clerical drudgery. While not a rich man, his timing was great; low land costs and high craftsmanship that couldn't be bought at present-day prices for three times the money. Marian indicated she'd never met the relative and had no idea why he had made her the sole heir to three acres and a view in Ouray County, Colorado. But she wasn't complaining.

As soon as the vehicles were unloaded and the cabby paid by Mrs. Brown with crisp bills carefully selected from a cavernous purse, the group dutifully marched into the house. Whitcomb let out a deep sigh which Dean ignored as he fumbled with the light switch.

"Make yourself comfortable. There's beer in the refrigerator. I'm going back to Ridgway for some food."

"Great place! Great place, Davey!" said Archer, sounding like a game show host as he wandered about the living room, his ever-present aluminum suitcase still dangling from his hand.

"How far is Sneffels?" asked Whitcomb curtly, stopping conversation. Dean couldn't have been more surprised if the man had asked for the Arctic Circle.

"Mount Sneffels?" he asked incredulously.

Archer jumped in, a bundle of nerves. "That can wait until morning,

15

Henry." He turned to Dean. "Dave, just pick up a few steaks, maybe a pie, and some ice cream. And eggs and a little bacon and juice for the morning."

Whitcomb glared at him. "This isn't some screw-around vacation, Archer. This is vital."

"I know, Henry, I know. We all do. But we're tired and it's been a long day...and your headache...I just thought we'd all be better off waiting until morning to talk about it."

Whitcomb muttered something inaudible and turned to Mrs. Brown. "Brown, give the guy a couple of hundred bucks for food."

He lit a cigarette, blowing out the smoke in a long puff. "There must be a bathroom around here somewhere. It is inside, isn't it?" He began to wander down the hall.

Dean called after him. "Please put out the cigarette. I'd appreciate it if you'd smoke outside."

Whitcomb was already out of sight down the hall. Dean turned to Neil Archer, ignoring Mrs. Brown who stood there, two crisp one-hundred dollar bills in her outstretched hand. "Neil, I'd like to have a word with you!"

"Later, later, Dave. Why don't you run down and get the grub? I'll settle things here. Really, it's okay."

Neil was off down the hall before Dean could protest further. Brown continued to thrust out the bills until Dean took them. She then followed Whitcomb and Archer. Dean was left to wonder which one held Whitcomb's wee-wee when he peed. He turned disgustedly, slamming the door as he exited.

The driveway was as black as an eight-ball and he stubbed his toe, cussing aloud as he groped his way to the car. Suddenly, he was startled by a sound behind him and turning abruptly saw it was Dorrie Briscoe.

"I'll come with you," she said anxiously, grabbing his arm in the darkness of the mountain night.

The American literature professor seemed to be a firm believer in the old adage "Silence is Golden", a particularly astute observation in view of Dean's foul mood. The short trip was made in silence. The Ridgway Market was empty of customers and near closing when they arrived. They quickly completed their shopping. The store's meat selection was limited at the end of the day so they supplemented the two remaining steaks with hamburger and pork chops and added the items to the large selection of breakfast food.

Dean's presentation of a hundred-dollar bill for payment was met with an upturned eyebrow. When the clerk seemed to have trouble finding change for the large bill, they scrounged through purse and pocket, finally pulling together enough from their own resources to settle up.

During the return trip, Dean was feeling guilty about the silent treatment and was about to open his mouth when Miss Briscoe was first to speak.

"You have every reason for being ticked at me for not explaining why we're here but..."

"Frankly, Neil Archer is number one on my – pardon the expression – pissed off list, with Henry Whitcomb, Mrs. Brown and maybe Crawford following closely. So far, you've been the only sane person in the group."

She laughed. "Thanks. But seriously, the less you know about this, the better. It's not because anyone's doing anything illegal or dishonest, it's just...so wacky. You've gotten a little dose of Whitcomb. Take my word for it; he doesn't improve with an increased measure and this is his show all the way. We'll be out of your hair soon, probably by tomorrow afternoon."

"So what happens between now and then?" he asked.

Dean found the answer, at least in part, not from Dorrie Briscoe who wouldn't say but from Neil Archer when they returned to the house. Whitcomb was in bed, having summarily confiscated Dean's bedroom. Mrs. Brown took over the other second floor room just as the two returned from shopping. Dorrie began unpacking the groceries and Hays Crawford saw the wisdom of helping her in the kitchen when David Dean grabbed Neil Archer by the collar and dragged him into the living room, fire in his eyes.

"Talk," he said in a no-nonsense tone.

"Sure, Buddy," Archer answered nervously. "We've got a lot of catching up to do."

"No, we don't."

"What do you mean?"

"You know what the hell I mean. Why are you and four strangers dropping out of the sky for a September vacation, with half of you acting like world class pains-in-the-ass and no one acting as if they want to be here?"

"Look, it's no big deal, really." He turned and walked toward the window, cracking his knuckles. "It's Whitcomb. He just wants you to take him to visit this place, Sneffels...not the mountain, the town."

"There isn't a town of Sneffels...."

"His grandmother's from there. He just wants to see it."

"I don't believe you."

"You don't have to believe me, but he wants to see it."

Dean sighed with exasperation. "Sneffels is a ghost town. There's nothing there but a few falling-down buildings and some rusty mining machinery. I went up there on a jeep tour a couple of weeks ago. I'm not even sure the road is still open."

"Why not?"

"Neil, did you see that white stuff on the mountains when you were driving from the airport? It's snow. Some of it's left over from last year but it's late September so this year's quota has already started falling, at least in the high country."

Hays Crawford wandered into the room and sat on the arm of the sofa, staring out the window at the darkness but listening intently. Dean ignored him and tried to get through to Archer.

"We're at about 7,300 feet elevation where we sit. Some of those mountains you saw top 14,000 feet! The town of Sneffels is at ten, eleven, maybe 12,000 feet."

"Shit, that's two miles up!"

"That's the first sensible thing you've said since you got here. Look, I signed on as a house-sitter, not a tour guide. Does Marian Anderson know anything about this?"

Archer ignored his question. "Let's stop arguing. I know I'm a pain-in-the-ass, but just take Whitcomb up and get it over with. He'll pay. He's a rich son-of-a-bitch."

"You don't hop in a Honda and drive to Sneffels," Dean said but Archer just gave him a "Why not?" look.

Dean plunked himself down in a chair, wishing he had never answered Marian's phone call.

Dorrie cautiously came into the room, carrying trays with food. She placed a plate with steak, fried potatoes and a warm roll in front of Dean. The smell was enough to distract him into taking the offering and he began to eat.

"Do you think I should knock on the doors upstairs and offer the others something?" she asked, to no one in particular.

Crawford answered. "Naw, Henry won't eat with a headache and let the old bitch starve. Maybe it'll improve her disposition."

"Mrs. Brown cooked up some hamburger before she went to bed," Archer said, his mouth half-full of pork chop.

Hays Crawford only nibbled at his food. "There's a real ghost town up there, huh? Just like the movies?"

"Not quite," Dean answered, "You don't see chairs and bottles and antiques lying around; just empty buildings or the remains of them. There's not much standing in Sneffels but some of the other ghost towns are remarkably well-preserved, especially the isolated ones. There are scores of hamlets in the mountains and most of the old mines had boarding houses or outhouses. If it wasn't so dark you could see mine buildings on the far side of the valley from that window."

"No shit?" Hays looked out into the darkness. "How do you know so much about this area? You just got here."

"I like history and I haven't had much else to do. The late tenant left plenty of books."

The four ate with plates on their laps, and the only further conversation concerned the food. Finally, when the meal was finished, Dean got to his feet. Maybe the history professor needed a history lesson.

"One hundred and twenty years ago the population of this area was thousands more than today," Dean began. "Gold and silver pulled the easterners in like a magnet. The miners laced the back country with roads and settlements and towns and then, almost as fast as it started, the whole party was over, or damn near so. Why? Because either the mines played out or the price of metal dropped so it was no longer practical to dig the stuff out of the earth. Before the turn of the century the big boom was over, most of the people had moved on to chase other dreams in other places, and most of the roads in the county went back to nature. Unless you want to hike, the only way to get to the back country is by four-wheel-drive vehicle. And that's a hell of a struggle."

"So," Neil Archer said triumphantly. "We'll rent a jeep!"

Dean shook his head.

"Look," Archer said, exasperation showing on his face. "You don't know Henry. He won't leave here until you do what he wants. There's no other way. Just do it and we'll get the hell out of your hair." The others nodded in agreement.

"Let him rent one himself. He doesn't need me to hold his hand. If he doesn't want to drive himself, there are lots of competent drivers he could hire."

Dorrie answered after the others looked to her. "Mr. Whitcomb wants to keep a low profile. He wouldn't want to raise any questions.

You've gotta do it, Dave, please?"

Dean sighed, a long and defeated sigh. The only way to talk sense to Archer was to not talk at all, just get rid of him, as soon as possible.

"You win. I'll get up early tomorrow and go into town and rent a damned jeep. We'd better get started by nine if anyone is going to do any poking around up there. And I'm not kidding you when I say it's a damn tough drive."

Dean remembered his only trip to the high country, two weeks earlier. He'd seen advertisements for jeep tours and his curiosity had gotten the better of him. The vehicle was an oversized, specially equipped jeep, driven by a local outdoorsman with years of experience. Seven tourists snuggled into the vehicle, at least half of whom were petrified from the moment they bumped over the first rock and swung over the first abyss. The ride had shaken his bones loose and his bullet wound, still tender, objected madly to the untimely excursion. Nevertheless, the country had thrilled him beyond measure with its beauty and unforgiving wildness. Although it frightened him like a schoolboy trip to the principal, he wanted to see more.

"I'll do the driving," Dean continued. "The rental jeeps only hold four, so two of you will have to stay at the house."

"Mrs. Brown won't go up there, I'm sure," Dorrie said, " but I'd like to see it. It sounds fascinating."

"I'll sure volunteer," Crawford added.

"Well," said Archer with reluctance no one believed, "it sounds like a piece of cake but, if you guys are so keen on going, I guess I can hold down the fort back here."

"Good," said Dean, "We've got the crew. Now for the rules. Keep Mr. Big-Shot off my back. Period. I'm running this affair and unless you want me to embarrass you, keep him in line. The same goes for everyone. When I say it's time to come down, down we come, no argument. I don't want anyone hurt, especially me. That's rough country up there and you have to respect it. And dress for it. I have no idea what we'll run into in the way of weather. If anyone is afraid of heights, they'd better spend the day in the corner rocking chair. This ain't Kansas, Dorothy."

Dean crossed the room and turned on the radio. "Maybe we can catch a weather report and find out what we're in for."

It was just after ten and the Grand Junction station was finishing up the news. The weather report followed; the overnight temperature would fall to the thirties in the high country but no mention was made of precipitation.

"You make it sound like we're climbing the Matterhorn, for God's sake. It's no big deal." Archer sounded bored with the whole affair.

"Don't be so sure. There may not be a major storm predicted but each level of elevation has its own weather pattern and it can change in minutes. Now, I know everyone wants to play let's-keep-a-secret but someone has to tell me where you really want to go. I can get you up to Sneffels. I assume the road's clear to there, but if your friend wants to go much beyond there, it's questionable."

"Byrd's Song," Crawford said. "Byrd's Song, Colorado."

"I never heard of it," Dean said.

"It was a settlement, a little over a mile from Sneffels," Crawford answered. "More like a single home site."

"Higher than Sneffels, I suppose." Dean didn't have to wait for the answer.

Crawford rose and began to saunter down the hall. "Come on, roomy," he called to Archer. "If I'm going to play Lewis and Clark in the morning, it's time to get to bed."

"He can't go yet," Dorrie called. "Dr. Archer promised to do the dishes and clean up the kitchen. But just so I'll be bright-eyed and bushy-tailed for the trip tomorrow, I'm calling it a night." She picked up her suitcase and began to climb the stairs. "Wish me luck that Mrs. Brown doesn't snore."

Neil Archer was wise enough not to protest the kitchen duty; little enough penance for what he had caused to date. Dean muttered a goodnight and went to the den to make his own bed; he'd had enough of the day. He opened the pullout sofa and fished a pillow and blanket from the closet but there was no linen in the room. He quietly climbed to the second floor and made his way down the darkened hallway to the small closet next to the bath. As he rummaged through the towels and bath articles, he heard a noise at the far end of the hall. Dorrie was standing in the shadows outside the closed door to the second bedroom gently knocking. "She's locked the door," she whispered back to Dean when he saw her.

"There aren't any locks on these doors."

"Then she's wedged something against it. It won't budge."

"Go away!" came a mumbled snarl from behind the door.

"Mrs. Brown, it's Dorrie. I'm supposed to bunk with you."

"No one sleeps with me. Find someplace else!"

"But, Mrs. Brown..."

"Good night!"

Dean smiled in spite of himself, shaking his head in disbelief. He marched down the hall and handed Dorrie the pile of linen. "The den," he said, "downstairs, down the hall, on the left."

"No, I couldn't. That's where you're to sleep..."

"Goodnight," he said, in a tone that cut off further conversation. He went back to the closet and gathered a second pile of linen just as the front door slammed; Neil Archer going out on the porch for a cigarette, no doubt. At least he had the courtesy to smoke outside, unlike Whitcomb, Dean thought as he descended the stairs.

Just as Dean returned to the first floor, Neil pounced back through the door, looking like he'd seen Marley's ghost.

"There's someone out there!"

"Neil," Dean said, not trying to hide his exasperation. "You're in the country. There are skunks, raccoons, deer, even a bear once in awhile. Go to bed."

"This was a man. I saw him. He was parked up by the road. I heard him leave."

"So?"

"He ran when he saw me. It scared the shit out of me! He was standing up by the driveway." Archer turned and wandered down the hall. "This whole deal gives me the creeps. Maybe we were followed."

Dean stepped outside but only the stars and cool night air greeted him. He didn't know whether or not to trust Neil's judgment but at this stage of the day, he hardly cared.

Returning to the quiet house, he stopped at the sink to splash water on his face. Archer had filled the dishwasher and dumped the pans in a sink of cold water before his alleged encounter with a prowler and toddling off to bed. Dean looked at the sofa and, with a sigh, turned out the lights.

CHAPTER II

A hurdy-gurdy labyrinth of sights and sounds had just begun teasing their way through Dean's brain when the shrill ring of the telephone brought him back somewhere close to reality. He struggled from the sofa, rapping his knee first on the coffee table and then on the rocker, before stumbling to the kitchen and lifting the receiver.

"Howdy," said a female voice, far more cheerful than the hour dictated.

"Do you know what time it is?" Dean asked angrily, looking at the digital readout on his microwave oven. It showed twelve-twenty.

"Sure. It's after two o'clock here but it's still early out west. Don't tell me you guys are in bed already!"

"Do I know you?"

"No. But you're the flatfoot, right?"

As Dean's mind began to register, he realized he was speaking to a child. "How old are you?" he asked.

"Fourteen. Now may I speak to my mother?"

"Briscoe or Brown?" he asked with a sigh.

She laughed with the same cheery ring as Dorrie Briscoe. "I like a man who has a sense of humor in the middle of the night. How old are you?"

"I'll get your mother," he answered, but Dorrie was already coming. He could hear the sound of her puffy slippers swishing down the hall. He held out the phone for her and retreated to the sofa, rubbing the sleep from his eyes, as Dorrie spoke in a muffled tone. A full moon was beginning its climb and he watched as it flowed across the deck, spilling whiteness through the sliding glass door, painting the room in angles and silhouettes.

When Dorrie finished her brief conversation, she shuffled over to the sofa and sat beside him. "Sorry," she said.

"Problem?"

"With Nattie? Never."

"Isn't she up a little late for a fourteen-year-old?"

"She's probably just getting started. When Webster was looking for a definition for the word 'precocious' he should have interviewed Nattie."

Dean chuckled. "I understand teenagers can be hell to raise."

"I haven't been 'raising' Nattie since she was an infant. She simply lives in my house and entertains me."

"What about her father?" he asked.

"She doesn't have one." The answer came in a tone that said "don't push it." She continued, "The neighbors next door are sort of babysitting but with Nattie that's a joke."

"That's a lot of freedom for a fourteen-year-old."

"She's only thirteen. Nattie counts the years differently from the rest of us mortals. Once she has a birthday, she starts counting the next year. My daughter won't be fourteen until November but she's already made her birthday wish-list. She wants a vibrator so she can experience 'this sex-business' in the privacy of her own room."

"She sounds like quite a child."

"That she is. Last week she came home with a fifth of vodka and carried it up to her room, along with a bucket in case she got sick. She wanted to learn about 'drunk.'"

"What did you do?"

"What any mother would do. I asked her where she got the vodka. Some kid sold it to her for five dollars. I told her to get some more if she could. Five dollars is a great price for Smirnoffs."

Dean chuckled as Dorrie continued.

"Really, I'm not quite that bad, but she is a handful. I feel like the Virgin Mary, blessed with this marvelous child that fell into my lap from heaven. I'm constantly in awe of her. I can't believe she's mine. My whole life is designed around somehow shepherding her to adulthood."

"What about Dorrie Briscoe's life?"

"What life? I don't have one. I live vicariously through others. Look at me? A shrink would have a field day! I have more hang ups than a coat rack. No husband. The only long term lover I ever had was the most unreachable man I could find and he's a shit. Every time I'm around a halfway decent guy, I come on as if I'm in heat and I don't even realize I'm doing it." She smiled at him. "Look, I'm sorry if I gave you the wrong idea today. I was juvenile. But the plus is you only have to put up with us for a few more hours and we'll be out of your hair."

"Are you always this frank to strangers?"

"It's just nice to be able to talk to a sane man for a change and I suppose I'm feeling guilty for not telling you why we're here."

"So why not just tell me?"

"Because that bastard Henry won't let us."

"You're a big girl."

"You don't know Henry Whitcomb and you can thank your stars you don't!"

"What makes all you people so damned uptight?" Dean asked as a cloud passed away from the moon, relighting Dorrie Briscoe's face in a pale glow.

"Because we're scared witless, that's why."

"Of Henry?"

"Yes. But that's not all." She rose and crossed to the sliding glass door, opening it.

"It's chilly out there," he said as she started to step outside. He reached across the back of the sofa, pulled off a quilt, draping it across her shoulders as he followed her into the cool night air.

"Let's stop talking about Henry-the-Prick and tell me about David Dean," she said.

"There's not much to tell. You'd find him kind of boring. He doesn't have a doctorate or a pile of money. He likes Mexican food, bicycles, a night at home, sports, and his own company. He doesn't like suits, crowds or pretentious people."

"That sounds like a high school yearbook! You left out, 'a simple guy who likes classical music and reads some pretty heavy books,'" she said. "Sorry. I've been peeking around the place, and American Lit is supposed to be my bag."

"Most of that stuff came with the house, but I'm developing a taste for it, especially the music."

"What else don't you like?"

"Violence," he answered, without hesitation.

"It sounds like you picked the wrong profession."

"I guess I thought I could help to put a stop to it. The naiveté of innocence."

"So now you want to hide from it." She quickly caught herself. "I'm sorry. That was out of line."

"No. It was deserved, mostly because it's probably true. But I am smart enough to know you can't get away. Let's just say I'm taking a vacation from it. But admittedly, it's nice to have the nasties of the world so far away from Ouray, Colorado."

"You really like it here, don't you?"

"I read the little weekly newspaper. The town cops spend most of their time checking to see that doors are locked or busting some tourist or trucker speeding down from Red Mountain. The paper lists the complete activities of the police in each edition; everything they do. I love it. I haven't seen a rape or a robbery since I got here. The closest thing to violence is a dog fight. I'm

25

not even sure they don't list the wrong telephone numbers!"

"It must be nice," she said, "I read the Philly paper and it's cut and slash daily. It makes me sick, little kids killing each other, hate in every direction. It's reassuring to think there are still places in the world like here where there is a little common sense left. There's probably never been a murder in the town's history."

"Maybe not recently but a hundred years ago this was an entirely different place."

"Oh, I'd forgotten about that." She paused, as if choosing her words carefully. "Did you ever think you'd like to live back then? Or maybe just visit?"

The seriousness of the way she asked it caught him off guard. "A hundred years ago? Like Flash Gordon and his time machine?" he asked, with a smile.

"Maybe."

"Nope. I'm a today sort of guy. Yesterday's finished and I'll let tomorrow take care of itself."

"I would," she said. "I'd go back. I'd do it in a minute." A strange look crossed her face but vanished as fast as it appeared. She changed the subject.

"Look at us. We've only known each other half a day and already we're philosophizing over some pretty deep stuff."

"The best conversations are between perfect strangers," he said as he followed her to the door.

"We'd better get some sleep if we're going to be tramping around Byrd's Song tomorrow. It has the makings of quite a day."

She closed the door with a knowing smile on her face, leaving Dean to further wonder what he was getting into with this bizarre collection of people.

CHAPTER III

A pleasant breakfast smell of bacon, eggs and coffee greeted Dean to Wednesday morning. Moments later, he felt the warmth of the first glint of sun as it broke the ridge on the east side of the valley. As his eyes began to focus, a human image took shape in the rocking chair across the living room. There sat Henry Whitcomb, dressed in what some catalog store undoubtedly described as high mountain gear. He casually sipped a cup of coffee.

"Mrs. Brown cooked some breakfast." He set his coffee down and lit a cigarette. "Wake up the others and let's get going. And, hey, I don't want you screwing around with Doctor Briscoe, you hear?"

Dean took a deep breath. "Look," he said, trying to stretch the kink from his back, "this is my place, at least temporarily, and I don't take kindly to someone telling me what I can and can't do. And I believe I asked you nicely not to smoke inside."

Whitcomb simply let out a bored sigh with a puff of blue smoke, rose and, turning his back on Dean without comment, climbed the stairs, growling a couple of orders to Mrs. Brown above. Hays Crawford strolled into the room from the kitchen, munching on a mouthful of something and laughing at Dean's encounter with Whitcomb.

"Welcome to the club!" he said.

"I don't remember joining," grumbled Dean as he rose from the sofa.

"With Henry you don't have a choice. He elects the members." Crawford gazed out the window. "I can see a building up there, across the valley, just like you said. Can we drive up there, too?"

"I'm not a tour director," Dean mumbled. "Besides, the road only goes part way. From there you have to hike."

"You got any binoculars?"

"In the closet," Dean said as he rose and left for the bathroom.

When he returned, Crawford was peering intently across the valley at the slope a mile or two distant. A fan-shaped tailings pile sloped downward, its tan color distinct against the underbrush surrounding it. There was a large wooden building visible above and to the right.

"I can even see a mine opening! Are there any of those at Sneffels?"

"You'll see in a couple of hours," Dean answered.

"No he won't." Archer said as he entered the room, his face painted in a pout. "Henry changed the passenger list. He wants me to go."

"Shit!" said Crawford, turning on his heels and leaving the room.

Dean ignored Archer, climbed the stairs and entered his old bedroom without knocking, picked out appropriate biking clothes, and left the house. As he peddled to town and the jeep rental agency, he second guessed his decision to take the group up in the mountains to Sneffels. As he saw it, there were but two choices; punch the son-of-a-bitch Whitcomb in the mouth and move into a motel, or go to town, rent the damn jeep, give them their high-country adventure and hope they got the hell out of his life. The motel idea sounded better and better the more he thought about it. He didn't care for situations where he was operating on half the story. But he'd made the commitment. Best bite the bullet and get it over with.

The early hour prolonged the rental procedure but the delay didn't stop him from taking time out for a leisurely breakfast, away from the hassle of his own place. When he returned, Mrs. Brown was apparently conducting some lengthy ritual in the bathroom as she remained there with the door closed. She was the only one to miss the fireworks that erupted as soon as Dean entered the house.

Hays Crawford was sitting on the floor, his back against the wall, casually dismantling a radio that didn't work and Dorrie Briscoe was on the sofa, thumbing through a magazine. Neil Archer was just coming down the hall from the den. Henry Whitcomb sat in the same rocker as earlier, holding a cup of coffee, a lighted cigarette in the ashtray next to him.

"Where in hell have you been?" Whitcomb snarled as Dean entered. "It'll be noon by the time we get up there!"

Dean took one look at the scene, crossed the room, picked up the cigarette, and casually dropped it into the coffee Whitcomb was about to sip. He then picked up the opened pack and a lighter, walked resolutely to the door, and tossed them across the yard. Henry glared at him with the severity of an S. S. officer at a Bar Mitzvah candidate.

"That was a gold lighter," he said coldly.

Dean turned and looked at him with equal ice. "From what I understand, you can afford it. I told you, I don't take kindly to orders in my house. And I've always found repeating myself to be an unnecessary waste of my time. Now, if we're going, let's get going."

Whitcomb rose slowly and went out the door. Whether he was going for his lighter, another smoke or to cool off, Dean neither knew nor cared. He went upstairs to his closet, changed clothes, showered and retrieved a second sweater. What the hell, Dean had the jeep and was going to go touring, even if the visiting king and his court had changed their collective minds.

But they hadn't. When Dean returned to the living room ten minutes later, Henry was waiting by the door, acting as if the incident had never happened. He carried the mysterious aluminum suitcase and wore a scowl on his face. Archer, Crawford and Dorrie Briscoe stood by, as if wondering what new calamity was about to occur.

"There isn't a room in this house that has a door that locks," Whitcomb said to Dean as he entered the room.

"Why would I need one?" Dean answered. "I hardly lock the outside doors when I go to town."

"It's imperative that this case is locked up while we're gone."

"What's the sweat, Henry?" asked Archer. "Hays and Mrs. Brown will be here. Nobody's going to steal it."

"I want it locked," Whitcomb replied. "I don't trust this jerk not to take off with it," he continued, glaring at Crawford.

"Thanks for the vote of confidence, boss," Crawford said, stuffing a piece of toast in his mouth.

"We'll lock it in his car," Whitcomb said, motioning toward Dean and handing the case to Neil Archer.

"Got the keys, Buddy?" Archer asked as he took the case and moved toward the door.

Dean tossed them to him and turned to Whitcomb. "Aren't you afraid I have another set?"

"You'll be up in the mountains with me. Let's get this show going."

A few moments later, when Dean was at the front hall closet pulling out extra clothing for Neil and Dorrie, Hays Crawford came up behind him.

"Do you have an extra set of keys?" he asked, in not much more than a whisper. "It's no big deal. I'm not going to steal anything. I just want to...look at something."

"No. As a matter of fact, they're back in Pennsylvania with my stepfather."

Dean didn't bother adding he wouldn't have given them to the young man if he had them.

Archer returned from the car, and gave Dean back his keys. The group was ready to leave. Just then, the front doorbell rang. Crawford, closest to the door, answered it. Standing there, bedecked in western garb, airline cat-cage in hand, stood a smiling Fred O'Connor, Dean's stepfather and roommate.

"What in God's name are you doing here?" asked a startled Dean. "You're supposed to be in Pennsylvania."

Fred O'Connor married Dean's mother late in life, while her son was in the service. Then Mary Dean succumbed to a heart attack only four months later, three days after Dean met Fred O'Connor for the first time. Sixteen years later the two still shared the same house.

"Me and Mrs. Lincoln decided you needed some company," Fred answered, holding up the cage from which the cat squinted nervously. "And it helped when number twenty-seven hit the Atlantic City roulette wheel twice in a row, just as the airlines started a price war. Aren't you going to introduce me to this crowd?"

As Dean, still dumbfounded, made the introductions, his stepfather continued. "This nice lady who lives in a place named Silverton gave me a ride from Montrose."

The old man set the cat carrier on the floor and opened the door. "Say 'hello' to the folks, Mrs. Lincoln."

The cat wandered out, looked first right, then left and made a dash for Dean. As he bent to pick up the pet he hadn't seen in weeks, the snobby animal trotted between his legs to a startled Dorrie Briscoe who had just crossed the room. She stooped and picked up the purring cat who looked as if she had known Dorrie all her life.

"Ungrateful dust-mop," Dean scolded.

"Where you're going in the jeep?" Fred asked, taking off his jacket.

"We're going to Byrd's Song. And we're late." growled Whitcomb. "We can continue this chit-chat when we get back." He went out the door with the others dutifully following him, all except Crawford who returned to the kitchen for more food, and Dean who lingered, taking his stepfather in hand.

"It's really great to see you, Fred! I'll explain about this bunch when I get back. Hopefully, by then they'll be packing to leave."

"That one fellow is a might on the touchy side, ain't he?"

"Wait 'til you meet his secretary. She has the personality of a drill sergeant."

"Well, then I'm glad I came if there's a lady in need of a little temperament adjustment."

"Ten bucks says even you can't warm her up!"

"Make it twenty-five and you're on!"

Just then, Mrs. Brown finally stepped out of the bathroom and took one look at Mrs. Lincoln who had curled up on a soft spot on the sofa, resting from her travel ordeal.

"Get that damned cat out of here!" she yelled.

"I thought you were sort of running this place," Fred said to Dean, as Dean turned to leave.

"I thought so, too," answered Dean. "I'll leave this little problem in your hands, Fred. Do you want to pay me the twenty-five bucks now?" Dean chuckled as he closed the door behind him, leaving Fred O'Connor facing scowling Mrs. Brown who stood with hands on hips, looking to kill. Dean climbed in the jeep where Archer was crabbing about the closeness of the back seat and Whitcomb sat drumming his fingers impatiently.

The sky was cobalt-blue, with only a hint of stringy white clouds drifting down the valley as Dean turned, not north toward Montrose and the lower elevations, but south toward the Victorian town of Ouray and the imposing San Juan Mountains that surrounded it. The temperature was chilly but pleasant with the sun peeking over the ridge to their left, dappling the aspen and cottonwoods along the banks of the Uncompahgre River, as it slowly warmed the valley. The river began to skip along at a quicker pace as the jeep approached the base of the mountains. Mount Abrams, dead ahead, with its classic pyramid profile, dominated the horizon while the sides of the valley closed in on the travelers as they neared the small town.

Rounding a curve, they passed the large hot-springs public pool, as the town spread out before them, sleepy houses, boxed on three sides by the vast mountains. Few people were up and about as Dean drove the jeep up the wide main street of shops and buildings, each with a western facade of a time gone by. The mountains towered so close and so completely, a first time observer might think there was no road to the south until a narrow highway appeared, switch-backing its way up the wall of stone directly ahead.

"It's called the Million-Dollar Highway," Dean said. "It runs from here to Durango, seventy-five miles of spectacular scenery, if your stomach can handle drop-offs with no guardrails."

"Is that where we're going?" asked Dorrie from the back seat, just as Dean turned right, onto a road that changed to gravel almost at once.

"Nope," he answered, "I've got something even better."

They crossed a bridge over a deep gorge with water bubbling through the bottom of the abyss as Dean shifted the jeep to four wheel drive. The vehicle began to climb steadily and Dean could feel Henry Whitcomb stiffen next to him. The road was relatively wide and well graded, and after the first turn a beautiful view of the town below opened before them. They climbed the western side of the ridge and at first the closeness of the mountains blocked out the sun. When the sun finally broke the top of the eastern peaks, they were flooded in welcomed warmth. For the first few miles the road was locked in a pine forest with only an occasional glimpse of the mountains before them until a curve in the road and a break in the trees opened their view. Although unprotected by guardrails on the right, the thick line of pines shielded them from the direct view of Canyon Creek, hundreds of feet below. Whitcomb looked petrified but said nothing.

Archer finally quipped, "This isn't so bad."

Dean said nothing, knowing this part of the road was practically a freeway compared to what lay ahead.

After two miles they crossed Canyon Creek and began to climb in earnest. The road remained wide and well graded, in better shape than some eastern byways in the winter, Dean thought. But the smoothness was of short duration. The road recrossed the creek and narrowed, climbing sharply, as it clung to the side of a sheer stone cliff, like a scratch on a wall, the width hardly sufficient for one vehicle.

"My God," Whitcomb cried, ashen faced, "we're not going up there, are we?"

"Some people do this in a regular car," Dean commented, trying to sound more blasé than he felt. "There are a lot more difficult roads up in these mountains."

"Keep to the right!" Whitcomb kept admonishing, the edge of fear clear in his voice.

"I can't look," cried Dorrie. Dean smiled, feeling like a veteran after his one previous jeep trip.

If anything, the scenery improved for those willing to open their eyes. A tiny silver waterfall trickled from a snow melt, far above and to their left, across the abyss of the canyon. Mountain blue birds fluttered in the green of the pine. They switched back sharply over open rock with the road bed deteriorating rapidly and they climbed, higher and higher.

"My ears just popped," said Dorrie.

"That's because we're over 9,000 feet up," answered Dean as he guided the vehicle across a wet section of road, washed by an open spring that flowed across their path before dropping down to the valley.

"How the hell high are we going?" grumbled Archer. "I think I'm getting a nosebleed."

"Another 1,500 feet, at least. The map shows Sneffels to be around 10,600 feet."

"And Byrd's Song is higher?" Archer whined.

Dean didn't answer as the road was again hanging on the side of the rock. The solid overhangs above them made the passage more a tunnel than a road. He gave a quick glance at Whitcomb who looked as if he might be sick. Dean smiled to himself and slid the jeep closer to the left side of the road out of pure spitefulness.

"That's United States Mountain up ahead," Dean pointed out in his best tour guide voice. "They pulled hundreds of millions in gold and silver out of there..."

"Who gives a shit?" Whitcomb snarled through clenched teeth. "Just keep your damn eyes on the road!"

"Anything look familiar?" asked Archer.

"Shut up!" said Whitcomb fiercely, just as a large bank of snow appeared on their left. It was filled with broken trees and stumps, bridging the stream below with its mass. Up the slope to their right, much of the vegetation had been sheared away by the racing snow slide.

"That's the remnants of an avalanche that ran last winter." No one spoke as they gazed up at the massive destruction, as if a giant hand had scraped the slope bare.

At the four and a half mile point from the highway the road opened up to display a large complex of metal buildings and other structures.

"The famous Camp Bird Mine," Dean announced. "That's the reason the road this far is so well maintained. From here on it's strictly four-wheel-drive."

"You mean it gets worse?" Dorrie asked.

"You betcha," Dean answered, shifting down and beginning the steep climb up the narrower road that forked to the right.

Occasionally, the broken trestle of a forgotten mine could be seen high up on the sides of the cliff above the canyon and Dean was pointing one out when Dorrie interrupted him.

"I think Neil is going to be sick," she said, the alarm sounding in her voice.

Dean pulled the jeep to the side and Whitcomb moved forward while Neil Archer scrambled out, stumbling to his knees by the side of the road.

"You don't look all that great yourself," Dean said to Whitcomb, but Whitcomb simply waved his hand.

"Just keep going," he muttered, his head thrown back against the seat.

"I think we could all use a break," Dean answered. It was a relatively flat section and Dean himself could use the pause.

"May I look," Dorrie asked hesitantly.

"Just be careful," Dean answered, pushing back his seat to allow her to exit.

She stepped out of the vehicle and cautiously crept to the left side of the road, stopping several feet from the edge. Dean took her hand and they moved forward. Far below them raced a beautiful waterfall, spilling and tumbling over rocks and broken trees, as it hurried downward, a scene of purely natural wildness.

"It's scary, but so breathtaking," Dorrie whispered reverently, gripping his hand vice-like as she peeked over the edge.

"As wild as it is now, imagine the scene in early spring. They get 300 to 400 inches of snow up here."

"I'm so light-headed," she said, her cheeks pink with the cool morning air, "but I don't feel nauseous."

"That's the elevation. We're around 10,000 feet here."

"Let's get moving," Whitcomb yelled from the jeep.

Archer crawled back in the vehicle, but Dean ignored the summons until he and Dorrie had taken their time drinking in the view.

Once they were underway, the road rounded a curve, opening up to a vast basin and Sneffels Creek, the stream that produced the waterfall below. The stream bed was much closer to the road level now, filling their ears with the sound of its fury. The mountains, wrapping around them on three sides ahead, contained fewer trees as they gained elevation and approached the tree line. Grassy slopes held the remnants of summer wildflowers and yellowing brush. Soon a derelict building came into view on their right, and then another.

"Welcome to Sneffels, Colorado," Dean said, "Home of no one but the ghosts of yesterday."

The road leveled out, following the stream to the left or south side, and further remains of collapsed buildings appeared. There was evidence of extensive mining operations across the creek but it appeared most of the town had been built to the north side of the road, on their right.

There was a sign next to the road and as Dean stopped, Dorrie, leaning across the front seat, read it aloud.

"It says, 'The Town of Sneffels, founded in 1875, originally called Porter's Peak. Population 2,000. Revenue mill and tunnel, access to Virginus Mine. Employed 600 men and produced gold and silver worth $1,000,000,000 today.' Wow, I'm impressed!"

"You have to wonder where they fit everyone." Dean commented as Whitcomb opened the door of the jeep and alighted, holding on to the side of the vehicle to steady himself. Archer, his head in his lap, simply moaned and stayed put.

Dean took his time and held back the seat for Dorrie. When all three were standing on the road, Whitcomb lit a cigarette and studied the scene intently.

"Well," asked Dean, "just like Grandma described it?"

Whitcomb, his hand shaking noticeably, muttered, "Yes." He continued looking, as if searching for something. "This is it. It looks so different without the buildings but the mountains don't change."

He turned abruptly and gazed up at a high peak behind him, to the north. "It's up there," he said, motioning with a wave of his hand. They followed his gaze to a spired peak towering above. "Under that rock. See the flat area just below the peaks? The grassy piece of land? That's Byrd's Song."

Neither Dorrie nor Dean said anything, and he continued. "There was a cabin and buildings. See the gray rock to the left? The trail came down around there, and then down the slope."

Whitcomb was pointing to a small meadow-like area just below a nearly-vertical cliff, the highest point visible from where they stood. He traced a line with his finger around the curve of the slope. Dean pulled out his map, trying to identify the location.

"I think the mountain is Potosi Peak," he said, "It's at 13,763 feet, the grassy area must be about 1,000 feet above us. We're at 10,600, so it's at almost 12,000 feet."

A steep slope of rock and meadow, and clusters of aspen and dead pine led up from where they stood, the details lost in the distance of the heights above them.

"The view up there must be fantastic," said Dorrie.

Whitcomb looked at her. "It is," he said in a voice he thought was out of ear shot of Dean.

"They skipped down there as if it was nothing," Whitcomb continued, his voice strangely out of character, with none of the brusqueness usually evident.

"Who?" asked Dean, but neither Whitcomb nor Dorrie answered.

"Ella's house was over there and the store was down on the road. Porter's store..." Whitcomb stopped, trying to catch his breath. "I can't walk fifty feet without feeling like I'm going to die," he stammered disgustedly.

"Yesterday you were at sea-level," Dean said, "and today you're traipsing around a couple of miles higher. You're probably breathing in less than half the oxygen you're used to. Give your body a break. It takes time to get used to the altitude."

"How much time?" Whitcomb asked.

"I was here a week before I felt normal and two weeks before I could do any walking without gasping for breath, and that was 3,000 feet lower."

Whitcomb looked up at the mountain again but said nothing. He moved a few feet away and sat on a rock, gazing at the remnants of wooden structures and the rusting metal of roofs, each marking the place of a former home, people and lives long since forgotten. Scars of the closed mines pocketed the hillsides, their tailings spilling down the slope below them while pockets of snow lay cradled in the nooks and crevices of the mountains above. Dean stood by waiting for Whitcomb to catch his breath while Dorrie returned to the jeep to look in on Archer who hadn't moved. When Whitcomb finally got up, he motioned for the others to stay put as he slowly walked around, kicking a fallen plank or stepping over the remnants of a derelict building.

"He's not going to be satisfied until he gets up there," Dorrie said, with a sigh. "It's an obsession."

"He's in no shape to make the climb and that's the only way up, unless you're a mountain goat." Dean gazed at the small area high above. "Who lived up there? Was it really his grandmother?"

"Just a little girl," Dorrie said in a wistful voice, and then added, "What do you bet he'll find a way to get up there?"

She turned away and walked off by herself.

Dean didn't disagree.

Darkening clouds were beginning to build. Dean called to the others and was met with less argument than he expected. Whitcomb was the slowest to return as Dean started the jeep for the journey back down the mountain.

The return trip was less trying than the climb up with at least the element of the unknown no longer plaguing the passengers. Archer remained near-comatose and Henry Whitcomb looked only slightly better. Everyone was silent until they were back on the highway and Neil Archer finally raised his head.

"God, that was terrible."

Dean couldn't help getting in a lick. "You ought to love it up there, Neil. That's history. You're the history teacher, aren't you?"

"History belongs in books and museums, not two miles up in the air, hanging off some cliff!"

He turned to Whitcomb. "I hope the hell you found what you were looking for, Henry, 'cause I'm sure not going back up to Puke City again."

"You'll go where I tell you to go," Henry muttered.

Nice to see the ornery bastard back to normal, Dean thought.

When Dean pulled in the driveway he noticed that his car was parked in a slightly different position than where he'd left it. Archer was still seeing double so probably didn't notice and Whitcomb was so deep in thought, he'd miss the second coming. Dorrie started to say something but held back.

When the four travelers entered the house, Mrs. Brown was the first to greet them. She stood by the door, her bag packed, while Mrs. Lincoln opened one eye from her cozy rocker as if to say "I won."

"There were seven calls, Mr. Whitcomb. I wrote them down. And Dr. Briscoe, there was a call from your daughter's baby sitter. She said it was very important."

Dorrie made a dash for the phone as Mrs. Brown handed Whitcomb his messages.

"Later," he said, dismissing his secretary as he started for the stairs.

Just then Fred O'Connor came down the hall from the den, the mysterious aluminum suitcase in his hand. "Welcome back, folks. Say, Dave, where did you get the electric helmet?"

"Oh, shit!" said Archer, and Whitcomb made a dash to Fred, grabbing at the case.

"Give me that, you thieving bastard!"

Fred pulled it back. "Whoa, Hank. This here was in my son's car. I don't see any call to be accusing folks."

Whitcomb, surprisingly, stepped back. "I'm sorry. I've been under a lot of strain lately. It is my suitcase."

"He's right, Fred. I let him lock it in the car for security. How did you get in? I have the keys."

Fred handed the case to Whitcomb as he explained. "I figured out here in God's country there wouldn't be a bus like back in Parkside, so I brought your extra keys. I just borrowed the car and went down to the library. They have a right nice mystery section and you don't have much decent reading material around the house."

"You don't have a driver's license, Fred." Dean muttered, but no one was listening.

Archer looked petrified, and Mrs. Brown was ready to kill someone, Dean wasn't sure who. Crawford was nowhere to be seen. Henry Whitcomb finally slumped down in a chair, holding the sides of his head and looking like a beaten man.

"Look at the bright side," Dean said. "At least you saw Byrd's Song from a distance."

"It's not enough," Whitcomb muttered.

"With a 'Y'," Fred O'Connor said from across the room.

"What?" asked Whitcomb.

"Byrd's Song," Fred repeated. "It was a homestead site, named for some miner in the1880s. I figured you folks knew that if you were going up there."

"How in hell do you know that?" Henry asked, a look of wonder on his face.

"While you were fooling around in the hills, I was chatting with a right pleasant lady at the library. I asked about Byrd's Song so I'd know what I was talking about when you got back. She had a dickens of a time finding something on it but called this other lady who located a mention of the place in an old book."

Whitcomb jumped to his feet and glared at Neil Archer. "You're the history professor! How come you can't find out shit and this old man does it in five minutes?"

He turned to Fred O'Connor. "Did Byrd have a daughter named Sarah?"

"Don't ask for miracles, Hank. I didn't do any in-depth detecting. If it's important maybe the 1880 census will tell you."

"How the devil do you know this stuff, Fred?" Dean asked.

"I used to see this lady who was into gynecology..."

"You mean 'genealogy'..."

"Whatever. Anyway, there's lots of info out there if you know where to look."

Mrs. Brown cleared her throat. "Mr. Whitcomb, the plane is ready any time you are. I called the pilot and told him to be on standby."

"We're not leaving...at least not just yet. I'm going to see Byrd's Song. If it takes two weeks until I have the breath to get up there, so be it. We're staying right here."

You could cut with a knife the shock wave that circled the room. Mrs. Brown let out a low moan, Archer said, "Oh, shit!", Dean gritted his teeth and Dorrie, who was just returning from the phone, said, "We can't!"

"Come on, Brown. We've got some phone calls to make," Whitcomb muttered, ignoring the reactions.

"Just a minute," Dean said coldly. "That's still my bedroom up there and I need a little time to clear it out." He crossed to the stairs, calling over his shoulder to Fred. "I hope you didn't unpack."

"There's no need for you to leave," Whitcomb said, his voice neutral.

"Look," Dean answered, "no one's told me diddly-shit since you people showed up, virtually unannounced. You dragged me over the meadow through the woods to grandmother's house and took over my house and bed, all with the common courtesy of a bad case of measles. Now we've graduated to electric helmets, whatever the hell they are, and at least two more people than beds. I'm sick of it. I'm sick of being the only jerk who doesn't have the foggiest idea what's happening and being played for a sucker. Have a nice vacation and lock the door after you finally leave."

"Wait a minute," Whitcomb called but Dean didn't wait. "Tell him."

Dean stopped. "Listen, Whitcomb, it's too late. You know what? I don't want to hear it. I really don't give a shit."

"You and the old man. At least listen. He's seen it; he might as well know what it is." Whitcomb turned to Mrs. Brown. "We've got phone calls to make."

"Henry, wait a minute," Dorrie called, "I can't stay. Nattie doesn't have a babysitter. The woman quit. Nattie's all alone. I have to go back."

"I need you here. Find another babysitter. And tell Dean about the turban. My head's killing me and I have to have time to think." He and Mrs. Brown climbed the stairs and were gone.

Dorrie sank into a chair and began to cry. "The bastard always gets his way! He's so damned uncaring!"

Fred put his arm around her, just as Hays Crawford came in the door. "Just take a deep breath and think of something nice, darling," Fred cooed to Dorrie. "The world can't be all that bad. Think about strawberry shortcake and Fourth of July parades and Christmas."

Dean simply shook his head.

"It was just like it was supposed to be up there, wasn't it?" Crawford said, grinning from ear to ear.

"Where have you been?" Archer asked Crawford sharply, ignoring the question.

"The old man skunked me in Backgammon so I went for a walk. Why?"

"All hell's broken loose," Archer said to Crawford. "Mr. O'Connor saw the turban."

"Oh, shit!"

"It didn't look like any big deal to me," Fred said. "So, what is it? A cure for the common cold?"

Dean, still disgusted with the entire affair, started for the stairs. Dorrie called to him.

"David, please listen." He turned. "Just listen. Then you can go. Someone else has to hear this. Please?"

He wanted very badly to continue up those stairs, pack his bags, and get the hell out of the place but those doe-like eyes brimming with tears told him he'd be in the same league as Whitcomb for bastard-of-the-month if he left her standing there. With all the enthusiasm of a school boy waiting for the school nurse to give him a shot in the ass, he reluctantly returned to the living room and sat.

"Shoot," he said, wondering what he was getting himself into.

"You tell him, Neil. You got us out here," Dorrie said, wiping her face and getting up. "I have to see about Nattie. I have to do something." She went to the kitchen and picked up the phone.

"Just because Whitcomb tells you something..." Dean started to say, but Dorrie cut him short.

"You just don't understand," she said, shaking her head as she began to dial.

Dean opened the sliding glass door to the deck and the afternoon. The clouds were still high in the mountains, but the lower elevations continued to be bathed in sunlight. Crawford, Archer and Fred O'Conner followed Dean and the four lounged against the rail as Neil Archer began to explain.

The history professor gave a deep sigh. "You're going to think we're all nuts."
Dean gave him a look that said it all.

"It started last March," Archer began. "I was picking up stuff for the college museum and writing an article on some of the wacky things, especially quack medical items, that dated from around the turn of the century. I'd picked up a couple of Heidelburg belts, electrical belts, that were supposed to cure everything from cancer to impotency. Remember, electricity was new and no one knew beans about it. People would pay big bucks for these gadgets that didn't really do a damn thing."

Crawford chuckled. "I'm not so sure. Women would wear some crazy contraption that looked like a chastity belt that was supposed to cure all their female problems. It gave them a little jingle of a shock in the ol' wazoo! Cheap Victorian thrill!"

"Anyway," Archer continued, "the whole fad died out in a couple of years. We fooled around with the stuff I'd collected, with Crawford testing it. They all worked basically the same way, just a little electrical current that didn't do any harm or any good. The only contraption that did anything was the Klaxton Turban."

"The electric helmet?" Fred asked.

"Yeah," Crawford answered. "It worked on the same principle as the belt except you put it on your head instead of around your waist or over your crotch."

"A couple of us tried it out and it was kind of restful, like a massage. If you had a headache, it sort of put you to sleep. No big deal, no wonder cure, but it was fun."

"Weren't you afraid someone would get hurt?" Dean asked.

"Hell, no!" Crawford said, disgustedly. "The thing is about as strong as rubbing your feet on the carpet in the winter and touching the radiator for a spark. It's a real nothing."

Archer continued. "So, one day last March, Jeremy Whitcomb tried it. He's Henry's son. He took one of my classes years ago and we're tennis buddies. I guess he had a hangover or something and we got talking about the turban. He tried it and it really helped. His old man was suffering these god-awful headaches after his wife and son died and Jeremy kept trying to convince Henry to try it. Finally he did. That's when the problems started.

"Crawford and I were the only two there when we plugged in Henry. Henry zapped out like sleeping beauty and was gone for about ten minutes. No problem; lots of people napped when they tried it, but when Henry woke up, he looked like he'd been waltzing with the ghost of Christmas past. He wouldn't say anything. He wouldn't answer us. He kept staring ahead, muttering to himself. It scared the shit out of us. I called in Dorrie and she finally got him to come around and say what happened."

Dorrie returned from the phone and stepped out on the deck. "Nattie's home...alone, unfortunately."

"You can't leave her by herself!" Neil exclaimed in a shocked voice that startled the group.

"I left a message on my sister's machine. Keep your fingers crossed Mary will come over and help, if she isn't too busy. She lives in Ardmore and owns a dry cleaning store." Dorrie, still looking worried, slumped into a nearby lawn chair. She dejectedly waved her hand for Neil to continue.

"Henry had a dream, but he said it wasn't like any dream he'd ever had. He was on a street he'd never seen and it was 1926. He read the year and state on a car license. It was Ohio. There were tall trees, nice wooden houses, and two people who walked by were dressed for the time. It was warm, probably summer, he said. He managed to read a street sign, Basset Street, but he had no idea what town he was in. Then he woke up."

"So?" asked Dean.

Dorrie sighed. "He insisted it wasn't a dream. He said he was really there."

"Oh, come on!"

"That's what we said," she continued, "but he was a basketcase, really shook. The way he described it, it was eerie. He said he could see everything, front, back, up, down. He could turn, he could smell, only he wasn't there! When he looked down, there was no 'him!' But he could move, take steps...sort of float-like, but he couldn't affect anything there, like pick something up, or feel something. He was an observer but not a participant."

"Could the people see him?" Fred asked.

"No, he wasn't 'there' to them either," Dorrie answered.

Archer sprawled his lanky frame on another deck chair and began to rock. "If it had been one of the students, I'd have kicked him in the ass for pulling my leg, but Henry Whitcomb? He practically owns the college..."

"And half the world," added Crawford.

"Yeah," Archer continued, "so why in hell would he be making up something like that?"

"What happened next?" asked Fred.

"We tried to get him to do it again, but he wouldn't. We started testing the damn contraption on student volunteers, but nobody reacted anything like Henry; just a buzz, like a massage, like before. Hays took the contraption apart again, but he still didn't find a damn thing. Then we spent weeks trying to locate a Basset Street in Ohio. Finally, in June, Dorrie convinced Whitcomb to do another session with the turban."

"After you found out where Basset Street was," Dorrie pointed out to Archer.

"Yeah," he answered. "In Brigham, Ohio. That's the only town that has a Basset Street. Henry swore he'd never been near the place; it's down in the southwestern corner of the state. I went out there with him, but the address is a parking garage and no one seemed to be able to find a picture of how it looked in the twenties.

"Henry was as nervous as a tic for the second session. He insisted Dorrie be there and swore us to secrecy like an atom bomb test. The only other person he told what was going on was Brown."

"Why the secrecy?" asked Dean.

Dorrie answered. "Because he was frightened to death he'd look like a fool! Something like that doesn't happen, and yet it had happened to him. Or so he said. He wanted a witness he could trust."

"The second session was a bummer," Crawford said glumly. "He had the same reaction but it only lasted about four minutes. There was some noise out in the hall and ol' Henry woke up like Christmas morning."

"So, where did he go this time," Dean asked sarcastically.

"He couldn't tell," Archer answered. "He said it was very barren, no houses or people. But it was the same sensation. He could move, see all around, even smell. But 'he' wasn't there."

Dean gave a look as if to say, cut the bull.

"Don't kill the messenger," Archer said defensively. "I'm just telling you what Henry told us."

"So, tell us about Byrd's Song," Fred asked.

"I'll get to it," Archer said. "There's a lot more. After the second session, Henry got very serious. He put us on his payroll; more money than we could say no to. We were the only ones he'd allow to know about what we were doing, the three of us and Mrs. Brown. No experts, none of that stuff. He fixed it up with the college so we're on a sabbatical, a special project. We're dead meat if there's a leak and Henry Whitcomb, financier, world-class bigwig, etc., etc., ends up on the front page of some supermarket gossip-sheet."

"There's been five more sessions," Dorrie added. "And a lot of experimenting. He becomes really hyper about going under, but it's a love-hate thing. He's scared to death, but fascinated at the same time, when it works."

"Does he really believe he's back somewhere in history? That he's some cockamamie space-time traveler?" Dean asked.

"Who in hell knows?" Crawford said disgustedly. "I don't think he has any more idea what's happening than we do. Only it's happening to him."

Crawford began pacing the room. "Here's what we know. The only adjustment on the turban is the intensity; mild, milder and mildest, but it seems to affect how far back his 'dream' takes place. We don't tell him how much juice we're using, so he can't fake it, but when we pour it on, he goes back. Like the fifth session, he was back in some early history, a biblical place, with everyone babbling in some tongue he couldn't understand."

"Sure," said Dean, "and a bearded guy carrying a cross came strolling by..."

"And you wonder why Henry doesn't want to talk about this!" Dorrie said sharply.

"What do you expect me to say? You have to admit this is about as bizarre as you could get. I don't know what he's smoking or chewing or what the game is, but I'm not buying it for a minute!"

"What controls where the dream takes place?" Fred asked calmly.

"That's been the brain-teaser," Neil answered. "There's no rhyme nor reason to it. There have been cities, open country, even the foreign place. And the time of day doesn't even seem to correspond with the time of day when we're doing it. Except for the approximate time in the past, it's all random. And the only control we have on the time is around five years or so, if we're careful. The further back we go, the wider the band."

"Why only seven sessions?" Dean asked.

"They seem to knock the shit out of Henry," Neil answered. "He swears it's the last one every time we do it. He's obsessed with knowing if what he sees really happened, and he's violent that no one else finds out about it. He guards the turban like the crown jewels, and yet he knows it's probably only a catalyst. It's his head that's doing the traveling, not the turban."

"It's driving him crazy," Dorrie added. "You'd have to know him. He's not used to not having complete control of the situation and here is this...thing that's happening to him, the last person in the world who'd want it...and he doesn't know what to do about it."

"The sessions are a bitch," Crawford said. "He needs absolute silence or he wakes up. If he has to take a piss or something, it queers it. He can't seem to go under every time he tries, only about one in three or four. We had finally set up perfect conditions and then Brown had to sneeze! I thought he'd kill her when it woke him up!"

"Finally, in late August we got in a good one, an hour and twenty-two minutes," Neil Archer said.

"To Byrd's Song," Dean said.

"Yeah," answered Crawford. "And Sneffels, a place we at least found existed. That's why he's going bonkers over getting up there."

Dean let out his breath. "Tell me, all of you. Who buys this stuff?"

They looked at each other but said nothing.

It was Fred who answered. "You've got to admit, it makes for some interesting head games. If a fellow really could do it, I mean."

The shrill ring of the telephone broke their concentration.

Dorrie hurried to answer it but returned at once saying it was for Dean. It was Marian Anderson, the owner of the house.

"David! For heaven's sake! Why didn't you tell me you had Henry Whitcomb out there?"

"Because no one told me, Marian. How did you know?"

"I just hung up from talking to him. He wants to stay on awhile but he's afraid he's putting you out. He sounded so nice. Do you know what the man is worth? Scads! He practically built Spinnersville College and gave it to them. Henry Whitcomb owns zillions of companies..."

"And he's a pain in the ass but what's your point, Marian? I have no problem with letting Mr. Whitcomb have the place for as long as he needs it. I just don't want to be here at the same time."

"He thinks you're the cat's whiskers, David, and he says he really wants you to help him see the sights, whatever they are. David? Please be nice to him! You won't embarrass me, will you? I'll say something sweet about you to Leland and maybe he'll give you a big raise when your ass gets better. Bye."

Why do rich people always get their way? Dean asked himself. Here was Marian Anderson, swimming in a five generation-old family fortune of her own, who just happened to be married to a lowly police lieutenant who was Dean's boss. Marian assumed that manipulating someone's life was as natural as mother's milk, and everybody did it. He loved her like an older sister but she was one of the most frustrating women he'd ever met.

David Dean, chump-of-the-month, was standing there, undecided about what to do, when sweet Mrs. Brown clopped downstairs, summoning Dorrie Briscoe. She turned to Dean.

"When Mr. Whitcomb is finished with Dr. Briscoe, he will see you." Brown said it with the efficiency of an English butler.

Dean hardly had time to make up his mind on the 'invitation' before Dorrie returned, a yard-wide smile on her face.

"Henry is flying Nattie out here! His son Jeremy is coming with some papers and he's picking her up! I didn't know what to say!"

"There will be sleeping bodies laid out like cord wood on the living room floor," Dean muttered. "Don't mind me, my brain's just spinning a little too fast. I'm happy for you. At least you won't have to worry where your daughter is while you're playing the dream game."

"You have to meet her! The two of you would get along sensationally!"

Dean smiled politely and went upstairs to his/Henry's bedroom.

Henry Whitcomb sat on the bed, feet on the spread, with a phone book and various papers stacked around him. He wasted no time getting to the point.

"Archer and Crawford will be moving to a motel in town tomorrow. Before you and the old man leave, I'm asking a favor, a small favor. I've made reservations in town for dinner, just the three of us. Give me that much. You know I've spoken with Mrs. Anderson?"

"Yes."

"The reservation is for seven o'clock," he said. Picking up the phone, he began to dial.

Dean, using the best of his detective training, deduced that the interview was over. However, there was a victory of sorts. There was no evidence of tell-tale cigarette smoke or spent butts in the room. Small victory but victory nonetheless, he thought sarcastically as he returned to the first floor.

Neil Archer was waiting for him in the living room, looking even more worried than usual. Dean was expecting to be questioned about his meeting with Whitcomb but in true character, Neil Archer was only concerned with his own problems.

"I've got this problem..."

"What's her name?" Dean asked, continuing to walk out the front door into the fresh air.

"It's not like the other times, really."

"It's never like the other times..."

"She's incredible. So incredibly beautiful and full of life. And she's so intelligent, so cerebral...for her age."

Dean turned. "For her age? Just what is her age, Neil?"

Archer began biting his fingernail. "Not old. Not very old at all...in years at least. But she's incredibly perceptive, 'way beyond her years. The questions she asks! She wants to know about everything! I'm going to marry her...even if I have to wait."

"Just how long would you have to wait, Neil?" Archer didn't answer. "Neil, how old is this girl?"

"Fourteen. Natalie's fourteen, nearly fifteen."

"Neil, that's sick! For God's sake!" And then the wheels began to click! "Natalie Briscoe! You're talking about Dorrie's daughter!"

"That's my problem," Neil said glumly. "I have to tell Dorrie. Natalie's coming out here! To this house! We were going to tell her mother sometime, but now I'm scared shitless Dorrie won't understand." He suddenly turned. "How did you know about Natalie?"

"She called last night, late, for her mother. Neil, tell me you're not sleeping with this child. You can go to jail for shit like that. In fact, I'd turn you in myself in a minute!"

"No! No! No! I wouldn't touch her! What do you take me for? I wouldn't touch her, not until our wedding night." He shuffled his feet. "Besides, she isn't a virgin anyway."

Dean turned away. "Neil, I don't want to hear this shit! Clean up your own mess!"

He abruptly left Neil, camped in a world of his own, his voice trailing after. "Some little son-of-a-bitch on the midget football team did it to her. I'd kill the little bastard if she'd tell me his name. She was a cheerleader, an innocent little cheerleader..."

Dean walked around the house and down to a grove of pinions and scrub oak and quiet, at least a momentary escape from the group of wackos who had invaded his previously tranquil mountain domain.

CHAPTER IV

The restaurant Whitcomb had chosen was in an old Victorian hotel in Ouray. The hostess led them to a corner table but Whitcomb ignored her and sat in an enclosed booth at the far end of the room. Dean shrugged at the embarrassed woman by way of apology as the three sat. As usual, Whitcomb was quick to get to the point and as soon as drinks were served, began his pitch.

"You've heard the story, so now you know what's going on but you haven't heard my side. I'm not going to ask you what you think about it. In the first place, you'd probably say something cute like 'who gave the bull the enema' and in the second place, I frankly don't give a shit what you think. But I have this problem. I'm knee deep in something I don't understand and look at the staff I have to help me! Neil Archer is an asshole, I wouldn't trust Crawford as far as I could toss him and Dr. Briscoe is a psychological grab-bag. Mrs. Brown is a marvelous secretary, but she isn't paid to think and usually doesn't. I need help and, believe me, that's a rare occurrence."

"With your money, you could hire anyone you wanted," Dean said as he sipped a glass of red wine. Fred remained silent. He hadn't spoken a word since the three left for dinner.

"Answer me this," Whitcomb asked, "suppose you're out on a lonely road in the middle of the night and a flying saucer came wop-wop-wop down in front of you and three little green men jumped out, took your picture, and took off. Would you tell anyone?"

"No, I guess not."

"Neither would I." Whitcomb formed the words with icy firmness as he stared back at them.

"So why did you tell the gang?"

"I didn't. They were there when it happened. Look, I'm sixty-three years old and feel eighty. I've been dreaming for probably sixty of those years and I'm telling you, what happened was no dream."

"How can you be so sure? You dream randomly, just like these sessions."

Dean picked up a roll and butter.

"Dreams aren't random. You can always think back to something that triggered them, something you did or at least thought about recently and they're focused.

"This was entirely different. If I looked up, I could see up. If I looked down, I could see down. I had peripheral vision. I could turn around. I could see everything except myself. I was there; only I wasn't there. I could smell, hear, sense. I could do everything but touch. If I tried to reach out for something, I'd pass right through it. I couldn't see me! I'd look down where my legs should be and there was nothing! I'd take a step and it was like floating; I could maneuver, sort of lope along with only the slightest sensation of the ground beneath me. I could move through objects, just pass through them. Does that sound like any dream you've ever had?"

"Could you walk on water?" Dean asked.

Whitcomb didn't answer, but continued. "I have to get to the bottom of this thing. I wake up with a headache that feels like my brain is going to explode three days out of four and this nonsense is a big part of it. Byrd's Song seems to be the first place where I have a shot at verifying if these places I'm visiting are real or some practical joke my brain is playing on me. I need the verification, nothing else. I need to know if those people really lived! Were they real? That's why I'm so gung-ho about getting up to Byrd's Song. I saw something up there that I'm sure is still around, if it ever really existed in the first place. And I know damn well I've never in my life been near Byrd's Song, Colorado, before this morning!" He paused. "But I need help."

"You're in no shape to make that climb and even if you did spend some time at high elevation getting in even minimum shape, the snow would beat you. It's September."

Whitcomb didn't answer but toyed with a roll, as if looking for an alternative.

"What about horses?" he asked tentatively.

"Horses are too smart to go up there. Besides, you're probably no more a rider than you're a hiker."

Fred O'Connor tugged at his ear and cleared his throat. "Just how hard did you try to check out them places you saw in those other sessions?"

"There wasn't much to check out. At least two were outside the country, God knows where. One was in New York but the session was too short to get any real information. Neil Archer is supposed to be a historian but he isn't worth a damn. He did manage to find Brigham, Ohio, but it didn't tell us much." He took a gulp of scotch, as if to fortify himself. "Look, I want to hire you two."

"No way!" Dean surprised himself with the quickness of his response. "I've seen how you treat the help and I don't want any part of it. Thanks, but

48

no thanks!"

"You wouldn't be employees. You'd have a contract. No conditions, no restrictions, a free hand to prove this is a world class hoax or the greatest thing since the first coming. You don't have to believe me, that's not part of the deal. All you have to do is prove one way or another that this shit I'm seeing really happened. I'm the one who needs to be satisfied, not the rest of the world. Archer and the others don't know what direction to turn. You're a detective, you're used to digging and the old man here has common sense. Besides, I imagine you're both so cocksure it's a joke you'll dig all the harder to prove you're right."

"No sale," said Dean stubbornly. "I don't want to be a party to giving credibility to a rip-off. Sorry."

The three ordered the evening special and there was no further conversation during salad and soup. As the entrees were being served, Fred O'Connor spoke up.

"Just what did you plan to do with our findings?"

Dean looked at the old man coldly and continued to eat.

"The information would be for me and me alone," Whitcomb answered. "As I told you, I'm not trying to prove anything to anyone else or sell this to anyone else. I want to know. Me alone. You know why? Think about it. It's useless to anyone else. There isn't anything you or anybody could ever do to absolutely prove that this is happening. If you prove anything, it's limited to just two things: one, it's a hoax, or two, it's a figment of my mind. You can't prove it's happening, just if it isn't. I'm the only person who knows for sure I'm not lying out my teeth."

"What about a lie detector test? Would you take one?" Dean asked testily.

"Sure, if it makes you happy, but I'll tell you what it will say. 'Inconclusive.' I took a test eight years ago, and that was the result – inconclusive. The operator said I was so strong-willed, I could probably beat it if I concentrated hard enough."

He took a drink and continued slowly. "I took another lie detector test two years ago in August. It came out the same."

Fred rubbed his chin and smiled. "So all you're hiring us for is to find that these things you see really did occur, just as you're seeing 'em in these here sessions?"

"Exactly. And if you want to waste your time working your ass off to try and prove it's a snow job, feel free. It doesn't bother me, it's your time. I already know the answer to that one."

"Answer me something," Dean asked. "Does all of this have anything to do with your wife and son being killed?"

The question obviously irritated Whitcomb, but he held his temper and answered in as chilling a voice as Dean had ever heard.

"No. Except if I am really seeing the past and I could somehow control the randomness of it, I wouldn't waste a minute going back to August 18, two years ago. I'd find out who slaughtered my son and kill the son-of-a-bitch with my bare hands!"

"Sorry," said Dean. "No sale. I have a full-time job, and my gut tells me there's too damn much about this business that smells like week-old fish."

Fred looked about ready to burst but held his tongue.

Whitcomb answered. "I'll get you a leave of absence from the Parkside Police force for however long it takes, fund all of your expenses and pay you one thousand dollars a week and a lump-sum of twenty-five thousand dollars when you're finished, regardless of your success." He wiped his lips in a dainty fashion.

Fred gulped. "Free hand, you said?" He looked like a county judge deciding the case of the year.

Whitcomb knew he had a live one and went in for the kill.

"We followed the last five sessions with intensive questions and Dr. Briscoe taped them. All that stuff is available, tapes, transcripts, everything. I'm available to answer any question you might have. I'll go anywhere you ask or do anything you wish within reason."

"Including more sessions?" Dean asked.

Whitcomb stopped and took a deep breath.

"If that's what it takes to get to the bottom of this. Frankly, that's one reason I'm staying out here; it's the quiet. I can't seem to get that back home. That and what I saw in Byrd's Song."

"No qualifiers whatsoever?" Dean pressed.

"Just one. No more people involved. I won't be made the town fool." Then he added, "I suppose I'll have to tell my son because he'll be here, but he's the last one who's to know. Far too many people I don't trust know about it already."

"We'll let you know in the morning," Fred said before Dean could finish his mouthful.

Whitcomb, to his credit, knew when not to push. Don't oversell; the rule of the successful salesman. Dean didn't argue the point.

Nothing further of substance was discussed during the meal. Fred prattled on about everything under the sun while Whitcomb pretended to be interested and Dean stewed. If someone didn't know any better, they'd think the bastard Whitcomb was actually a regular human being.

By the time the three left the restaurant, the wind had picked up and there was a decided chill in the air. Snow in the high country tonight, Dean said to himself.

When the trio of Whitcomb, Dean, and O'Connor arrived home, everyone was in bed except Dorrie Briscoe. She sat on the sofa, bedecked in a bathrobe and slippers, amid sheets, blankets and pillow, reading a leather-bound copy of The Scarlet Letter. Whitcomb simply nodded and continued toward the stairs but Dean and his stepfather paused.

"Hi," Dorrie said in a cheery voice. "I'll take the sofa tonight. The pullout in the den opens up enough for you two, at least for one night. I pulled out some extra bedding."

"The old man can sleep on the sofa," Whitcomb called over his shoulder in a matter-of-fact voice, "Dorrie will sleep with me."

Dean turned in time to see the startled and hurt look on Dorrie's face.

"Don't act as if it's the first time," Whitcomb added sarcastically as he stomped up the stairs out of sight.

The tears came in torrents as Dorrie made a dash for the deck outside.

"Something of a heartless bastard, ain't he?" commented Fred as he took off his coat.

"I'll see what I can do," Dean said, pulling the quilt from the back of the sofa and moving to follow Dorrie. "Stay here for a bit until we figure out who's on first."

"Gotcha," Fred answered. He reached up and turned off the lamp, leaving only a night-light as he slumped down on the sofa. "Give me a shake when we work out the score cards and point me toward the right bed."

Dean stepped out into the cool night air, crossed the deck, and wrapped the quilt around Dorrie's shivering shoulders.

"Didn't we play this scene last night?" she asked with a sniff.

"You don't have to talk."

"Yes, I do," she answered, wiping her eyes with a balled-up handkerchief. "I want to. The bastard! The no-good bastard!"

Dean said nothing.

"I was dirt-poor when it happened. They had just repossessed my car. Nattie wanted ballet lessons and horseback riding lessons and every other kind of lesson I couldn't afford. I didn't have squat. Henry made a play for me and shy little Dorrie Briscoe fell all over herself clawing her way to his bed. God, even talking about it makes me feel like a Tenth Avenue street walker."

"Are you still...involved?"

"Fucking him? No, thank God! At least I wasn't, not for two years. But just being here is bad enough. God, he's such a controlling bastard. I look at him and I'm a two-dollar whore."

"At least you broke it off. That's something," Dean offered.

"I couldn't live with myself...and Nattie didn't like ballet." She paused. "Who am I kidding? I didn't break it off. He did, when his wife and son were murdered."

"Were the two of you serious?"

"In love? Henry Whitcomb? Are you kidding? Henry's incapable of love. I was in awe of him, if that qualifies for love. It's so damn long ago, I don't really remember. Besides, I'm not sure I've ever been in love so what do I have to compare it to?"

"Did the stork bring Nattie?" Dean asked cautiously.

She laughed. "No, but love didn't have a damn thing to do with it either!" She paused for a moment, as if wondering whether or not to relate the story. "We were still playing nineteen-sixties, twenty years later. Burn your bra, love everybody, fuck like the Irish Navy, totally uncomplicated sex, the whole bit. We were waving flowers and screwing our brains out, and so damned positive we had all the right answers. God, it was so stupid. A bunch of us went to Fort Lauderdale from college for spring break. But instead of fun in the sun, it was pain in the rain, like a monsoon for four days. So we had a party, a party to end all parties, a real honest-to-God '60's party. Good ol' fun-loving Dorrie who'd do anything got herself so shit-faced drunk she lost a day or two. When the sun finally came out, I knew I had had sex. God, I felt like I'd taken on the Southwest Conference football schedule, but that wasn't exactly a novel feeling in those days. After I pulled it back together, I didn't give a thought about what happened until I missed a period or two."

"So what did you do?"

"God, I'd never even seen the boy…, or boys. I had no idea who he was. There were hundreds of students in the hotel. I only knew I was pregnant. Would the baby be black or Chinese or a midget or the next center for the New York Knicks? Who knows? I never felt so lonely in my life, but having an abortion never entered my mind. I gritted my teeth, took off a semester and hitchhiked around Europe on my grandmother's inheritance. Then, bingo! There was Nattie, this beautiful little woman-child!" She looked up at him.

"Why am I sitting out here in the middle of the night, freezing my ass off, telling you my life story?"

"So you don't have to go up to Henry Whitcomb's bed?"

"I guess you're right. Don't listen to me. I'm all screwed up. Half the time I don't mean what I'm saying. God, how can anyone fuck up their life the way I have?"

"Don't be so hard on yourself. It seems to me you've done a pretty fair job in some areas. You managed to get a doctorate, raise a smart kid and hold it together. We all have a few loose ends once in awhile."

She smiled, at last. "Some loose ends. But thanks, that was a nice thing to say even if it is a bold-faced lie."

David Dean, cold as a clam on ice, was ready to call it a night, but Dorrie Briscoe, in a mood to remember times gone by, was just getting started.

"When I was in college," she continued, "before Nattie, I had a roommate named Sue Ellen. She wasn't really a friend of mine; we were sort of tossed together, you know, luck of the draw. I was Miss Personality, in with the right crowd, always with plenty of boys chasing ol' Dorrie who'd do anything on a dare. I was tons of fun. Poor Sue Ellen. She was pretty enough, I guess, but she never fitted in. She had this boyfriend, Tommy Something-or-other. He went to school around Philadelphia, Drexel, I think. Sue Ellen spent nearly every waking minute writing to him, dreaming about him, talking to him on the phone. The rest of us would be out boozing up our Friday nights with our fake IDs, having a hell of a time, while poor little Sue Ellen would be back in her room rereading every one of Tommy's letters for the thousandth time.

"About once a month or so, Tommy would come down to Spinnersville. He was a nice enough guy, kind of quiet like Sue Ellen. But when the two of them were together, something weird happened. It was like the rest of the world was closed off. I'd see them walking around the campus, holding hands or snuggled in some corner of the rec hall. At first we kidded Sue Ellen about what a sap she was for falling head over heels for one guy when there was a college full of hunks floating around. But, you know, she wouldn't pay us any mind. We'd tell her you can't get that close to someone; you'll get hurt. But it was as if she didn't care. She'd just smile and go on spending every waking minute worshipping the ground Tommy walked on. I asked her one time what the two of them found to talk about. They didn't really do anything exciting, not even when he came down to visit. God, I don't even know if they were sleeping together! Sue Ellen just looked at me and smiled and said, 'We talk about everything – every thought I've ever had, every wish, every dream, all the things that scare me, everything.' I told her there wasn't a guy born I'd ever tell my secrets to. She just looked at me and said, 'That's sad,' and walked away."

"Whatever happened to her?"

"Oh, I don't know. We exchanged Christmas cards for a couple of years but we really weren't friends. She sent me an invitation to her wedding but I made some limp excuse and didn't go." Dorrie sighed and waved her hand in dismissal. "Oh, maybe Tommy beat her every night of their married life and they've been divorced for years, who knows."

"But that's not the point, is it?"

"No, it isn't. Nattie was two or three years old before I finally did get the point, when it finally sank in that Sue Ellen was right all along. You know, there probably isn't one in a 100,000 or maybe a million relationships that two people are as much in love as Sue Ellen and Tommy. We made fun of them and all the while they knew that when the two of them were together, there was no one else in the world. Nothing else mattered. Each had someone that loved them just as much as they loved; no doubts, no fears, no jealousy, just pure love. Perfect."

"Perfect in your mind."

"Maybe. Maybe it was just in my mind." She looked up at him, the chill of the air causing her breath to come in little puffs. "But that's why 'kiss and fuck and say goodbye' romances disgust me." She turned and walked to the far edge of the deck and spoke with her back to him. "Don't get me wrong, I'm not frigid or something. God knows I do it enough. But that doesn't mean I like it. Don't mind me, I don't know what the hell I want."

"Maybe you want a Tommy something-or-other."

She turned and he could see her smile. "But I won't get him. Because I'm not a 'Sue Ellen.' I'm too damned frightened to give away as much of myself as it takes to get a Tommy-love in return."

David Dean didn't know what to say.

Finally, Dorrie Briscoe took a deep breath. "But I do know what I don't want and that's to have sex with Henry Whitcomb." She bit her lip.

"If I go back in there he'll just come down and get me." She turned to Dean.

"Sleep with me tonight. Not sex and all that stuff, I just want someone next to me, someone to hold on to." She kissed him, lightly on the lips and took his hand. She tasted like cigarette and something minty and ineffective, designed to not make her taste like cigarette. "You're a nice man," she added, "please?"

They crept past a lightly snoring Fred O'Connor, draped the quilt over him, turned out the night light and tiptoed to the den.

Dorrie Briscoe was right about one thing. Dean should not have paid a lick of attention to what she said. It was all bullshit. She certainly had someone to hold on to but the "just sleeping" part was pure fantasy. Dean's mind took the night off from truth and consequence and all matter of secular concerns like the national debt, world hunger, a certain lady back in Pennsylvania, and Henry Whitcomb's ridiculous proposal.

CHAPTER V

Dean was up before the first light, exhausted but unable to sleep. He left the naked figure of Dorrie Briscoe, curled up like a contented kitten, making purring noises as if all was right with the world. The sound of an early-bird body stirring in the kitchen had shaken him from the misty level of half awake to the shock of full consciousness. He dressed soundlessly and shuffled down the hall to the kitchen, feeling along the wall for direction and trying to get the accusing picture of Cynthia Byrne from his guilty mind. There, sitting with elbows on the table, spooning up cereal and drinking a cup of black coffee, with Mrs. Lincoln in her lap, was what had to be Dorrie Briscoe's daughter.

"Hi, I'm Natalie Briscoe." She was a pretty little half-child, half-adult with long brown hair and an infectious smile.

"And your friends call you Nattie." Dean answered, rubbing his eyes at the light.

"My mother calls me Nattie, just to annoy me."

"Hi, Nattie."

She smiled. "You adults are all the same. Okay, I'll let you call me Nattie just because you have possibilities." She reached for the coffee, spilling a few drops on an open notebook next to it.

"Damned! Now see what I've done!"

"What are you doing here before dawn?"

"Jerry and I flew in to Denver late last night. We couldn't get a flight over to this side of the mountains, so we rented a car and drove. It's over three hundred miles. Jerry crawled to town to get a bed but I'm in better shape so I had him drop me off. Who's the geezer on the sofa, sleeping in his clothes?"

"My stepfather."

"And you're the flatfoot." She didn't ask it; she just made a statement and began writing in her notebook.

"That's me," he said, pouring a cup of coffee and sitting next to her.

"Don't mind the interruption, I'm just getting down my first impression of this place."

"Welcome to colorful Colorado."

"We'll see. At least it beats spending a week with 'Mary Queen of Spots' and her dry cleaning shop." She looked up at him with a smile.

"Are you sleeping with my mother?" She asked it matter-of-factly, causing him to gulp at his coffee, vying for time to set up a really intelligent answer. He wasn't near quick enough.

"Bingo!" she said with a laugh and continued to write. He started to say something cute but his brain was on hold. "Was it 'True-love' or 'Help-me-make-it-through-the-night?' Never mind, you don't have to answer. Either way, chances are, one night is all you'll get. Dorrie is a classic case of next morning regrets. She'll be in her penitent mood all day. But don't feel badly. You just happened to be in the store window when Dorrie had an urge to go shopping."

"You really know how to make a guy feel swell, don't you?"

She smiled that infectious family smile and put down her pen. "Don't blame me that my old lady is easy. No trouble getting in her pants, you just can't get into her head. Dorrie doesn't believe sex is any big deal, at least until the next day."

"And you don't agree with her?"

"I don't agree with Dorrie on lots of matters and sex is sure one of them. If I contribute to the next generation I'm going to know who the old man is and I'm going to pick him very carefully."

"Freud would have a lot of fun with that."

"What do you mean, because I'm Nattie-the-bastard? That doesn't phase me. But Dorrie just got lucky. How many times is that going to happen? I turned out to be one fabulous kid but it was simply pot luck. And she screwed me out of the opportunity to know my old man and be able to check him out. No hard feelings but you've got to admit, it was pretty irresponsible."

"No comment," Dean answered.

"I've got this theory, see," she continued, "stuff is passed on to your kids through your genes, right? So it stands to reason the older a guy is, the smarter his genes are." Dean laughed. "I mean, if I start fooling around with a fourteen-year-old, what does he know? And what do his genes know? And that's only part of the problem. From all I hear, this sex stuff is one fabulous trip. Dorrie sure thinks so. I don't want to wait around 'til I'm gray before I get on the hayride. This whole sex and love business is one confusing subject."

"A lot of very intelligent people have grappled with the birds and the bees for a very long time. I wish you luck."

"Oh, I'll figure it out. Just give me time. Like selective breeding," she continued. "I've given that some thought, too. Like maybe they should save the sperm of all the intellectual he-men and mate it to all the super class beauties. But then all you'd get would be a bunch of Barbies and Kens with super IQs and that would be a B-O-R-E!" She smiled that pretty smile again. "I don't have all the answers but if I don't ask the questions, I'll never get 'em!"

He laughed. "You'll get most of the answers. I'm sure of that. What's in that notebook? All the great thoughts of the world?"

"All the great thoughts of Natalie Briscoe. You'll be seeing this in the Smithsonian one of these days...or your kids will. I'll probably outlast you."

He laughed. "By years and years."

"Did you really toss the tree-maker's cigarettes out the door?"

"Tree-maker?"

"You know, the poet, Joyce Kilmer? 'Poems are made by fools like me...'"

"'But only God can make a tree,'" Dean finished, nodding. "Yes, I pitched his butts out the door."

"That's cool. You really do have possibilities." She picked up her cereal bowl and drank the remaining milk.

"Does the tree-maker still pretend he's 'Timmy Tuttle and the Time Machine?'"

"What do you know about that?" Dean asked quickly.

"Lots."

"How?"

"I monitor Dorrie's phone calls. I read her mail and stuff like that, too." He looked at her with raised eyebrows. "Hey, if I'm going to look out for her, I have to be informed, don't I?"

"Does she know you're the local CIA agent?"

"Probably. We have a cool relationship. She depends on me a lot, but she gives me space. Like, she wouldn't dare read my diary."

"She'd probably be shocked."

"No doubt about it. Hey, maybe you and I should have an affair. We think alike." She spoke with all the seriousness of a black-robed judge.

"And shrink poor Doctor Archer to a blob of jealous waste?"

"Uh-oh. So the kitty's out of the can on that one, huh?"

"'Fraid so."

"Dorrie-the-big-mouth?"

"No, the heartsick lover himself. Dr. Neil told me."

"And I was going to let him down gently. I hope he doesn't jump off a bridge or do something gory. Oh, well, at least the filial-maternal interdependence bit is still intact."

She poured herself another cup of coffee. "There's not much that gets by you, is there?"

"I'm a detective. I'm supposed to know what's going on."

"Are you 'on the payroll'?"

"There's been an offer. I'm still considering it. What's your opinion of this whole business?"

"It's pure bullshit."

"Wash your mouth out with soap!"

"That's been tried before, too. But, okay, I'll clean it up in deference to your advanced age and obvious conservative upbringing. And to answer your question, that's easy. I think you ought to grab the money and run."

"What do you think the whole thing is all about?"

She thought a minute. "I haven't figured it out yet, but I'll give you something else to chew on. I think whoever killed Henry's wife and his son Mike is right here and it's all slopped together like a Cajun soup."

"Why?" he asked with surprise.

"You're the detective, you figure it out."

"Perhaps Whitcomb should hire you!"

"Yeah, except adults have this prejudice that says everybody is stupid until they reach the age of twenty-one. They're too dumb to know most of the time it's the other way around!"

He shook his head. "You're really something!"

"That's what I told you. Look at the opportunity you're missing!"

He just smiled and she shook her head glumly. "If you're not interested it's going to get awfully boring around here. The only other male is Sparky-the-Geek and I'm not that hard up. Besides, I think he's gay."

"Hays Crawford? Really?"

"Scouts' honor. But mum's the word. The closet door's still shut. Really low profile. No one's supposed to know."

"Except Nattie-the-know-it-all. Who told you?"

"It was something Dorrie said. She's got the lowdown on all the boys."

"It's not lady-like to go around spreading rumors."

"I don't, usually. But you're a detective. I'm just giving you a head start."

"Does Archer know about Crawford? He's bunking with him."

"God, no! Neil's so heterosexual it's disgusting! He'd roll over and die if he had a hint."

Dean shook his head. "I can see Neil Archer didn't have a prayer of a chance courting Nattie Briscoe. Are you always that cruel to your ex-boyfriends?"

"Dr. Archer deserved it. Imagine him, coming on to a little kid like me! It's disgraceful! And he had the balls to try and read my notebook! Besides, he's all wrong anyway. He has a two-syllable last name. I need a guy with one-syllable, like 'Dean.' 'Natalie Briscoe-Archer' wouldn't hack it. Now, 'Natalie Briscoe-Dean' sounds cool."

"Sorry. What about Jeremy Whitcomb?"

"Nice guy but far too serious. And he's a two-syllable, too. Besides, he's so uptight with his father, it's got his head all messed up. The old man treats him like stale bread."

"You could have a lesbian affair with Mrs. Brown," Dean offered.

She laughed heartily. "I like you. You have a kid's sense of humor!"

"Believe me, you need it around this place."

"But you're not much help in the love business. Here I've been connubial for almost two years now and...nothing. Virginity is such a bore."

"'Connubial?'"

"Yeah, isn't that a neat word? I read it somewhere."

"What about the alleged torrid affair with the midget football player?"

She laughed. "I just tried that fairy tale out on Doctor Neil for kicks. He was ready to take on the starting lineup of The Spinnersville Spartans just to protect my honor!" She got up from her chair.

"I think I'll just mosey down the hall and hop in Dorrie's bed. It ought to give her a shock when she wakes up! See you around, flatfoot!"

Nattie sauntered out of the kitchen, her notebook under her arm and Mrs. Lincoln trotting on after her. The cat was a sucker for anything that held promise of excitement.

Dean had no desire to stick around and see the action nor did he want any "next-morning" conversation with Ms Briscoe, Sr. He was already suffering from guilt-regrets of his own as thoughts of Cynthia Byrne kept sneaking into his brain for a peek at the future. There were other pressing matters as well; rich uncle Henry and his pot of gold, for one.

Dean went over to the sofa and gave Fred O'Connor a shake. "Rise and shine. We've got some decisions to make. You like to take notes and make lists. Grab a paper and pencil and I'll meet you outside. I'll even spring for breakfast."

The old man grumbled but started to stir as Dean stepped outside to the back yard.

There had been a frost, the first of the season at this elevation, although the mountains had been dusted for weeks. Lightly painted white crystals glistened in the first rays of the sun. Looking up, Dean could see the mountain tops, powdered not only in frost but in snow, well down below the tree line. It was a beautiful sight, but it negated any plans for a hike to Byrd's Song, at least for a few days. The trail would be impassable. Even a few days' wait wouldn't ensure the path would melt before the higher altitudes became locked in winter-long ice.

A black Buick pulled in the driveway and a heavyset man in his early thirties alighted. He was dressed in an open necked sport shirt, slacks and a light golf sweater and grasped his arms about himself in an effort to ward off the cold as he stepped from the car.

"It's not supposed to be winter yet," he said as he extended his hand to Dean, a nervous smile on his face. "I haven't even closed my swimming pool back home!"

"Any swimming pool here would be a skating rink this morning," Dean answered.

"I'm Jeremy Whitcomb."

Dean shook his hand and introduced himself. "I'm afraid you're not dressed for the mountains. But the sun will warm it up to the 70's a little later. Did you find a hotel?"

"Yes, and I surely could use a few hours trying out the bed but I have to see my father. Dad called me in from California, but I had to fly back to Spinnersville before I came out here. I'm bushed. I haven't slept in days."

Jeremy Whitcomb was a pleasant enough individual but had the air of a man who'd spent his life being pushed around, by anyone and everyone. You could picture him having his lunch money ripped off or always being passed over for everything but the dirt details of life. Henry Whitcomb would eat his son for lunch like a Chinese takeout and still be hungry by three.

"I suppose the gang's all here?"

"Sleeping, except for Nattie."

"Sleeping is not part of her agenda," Jeremy laughed, just as Fred O'Connor walked up to them, struggling with the buttons on a plaid parka. Dean introduced the two and walked Jeremy to the door before leaving for breakfast with Fred.

"We'll have to talk later," he said.

During the drive into town, Fred wasted no time in cutting to the chase. "Are we here to put together a plan of action on this business or are we still trying to make up our minds if we should take Whitcomb's money?"

"I already know we'd be fools to get involved with that guy, but I don't suppose you'd be fit to live with if I said no."

"Don't go blaming me. This is 100 percent your decision. I'm just along for the ride to offer whatever little help I might give. That is, if you should decide to take on the caper."

Dean rolled his eyes and started to say something but Fred didn't give him a chance.

"And," he continued, "twenty-five grand is a fair piece of change. It could get you and me and Cynthia Byrne started off really nice, if you can keep Miss Dorrie Briscoe out of your bed long enough."

Dean winced and said defensively but with little conviction, "Cynthia and I don't have a celibacy pact."

"I suppose that's what she says when those sharp doctors down at her clinic make a pass."

"Let's change the subject," Dean grumbled. "We've got business to talk about."

Fred didn't even bother asking again if they would take up Whitcomb's offer.

"The way I figure it," he continued, "we best interview each of 'em separate; divide and conquer. That way we'll know if they all have their stories straight. That's how all the great detectives do it. I say we..."

"Whoa!" said Dean. "I can't think on an empty stomach."

The two men took a table by the window in the Silver Spurs Cafe. Fred ordered eggs, sausage, hash-browns and pancakes while Dean settled for French toast. The snow glistened in the view before them with Cascade Creek spilling down the sheer cliffs of the Amphitheater, the large glacial cirque that dominated the scene to the east side of the small town. Just as the coffee arrived, the sun peeked above the cliff, sparkling the snow like so many jewels.

"If we're going to take Whitcomb's dough, we'll give him full value for his money," Dean said, as he started in on his meal.

"You betcha," Fred answered.

"That means digging like a hungry miner for every bit of information we can get. I don't disagree about talking with everyone individually but, before we do that, I want to listen to those tapes and read those reports."

Fred nodded, wet his pencil, and, in large block letters, made a note on his yellow pad.

"One, read reports. Two, listen to tapes. Three," he continued, "dig into the Byrd family." He looked up at his stepson.

"I'll get a bushel full of detail. If Whitcomb fabricated this story it's one thing. But if it's real and he has inside knowledge of the family, maybe we can trip him up. This may be a small town but they like their history. The museum and historical society would put Parkside, Pennsylvania, to shame."

"I've got some work to do myself," Dean said. "I don't want Whitcomb to know it, but I'm going to dig out every detail I can about the murder of his wife and son."

"You think the killing has something to do with this turban business?" Fred asked as he mopped up the last of his eggs with a piece of toast.

"I don't know but when two off-the-wall events happen to the same people, it makes me wonder. I'm no big fan of coincidences. And another thing; Whitcomb is a guy who likes to control everything. It strikes me as rather convenient that Whitcomb controls this whole affair, too. The place he 'goes back to,' what he sees, how long he's 'there,' it's all just his word."

"Interesting, ain't it?"

"Maybe that's why I'm being a gullible jackass and taking it on. The whole thing is interesting." Dean sipped his coffee and sat back. "That and 25,000 bucks."

"Yeah, it's interesting. But it ain't a fraction as interesting as it'd be if the whole thing isn't 'Let's pretend.'"

"Wake up, Cinderella. You're back in the pumpkin patch." Dean muttered.

"All I'm saying," answered the old man, "is keep an open mind. That's what makes objectivity."

Over a second cup of coffee they agreed to listen to the tapes and read the reports together in the privacy of the downstairs bedroom they were now to share. Hays and Archer were to vacate that room and move to the hotel while Dorrie and her daughter would share the den.

Dean would inform Whitcomb he and Fred were willing to take on the project and ask that he, Whitcomb, advise the others to cooperate fully. Dean and O'Connor would then interview everyone with Fred handling the women and Dean the men. Somewhere in between Dean would call his police friends back in Pennsylvania and pump them dry about the two-year-old murder investigation. Fred would begin researching locally whatever information he could find on the Byrd family.

As they rose to leave, Dean sighed deeply, wondering just what they were getting themselves into.

CHAPTER VI

When the two returned from their breakfast council, Dorrie and her daughter were sitting at the kitchen table, munching on English muffins and jam. Dorrie muttered a greeting but would not meet Dean's eyes while Nattie sat there smiling like a juvenile version of the Cheshire cat. Fred joined the women while Dean went upstairs where he found Whitcomb and Mrs. Brown in the bedroom in close conversation. Mrs. Brown made no move to allow Dean to speak in private so he conveyed his acceptance of Whitcomb's offer with her standing stoically by. He added the proviso Whitcomb speak with the others and require their full cooperation. Whitcomb agreed, with a look that said he hadn't doubted for a minute Dean would accept. He ordered Mrs. Brown to draw a check for a one thousand-dollar advance and turned to pick up the phone, a gesture that was fast becoming his stock sign of dismissal. If moneybags bore any animosity toward Dean for usurping his bed partner of the prior evening, Dean couldn't tell. Whitcomb always looked so pissed off at the world, a rise in his level of nasty was impossible to detect.

Neil Archer was pacing the living room when Dean returned to the first floor. The cradle robber was nervously trying to get Nattie's attention without her mother seeing but Nattie was having none of it, pretending not to notice him. Archer's suitcase was by the door and Hays Crawford soon joined him, his luggage in hand, both about to move to their new digs in town. Before they left, Whitcomb, true to his word, gathered the group and told everyone in no uncertain terms to cooperate with David Dean and Fred O'Connor, as he put it, the two new members of the team. Everyone would make himself or herself available to be interviewed.

Whitcomb and Brown planned to go to town to buy a jeep. Renting was apparently only good for the common folks. Whitcomb also wanted to round up the gear he felt would be needed for the assault of Byrd's Song, hopefully after the snow melted.

Dean said nothing. The town could use the off-season business, no matter how silly the purchases.

Before the group left, Dorrie Briscoe came out of the den and, without comment, dumped a suitcase full of tapes and papers on the coffee table. Much as Dean regretted the nightlong wrestle, he was beginning to wonder if he were the world's worse lover or had just missed a couple of chapters. He was pondering the subject when the phone rang.

With the entire group lingering in easy earshot, Dean answered. It was Cynthia Byrne, calling from Parkside, Pennsylvania. Much as Dean loved her, she was the last person in the world he wanted to talk to with the entire Whitcomb clan, and especially Dorrie Briscoe, seeming to hang on his every word. None of them seemed even slightly interested in getting on with what they were doing and giving him the crumb of privacy he deserved.

After a jaunty remark about unexpected company and some general banter he admitted that, yes, some of the company were females but it was business and, 'the business' was sort of hard to explain. He then tried to keep his responses limited to monosyllables but the change of her tone made him feel he was digging his own grave. Finally, Cynthia got the hint that the timing of her call was not welcomed and, with a chill equal to the morning air, she quickly ended the conversation.

Dorrie Briscoe glanced at Dean for the first time since getting dressed, raised her eyebrows in censure and looked away. She then waltzed a semi-reluctant Nattie out the door muttering about showing her daughter the town. Surprisingly, they left in the car with Henry Whitcomb. Hays Crawford and Neil Archer were close behind. The wholesale emigration left ace detectives Fred O'Connor and David Dean alone to begin their detecting in peace.

Dean was about to plug in a little Franz Liszt to soothe his frazzled nerves when the ever-ready Fred O'Connor popped up with a fist full of hay-raking music. He triumphantly spread out a half dozen tapes and plugged in Waylon Jennings before Dean could stop him.

"We need some music with words around here, not just tooting and plunking and picking," Fred grumbled as he started in on the stack of files.

Dean looked to Mrs. Lincoln for support. She opened an eye but was too exhausted to protest the music, having completed sniffing out the entire premises. After deeming the place acceptable, the cat simply settled down in a sunshine corner for a well-deserved nap.

Mrs. Lincoln was a homebound feline of genteel tastes. At one time she may have considered the outside life but summarily dismissed it. The hunting, killing, dissecting, disemboweling and eating of wild rodents, washed down with muddy puddle water bore no civilized comparison to food and liquid in a dish and a warm lap available on demand. The great outdoors might be swell for some pussy cats, but she'd get what little excitement she needed on the safe side of a window pane, occasionally pawing on the glass at feeder-birds who paid her no heed whatsoever. All in all, it was a most pleasant life, even though the music was sometimes raucous. She closed her eyes and went back to sleep.

Dean sighed in defeat as he went to the phone and dialed the number of the Parkside, Pennsylvania police department. The familiar voice of Rita Angeltoni answered on the first ring. Rita was the department's woman wizard of all things with the possible exception of personal appearance and, after an exchange of pleasantries, agreed to contact the Spinnersville police to obtain details on the two-year-old Whitcomb murders. Not surprisingly, Rita was a fourth cousin-once-removed, or some other equally tenuous connection, to someone at the Spinnersville station. No sweat. She'd get the info post haste.

When Dean returned to the living room, Waylon was crying for a lost love, with Fred attempting to harmonize. Mrs. Lincoln had moved to his lap, a prop for a pile of typewritten papers.

"Here are the highlights of the seven sessions," Fred said, in his Nero Wolfe voice. "The first one we pretty much know about. That was Basset Street in Brigham, Ohio. They didn't take any notes 'cause they didn't know it was going to happen. The second session only lasted four minutes. Whitcomb claims he was in a desert-like area with no one else anywhere around. It looked like pictures of the far west, maybe Utah or Nevada, but he couldn't tell. No idea 'when' either but he was insistent he was actually there. It was no dream. He got snippy as hell at 'em when they questioned him."

"A zero," Dean muttered, taking a seat next to his stepfather.

"Number three had real possibilities," Fred continued. "Whitcomb was in an office building, a dozen or so stories high. It was New York City, he could tell by the skyline, and he guessed it was the '60s by the way people dressed and there were real estate papers dated April 1967. The bad news is that he was only there three minutes. Mrs. Brown sneezed and he woke up or came out of it. I guess he damned-near killed her."

"Convenient as hell, wasn't it?" Dean muttered and Fred nodded as he continued.

"It took him a long time to go under for the fourth session. The notes talk about him being nervous and not himself. Finally, on the sixth try, he went...to a farm, for twenty-six minutes. This is where he first experiments with moving around and covering more territory. He couldn't tell exactly where he was but there was an Iowa newspaper dated June 1943. He describes the people in detail, little things like poor teeth, and pockmarks. There are five of them, a man, a woman and three little kids. He can't find anything to place the location and everyone is sitting around not talking much so he tries to go down the road to another farm. He doesn't make it before he wakes up. Noises outside this time."

"You didn't listen to the tapes yet?"

"No. Just Dorrie's summaries. They're pretty detailed."

Dean went to the kitchen and poured two cups of coffee.

"What happened next?" he asked over his shoulder.

"Crawford caught hell over the fifth session. It seems he turned the gizmo 'way up and sent Whitcomb on a ride to antiquity, or so Henry claims. He was in some biblical scene, a crowded street with dirty, smelly people babbling in some foreign language, hawking wares, begging, crapping in the gutter, babies hanging off breasts, the whole bit. Whitcomb stayed eleven minutes but couldn't wait to get out. Dorrie says he tried to memorize some words but then she thinks he got frightened he might get stuck there! It was the first time he bailed out on his own, so to speak."

"I guess that was how they figured out intensity sets the time period," Dean said as he handed Fred a cup and sank down on the sofa.

"Yeah, but they didn't understand it until after session number six. That one was a bummer, too. He was in France, in the mountains, forty-two minutes worth. He thinks it was the 1930s but there was nothing to verify it. He was outside a village but spent most of his time trying to get close enough to get in a building. Another dead end. We can listen to all the details but I don't know what it'll get us. The bottom line is the only session worth a hoot is Byrd's Song."

"I figured that would be the case. Let's listen to Whitcomb's version of a couple of the early sessions and then play the tape of Byrd's Song. How long was he there?"

"Eighty-two minutes, an hour and twenty-two." Fred rose and cut Waylon off in mid-pleading. He shuffled through a stack of cassettes and inserted one.

Henry Whitcomb's nervousness oozed through on the tapes, especially the earlier sessions. There was no doubt he was a different man after undergoing something that strongly affected him. While he became more subjective with each passing session, his voice and tone continued to sound totally unlike the Henry Whitcomb that Dean had grown to detest. Most of the questions during the post session interviews were asked by Neil Archer with occasional input by Dorrie Briscoe. Hays Crawford was silent. Apparently his sole job was to run the Klaxton Turban. There was a continual insistence on Whitcomb's part that he was not dreaming. He became irate when Archer once referred to a session as "while you were sleeping."

Whitcomb experimented in propelling himself and by the fourth session was able to move, at a pace he described as approximating jogging in slow motion, like 'walking on the moon.' He repeatedly expressed his frustrations at being devoid of the sense of touch, being unable to pick up an object or move it. In session six he was particularly frustrated when he couldn't turn a newspaper to read a date. The seventh session, Whitcomb's "visit" to Byrd's Song, was far and away the most detailed and interesting. Dean and his stepfather listened to the thirty minute summary three times.

Whitcomb's voice alternated from wonder to excitement to futility as he attempted to remember as much as he could.

"I was standing at the top of a steep trail high in the mountains, spectacular mountains. It was sometime in midday by the look of the sun. There was a house, a shack really, in front of me and a couple of sheds around. The house was small, maybe twelve by fifteen or eighteen feet at the most. There was a tin stack with a curl of smoke coming out; I could even smell the wood. It was pine. The place was on an outcropping of a cliff and down below, hundreds of feet below, there was a town of sorts, a collection of buildings that ran along the side of a dirt road. On the other side of the road there was a river or a stream and beyond it, a factory or maybe a mine, with large wooden buildings and long sheds. Donkeys or mules were everywhere, maybe a hundred or more of them. I could even smell them, as high as I was, and hear the noise the men were making. It must have been a mine because the workers were loading heavy sacks on the animals, one on each side. There were pockets of snow all over the place, not on the ground where I was standing but up in the crevices of the mountains. The town was a mire of mud and rivulets of water were everywhere. The mountains were all around me, spectacular mountains, and I was taking it all in when I heard a noise behind me and turned around just as a young girl was coming up the trail. She was a pretty thing, a little on the skinny side. She wore a faded cotton dress that came down to her ankles and she had some sort of boots on. I'm trying to remember everything. She wore a locket, a gold locket in the shape of a heart with tiny pearls around the edge. Her hair was tied back in pigtails and she was maybe thirteen or fourteen-years old. I felt as if I could reach out and touch her she was so real. She carried a basket with a red cloth covering the contents and had a big grin on her face. The girl called out 'Sarah' just as she passed me and climbed up toward the shack. A woman who looked to be in her thirties came out of the building followed by a second young girl about the same age as the first. The second girl was dressed like the first but without the locket, and she had on an apron. Her hair was shorter and she was prettier but she had a frail look about her.

"The first girl handed the woman the basket and said, 'Ma was baking some bread so when I told her I was coming up to Byrd's Song she packed you a loaf.' The woman looked very pleased and said 'thank you' a number of times and asked about someone's health but she had her back to me by then and I couldn't hear clearly. I think she called the girl 'Ella' but I'm not sure. She said it quickly and didn't repeat it." There was a long pause, as if Whitcomb was straining his memory. Finally, he continued.

"Ella, the visiting girl, remarked how beautiful it was up there and how she wished she didn't have to live down in 'Sneffels.' That's how I found out the name of the town."

Archer asked about the older woman but Whitcomb only said she looked pleasant but tired and was dressed in similar fashion to the younger girls. After the 'thank you,' she went into the cabin and proceeded to work on the preparation of a stew.

Whitcomb followed her and described the cabin as having two rooms, a main living area and kitchen room with a curtained off bedding area, apparently for the young girl. There was a small separate bedroom containing a double bed, presumably for the parents. Articles of men's clothing lay about. Later, the girl mentioned a father "off digging." Whitcomb could find no direct reference to date or location in the cabin so after noting the description of the room in his mind, he went back outside to listen to the girls.

Whitcomb provided minute details of the young ladies' conversation as if trying to remember every word spoken. They were apparently school chums and their discussions were not unlike what might occur today; talk of boys and teachers and an upcoming dance in the town.

Unfortunately, little was said about names, places or dates that would help Dean and Fred.

When the girls sat looking down on the town, Sarah mentioned she wished she had a spyglass so she could 'see Tommy when he went to Porter's store.' That was the only other reference to a name.

Whitcomb's physical description of the location was equally detailed. The shack, or cabin as he later called it, was built nearly under the overhang of a high cliff. The wood was described as rough-cut lumber and the roof tar paper. There were but two windows, both facing toward the town below. The out building was a tiny woodshed with an attached privy.

Dean had to admit the general description bore a remarkable resemblance to what he assumed the view would be from that ridge above Sneffels that Whitcomb had pointed out a day earlier. A fleeting thought passed through his mind, suggesting Henry Whitcomb had actually stood on that high cliff when Sneffels, Colorado, was inhabited by more than the ghosts that dwelt there today. He quickly dismissed the notion as nonsense.

"I have one major problem," Dean said when they had finished listening. "What did Whitcomb see up there that makes him so sure he can verify it's the same place?"

"Nothing he admitted to in the tape, that's for sure," Fred answered.

"But something else is fishy. What Henry described didn't take any eighty-two minutes. The old boy is holding out on us."

"At the very least." Fred sighed. "I guess we'd better go 'Byrd hunting.'"

Before Dean could respond, the phone interrupted.

When Dean answered, a male voice introduced himself as Harry Hammond, police chief of Spinnersville, Pennsylvania. Rita Angeltoni certainly had connections, Dean thought. Hammond first expressed curiosity about Dean's interest, but after Dean explained Whitcomb and his friends were in Colorado, and he had hired Dean to investigate another matter, the gruff-sounding police officer was more than cooperative. He had known Whitcomb and his family for years and was intimately involved with the investigation of the murders. As there was a voluminous amount of information, Hammond had decided to call Dean and highlight the details.

The murders had occurred on the afternoon of August 18, slightly more than two years before. There was no sign of forced entry and nothing had been taken. Both victims had been shot in the head, both at close range. Although the coroner's findings were inconclusive, there appeared to be a lapse of time between the deaths; best guess, an hour or so. The house was wired with a highly sophisticated alarm system which remained operational.

"Phyllis Whitcomb was always a bundle of nerves," Hammond reported, "She would never be in that house without the damn alarm engaged. The place was like Fort Knox. She had silent alarm buttons in every room. If there was the slightest hint she was in danger she would have signaled. God knows she'd done it in the past. We were out there on half-dozen occasions chasing ghosts she thought she heard."

"Any chance they were the real thing and she wasn't just crying wolf?"

"Naw. It was common knowledge the place was impregnable. It was like a joke around town. Besides, Spinnersville is as safe as a sultan's harem. We don't have even ten break-ins a year and those are just kids. Besides, everyone knew the place was wired. Why hit Whitcomb's fort when any other place in town is easier?"

"What are you telling me?" Dean asked, guessing the answer.

"It was an inside job." Hammond made the pronouncement in a sober voice with a conviction that sounded like he'd reached the conclusion after a considerable amount of thought. "I figured that from the start. We just mouthed the case the other way."

"A bullet in the head sounds more like a suicide or a gang hit than a crime of passion," Dean remarked.

"Two shots to the head each, first one killed 'em, second for good measure, and no gun. It might look like a gang hit but I don't buy that either. We're still singing random to the public but humming friend or family to ourselves."

"At the coaxing of Henry Whitcomb maybe?"

"Henry doesn't pressure anyone, his presence alone does that. Besides, we didn't have a lick of proof to go around accusing anyone."

"No one heard the shots?"

Hammond chuckled. "You wouldn't ask if you saw Henry's place. It's so far up on the hill you could fire a canon and no one would know."

"You're pretty up on this for a two-year-old case, aren't you?"

"Have you ever been in Spinnersville?" the police chief asked.

"I went to college there years ago and but I haven't been back except to bike through it a couple of times on tours. It's a good seventy-five miles from Parkside," Dean added.

"First off, things like this don't happen in Spinnersville. If the college stopped operating, the half dozen businesses here would close their doors the next day. That's how small we are and that's why this murder was such a shocker. Secondly, I knew Phyllis Whitcomb very well. We went to high school together. She was a class lady who had the misfortune to marry a prick."

"Give me a read on Henry Whitcomb," Dean asked. There was a short pause before Hammond answered.

"Henry Whitcomb wouldn't pick your pocket, but if he sold you Girl Scout cookies, chances are they'd be stale. Don't underestimate Henry. You don't make the kind of dough he's accumulated playing in that league without working all the angles and being one smart son-of-a-bitch. He may do some things that seem dumb as hell, but he's nobody's fool. Henry always has an agenda."

"Sounds like you know him pretty well, too."

"He stole Phyllis Riley away from me thirty-five years ago and I knew him years before that."

"It sounds like there's no love lost."

Hammond let out a deep sigh. "It wasn't just his stealing my girl, it was the shitty way he treated her all these years while she never stopped worshipping the ground he walked on. Phyllis was a sweetheart, full of piss and vinegar, 'the girl most likely,' cheerleader, beauty queen, sharp as a tack. By the time Henry finished with her, she was damn near a recluse. Her whole world shrunk to Henry and her sons. 'Peculiar,' that's what the town kindly said, or, 'the housekeeper,' when they weren't so kind. All she did was run around cleaning up after Michael or whiping Jeremy's nose and doting after 'Daddy' as she called Henry."

"True love, it sounds like."

There was a long pause before Hammond continued. "No, it wasn't like that. You'd have to have known her, seen the change over the years. Granted, she was obsessed by him but it wasn't love."

"Fear?"

"Who's to say? It was a compulsion. Henry was her life. Period. It was as if some force had assigned Phyllis Whitcomb to toss roses in Henry's path to keep his feet smelling clean while she withered away. Neighbors wouldn't see her for weeks sometimes and then spot her in the woods behind their property, talking out loud, without anyone else around. Toward the end, she really needed help, but that might have soiled Henry's perfect reputation." Dean could detect the hatred stewing in the police officer's voice. "Now he treats his son Jeremy damn near the same way."

"What about Michael?" Dean asked.

Hammond laughed. "Crank up the gramophone and play the other side. Henry worshipped the kid; Michael could do no wrong."

"Did he?" asked Dean. "Do wrong, that is?"

"Naw. Michael was an okay kid. He played the old man, enjoyed the adulation. But I'll tell you this, Henry is obsessed with the murder. I think he'd do anything to know who killed his son."

"And his wife," Dean added.

"Yeah, her, too. But, believe me, that's two different matters. Henry's out at the cemetery once a week or so, putting flowers on the grave, standing around, maybe even praying. But he's not at his wife's grave."

Dean didn't comment. "Tell me about the rest of the people. Who could be involved in the murder? Who's at the top of your list?"

"You're a cop. You know. Nine times out of ten it's the spouse. Whitcomb was screwing around, you probably already know that. He's my first choice."

"But not to kill his son!"

"Maybe the son caught his old man killing his mother and got in the way somehow. Or maybe it was a hired job and the killer wasn't so discriminating. Maybe I'm all wet about Whitcomb and it's his sweetie. Maybe Miss Professor wanted old Henry to make her an honest woman." Somehow Dean couldn't see Dorrie Briscoe killing two people in cold blood.

"Any evidence Phyllis Whitcomb might have been having an affair, too?"

"Frankly, she was too strange near the end, unless someone was taking advantage of her. I wondered if her husband suspected it but we couldn't dig up a hint. As I said, she worshipped the ground Henry walked on. It would surprise the hell out of me if she ever fooled around. She almost never left the house, except for her walks and church. But I'll say this, if she were having an affair, Henry's ego would have gone bonkers. You just don't piss in Henry Whitcomb's pea patch and get away with it."

"What's Whitcomb's beef with his other son, Jeremy?"

"Jeremy's a nice sport but he's too soft for his old man's liking. Remember the old Charles Atlas advertisements when we were a kid? Jeremy could have posed for the guy getting sand kicked on him. Papa was always comparing his two sons and Jeremy came out on the short end. The kid was a mama's boy and that didn't sit well with his dad. The old man can be a first-class bastard if you haven't already discovered that. It's funny, though, in spite of it, Jeremy thinks senior is God. He'd do anything for him."

The tree-maker, thought Dean. Then he asked, "How did the sons get along with each other?"

"Pretty well, by all accounts. They traveled in different circles but there didn't seem to be any animosity there. Michael didn't have any reason to be jealous of Jeremy and Jeremy is too kind a soul to know what jealousy is."

"Any girl friends?"

"None special, at least at the time of the murder. They both dated, Michael more so, big-man-on-campus and that stuff, but no serious involvements. Jeremy seems to always be doing the old man's bidding to such an extent he doesn't have time to piss, much less enjoy himself."

"Tell me about Hays Crawford."

"A friend of the boys, a neighbor. He's a crackerjack electrician. It was Hays who wired the house for Whitcomb. Crawford has a police record. Nothing really serious, just some possession charges, teenage indiscretions. He was pretty spaced out for a while there but he's been clean for three or four years now. Still a little weird but clean."

"Any evidence he's gay?"

Hammond sounded surprised. "If he is, he hides it well. Frankly, I'd be surprised. Crawford didn't run with that kind of crowd and this is a small town. Besides, there was a story a few years ago that pointed him out as a daddy to one of our local free spirits."

"If he put in the alarm system, couldn't he screw around with it?"

"He claims he couldn't, at least not from the outside. It was made foolproof, or so he says."

"Tell me about it."

"It's heat and motion sensitive and covers the place like an Eskimo's long-johns. It even records the time of each legitimate entrance. Word is, the old man wanted to know the time the boys came in and he didn't want to stay up and wait for them. And, before you ask, on the day of the murder, there were three recorded entrances, one-seventeen, two-oh-nine, and five-thirty-three, all p.m. The last one was Jeremy Whitcomb when he discovered the bodies."

"You said it recorded the entrances. What about the exits?" Dean asked.

"There's a switch inside you flip when you're leaving, unless you're not familiar with it, like if you're a burglar."

"So the killer came in at one, and stuck around for a little over an hour, killing first one and then the other. Doesn't make sense, does it?"

"Nope. Or, the killer murdered one and then the second person walked in on it later."

"Who died first?"

"If the coroner's right, Michael died about one-thirty to two o'clock and his mother between two and two-thirty. They both died immediately. They were shot at close range, powder burns and all."

Dean sighed. "Let's get back to who's-who. The only one remaining is Neil Archer. How does he fit in?"

"Another Whitcomb whipping boy. Archer got in trouble over a freshman coed a few years ago, got her pregnant and was about to be canned. Whitcomb went to bat for him with the board and saved Neil's job. God knows why. But now he has Archer in his debt for life. That's how Henry works; he gathers chits on you and then turns the key."

Dean remembered Henry Whitcomb's secretary. "Did you check out Mrs. Brown?"

Hammond laughed. "To be honest, I don't remember. I suppose she was at work. I hear she hasn't missed a day in twenty-five years. The old bag is a cracker-jack secretary with as much personality as the federal register. If Whitcomb ever smiled at her, she'd die of acute orgasm, but there's no chance of that."

"No skeletons in her closet?"

"Zero rumors around town."

Dean thought a moment. "If Brown has the hots for Whitcomb, why wouldn't she be as much a suspect as anyone else?"

"Oh, I don't know," Hammond answered casually. "I guess it's just difficult for us to take her seriously. Besides, it's been two years since the murders and nothing has changed for her. She's still just his secretary."

"Nothing much has changed for any of the others either," Dean noted.

"I guess you're right. The only thing that's happened is Briscoe is out of Henry's bed and Jeremy is, reluctantly by the looks of things, a vice-president of some kind. Everything else is business as usual."

"Did they all have alibis at the time the killings took place?" Dean asked.

Hammond went down the list methodically.

"Henry Whitcomb was in Atlanta on business and flew back later that evening. However, he could have let someone else use his ticket and taken an earlier flight under another name," he explained. "No one remembered seeing him but business travelers tend to be pretty anonymous and Whitcomb is used to maintaining a low profile."

"Until he opens his mouth and starts directing traffic," Dean added.

"Hays Crawford was supposed to be in a college class all afternoon but they don't take attendance in grad school and a few weeks had gone by before we got around to checking him out as a possible. No one could remember for sure. Archer was on vacation at Margate on the Jersey shore, by himself. The honey he was with left the night before in a snit. I guess he wasn't all she'd hoped for. Any way, no corroboration. The Briscoe dame was shopping in Philly but alone. She produced some dated receipts but they don't list the time."

"What about Jeremy?"

"Driving down from a business trip in Boston, again, alone. He can prove he was in Massachusetts the night before, but that's it. It's a six or seven hour drive but he didn't discover the bodies until after five and that leaves a lot of unexplained time."

Dean had run out of questions. He promised to keep Hammond posted if there were any developments in Colorado although he was vague about Henry Whitcomb's reason for traveling west except to say the trip didn't appear to have anything to do with the killings. He ended the conversation by thanking the Pennsylvania officer for his gracious help.

Fred had moseyed upstairs and picked up the extension, at first to Dean's chagrin, but at least it negated Dean having to take detailed notes of the call. Fred came downstairs with his ever-present pad, full of scribbles.

"Looks like we might be chasing more than just ghosts, doesn't it?" he said, with a smile.

Dean took hold of both of the old man's shoulders and looked him straight in the eye. "Look," he said, "if this thing gets the slightest bit hot, I want you out of here. We went down this path once before and I was a nervous wreck. I'm the cop. I'm supposed to be exposed to danger. You're not. This isn't one of your mystery books. Understand?"

Fred gave him the classic "look-of-wonderment" and pledged all the right assurances, none of which Dean believed for a minute. But at least the warning was on the record, hopefully unnecessarily.

"Seems like quite a coincidence," Fred said sagely, "that all the people Hammond thinks might be suspects in the murders are here under the same roof as Henry Whitcomb. It's like he's putting 'em on trial, and he's the judge and jury." That same thought had occurred to David Dean.

The two men went over a list of questions for their upcoming interviews and agreed to get back together before dinner to compare notes. Fred was anxious to go into town to the library and historical society to get started on the Byrd research as his assignment was limited to only two interviews, Dorrie and Mrs. Brown. Dean drove him in, grabbed a sandwich, and arrived back at the house just as Crawford and Archer followed him up the drive.

Dean began his interview sessions with Neil Archer but learned little of substance from him. Much of the information was the same as he'd read, heard on the tapes, or been told by Archer the prior day. He felt the professor was giving Whitcomb lip service, while pretending to be objective, probably because Whitcomb was paying him more money than he could possibly make from his college position. When Dean pressed him, he was evasive, but admitted his surprise when he found a Byrd family really existed. He dismissed the Basset Street, Brigham, Ohio, connection as a fluke. While Archer didn't suggest Whitcomb was faking the sessions, Dean figured he was secretly convinced the whole thing was in Henry's head.

Archer also purported to now be an expert on the feasibility of time travel. "We must have read everything in print on the subject, hundreds of books."

"Fiction, I presume," Dean said sarcastically.

Archer ignored him and continued to expound. "Most of the scenarios on trans-time exploration had people going back and changing history, you know, righting the wrongs of the world? But that's kind of hard to buy, too many 'what-if's?' The way it appears Henry is transcending time makes lots more sense, scientifically speaking; his being there, but not really being there, just being an observer."

"As far as I'm concerned, the whole thing's kind of hard to buy, but that's not my job."

"Think of it like a magic trick," Archer said. "Just because you don't know how the magician saws the girl in two doesn't mean he really cuts her. Just think what it would be like if the turban really does work!" His eyes brightened and he waved his gangling arms in animation.

"You could stand back and watch Picket's charge at Gettysburg, Antietam, Vicksburg, all the great battles! Watch Ulysses Grant, hear his attack plans first hand!"

"Yeah," added Dean, "see the bodies, hear the screams and anguish of the kids getting killed, and not have to even worry about getting splashed with their blood."

"You've got no sense of history," Archer said angrily. "Who wouldn't want to meet Lincoln, Napoleon, see Marie Antoinette on her throne?"

Dean was sure Neil Archer would spend more time leering at Marie Antoinette in her bathroom than gazing at her regal highness in awe-struck wonder but he held his tongue. He changed the subject to Henry Whitcomb, the person.

Archer was coy about his overall opinion of Whitcomb. While the others were vocal about their dislike for the man, Archer, out of loyalty or otherwise, would not speak ill of his boss. Dean considered broaching the subject of the murders but thought better of it. Meanwhile, all Archer wanted to talk about was Nattie Briscoe, but Dean put him off, saying he had to interview Crawford and the others and didn't have time.

Dean's discussion with Hays Crawford was far more interesting, perhaps because Crawford, although brash and somewhat obnoxious, still maintained the candor of youth. As he put it, he tossed his cards on the table early in the conversation.

"Seeing as you're a detective digging into all this shit, I might as well save you some time and tell you up front I've got a record."

Dean didn't admit he already knew and let Crawford fill in the details.

"A couple of drug busts years ago. I did thirty days in Maryland one time, but now I'm clean, clear and free. But boy, I was sure whacked-out for four or five months."

"What turned you around?"

Crawford laughed. "I saw the light! I went on a personal crusade, painting, 'Jesus Saves' on every highway overpass across the United States! Great way to see the country."

"I think I've seen your work," Dean muttered.

"Damned, I was good. I could handle a spray can, neat as a pin, hanging upside-down, thirty feet above the concrete, at four o'clock in the morning!"

"Everyone needs a specialty now-a-days. Tell me about the Klaxton turban."

Crawford rattled off the information in rote. "Albert Klaxton, born in Minnesota in 1866, worked in Menlo Park with God himself, messed around with various electrical gizmos for a few years, marketed the turban for three years, went bust and ended up a bookkeeper for an auto company in St. Cloud. The turban bombed. He probably didn't sell a hundred of them."

"Why?" Dean asked.

"First off, he was too late. Fads move quickly. Second, he had no marketing plan. Sears, Roebuck was carrying the 'Heidelberg Alternating Current Electrical Belt' at prices from four bucks to eighteen bucks, depending on the gauge of the current; C.O.D., ten days free trial. Klaxton was a dead duck. He was trying to sell the turban from the back of a wagon, one at a time."

"What were those things supposed to cure?" Dean asked.

Crawford pulled out an old circular from his back pocket and began to read. "For nervous diseases and weakness of all kinds in men and women, including, but not limited to, nervous exhaustion, gaining back lost strength and power, over brain-work disorders, impotency, insomnia, melancholia, kidney disorder, Bright's disease, dyspepsia disease of the liver, female weakness, poor circulation, weak heart action and almost every known disease and weakness. The constant, smooth, soothing alternating current will improve your circulation and calm your mind to utter tranquillity." He looked up at Dean, a smile on his face. "So, how could you say 'no?'"

"And they let them get away with that?"

"Times change, thank God. But fifty years from now they'll laugh their asses off at what we're doing to ourselves today. Don't be too harsh on grandpa. Remember, a few years before that they were drawing blood, slapping leaches all over your body and feeding you God-knows what. Besides, do you really think half the vitamins and shit we put in our bodies today are worth a damn?"

Crawford had been present at the post session interviews but had not asked questions, as he said he "frankly didn't give a shit what Whitcomb saw."

"Why?" asked Dean, surprised at the answer, and not entirely certain Crawford was telling the truth.

"Listen, I've taken more trips than a train conductor and I know one when I see it. After you've spent a few months with druggies, nothing surprises you. You know the routine."

"Are you saying Henry Whitcomb is on something?"

"Hell, no! I'm just saying his mind is taking him on some neat little excursions, without a bucket of chemicals to screw up his body. It's terrific! Think of the potential! The big elevator ride with no down button! No harm to the bod. Just plug it in when you want to take a little trip! If the thing really worked, it would be worth a billion!"

"So you're not convinced it works?"

"Oh, it works on Henry okay, but I can't figure a way to get it to work on anyone else. Maybe it just doesn't. That makes the most sense, that it's Henry's mind, not the turban that's the travel agent. But the potential is so great, it's worth pulling out all the stops."

"Let me get this straight. Then you don't buy the reality of it, that the stuff he saw really happened?"

"Give me a break, Alice! Get out of your hole and return to the garden!"

"The potential?"

"Look, my interest is purely psychedelic. I don't give a shit about the history bit. Henry's barking up the wrong tree. He should stop chasing the past and sit back and enjoy the ride."

"What about Basset Street?"

"Come on! Ohio is a big state! It's more of a surprise there was only one town with that street name."

"How do you explain the 'where' of the sessions?" Dean asked, playing the devil's advocate.

"Just like your dreams, crazy connections to reality, but if you think about it, you can usually come up with the tie. Like maybe Henry was watching a beer commercial the night before he tripped to the Rockies!"

Hays rose and crossed to the window.

"I guess it would be cool if it really did work, wouldn't it? It would be a gas to go up there and sit in with a bunch of miners, guys from all over the world, working together to scrape a fortune out of the ground."

He peered out the window and then turned to Dean. "Have you ever been up to that old bunkhouse?"

"No. I'd guess it's quite a climb. I've driven up the dirt road just below it."

"But not as tough as Byrd's Song."

Dean had taken longer than planned with the Hays Crawford interview but it was time well spent. There was a strong element of common sense in the young man's pronouncements on the "how" of the Klaxton turban, but David Dean had a lot more digging to do before he admitted to having any answers. And he felt Crawford was a point or two less than one hundred percent in his candor.

CHAPTER VII

Long before the first scruffy band of white men traversed Engineer Mountain from Lake City, Colorado, in search of gold, the Ute Indians wandered for uncounted millennia throughout the area of the San Juan Mountains and the Uncompahgre Valley. Besides the beauty of the land and the abundance of game, there was an additional attraction: the bubbling, steaming, ever present, hot spring pools. While the mystical reverence with which these waters were once held abated with the so-called advance of civilization, the pools continued to flourish and be utilized, thanks to the ingenuity of decades of town fathers who constructed and maintained a public facility that now operated on a year-round basis. Many a visitor rounding the curve on the northern approach to the town of Ouray on a winter evening blinked twice when they saw clusters of ghostly swimmers, their heads bobbing in the steam, like apples at Halloween, frolicking amid the snow and ice of the season.

Now Henry Whitcomb had discovered the place, appointing it his personal training spot to drill himself into shape for his assault on Byrd's Song. The pools, with their three different levels of water temperature and the adjoining exercise facility, were just what the money merchant needed. Or so he said as he made the pronouncement when he returned to the house just after four o'clock, chipper and, as he reported, feeling better than he had in years.

Crawford and Archer were assigned to join him for the evening workout, how willingly could only be guessed. Whitcomb pulled up in a new bright red jeep with only Mrs. Brown accompanying him. Neither Dorrie nor her daughter was anywhere to be seen. Brown immediately appropriated the upstairs bath with not so much as a wave of greeting and commenced one of her marathon showers.

"The others are flitting around town," Whitcomb said, after putting down an armful of packages. "We saw them all at one time or another. Jeremy will drive them back. By the way, I had lunch with Jeremy and brought him up to speed on the turban. He may want to talk with you. Unfortunately, the child knows, too." He was off to his room without further comment.

Dean moseyed to the kitchen, wondering if anyone around the place ate. No one mentioned meals so he cooked himself a steak and a fist full of frozen French fries. Every man for himself. He had spent the time since Fred left going over the material on the sessions in more detail, learning nothing further. There were, however, some pointed questions to ask Henry when the opportunity for that interview came about. Dean was also curious about what Fred O'Connor might have found in his discussions with the women.

It was nearly six-thirty when Jeremy's car pulled in the drive, chauffeuring Fred, Dorrie and Nattie. Nattie was first in the house, looking as mad as a wet hen.

"I still don't believe you'd do that!" she shouted over her shoulder to Fred O'Connor who wore a yard-wide grin above his plaid bow-tie. "You're unbelievable!"

Fred moved around her, waving a salute to Dean with a large manila package and made for the downstairs bathroom.

"First in the bath," he called to Nattie. "Take the one upstairs if it's free. We don't have a whole lot of time if we're going to eat before we go." Dorrie crept by in the confusion and escaped to the den, banging the door behind her.

Dean looked at Nattie, his eyebrows raised, asking for an explanation.

"That old man is a fool and a meddler! I can't believe what he did! Listen to this! We all had a snack in this little deli place and the old geezer starts a conversation right out of the blue, with this jeans and flannel shirt dude. The next thing I know he's introducing all of us and arranging a date for me! It's like something out of the middle ages! And you won't believe where we're going! An Elk's dance!"

"How old is this man?"

"I don't know, fifteen, maybe sixteen. He can drive. Maybe out here in the wilderness you can drive at ten, I don't know."

"And what does your mother think about this?" asked Dean with a smile.

"Oh, she thinks it's the funniest thing since Clarabelle, the clown. But that's only the half of it! We're double-dating!"

"Your mother's going?"

"Hell, no! Gramps-the-geezer and Miss Personality! Mrs. Brown! Can you believe it? And Ron, that's the cowboy's name, is picking me up! He'll probably be driving a pickup with a damned dog prancing around the back!"

She turned and shouted over her shoulder, "If he shows up in a truck, you and Brown can sit on the hay with Rover!"

Dean couldn't help smiling. "Fred O'Connor talked Mrs. Brown into going dancing with him? Now I'm the one who can't believe it!"

"He's one smooth gent for a hundred-year-old. She wasn't going to give him the time of day, but he put a sweet-speech on her that would charm a spider out of its web. In about ten minutes, he had her number. He spread it on like chocolate frosting, about it being business and how King Henry told everyone to cooperate and all. She couldn't say no, not that I'm sure she wanted to."

"What about Doctor Neil, every child's friend?"

"He's in mourning but it'll be short-lived. Wait until he gets to ogling the local honeys in the hot tub tonight with Hays and Henry, if he isn't too exhausted from pumping iron." She slumped down into the sofa.

"By the way, count on a full night's sleep tonight. Miss Dorrie scratched you from her most wanted list. But I did convince her to talk to you. I figured if you're going to get anywhere with the 'yesterday project' you'll need all the help you can get."

"Thanks," was all Dean could muster.

"All I have to wear is a dress, if you can believe it! And I don't even know how to dance to chicken-plucking music!" She turned, striding off to the den.

Dean had assumed Jeremy had returned to town as he hadn't come in with the others but later, when Dean stepped outside for air, Henry Whitcomb's son was there, gazing down the valley.

"Are you getting a breather from the zoo?" Jeremy asked with a smile.

"You betcha," answered Dean, shoving his hands in his pockets against the cool evening air. "Are you sticking around the house or going back to town?"

"Oh, I'll go back in and get a bite to eat later." He turned to Dean. "May I be candid?"

"I wish you would be candid. It would be refreshing for a change."

"What in hell is my old man into?"

"I thought he told you."

"Telling me doesn't mean I understand it!"

Dean chuckled. "I'm not sure any of us do. And to hear your father talk, I'm not sure he comprehends it himself."

"Look, is this just some damned seance to see who killed my mother and brother?"

"That's not the way your father is selling it."

Jeremy kicked at a clump of fallen aspen leaves and walked a short distance away, irritated. "Why won't he leave it alone?"

"Why should he? Or, why should you for that matter? They were your family!"

Before Jeremy could answer, a car pulled in the drive. It was of a vintage Dean hadn't seen in years; a '60s boat of a vehicle, pinged and scraped and dappled with rust but still damp from a recent wash, probably its first in years.

A young man stepped out of the car and walked toward them with a pace that was neither cocky nor timid. Dean could smell the Old Spice at ten paces.

With a kind of shy confidence, the young man held out his hand to Dean who had stepped forward.

"Hi. I'm Ron Adams," the young man said. "Is Miss Natalie and the others ready to go?"

Dean brought Mr. Adams into the house and rounded up the group. Nattie looked delightful in a dark blue dress, certainly not one of her choosing yet a picture-pretty memory of days gone by. Even Mrs. Brown was polished and trimmed to a new high, as she made her Loretta Young corseted entrance down the stairs, albeit with an air of reluctance. And Fred, always the dapper gentleman, led the parade, as spiffy as a Victorian gent.

Before the foursome left, Fred pulled Dean aside and handed him the large manila envelope. "These are photos taken around Sneffels, most in the 1890s. A kindly lady stuck her neck out and lent them to me so be careful. I photocopied a few newspaper accounts, too. The library doesn't have a copier and I had to go to the court house for the photostats so I didn't get many. When we get back from the dance, we'll talk."

"Did the place look like Whitcomb described it?" Dean asked.

"To a tee. But George Porter, the fellow who owned the store, was something of a photographer. There are probably lots of copies around in libraries and books. Henry could be describing what he saw in print."

Dean took the folder. "You're beginning to sound as cynical as me. I took you for a true believer!" Then he added, "I didn't know you were an Elk."

"I'm not," he called. "I'm a Moose. Close enough though; they both have horns. You owe me twenty-five dollars!"

Whitcomb followed the exodus of the main group, dressed in what he probably considered his bum-around clothes, last year's cashmere golf sweater. Before he left, Dean stopped him.

"I want some time to talk with you," Dean said. "We've interviewed the others and I have some questions."

"Okay," Whitcomb answered. "As soon as I'm back from the swim. I'm interested if the old man found out anything today, too."

Whitcomb left, virtually ignoring his son who was seated on the sofa.

Dean fed Mrs. Lincoln, put a Boston Pops piece on the stereo and after filling the washer with a week's worth of clothes, flopped into a living room rocker. His backside was acting up again, too much up and down and running around.

"How did you get out of the big swim session?" Dean asked Jeremy, more for polite conversation than the answer.

"I'm not on Pop's list of social friends and he has a full complement of whipping boys already assigned. Do you really believe this shit about going back in time?"

"Your father hired my stepfather and me to find out if what he says he saw really happened, that's all. We're not obligated to believe or not believe it."

"Answered like a politician. Are you saying you're not on the payroll to find out if one of us killed my family?"

"My job has nothing to do with the murders in any way. Your father made that clear. In fact, he acted annoyed when I mentioned the subject." He paused. "But that doesn't stop me from being interested personally."

"Do you think that's wise?" The question didn't come in the tone of a threat but the words sounded strangely out of place.

"Why wouldn't it be? Do you think one of the group out here in Colorado killed your mother and brother?"

"No. It was a bungled burglary. And they're not going to catch whoever did it. It was someone just passing through. Period. How's that for an opinion? Strong enough?"

Dean wanted to pursue the subject but knew he had to be careful.

"There seems to be a feeling in certain quarters that it was someone close to the family, something about the alarm system, and the fact that your mother wasn't too open about letting in strangers."

"Mom could be conned like the rest of us. She wasn't always fully lucid, if you must know. Someone put a story on her and she let them in. That's all. Maybe it's exotic to think of a sinister family plot like some who-done-it thriller but death is like taking a shit; a body function. There's nothing romantic about it. It's dirty and brutal. You should know that, you're a cop." He rose, putting on a new coat.

"Sleep tight," he said, closing the door quietly behind him as he left, leaving Dean alone in the house, with a spinning washer and Dorrie Briscoe.

There was no sound from the den where Dorrie remained closeted since she had waved her daughter off to The Elks. Later when Dean was exiting the bathroom, he literally ran into her in the hall.

"Hi," she muttered, looking down at the ground.

"Hi, yourself," he answered. "Did you have any supper?"

"No," she murmured. "I thought I'd fix myself a sandwich."

"I'll broil you a steak." He went out to the kitchen before she could answer. She followed behind. "Look..." she said.

"No speeches necessary. We're starting all over again."

"I'm sorry,..."

"Rare, medium or well done?" he asked, opening the refrigerator door.

"Medium, and thanks."

Dean fired up the broiler, removed a steak from the refrigerator, pierced it on both sides with a fork, and rubbed in pepper and garlic salt and pushed it under the flame. Dorrie followed him into the kitchen and perched herself atop the counter. She wore a short red skirt, very short but seemed oblivious to it. Dean was not. He opened the freezer door and took out a bag of frozen French fries, scattering them on a cookie sheet.

"These things aren't very good but at least they're filling. Want another vegetable? I have them canned or frozen."

"Why are you doing this?"

"I'm basically a nice guy," he answered as he shoved the fries into the oven on the shelf under the meat. "Besides, my mother always told me to be kind to house guests."

He could hear her sigh. "I rolled over and reached for you this morning," she said in a softer voice than he wanted to hear.

"And found Nattie," he answered, not turning around to face her knees.

She sighed again. "God, I was embarrassed. Nattie's always doing things like that. It's her way of showing disapproval. Another chapter in her damned notebook."

"She's quite a kid," he answered, turning around to face her. "You can be proud of the daughter you raised."

She smiled. "Nattie thinks you're pretty special, too. Did you see her tonight? Didn't she look sweet? What a pretty girl! And that boy! He almost reminded me of Sue Ellen's Tommy!"

"Be careful," Dean cautioned. "They're just kids."

She started to answer, but changed the subject instead.

"I stopped by the school today. I don't know how long Henry will keep us here but I hate to keep Nattie away from studies too long. They can't enroll her but I finally got them to agree to let Nattie sit in, starting Monday, sort of like a visitor; very informal. It's a small school, under two hundred students from kindergarten through high school, but they were very nice, no hassle at all."

"What does Nattie think about that?"

Dorrie chuckled. "She's convinced the children here are still learning their multiplication tables on a slate tablet with a piece of chalk! I think she's in for a surprise."

"Bigger isn't always better," Dean answered as he pulled out the steak and placed it on a plate. "A few days out here may be good for her."

He went into the living room and began sorting through the information Fred had compiled while Dorrie ate her meal, chatting intermittently between bites. When she had finished eating and picked up the dishes, she moved beside him on the sofa.

"Thanks for not wanting any postmortems on last night."

"No problem. I'm feeling as guilty as Adam anyway. I guess I told you I'm rather committed to a marvelous lady back east. I was a very bad boy."

She laughed. "That was the marvelous lady on the phone, wasn't it? I could tell by the way you squirmed and sweated!" She patted his knee. He wished she wouldn't do that. "Never mind, you were really terrific anyway!"

He felt like the third grade dunce who was patted on his head by the teacher for spelling his name right.

"What are these?" she asked, picking up some of the pictures.

"Mostly the town of Sneffels in the 1890s and around the turn of the century," he answered. "Fred picked them up at the library and historical society."

There were dozens of photographs, most showing mustached miners and calico women amid buildings that looked like they'd been constructed on short notice. Hurry-up work before the gold and silver ran dry. Fred had listed a chronology of each photograph in an effort to pinpoint the date on which they should be concentrating.

"Will it be difficult to find out what year Henry is talking about?"

"I wouldn't think so," he answered. "The town went up like a rocket ship but came down just as fast. It says here the first cabin was built in 1875 and by 1890 there were two hundred and seventy people in the area. Not too many years later there was only a handful. Henry mentioned a lot of buildings and Porter's store, but he didn't mention the Atlas mill across the stream. The mill was built later. I'd guess Henry is talking about 1888 to 1892, at the latest."

Dorrie picked up a picture of eight children of various ages, all standing in a row next to a dour woman who reminded Dean of Mrs. Brown.

"I wonder if one of these children is Sarah Byrd," mused Dorrie. "What a collection of rag-a-muffins!"

"Tough times, tough kids."

"I wonder how today's children would have survived up there?"

"You can't help getting involved in history in this part of the country. It's all around you. I've read a little about it. It was an incredibly difficult environment, especially the winters. You have to give those people credit – not just the kids, everyone. They left the security of towns and cities to live and work at a 10,000- to 12,000-foot elevation, amid hundreds of inches of snow, miles from medical help. Scores were killed or maimed in avalanches or mining accidents, and yet they stayed, at least until the mines shut down."

"The greed of gold," she said, picking up a picture showing two men with pick axes standing outside a mine portal.

"Maybe not greed as much as a dream of a better life. Times were difficult all over and people just wanted their families to have more than they did growing up. A lot of the men were Civil War vets who couldn't find work when they returned home. Economic conditions were God-awful after the war but at least the West offered opportunity for those willing to work. Don't forget there were thousands of immigrants, too, from all over Europe. Remember the Irish Potato Famine? Hundreds of thousands dying. The ones who made it to America were the lucky ones. In spite of the hardships they faced here, at least they were alive. But you had to work. No one was handing out welfare back then."

They continued to sort through the old photographs.

"No mention of Byrd's Song in any of these pictures?" asked Dorrie, holding up a print of a long line of mules hauling ore.

"No, unless Fred picked up something he can tell us that he didn't write down."

Mrs. Lincoln perked up her ears moments before either Dean or Dorrie heard automobile tires on the drive followed by footsteps on the porch. Henry Whitcomb opened the door looking spry and invigorated, his wet hair uncombed. He carried a wet bathing suit beneath his arm.

"I'm surprised you two are still out of bed," he said, causing Dorrie Briscoe to blush and turn her head away.

"Ready for our talk?" Dean said, ignoring the comment.

"Sure," Whitcomb answered. "Just let me get a towel for this hair. There's nothing like a swim out-of-doors when the temperature is hovering around freezing to set your body right."

Dorrie made an exit to the den without comment while Whitcomb was in the bathroom. She closed the door tightly behind her.

Whitcomb returned with a towel wrapped around his head like a 1950's shampoo commercial and spotted the pictures.

"Let me see," he said, reaching for them.

Dean held up his hand. "After I've asked a few questions."

Whitcomb sat on the sofa and kicked off his shoes as Dean explained that he and Fred O'Connor had read the files, listened to the tapes, and were just about finished with the interviews.

"There weren't many surprises from the way Neil and Dorrie explained it yesterday, except for the missing time when you were at Byrd's Song."

"What do you mean?" Henry asked it slowly, looking directly at Dean.

"It's pretty simple. You didn't fill in an hour and twenty-two minute's worth of chitchat in the report. There was more."

"Okay, you're right. It's just a little personal holdout. No big deal. Maybe I hired a pretty good detective after all."

"The 'something' to confirm to yourself you weren't dreaming?"

He looked at Dean long and hard. "Whatever it is, it isn't 'dreaming.' But yes, it's my form of confirmation."

"Then why hold out?"

"Because if someone besides me knew about it, I could never be certain, one hundred percent sure, that somebody hadn't gotten up there ahead of me and faked it."

"So now just two of us will know," Dean answered, picking up a pen and pencil. Whitcomb started to protest, but Dean dismissed him with a wave of his hand.

"One hundred percent candor, remember? Besides, your concern is bullshit. Nobody can get up there any sooner than you can, if at all. There's probably a foot of snow at Byrd's Song."

"It's supposed to warm up tomorrow, like Indian summer."

"When it's warm enough to go to Byrd's Song, we'll both go to Byrd's Song, if we're able."

Whitcomb thought a few minutes before he answered. Finally he explained. "Sarah Byrd had a pet, sort-of. It was a pack rat. He used to come at night and swipe little things from the cabin."

"That's a fairy tale! There's no such thing!"

"Yes, there is. I wasn't sure either but I looked it up in the encyclopedia. A pack rat isn't really a rat. It's a large wood mouse. And, among other places, they live in the Rockies! The book said they have a strong curiosity about things, especially shinny objects. That's what Sarah was telling her friend, Ella. Her pack rat, she named it Cinnamon Sam, stole a pin of hers, and later a button. He left her a nail and a few nuts. The encyclopedia says they don't really swap. They have one object in their paws and when they like something better, they leave the first object."

"So what's the point?" Dean asked.

"Let me finish the story. Sarah finally spotted the pack rat one night after playing trading games with him, and she managed to find his nest. It had all kinds of junk in it, even some pennies and a gold button. After that, she'd leave food and things for him but mice kept getting into the Byrd's food so her father put out a trap. He caught Cinnamon Sam by mistake."

"Too bad," said Dean, with little feeling.

"Yeah," continued Whitcomb. "She was telling her friend all this. She laid Cinnamon Sam in a tin box, with some of the treasures from his nest." He paused. "Then Sarah and Ella held a funeral, with me watching. I know exactly where she dug the little grave."

"You're pulling my leg!"

"Sure, it's been a hundred or so years, but maybe it's dry enough up there and something survived. At least the coins and buttons might be recognizable!"

"If she didn't decide to dig it back up a few months later."

"Who digs up dead pets? Look, this is my ace in the hole. If this proves out, I don't give a damn about anything else. I'll know these sessions are for real."

Dean rolled his eyes in disbelief. "I'm giving this gig my best shot, Henry, but I've got to tell you, I'm having a hell of a hard time playing the circuit. For instance, what's the point of having this group of us chase all this junk down if you can satisfy yourself by peeking in a century old mouse-grave?"

"You know something? The whole damn thing is pretty hilarious, isn't it? I mean, here I am, a multimillionaire, chasing a nothing little girl who lived, if she lived at all, ages ago. Why should I give a shit? She doesn't mean squat to me. But this whole business has me so damned up tight, I have to get some answers or I'll go bananas. Why the double and triple checking? I don't know. I guess the truth is, I don't really believe it myself, and I'll need a shitload of convincing to show me I'm not nuts!"

"One more question, Henry. How did you know Sneffels was in Colorado? You were clear that the girls mentioned the name of the town but no one told you the state."

Henry Whitcomb had a quizzical look on his face. "I don't know. Maybe we assumed it,...mountains and all..."

"Just like Wyoming, Montana, California, even Canada...Sneffels isn't on any current maps. You would have to do a peck of digging to find it."

"Someone suggested it, I suppose. A good guess?" But Dean could tell even Henry was not convinced.

Dean handed the stack of pictures to Whitcomb and went into the kitchen for a beer. As he was opening the can, Fred O'Connor, Nattie Briscoe and Mrs. Brown returned, amid a flurry of slamming doors and animated chatter, mostly from Nattie. Mrs. Brown went upstairs immediately, but Dean caught what looked like a smile at Fred before she exited. Dorrie called to Nattie from the den and the young lady, with a roll of her eyes, answered her mother and went to the room. Fred slumped into the rocker with a smile.

"I'm getting too old for this much excitement."

"Did the twinkle-toed dancers have a good time?" Dean asked.

Fred started to answer when Henry let out an exclamation that caught them both by surprise.

"That's her!"

Both men looked up to see a shocked expression on Henry Whitcomb's face. His color had drained as he pointed to a picture in his lap. It was a group picture of eight children of various ages and his shaking finger rested on a girl standing at the far right.

"She's older, a year or two. Her hair's longer and it's a different dress, but the same style."

Dean looked closely at the picture. It was the group picture with the Mrs. Brown look-alike and eight children. It showed six girls and two boys standing next to the stern woman in front of a wooden building Dean took to be a schoolhouse. The children ranged in ages between five and perhaps fifteen, the age of the girl Whitcomb was pointing out.

"That's Sarah Byrd?" Fred asked, peering over Henry's shoulder.

"No, no. It's the other girl, Ella. My God, I'm sitting here staring at a hundred-year-old picture of a girl that I listened to and saw with my own eyes last month!"

He slumped back and his breathing became labored. Dean thought to himself, if he's faking this, he's due an Oscar.

"Do you have a magnifying glass?" Fred asked Dean.

"It's in the den, in the desk," Dean answered as he studied the picture.

Fred knocked lightly on the den door and went in. He returned at once, followed by Dorrie, clutching a bathrobe to her throat. Nattie was at her heels, similarly attired.

Henry reached for the magnifying glass and squinted through it at the picture. Dorrie stood behind Dean. He was not unaware of her hand lightly on his shoulder.

Henry gasped, "She's wearing the locket!"

He slowly handed the picture and glass to Dean. Dean looked, moving the picture and glass for a better focus. Whitcomb was right. The girl was wearing a locket and by holding the magnifying glass at the distance that gave the highest focus, Dean could make out the heart shape, and a border that may have been tiny pearls.

Dorrie leaned more closely against Dean and he could feel her racing heart against his back. Even Fred O'Connor looked shocked.

Henry Whitcomb grabbed Fred's arm. "What is this picture?"

"It's a school picture, I suppose of the Sneffels school. I don't know what year, probably early 1890s."

"Then maybe her children are still alive! Or at least her grandchildren! Someone who's seen her! We've got to locate them! What else did you find out?" His voice had a sharpness to it that verged on panic. You could cut the tension in the room with a knife.

Fred answered slowly. "Byrd was there, at least in 1890 and 1891. His name was Thomas Byrd, that's all I know. He had a mining claim but probably worked for the Virginius mine that was in the Sneffels district and only worked his own claim part-time. A lot of the miners did that. I couldn't find out what happened to him after 1891 but I'll be digging more tomorrow. No mention of his family."

"What about the other girl? This one?" Whitcomb pointed at the picture.

"I couldn't find any mention of someone named Ella, but it might have been a nickname. The school pictures didn't identify the children."

Whitcomb began to impatiently shuffle through the other photographs but failed to locate another picture of the girl. "Are there more pictures where these came from?"

"Some shots of Sneffels but no more school pictures. The school probably only went up to the sixth or seventh grade. I'd guess the children would then come down to Ouray or, more likely quit. The school only lasted a few years. Besides, the miners floated in and out of the area. The family might have moved on."

Dorrie squeezed Dean's shoulder tighter. "Does this mean it's real? That Henry really...went back in time?"

"There are eight children in that picture," Dean said without emotion. "That means there were at least seven more copies of the picture floating around."

Whitcomb stared coldly at Dean but said nothing. Dean then turned to his stepfather.

"Come on, we've got work to do before bed." He went down the hall to their room with Fred following.

"A little abrupt back there, weren't you?" Fred said as Dean closed the door behind them.

"Look at it this way. Whitcomb's not paying us to roll over and pant at the first sign of a cookie. Besides, he was right about one thing; there's nothing we can come up with that proves conclusively he isn't faking it, however concrete the clues seem. What did the other pictures of Sneffels show?"

"They were pretty much as Whitcomb described. A fellow named Ashenfelter owned a livery of mules for hauling ore and he had stables across the stream. There were hundreds of animals. But there were dozens of the pictures as well and Henry could have easily gotten hold of one."

"I'm glad you're showing some objectivity."

"Any guesses how he might have faked the locket bit?" Fred asked.

"No, but frankly, I'm happy about it. At least it gives us something to go on. You've proven at least Byrd existed. That tells me Whitcomb put this fairy tale together with info he probably picked up from some living person, most likely a descendent. All we have to do is locate the person. That's a hell of a lot more up my line than chasing hundred-year-old ghosts."

"I guess I can deduce you're not buying the tale today any more than you did yesterday," Fred said glumly.

"Not for a minute, Watson. Not for a minute."

Dean sat on the bed and brought Fred up to date on his earlier conversation with Whitcomb, relating the story of the pet pack rat, Cinnamon Sam. They both agreed it would be nearly impossible for Whitcomb to fake a hundred-year-old grave site but the chance of finding it would be equally remote. He'd most likely "find" an alleged spot but be unable to locate any detailed evidence.

Dean could hear Whitcomb climbing the stairs and Dorrie and Nattie returning to the den as he asked Fred about his interviews.

"Dorrie didn't tell me much we didn't already know," the old man said, "except she isn't as inclined to dismiss the affair as quickly as the others. She gave me a good dose of 'Brain Study 101.' Apparently that's her specialty, getting into people's heads. Other peoples, not her own. It's as if she's really hoping it's possible the gizmo works and you can go back. The girl is a real dreamer."

"Did she detail her affair with Henry?"

"Only in passing. She assumed I knew but it didn't seem to bother her."

"Tell me about Brown. I couldn't believe she'd consent to go dancing with you! You deserve a trophy."

Fred smiled his pretend-modesty smile. "She's a tough one but a nice woman. And a hell of a good dancer!"

"What does she have to say about all this Byrd's Song business?" Dean asked.

"Brown was a little strange on that count. Once I was able to get her to open up, she was pretty candid. The lady is mostly all business, doing whatever Whitcomb asks her to do without offering her opinion, but when pressed, she'll tell you what she thinks."

"And what's that?"

"That if the Klaxton Turban really worked, she'd grind it up like a Brillo pad and toss it."

"That may be the smartest observation anyone's made to date."

"Maybe," Fred mused, "but it was the way she said it. She's frightened of something. Something in her past. The idea that there aren't any hidden secrets from times gone by scares the daylights out of her."

"Interesting. I wonder if it has anything to do with August, two years ago."

"The murders? We keep coming back to that, don't we?" Fred yawned deeply. "Try not to snore too loudly," he said as he pulled down the covers of the bed.

It took Dean a long time to nod off. His mind kept retracing the events of the day as he tossed about, hearing all the small sounds of the country house. The bedside alarm glowed one o'clock when he heard a human noise, a door slowly opening and the telltale brush of fuzzy slippers on the hall carpet. He waited but the sound didn't come his way. It moved up the stairs to the second level, padding across the floor above him to the bedroom of Henry Whitcomb.

Chapter VIII

"Wake up, Davey Dean,
Turn on your smile machine,
Chase those sleepies far away,
Jump up to a brand new day!
Up! Up! Up! And away!"

It had been thirty years since Dean's wizened grandmother had shaken him out of bed a thousand times in a row with that despised ditty; a gray-haired pug, cotton apron and holey sweater smiling down at him when the hour of the day warranted anything but a happy face. But for some reason known only to God, the simple doggerel from decades past kept singing its way through his brain the next morning until he stopped fighting the demon chorus and opened his eyes. The sun hadn't even seen fit to rise, but to escape the hated verse raging in his brain and the memories of cold mornings and dreaded school, he stumbled to the bathroom, splashed his face and brushed his teeth, until the singsong verse floated back to where it belonged; misfiled in some hidden recess of his subconscious. After pulling on pink jockey shorts (a slight washing machine miscalculation with a red golf shirt), jeans and sweater, he ambled out to the kitchen.

Nattie Briscoe had beaten him to the breakfast table for the second morning in a row and sat surrounded by her ever-present notebook, powdered sugar, crumbs and a doughnut, half on the table and half stuffed in her mouth, with a cup of coffee poised to wash it down. She wore a pair of men's pajamas, tops and bottoms, a Kelly green plaid that made her look like a circus clown. She smiled when she saw him. "Like the outfit? One of Dorrie's one-nighters left town and I confiscated it."

"You look great in anything, twinkle-toes," he answered, as he pulled on his socks and shoes. "How's the queen of the Elks ball the morning after?"

"Troubled," she answered in a somber voice. "Grab a cup of coffee and pull up a chair. I need some old-fogey advice."

"You chose the right guy," he answered as he rinsed out a mug in the sink. "What's the problem? Did Ron-the-woodsman use the wrong brand of snuff?"

"No, we had fun...sort of. He's a nice guy. But he isn't anything like the boys back in Pennsylvania. I can't seem to impress him worth a damn. You know what the jerk told me? That I'd better wise-up if I ever wanted to have a 'meaningful relationship' with real guys. What nerve! He stands there looking like a Marlboro commercial and talking like some Ivy League grad-student telling me what to do!"

Dean just smiled as she continued. "And he knows what he wants out of life; he's going to college and then come back here! To sticks-town, USA! He wants to start a business, a zillion miles from nowhere! Can you believe it?"

"Is that so bad?"

"Everybody back home wants to go to New York or L.A. or tour around the world. Nobody but nobody likes where they are! And where they are is a whole lot more exciting than No Place, Colorado!"

"Some people must like it where they are or there'd be a hell of a traffic jam on the highways."

She ignored him. "And he wants me to meet his parents! I'm supposed to go over there for dinner tonight!" She wiped the crumbs from her face but the end-of-the-world look remained.

"Are you going?" Dean asked as he sipped his coffee.

She stared glumly for moments before answering, picking up crumbs one by one with a wet finger.

"I don't know. I want to talk it over with Mom, if I can find out what bed she's in long enough to ask her. That's why I got up before the chickens so she can't sneak back to her own sack and miss out on the guilt trip I'm about to lay on her."

Don't look in my bed, Dean thought but filled his mouth with a doughnut instead of putting forth a comment on a still-touchy subject.

Nattie stood up and began to pace, holding up the lengthy pajamas.

"Meeting Ron's parents is like something out of 'Little Women.' The boys I know refer to their father and mother as 'Mr. and Mrs. Dork,' or 'the turnkey and his squaw.' Nobody would actually want someone to meet them, for God's sake!"

"You're not worried, are you?"

"No. Well, yes. Sort-of. I don't know what to say to 'em. They'll probably talk about branding cows or shooting Indians or something and I'll be sitting there like Natalie-the-nincompoop. I don't know how to act!"

"Act like Nattie Briscoe, and do a bit more listening than talking. And ask questions. That's the best conversation tool around."

"Like, 'gee, what's the name of that beautiful dead cactus in your driveway?' Thanks," she added glumly. "It'll be a miracle if I get through it without looking like the fool on the hill."

"You'll knock 'em dead!"

She quickly changed the subject. "About that picture last night, the one of the kids up in Sneffels?"

"What about it?"

"It really gave me the willies, sort of made me sad. I don't know why. Old stuff was always dates and grungy books in class but they looked like real people. It's as if I knew them or something. Do you believe in that reincarnation junk?"

"No."

"Me neither." She gave him a peck on the cheek. "I've got to run!"

"Where are you off to?"

"I've got to roust the geezer out of bed. I'm helping grandpa with his research on the tree-maker's visions. Pops got the chief bookworm at the library to open up over the weekend. I'm helping before Dorrie dumps me off at school on Monday and kills any chance of fun. And I've got to peek under all the sheets 'til I find my beloved matriarch. Neat word, huh? Busy day." And she was gone.

Dean was not looking forward to the awakening of the rest of the household so after donning a sweater and a wind-breaker, he pulled his bicycle from the storage shed and began peddling down the drive. The temperature was a pleasant surprise, several degrees higher than the prior day. The Rocky Mountain sun was just splitting two mountain peaks to the east. Once it climbed a few steps, the snow would begin to melt like a May day. Perhaps a trip to Byrd's Song wouldn't be out of the question after all.

Biking had always been Dean's passion, intensified after the 'Tour the Rockies,' a one week trek he had undertaken the prior June, a trip that marked his first visit to Colorado. But the gunshot wound a few days after returning to Pennsylvania had curtailed any serious biking activity since then. The forced hiatus in no way diminished his enthusiasm or love of the sport, however.

Periodic adjustments in his seat position reminded him of the still-tender bullet wound but the discomfort was more of an annoyance than anything serious as he rolled along. An occasional pickup truck or jeep passed him but the early morning traffic was very light. Dean found himself more interested in drinking in the scenery than beating his body into shape. He was pleased the five-mile jaunt into town to rent the jeep two days earlier caused no adverse reaction so he was determined to at least double the distance. He rode along higher in the saddle, no longer in the tuck position with its limited field of view, the pavement six feet in front. More like Mary Poppins than Greg LeMonde, he thought as he took in the beauty of the autumn day.

Breath came in unaccustomed puffs and his legs reminded him with a tingle that it would take a lot of work before he regained anything close to his earlier condition. But, what the hell, he had to start somewhere.

Biking had always given Dean the solitude and time to sort out his thoughts and problems yet today he was content to forget the matters at hand and pedal for pure relaxation. Just the cool breeze carrying the scents of the morning, a hint of wood-smoke and pine, and the familiar rhythmic motion of his churning legs. Enjoyment, pure and simple. That was just what he was experiencing until he turned from the main street of Ouray and saw Hays Crawford.

The young man was seated on the passenger side of a new car carrying on an animated conversation with the driver, an older man in a business suit whose head was half turned away from Dean. The car had a rental sticker on the rear bumper and a clothes bag hung from a hook over the back seat. Crawford was far too engrossed in his discussion to notice Dean who swung his bike around and stopped several feet up the sparsely traveled side street for a closer look at the two.

The driver had black hair, beginning to turn white at the temples and wore glasses. His arm was crossed over the steering wheel making it difficult to get a good look but there was something familiar about him. He was doing more listening than talking and it appeared Crawford was trying to convince him of something but he was still undecided. An aluminum siding salesman with a hot but reluctant prospect.

Dean stayed long enough to note the plate number and catch a partial glance at the driver's features before reversing his direction and peddling away from town, wondering if he'd seen the man somewhere before. The chance of Hays Crawford knowing someone in Ouray, Colorado, was too remote a possibility. Dean had an all-too-familiar feeling the young man was up to no good.

Dean's mind mulled the question during the ten-mile run north, back past the side road to his house, into Ridgway where he stopped at the bakery, five miles in the opposite direction from home. He poked his way through two more cups of coffee and a fresh baked cinnamon roll trying to decide if he should question Crawford about the meeting. He decided against it. Instead he'd slip back to Ouray later and try to find the visitor. If he were staying in town that would be little problem. There were few enough motels and hotels in season and a number had already closed for the year.

When Dean returned to the house, Fred and Nattie were gone along with Mrs. Brown who, according to Whitcomb, had driven the two to town. As for Dorrie Briscoe, no mention was made of her nor could Dean tell if she were still in the house.

"I called the weather bureau," Whitcomb remarked as he surgically sectioned a grapefruit at the kitchen sink. "They're calling for warm temperatures through tomorrow. Let's make a run at Byrd's Song before more snow comes."

"One evening in the hot spring pool doesn't put you in mountain climbing shape," Dean answered, "but you're paying the bills. Who else do you want to go?"

Whitcomb thought a moment. "Just the two of us."

"Two's a poor number. If one of us gets hurt, he'd be left alone when the other went for help. We should have at least three."

"If I suggested the trip to Archer, he'd puke and I don't trust Crawford as far as I could toss him." He began to eat his fruit.

"What about your son?"

Whitcomb dismissed the suggestion with a wave of his hand. "Jeremy is too fat and soft."

"You're a little hard on him, aren't you?"

"Mind your own business," Whitcomb answered sharply. "You're not being paid to snoop in family relations. The two of us will be fine."

Dean let the comment pass. "You're being a little chauvinistic, aren't you? What about the women?"

Whitcomb dumped the remains of his grapefruit in the trash, ignoring two seeds that fell to the floor.

"You don't quit, do you?" He didn't wait for Dean to answer.

"We'll take the little girl. She's probably in the best shape of any of us." He looked directly at Dean. "Besides, she's about the same age as Sarah Byrd."

The sound of a car in the drive interrupted them.

"That's Jeremy. He's driving me down to the pool."

"Get all the exercise you can," Dean said as Whitcomb left. "You'll need it." He stooped and picked up the grapefruit seeds.

If Dorrie Briscoe was still behind Whitcomb's closed bedroom door, she was as noiseless as a tombstone. Dean showered off the sweat of his bike trip, still wondering if he were alone in the house. He dressed much the same as before and had another cup of coffee before his curiosity got the best of him. A light knock on the upstairs bedroom door brought no response. The room was empty. So was the den where Dorrie's suitcase was neatly closed and the bed made with no purse or jacket about. He returned to the kitchen, feeling a little like a snoop, and then, as if to appease his conscience, tried to telephone Cynthia Byrne in Pennsylvania. No luck there either.

On the spur of the moment he dialed his old workplace, the Parkside, Pennsylvania police department. Rita Angeltoni answered on the second ring.

"I'm glad you called," she said. "I've got some backroom poop on your Spinnersville murders. There's a hot rumor they think it was an inside job, not a robbery. It's all hush-hush." Dean confirmed he'd spoken to Hammond with much the same result. Rita had no further details and after bringing Dean up to date on the rest of the office happenings, Dean got around to the real reason for his call.

"Do me a favor, Rita? Have the florist send Cynthia Byrne a dozen red roses and bill me, will you?"

Rita let out a sigh so deep it nearly blew the receiver from Dean's hand. "Sleeping around again," she said in an exasperated voice. "David Dean, when will you ever learn? Here you have this sweet woman you care about, who cares about you, and you go off fiddle-fuddling the first woman who comes down the pike! You ought to be ashamed!"

"Wait a minute!" Dean interrupted, to no avail.

"Just because you're good-looking, have a pleasant disposition and incredible buns, every time some woman wants to try you out, you don't have the you-know-whats to say no! When are you going to grow up?"

"Rita!"

"There's more to life than sex! That's a dangerous game you're playing! There's lots of stuff going around and not just AIDS!"

"Rita, I just asked for flowers..."

"I'll send the flowers. A dozen guilt-red roses. It's the color of a deep blush. I hope it works." She slammed down the receiver before he could comment.

The phone rang again before his hand was off the receiver. It was Lieutenant Anderson, Dean's precinct boss.

"I tried to get Rita to transfer the call but she was too pissed off at you. When are you quitting your vacation and coming back to work?"

Dean tried to explain the situation without volunteering his moonlighting activities but Anderson brushed him aside.

"Marion told me all about Whitcomb. All the more reason for getting the hell out of there. Come on back to work. It was only a bullet in the ass; you can stand up!"

The two chatted further and ended the conversation with Dean promising to consider returning by the first of the month, ten days distant. Anderson made some conciliatory comments about not rushing it and how he'd been kidding but both of them knew he was starting to press the issue.

Just before noon Dean climbed into his car, more for something to do than with a purpose, and drove into Ouray.

Jeremy Whitcomb's car was parked next to the hot spring pool as Dean passed by and he guessed one of the heads bobbing beneath the steam like a pea in boiling water was Whitcomb senior. He continued to the library where he recognized Whitcomb's new jeep. Fred and the two generations of lady helpers were presumably chasing down the elusive Sarah Byrd. He'd check in on them later. First there was the question of the rental car and the man Hays Crawford had been talking to that morning.

Dean had little difficulty locating the car. He spotted it in the parking lot of one of the larger motels at the south end of town, near Box Canyon, a scenic waterfall that attracted summer tourists. Nearby was a favorite spot with ice climbers when winter turned a deep, ice-covered gorge into a silent but awesome world-class challenge.

Dean pulled his Honda to the left of the automobile and pretended to busy himself with papers in his glove compartment while he looked around to make sure no one was watching. The car was locked and there was nothing inside of a personal nature. Dean was wondering what to do next when he noticed the vent window on the driver's side was not fastened. A smoker, he thought. No one cracks the vent window but a smoker.

Dean slid out of his car, trying to look as nonchalant as possible, and moved around to the opened window. He quickly reached in and turned on the headlights, closing the window behind him. He strolled into the lobby of the motel, whistling a cheery tune, feeling proud of himself.

A pretty but overweight woman, probably in her forties, sat behind the counter watching a television across the room. She immediately looked up and smiled as Dean entered.

"Hi," he said. "I just wanted to tell you one of the guests left his lights on. The blue Ford near the corner." The woman frowned and came out from behind the counter to look.

"That's funny," she said. "I just came by there a few minutes ago. You'd think I'd have noticed."

"It's probably the little fairies that live up in the pine grove," Dean said with his best charm-the-ladies smile. "You know what those rascals can do."

The woman returned to the counter and smiled. "Thanks. It was nice of you to stop."

Much to Dean's disappointment she began dialing a room without having to look up the number.

"That's pretty good," Dean said, stalling. "Do you know the room number of everybody in here?"

"This time of year it's no great challenge. In the summer it gets too busy." She turned away. "Mr. Griffin? I'm sorry to disturb you but you left your lights on in your car." She listened a few seconds. "Yes, a blue Ford." She repeated the license number but the party apparently hung up before she could say anything further.

She turned to Dean, a look on her face somewhere between shock and anger. "He hung up on me. He said I'm mistaken and I shouldn't have bothered him."

"Hey," Dean said. "You should at least get an 'A' for effort."

"What nerve! Now I don't feel so bad calling him Griffin-the-grouch! All he could do was, pardon-my-expression, bitch about everything; the town, the drive here, no bellhop to help him with his bags and cameras, the fact we didn't have a pot of coffee on at three o'clock in the morning, for God's sake!"

Dean laughed. "Where's he from?"

The woman pulled out a registration card and Dean looked over her shoulder. "New York, New York. The Big Apple and he can have it." Dean memorized as much as he could see, a Manhattan address and a business firm with the word 'Star' as a part of it.

"Just let his battery run out. I'll never tell. Then he'll have something else to bitch about in the morning. It will serve him right for being snotty to a nice lady like you." Dean turned to leave.

"Thank you, Mr. Dean," the woman said, stopping him in his tracks. She laughed when she saw his reaction to her knowing his name.

"Didn't you know everybody knows everybody else in a small town like Ouray?" He started to say something.

"I'm just kidding. I'm Alice Adams, Ron's mother. Ron went to the Elk's dance with the young lady who's staying with you."

Dean smiled and shook her hand. "He's a nice young man. I met him when he picked up Nattie. I hope she didn't give him too rough a time. She's a rather precocious young lady."

"So I gathered. But Ron is very impressed with her, in his own way. He's asked her over to the house to meet us."

"So I understand. I'm all for it. Nattie needs a little real-world sobriety. She's led a rather hectic existence, but she's a sweet kid. You'll like her."

Dean left the motel still feeling pretty good about himself. "Sam Spade, eat your heart out. Ace detective David Dean is on the job, knocking off the bad guys like ducks on a pond."

As he drove down Main Street he noticed a store that advertised hiking and camping gear and pulled into an open spot in front. After chatting with a friendly young lady he purchased a topographic map of the area and two light weight ponchos. At least they'd provide some protection for tomorrow's adventure.

From there he drove the three blocks to the library to check with his cracker-jack associates, busily digging for clues. Never mind that the team consisted of a thirteen-year old girl, an old woman candidate for grouch-of-the-year and Fred O'Connor who defied description.

During the short drive Dean speculated about the New York visitor with whom Hays Crawford was carrying on such an animated conversation. He was certainly selling something. And the only product that made any sense was Henry Whitcomb and his alleged visits to the never-never land. Was Griffin perhaps the Tuesday night prowler who had scared Neil Archer out of his socks? Dean could have kicked himself for not asking Mrs. Adams what day Griffin checked in.

Did Dean owe it to Whitcomb to tell him about the meeting between Crawford and the stranger? After all, Dean was taking the old man's money. He hadn't made up his mind by the time he pulled into a parking space in front of the library.

The Ouray Public Library was located in the rear of a building that held the city offices on the first floor and a community center upstairs. Dean was surprised at the size of the facility in view of the small, less than 800, population of the city. The library smells brought Dean back to his grade school years, when a perceptive teacher drew him out of his poor reading habits and introduced him to the wonderful world sandwiched between the covers of those timeworn volumes.

Dean spotted Fred O'Connor seated at a back corner table, busily writing on a yellow pad, with a half dozen books spread out before him. Nattie Briscoe was putting on her coat, about to leave, and smiled broadly when she saw Dean.

"Hi, flatfoot," she called.

"Hi, brat. What are you up to?"

"I'm off to the historical society museum up the street. I'm in charge of sorting through 10,000 photos, trying to find Miss Byrd's Song of 1891."

"Any luck?" Before she could answer, Fred wandered over.

"Nattie here is doing a first class job. She reports every hour and we compare notes." He gave the young girl a hug. "She's found five school pictures. We can pretty well put them in order by the way the kids grew. No sign of Miss Byrd but the other young lady is in three of the pictures. Then she drops out of sight. I expect her family moved on. The mining got tight in the mid-1890s when the government stopped supporting the price of silver. I'm checking the old mining records. It looks like someone took over the Byrd claim in 1892."

Fred explained that Mrs. Brown was downstairs, looking at old newspapers on microfilm. Later, she was to go to Montrose and visit the Family History Library of The Church of Jesus Christ of Latter Day Saints. "The church is big into genealogy. They have lots of old records on film and on their computer."

"Great! Maybe we'll find something by tonight." Dean then reported how Henry Whitcomb planned to tackle the trip up to Byrd's Song in the morning.

"Put on your hiking boots," he said to Nattie. "Daddy Warbucks commissioned you to accompany him and path-finder Dean to the high country."

"All right!" Nattie said with a wide grin. "Maybe I'll get some heavy vibes about Sarah and Ella!"

"That's no stroll in the park, tootsie-pop."

"No problem. I'll leave you two geezers panting. I'm just worried about lugging the tree-maker back down if he drops dead."

Fred sighed. "Well, it's as warm as a June bride outside today. If he's going to try it, I suppose he'd best get on with it. Either one of you old timers up to the trip?"

"We'll soon find out."

Nattie turned to leave. "Bye. I've got work to do and I have to quit early."

"Have you seen your mother?" Dean asked.

"Nope," she called as she dashed out the door. "I haven't seen her all day. But I'm going to Ron's anyway."

Fred chuckled. "Nattie has a big dinner-date tonight."

"Yes," Dean answered, "I just met the mother."

He explained about his detective work at the motel, Mr. Griffin and Griffin's earlier meeting with Hays Crawford. "It might have been as simple as Hays giving him directions but I wanted to check him out."

Fred snorted. "You don't get in the front seat to give directions. Besides, that lad couldn't direct his way out of a one-street town. He was up to no good. Take my word for it."

"Have you seen him around town?" Dean asked.

"Nope," Fred answered. "But Neil Archer came in here snooping. I think he would have stuck around but Mrs. Brown gave him the evil eye and chased him out. I haven't seen Dorrie either."

"It's a funny thing about Dorrie," Dean said.

"How do you mean?"

"You and the ladies took the jeep, I took my car and Jeremy picked up

Henry. So how did Dorrie leave?"

"Maybe she just went for a walk."

"Maybe," Dean answered, but neither of them believed it. Fred went back to his mining reports and Dean began to feel like the only member of his ace detective group who was dogging it. Finally he asked if there was anything he could do to help.

Fred suggested Dean relieve Mrs. Brown on the newspaper detail. "But, I've got to warn you," he added, "it's a quick route to a stiff neck and a headache."

Mrs. Brown actually smiled when Dean took over the chore in the small basement room. She didn't extend any friendly chitchat, but the smile was a start. Soon after, she and Fred left for Montrose, leaving Dean alone to wade through the up-to-the-minute happenings of 1891 via *The Ouray Argus* and *The Solid Muldoon*. Dean found it fascinating to peruse the happenings of the town a hundred years ago but *The Solid Muldoon* would have made delightful reading even if the Byrd situation had never come up.

David Day, the irascible publisher of *The Solid Muldoon*, named for a popular New York city fight promoter, could never be accused of not telling it like it was. The paper was peppered with caustic and raucous comments on everybody and everything. Woe be to the poor soul who found himself on the wrong side of Mr. Day's piercing pen. According to the librarian who stopped by to see if Dean needed any help, David Day had as many as forty-two libel suits pending at one time and a readership that extended to nearly every state then in the union and a number of European countries. Not bad for a small-towner who had been illiterate until he volunteered for the Civil War at the age of fourteen!

No one had a chance to pad history while it was happening and Dean learned far more about life in the town from the few hours of peeking at its newspapers than any after-the-fact third party opinion could have given him. Ouray was much larger then. The advertisements alone boasted a wide variety of stores and businesses as well as the ever present girlie-clubs. Politics were taken very seriously in the 1890's and it didn't take a mental wizard to know which candidate a paper supported! Terms like 'lily-livered coward' and 'snake-in-the-grass' appeared with regularity. Editorial freedom was unquestioned, where at times, good taste was not. Dean read a particularly gruesome and detailed account of a hanging at Canon City and reference to blacks and Chinese were particularly pointed and often cruel.

After plodding his way through 1891, Dean switched to the Ouray county census records, also on microfilm. 1880 listed only fifty-seven hearty souls in Sneffels, nearly all miners. The real growth spurt had not yet begun.

Apparently, the place was simply a mining camp at that time as only one housewife was listed and there were no businesses. The diversity of the working men surprised Dean. The census listed seventeen different states and five countries represented as places of birth! He could picture the babble of accents and languages among the hardworking men, many probably Civil War veterans, fleeing the harsh economic conditions of most of the country. Ulysses Grant had been a much better general than president and Dean recalled from his history the abysmal depression that followed the War Between the States.

Dean paged his way through the census of the town of Ouray as well. Here, in addition to the miners were listed barbers, doctors, attorneys and grocers, just like a small town of today. But interspersed were blacksmiths, milkmen, mule skinners and even a card player, giving a hint to the differences existing in a western town of the last century. The prostitutes were surely there, too, but protocol must have somehow disguised these ladies of negotiable affection as none of their profession were listed.

Dean was unsuccessful in finding the 1890 census. When he inquired, the librarian told him that nearly all federal census records for that year were destroyed in 1921 in a fire in the basement of the Commerce Department building in Washington. Disappointing. Sneffels was less than five years old in 1880 and when Dean reviewed the 1900 census, the "Byrds" had flown the coop, along with most of the population. By then the short-lived heyday had passed and Sneffels had begun its slow decline to oblivion, just another ghost town in the Rockies.

Dean returned to the newspapers, working his way into 1892, and was lapsing into a discouraged stupor when his bleary eyes recognized a name. It was a small article and he nearly missed it. It read, "Thomas Byrd, a miner, age forty, died suddenly at the hospital last Tuesday of pneumonia, having been sick for six weeks in the mountains prior to being brought to Ouray. His funeral was yesterday from the Catholic Church with internment in the Cedar Hill Cemetery." There was a final line. "Byrd was from Ireland and there are no known relatives here." The paper was dated March 25, 1892.

No Sarah Byrd, no Mrs. Byrd, only a lonely Irish miner dying in the mountains thousands of miles from home. The notice had a sobering effect on Dean. It was as if he knew the man, a relative, someone whose life he'd touched, however slightly, and here was a notice of the man's death as if it had happened last week instead of a hundred years before. A death that wouldn't have even happened in current times, given today's communication and medicine. Dean dismissed the feeling. After all, what did it mean? Yes, there had been a Thomas Byrd but no Sarah or her mother. Thomas had died shortly after Henry's supposed trip, seance, or what-ever-you-call-it, but someone or something survived to enable Henry to come up with his little fable. But Henry had screwed up unless there was more than one Byrd that didn't fly. Dean copied the article word for word after rereading it a half dozen times.

Fred had been right about one thing. Dean's neck and head hadn't felt this sore since he'd crammed for a chemistry final in high school. When Nattie popped in a little before four, he was more than ready to call it a day. Young Miss Briscoe hadn't found any other people-pictures, but she was thrilled with a photo of the town of Sneffels taken from several hundred yards north of the town that seemed to show a faint outline of buildings high above, where Henry Whitcomb had pointed out Byrd's Song. Dean praised his young detective but said nothing about his find. She didn't ask specifically so he didn't have to lie. He needed time to digest it, and time to stay a step or two ahead of Mr. Henry Whitcomb.

Nattie was content to run an uninterrupted line of chatter about Ron Adams and her upcoming dinner engagement and Dean let her do all of the talking on the trip home. When they reached the house, instead of going in with Nattie, Dean told her he had an errand to run and drove the half mile further down the highway to the Cedar Hill Cemetery.

The cemetery was visible from Dean's house. He could look down on it, a mile or so down the valley, on the far side of the highway. He had passed it many times but had never had reason to visit. According to the library, the fourteen-acre facility had been used for burial since at least 1870 with the first marked grave dated 1878. In years gone by the cemetery had been locally known as "Rowan's Farm," named for a town doctor. The man must have either had a sense of humor or been less than pleased at the obvious reference to his lack of professional success.

Dean didn't expect to find a gravestone for Thomas Byrd as he drove around the well-kept grounds so he was not surprised when he didn't. After all, who would bother to mark the burial of a lonely Irish miner, a short-time resident and a short-time remembered, who died without kin of any kind and perhaps without a friend. Dean got out of the car and wandered among the markers, feeling the same quiet sadness as when he made his infrequent visits to his own parents' graves. He realized he was probably the first person in a hundred years to even think about Thomas Byrd, buried somewhere here beneath the yellowing September grass. That's one more visitor than will remember David Dean a hundred years from now, he thought.

His reverie was broken by the sight of Mrs. Brown and Fred O'Connor passing by on the highway driving up to the house. He returned to his car and followed. Before he did anything with the news that Thomas Byrd died without heirs, he wanted to discuss his findings with the old man. But Mrs. Brown motored past the cutoff to Dean's place as if she never saw it and continued south on the road toward Ouray. Dean wondered what the two were up to but didn't bother following them. Instead he proceeded back to the house alone, irritated at cutting his cemetery visit short.

Dean was welcomed home by the impatient shrill of his telephone in concert with the sound of running water from the downstairs bath. Nattie was taking a forty-five minute shower, he thought, as he picked up the receiver.

"Hi." He recognized Dorrie Briscoe's voice without her introduction.

"Hi, yourself. Where did you scoot off to?"

"I'm...running an errand, sort of. Is Nattie there?"

"She's in the shower, trying to deplete the water supply of western Colorado. How did you leave?"

"I...walked to the road, and a guy gave me a ride."

"You hitchhiked? Look, is there a problem?"

There was a pause before Dorrie continued. "No, no. Everything's fine. Look, I need a colossal favor."

"It doesn't sound fine."

"I really need this favor."

"Try me," Dean said cautiously.

"I'll be gone three or four days. Could you sort of keep an eye on Nattie for me? She's self-reliant and all and there are lots of people around. She should be fine. Just make sure she gets to school on Monday and stuff like that."

"Henry wants her to go with us tomorrow when we hike up to Byrd's Song. I told him to ask you."

She yelled the answer. "No way! Tell the son of a bitch she's to stay down at your place or he doesn't get...he'll know what."

"Tell him yourself! Where are you?" he asked with a knife-sharp edge in his voice he didn't try to disguise.

"It's not important. I'll be back. And, really, thanks for everything. You're a prince." She hung up without giving him a chance to snarl his opinion of her actions, leaving him standing with his hand still on the receiver.

A barefoot Nattie dripped her way into the kitchen, swaddled in half the supply of towels.

"Oh," she said when she saw him, "I didn't know anyone was here to answer that." She turned and plodded back toward the den, calling over her shoulder,

"You really should have an extension phone in the john. Everybody does."

Dean followed her to the door. "Look, that was your mother. You're scratched from the big hike tomorrow."

"Shit!" And then she called, "Fine. Good luck in hauling the corpse down the mountain alone. Where's Mums?"

"I don't know where in hell she is but she's out of town for a few days."

"Don't tell me," Nattie sighed through the door, "you're the designated babysitter!"

"Right," he muttered, and added, "Be home by eleven."

During the seven-plus weeks of Dean's solitary convalescence, the only time the phone rang was a return call from Cynthia or a "how's your health?" call from Fred. Now, the damn thing wouldn't shut up.

"I'm sorry to bother you," said an unfamiliar voice when the phone rang once more. "This is Mrs. Adams. From the motel?"

"Ron's mother, yes," Dean answered.

"I don't know if I should be telling you this, but that man, Mr. Griffin?"

"What about him?" Dean asked cautiously.

"He asked about you, by name. I thought it was rather funny since you were the one who reported his headlights on." Dean started to say something, but she continued. "You turned them on yourself, didn't you?"

"It's a little complicated," Dean muttered, somewhat embarrassed. "What did Griffin want?"

"He wanted to know if I knew where you lived."

"Did you tell him?"

"Gosh, no. I've seen enough detective stories to not be that dumb. I told him I thought you lived up at the top of the Dexter Creek road, 'way up at the end. You know, that itty-bitty dirt road that clings to the east side of the ridge?" She made a noise that sounded like a giggle. "He's sure to get stuck up there."

Dean's father, who had been dead since Dean was twelve, used to use the expression "It's a long alley without a trash barrel." Dean never fully understood exactly what the saying meant but now it somehow seemed to apply.

He laughed. "Thank you, Mrs. Adams," and then added, "Assistant Detective Adams."

"And his real name isn't Griffin," she added. "He had me change a hundred-dollar bill and I caught a peek at his driver's license when he opened his wallet."

"What is his name?" Dean asked cautiously.

"I didn't see it clearly but it ended in a vowel; Italian, I think."

"Great! By the way, when did Griffin check in?"

"Tuesday..., no, Wednesday morning, at three."

"Good work...First Class Detective Adams.

She laughed. "Maybe someday you can tell me all about it."

"I hope so. You deserve it."

"But now, I've got to get back to my supper. Big doings tonight."

"Good luck. And, don't take any guff from our Miss Nattie and slap her fingers if she grabs for seconds on the pie."

Wednesday morning. Too late, unless Griffin had spent the early evening prowling around Dean's place. But then why would he ask directions if he'd already been there?

CHAPTER IX

Nattie Briscoe, combed and polished and bedecked like a princess in a fourth-choice skirt and blouse, had finally exited with cowboy Ron to her, as she called it with more nervousness than conviction, "dinner-in-hell." Dean himself felt like "Father of the Bride" as he sent prim Miss Briscoe and her proud-as-punch escort on date number two, leaving the house as empty as the refrigerator. Dean fried the last two eggs left in a carton on the kitchen counter and toasted two heels, all that remained of a loaf of wheat bread.

Henry Whitcomb had probably coerced his son Jeremy and Neil Archer into working out at the pool but Hays Crawford was still missing in action. Perhaps he was doing the town with the strange Mr. Griffin, plotting who knows what. Even faithful Fred was catting around with Mrs. Brown, leaving Dean still in the dark over what, if anything, they had learned in Montrose. He was impatient to share his findings from the old newspaper account of Byrd's death. Dean had spent the past few days bitching about too many people spoiling his reverie, but now he had to admit he felt uncomfortable alone.

After Mrs. Lincoln had pestered him for her cat food dinner, even she left him to his own company, content to curl up by the wood stove he had fired up to ward off the growing chill. Feeling too lazy to seek out a phonograph record, he began to absentmindedly punch away at the radio in search of mindless music. But music was in short supply. The garble of static was finally replaced by a sweet-talking woman; Doctor something-or-other, explaining to a befuddled caller that the volume of semen he ejaculated into his sixty-year-old wife had no bearing on her sexual pleasure.

"That's what I should do," Dean thought as the caller whined away with his sorry story. "Call a radio shrink and let her try and make some sense out of these whackos." After five minutes of airway dribble he shut off the radio with a sigh and leaned back in his seat knowing the only path to a logical resolution lay in thinking the matter through.

"Premise number one," he began, preaching to himself like a boarding school teacher. "You can't go back in time. It's pure bullshit. No matter what the facts seem to say, consider that as an absolute. "

"Besides," he mused, "I'd be a hell of a detective if I chalked up to ghosts, goblins, and things-that-go-bump-in-the-night, every unanswered question that popped up."

"Premise number two. Someone, singular or plural is trying to make believe premise number one is a crock of do-do. Top candidate for honors is 'His nibs, star of the show, Mr. Number-One, Henry the tree-maker Whitcomb.' If it is Henry, 'why?' and 'how?' If it isn't Henry, a whole list of other questions open up like 'who?' and 'how?' and 'why?'"

Then there was the problem of Byrd's Song. If it really did exist as Henry so described, someone must have told him about it in great detail, someone who'd been there, first or second hand. It stood to reason Whitcomb had never set foot near the place so who was the tale-teller? The prime candidate would be an heir of the young girl, if in fact she existed. Somehow, Dean believed they would find out she did. Regardless of who put this plan together they'd be a fool not to make sure simple details like the existence of the Byrds weren't factual. The trip to Byrd's Song the next day would be important. Whitcomb had something in mind, something he planned to pull off if the two made it to the tiny settlement site high above the ghost town of Sneffels. It was a head game, Dean was sure of it, but the reason still eluded him. The only edge he held would be information he or Fred O'Connor developed independently. All those facts spoon-fed by Whitcomb needed a hearty washing before they could be digested.

If Henry Whitcomb knew in advance all the answers Dean and Fred would discover and he was simply using the two for confirmation, what would happen if they fed him a foul ball? Some piece of incorrect fact. It might make for an interesting reaction. He'd have to consider it. But first he'd play out the trip to Byrd's Song in the morning.

Putting Henry Whitcomb out of his mind, Dean reached for the phone and dialed Cynthia Byrne in Pennsylvania, wondering to himself if he were calling out of guilt or loneliness.

Randy Byrne, Cynthia's teenage son answered on the first ring. He was home for the weekend from college and after a few banalities about school, Dean asked to speak to Cynthia. Randy hesitated before answering.

"She's not here."

"Have her give me a ring when she gets back," Dean replied, trying to disguise the disappointment in his voice. "There's a two-hour time difference so I'll still be awake."

"She's gone for three days," Randy responded reluctantly.

"Where?"

"A convention." Then he added, in a tone that suggested his disapproval, "With Doctor MacNaught. In Las Vegas."

Dean didn't know what to say as Randy continued.

"I guess she didn't tell you, huh?"

"No." Dean fumbled for something really original and finally mumbled, "It was probably sudden...something important to her job."

Randy let out his breath. "I saw the brochure around here last week. MacNaught's a real dude, Mr. Dean. He drives a Jag and he's single. He dresses like he owns the store."

"That's nice, I guess," Dean answered glumly.

"I think Mom's a little pissed at you. Your flowers got here...but she'd already left."

"Well, I hope you're enjoying them."

"Mr. Dean? If you're going to make a move, I'd get busy if I were you. This MacNaught is big league. Gotta go, Jen's waiting," he said, referring to his high school steady, and hung up.

Big league. Dean felt like the minor leagues, class double D, if there was one. Visions of riding the bench crowded his mind. And here was a kid only weeks out of high school playing the coach. What was even more irritating, he was right. Maybe Dean ought to take heed and get off his ass, if it wasn't already too late.

The idea of Cynthia Byrne in the arms of a stud doctor in sin-city Vegas kept his temperature rising as Dean moped to the kitchen and pulled out the dregs of his only remaining bottle of booze. There was nowhere near enough of the amber liquid to do the trick. He was splashing some water in the glass to make it last longer when Mrs. Brown banged open the front door, with a sober looking Fred O'Connor trailing behind.

"Let's go outside and count the owls," Fred said, as soon as Mrs. Brown made a bee-line for the water closet, her favorite room.

"Where in hell have you been?" Dean asked as soon as the two stepped out to the cool night air and the smell of pine and wood smoke.

"Doing some in-depth detective work," Fred muttered, "over a glass of social wine."

"While I've been solving the case on my own," Dean responded. "Papa Thomas Byrd died of pneumonia on March 25, 1891. I found it in the newspaper after you left." He reached in his shirt pocket and handed Fred his transcript of the article.

"Did you tell his highness?" Fred asked as he read the notice.

"I haven't told anyone, at least not yet."

Fred let out a noise somewhere between a grunt and a mumble as Dean continued.

"That proves there was a Byrd family. I figure it's like we said. One of Sarah's descendants is in touch with Whitcomb and fed him the story."

Fred looked up at him. "Sarah Byrd didn't tell anyone anything. Sarah and her mom died the winter before her father, 1890. Thomas Byrd was the only survivor and now you tell me he checked out the next year. And before you ask, Sarah didn't have any sisters or brothers. The whole clan's as dead as Sarah's pet rat, Cinnamon Sam and they've been dead over a hundred years."

"Shit."

"That just about sums it up. Nobody survived."

"How did Sarah and her mother die?" Dean asked.

"It didn't say. I expect the flu or pneumonia or something. They were dropping off like flies that winter. Or in an avalanche, those were plentiful, too. They buried more miners in snow than stone."

Dean turned to Fred. "Well, we earned twenty-five grand, old man. All Whitcomb wanted us to do was prove the Byrds really existed and we've done that."

"So how come you're not dancing a jig and running to the bank?"

"Because it stinks. And I feel like a three-dollar whore for playing his game. We're being manipulated."

"That's nothing new. We knew that from the starting gate but it didn't stop us from getting in bed with the bastard."

Getting in bed was a sharp reminder to Dean. The bright lights of Vegas began sneaking back to mind as the two wandered down to the edge of the property, pausing at a rock out cropping that looked down on the highway far below. "What about the school records, the names of the children? Little Miss Locket? What was Sarah's friend's name? Ella? Any luck there?"

"None of the rosters of pupils seemed to have survived. The census records give the ages of the children in the Sneffels district so we could probably identify some of them but we could never be positive about which one was which. Chances are Ella was gone by 1900, the year of the next federal census. But I don't suppose it really matters, does it? We know there was a Sarah Byrd from her death record. Are you going to tell Whitcomb?"

"One of these days. But there's something I want to see first."

"What's that?"

"I want to witness one of his sessions, his little trips to the world beyond, or whatever you call it. That and the little excursion tomorrow. I want to see Byrd's Song first hand."

Fred glanced at Dean. "You're thinking what I'm thinking?"

Dean smiled. "I'm getting curiouser and curiouser about what's up there. If Henry is planning to put on a show for my sake I don't see any reason not to attend. And there's no benefit in our laying all our cards on the table either, not before we find out the ante."

"Glad to see you're starting to figure things my way, son," Fred said sagely. "There may be hope for you in this detecting business yet. Now if you'd only read more crime stories, you'd think like me all the time, not just when genius strikes you!"

Dean just shook his head and smiled. He then mentioned his idea about misinformation and the two agreed it might become useful later but to hold off for the present. There was still more information to gather; Griffin's presence and his connection with Hays Crawford for starters. And there remained the question of the two-year-old murders.

Dean then updated Fred O'Connor on his conversation with Mrs. Adams at the motel. They both decided Fred would try to get more details on Griffin or whatever his name was while Dean and Whitcomb were attempting to reach Byrd's Song the following day. The two started back for the house.

"That Miss Dorrie Briscoe is a really weird lady," Fred said, in the tone of a learned counselor. "If I were you, and mind I ain't, I'd give her a wide berth and mend a few fences with the lady back in Pennsylvania."

Dean reluctantly told Fred about his phone conversation with Randy Byrne and Cynthia's trip to Vegas. The old man just chuckled, smiling like one of those silly dolls you can never knock over at cheap carnivals.

"Serves you right," he said, and then muttered some old turkey about the goose and the gander. Though Dean would have cut his tongue out before he'd admit it, it was advice he wished he'd heeded two nights earlier.

When the two returned to the house Fred O'Connor strutted off to his room to make a few more lists and devour another detective novel with Mrs. Lincoln trailing behind. Dean finished his drink and wanted another. The bottle was as dead as his brain and he'd had enough conversation with Fred so he pulled on a coat and drove into Ouray.

The Black Horse Tavern, one of only three watering holes in town, was down to the last half-dozen patrons when Dean pushed open the door. The place was weathered boards, too much cigarette smoke and a murmur of a few old stories heard too many times before. Dean had stopped by the saloon a couple of times in the past when he felt the urge for some human contact but hadn't been there often enough to be known by name. After nodding to the bartender he started to pull up a chair when he noticed Jeremy Whitcomb sitting by himself in the corner, emptying a beer. Henry Whitcomb's son was slouched down, exaggerating his excess weight and looked as if the beer was far from his first. Dean walked over to him.

Jeremy smiled and made a motion for Dean to be seated. Dean ordered two beers and complied.

"Out on the town for the evening?" he asked.

Jeremy thought about the question before answering. "You know, everyone back home would think this town is about as lively as a hospice but I like it here. I've only been in Ouray a day or two but I can sit in this place and recognize three or four guys I've seen, at the cafe, on the street, driving by. It gives you a sense of belonging you don't get in the East."

"You're sounding pretty mellow, almost philosophical."

Jeremy laughed. "I think half-loaded is more like it. But what the hell, I haven't anything better to do. The old man put his whip away for the day. But what are you doing here? I hear you and Pops are going to assault the mountain in the morning. Shouldn't you be pumping metal or sleeping or something?"

"I may not be a triathlete but if I can't keep up with your old man they ought to shoot me. Besides, I needed to get out of the asylum for a while."

"I can't blame you. So tell me, what are you looking for tomorrow?"

Dean took his time to respond. "Some proof for your dad so he's satisfied he isn't nuts. That's what he says."

Jeremy smiled and waved to the bartender for two more beers. "But what do you say?"

"I say it's his party, let him play any game any way he wants to. Why should I give a shit?"

Jeremy just shook his head. "That's a stack of crap a mile high. You're far too curious to take an I-don't-give-a-damn attitude. It's got to eat at you not knowing what he's up to. You're too smart not to know he's holding something back. And you think you're smart enough to figure out what it is, only that's where you're wrong. Nobody beats my old man." He said it in a voice not bragging but dripping with resignation, a loser who'd lost a thousand times before and knew a thousand more were waiting for him.

"So you tell me. What's it all about?"

"That's easy. It's about the death of my mother and brother. How does it fit together? Don't ask me, but it has to come down to that. Why else get us all involved out here? He doesn't need us here. But he can't buy the killings as a simple burglary gone wrong; he's positive one of us is responsible. He's going to go too far. If he isn't careful, someone else will die."

Dean was startled by the statement. "Why do you say that?"

"Maybe it's just the booze talking," the young man answered, trying to make light of it. "Besides, Dad is in piss-poor health in general and he's afraid he'll croak before he finds the answer."

"I suppose not knowing for sure what happened must tear him up."

"You don't know the half of it. It's become his life. Last month he took me out to dinner...one of the few times in years. My stomach was on the fritz so I wasn't drinking but dear old Dad knocked off a whole bottle of some hundred-dollar wine. He was pretty mellow. He looked me in the eye and said 'I'd give up all this shit for just five minutes in that room to see who the son-of-a-bitch was who killed my son.' He didn't have to say what he'd do to the person, his eyes told it all." Jeremy looked at Dean. "I can tell you. It scared the hell out of me. It wasn't just what he said; it was the intensity of how he said it. You knew he meant every damn word. Nothing else in the world matters to him. He's had it all and there's no more challenge in life, only the murders. I'll tell you something else, he looked at me as if he thought I killed them."

"Did you?"

Jeremy laughed. "I'll give you credit for being straightforward if nothing else. And to answer your question, no."

"But you know more than you're telling." Dean sipped his beer but didn't move his eyes from Jeremy.

Jeremy thought a minute. "Let's just say, I know the players better than anyone else, my father included."

"Do you think he's faking this Klaxton Turban business?"

The young man thought a few moments longer and finished his beer. "He'd do anything to accomplish his goals, whatever they are. That's a one-line description of my old man. He could fake it, there's no doubt about that. But somehow it's not his style. He's more direct. More in control. And this turban business definitely has him on edge." Dean started to answer but Jeremy raised his hand. "But maybe it's being done to him."

"By whom?"

"By himself. Maybe he's..." he struggled for the right word, "like willing it...in his subconscious. You have to admit stranger things have happened to people. What about ESP? People wake up out of a sound sleep at the exact instant a loved one dies, or is in peril. That stuff happens, you know it does." He threw up his hands. "Shit, I don't know. You're the detective. You figure it out."

"People keep telling me that. Tell me about finding your mother and brother."

"No." He stood up and waved at the bartender for more beers. "Look, I just don't want to get into that, okay?"

"Do you really believe they were killed by a burglar? You were pretty insistent the other day." He again looked Jeremy straight in the eye, trying to read the young man.

"Yes," he answered, returning the gaze. Then he turned away. "Or maybe I just don't like the alternatives."

Dean finished his beer and left, leaving Jeremy Whitcomb with two fresh ones on the table. He knew the young man would make good use of them.

CHAPTER X

Neil Archer made a token appearance the following morning for the sendoff of Dean and Whitcomb's assault on Byrd's Song. Nattie and Mrs. Brown stayed in bed and there was no sign of either Hays Crawford or Jeremy Whitcomb, who Dean was sure was nursing a world class hangover. Fred O'Connor was up and about but sat in the living room saying little. Whitcomb insisted on a full breakfast and as nearly all the provisions were depleted, Archer was directed to town for meat, eggs and bread. The two mountaineers waited in silence until he returned. It was after ten by the time the pair had eaten and were ready to leave.

They loaded the new jeep with more gear than an Abercrombie & Fitch catalog and left to a gorgeous but cool September morning. The bright red vehicle was not unlike the rental jeep but it had the stiffness and feel of a new car with only the telltale whiff of Whitcomb's cigarettes tingeing the new car smell. It felt good; a far cry from Dean's Honda. There was no conversation on the drive up and Dean couldn't tell if Henry Whitcomb was nervous or simply bored with Dean's company. The road was less intimidating without the gasps and cries of Neil Archer. Maybe repetition breeds confidence after all, Dean thought. The near silence continued after they parked the vehicle and began the slow climb up the trail.

If the truth be known to any observant deer or ground squirrel, the two made a pretty sorry pair. It was a bit of a case of macho versus macho. Each carried a backpack with all the provisions of a modern high country hiker. There was a tape recorder to enable Whitcomb to preserve impressions, a cellular phone, first aid equipment, a small shovel, binoculars, some food, enough clothing for a Marine regiment and a large variety of what every Yuppie camping magazine lists as mandatory. Whitcomb had searched high and low for a metal detector in Ouray but without luck. The only other items missing were a television and kitchen sink.

In spite of his still-not-completely-healed bullet wound there wasn't any way Dean was going to let that nasty old son-of-a-bitch out-hike him. It was obvious that Whitcomb, stubborn as a Missouri mule, felt the same way. Each pretended to stop to admire the spectacular view with ever increasing regularity as they tried to hide their labored breathing through clenched teeth.

But the more they climbed, the more the scene below them became clothed in a shroud of misty fog and roiling clouds until the spectacular scenery resembled a laundry basket of drab sheets.

At the start of the hike, if you'd stuck a pipe in Henry Whitcomb's teeth he'd look like Mark Trail on a holiday, but as the journey progressed the look was more a street person lugging a sack of soda cans to a redemption center. David Dean, high school sports hero, intrepid outdoorsman, just as at home in the woods as the corner barroom, wasn't much better off.

By the time Whitcomb collapsed for smoke break number seven he'd given up the charade, willing to let Dean pretend he was suffering less. He fell backward on the ground, spread-eagle, oblivious to the wet pine needles and muck clinging to his Eddie Bauer three hundred dollar jacket.

"How much further?" he gasped.

Dean whipped out his topo map as if he knew what he was doing and examined it closely, folding it until he centered the ghost town of Sneffels and the area above it. It had nothing to do with neatness; he was just trying to catch his breath before opening his mouth in learned explanation.

"Probably no more than a half mile or so, but it's four or five hundred feet above us in elevation."

"How the hell can you tell that?"

Dean pointed out the contour lines on the map. "Each one of these represents twenty feet of vertical rise. Where they're really tightly bunched together on the map it's the steepest part." He was proud as punch with himself, as if he'd known this crap all his life, not just learned it from the tawny girl in the Ouray shop who'd sold him the map the day before.

He continued to point out details to Whitcomb, sounding like Edmund Hillary on his final assault of Everest, until the old man stumbled to his feet, cutting the lesson short. Too bad. It was great for the ego to instruct an audience who didn't know his knee from his nose about the subject matter.

"Who gives a shit?" Whitcomb mumbled as he staggered to his wobbly feet and continued up the trail.

They hadn't gone fifty feet when the clouds let loose and rains hit. Without warning, silver dollar dapples poured from a blackened sky, earlier as blue as the sea, soaking them to their shorts faster than Dean could rip the two plastic ponchos from his knapsack.

Dean reluctantly, but silently, gave Whitcomb credit. The older man continued to slosh forward as the path upward turned to a mountain stream, cascading brown mud and mushy leaves and branches over their boots and ankles.

"It's a good thing we left Archer and Jeremy at the house. This would kill them," Dean commented during one of the rest stops that were coming with more and more frequency.

Whitcomb grunted. "My son Michael would have jogged up this hill."

They were above the tree line now and no overhead canopy of vegetation defused the soaking downpour that pelted like stinging bullets from a dark and sinister cloud camped directly above their heads; a vulture waiting for lunch. The two stumbled forward, up a section of trail as steep as lighthouse steps. Whitcomb was in the lead, and as he picked his way over a boulder the size of a Volkswagen, his feet flailed out behind him, sending him sprawling, face forward in the mud. He fought his way to a sitting position amid a litany of expletives, wiping the goo from his body, while Dean stood back, pretending to be concerned. To Dean, it was the highlight of the trip. Without a lick of conscience he absorbed the scene with concealed relish. He hadn't been happier since Mary Lou Regan kissed him at her fifth grade birthday party.

Dean simply couldn't let the stumble pass without comment.

"Where's my Nikon when I really need it? If the boys in the boardroom could only see you now," he said with the broadest smile he could muster.

Whitcomb said nothing. He simply scooped the mud from his pockets, out of his collar and off his face, and retrieved his spilled knapsack. With a grunt he turned and continued to limp up the trail.

The rain halted as quickly as it had begun; no sunshine or rainbows but at least there was less mud as the path began to finally level out near the summit of the ridge. Dean expected Whitcomb to be in a hurry once they neared the top but the millionaire surprised him.

"I want all my wits about me when I get there," he said by way of explanation, as he slumped down and undid his pack.

Both men seemed to put their discomfort on hold as they collapsed against a large rock and ate the peanut butter sandwiches Dean had packed, washing them down with gulps of warm but welcomed water.

It had taken them nearly three hours to make the ascent and in spite of frequent rests, no stop felt as good as the twenty minutes leaning on a boulder and gazing at the clouds skipping by the massive mountains. When Whitcomb finally rose, he actually smiled, the first that seemed to represent some degree of pleasure. He stretched his arms to the horizon and took a deep breath of the Rocky Mountain air.

"I did it," he said, oblivious to the mud and grime. Then, with a "let's-get-back-to-business" shrug, he turned and started up the last few yards of the trail.

Several large rocks shielded the pair from a view of their objective but as they turned the corner, Byrd's Song, tiny as it was, spread out before them. They were on a shelf, perfectly flat, a sculptured platform some prehistoric trick of nature had carved from the towering cliff that rose and fell around them. The entire area covered less than an acre. The remnants of buildings were clearly visible, interspersed with stalks of wildflowers, now past their brief summer glory, struggling for life in the thin mountain soil. Ancient planks and timbers, mingled with rusted metal and shards of tar paper, were scattered about, all reduced to ground level from the snow of a hundred winters. A rusted can or two spoke of more recent visitors but even that debris was of many decades past. The location was truly remarkable and one couldn't stand here without marveling at the majestic view of the world the location amply offered. Nor could you but marvel at the heart of those who'd wintered here, hearty souls, clinging to a perch more suited for eagles than mere mortal man.

Dean experienced a feeling of reverence, not unlike his cemetery visit, as he gazed at a homesite so accurately described by Henry Whitcomb just two days before. Everything matched. Dean could almost hear footsteps, Ella, basket in hand, long cotton dress, pearl-bordered locket and infectious smile, waving to her friend as she climbed the path where he stood. He felt a gnawing envy of Whitcomb, a wish to have visited the spot and spied on two young girls and their nineteenth century afternoon visit.

"This was the house," Whitcomb murmured, with an air of near veneration. "The other building was the shed." He gestured off to the left.

"There was a clothesline tied to a bush, a small tree, over by the cliff and there was a little spring behind it." Whitcomb stood on the rubble, kicking the boards with his feet.

"The kitchen was on this side," he said, more to himself than to Dean. "The bedroom back there," he gestured. "There were some flowers planted out front, in a clay crock; I'd forgotten them."

He lifted a board with his toe, as if trying to raise a ghost. "I wonder how long the place has been abandoned?"

Dean wanted to answer his question, tell him that Sarah and her mother were dead more than a century past but held his tongue. He closed his eyes in reverie, as if waiting for their ghosts to appear. Finally he shook himself and asked, "Where did Sarah bury her pet?"

Whitcomb looked at Dean as if he were being interrupted. He sighed, "Behind the house. It's up the trail only a short way, against a rock." He turned and started to walk away from the building site, up an overgrown depression that was hardly recognizable as a path. It led in the opposite direction from the way they had hiked up from the townsite of Sneffels below.

While yellowed grass was overgrown on the path they walked, you could see where the ground was indented, worn slightly lower than the surrounding earth, by a thousand footsteps long since silent. Dean had read that vegetation grew slowly in the high country and a careless hiker might cause damage that would take a decade to re-germinate in the tundra climate. He felt a pang of guilt with each careful step as he pressed tiny stalks beneath his tread.

Henry Whitcomb started off unerringly, almost as if he were counting his paces, following a treasure map in his mind. He walked under a cliff overhang about a hundred feet from the rear of the homesite, an area with a hint of a different color green, perhaps a garden of non-indigenous flowers long ago spent. Whitcomb stopped at a near perpendicular wall of rock at a slight curve in the trail. He had not hesitated an instant, going directly to the location, as if following a compass beam in his mind. Shaking his head slowly, a smile spread across his dirt stained face.

"This is it," he said with a conviction that left no room for doubt.

Kneeling, Whitcomb began to examine, not the earth, but the rock wall behind it. Dean knelt down beside him as he traced a nearly invisible cross, about six inches high, etched in the stone of the cliff. It would not have been noticeable, even from inches away, if someone was not looking for it. Time had discolored the mark, more a slight indentation than scratch, so it blended nearly perfectly to the surrounding surface. The overhang provided protection from the elements so the earth below it remained dry; tightly packed dust and struggling vegetation.

"God, it's real," Whitcomb murmured with an air of reverence befitting his kneeling position.

He yanked off his knapsack and rummaged for a small trowel. Digging as cautiously as an archeologist, he carefully opened a small hole about one foot square. The earth was firm, its clay-like texture turning to dust with each shovel. It appeared to Dean to have rested undisturbed for a lifetime.

"I have to be careful, the box might have rusted through," Whitcomb muttered.

"It takes moisture to make rust," Dean answered. "This place is as dry as the Sahara. How deep was it buried?"

"Not deep," Whitcomb grumbled as he scraped away the earth.

"Describe it," Dean said quickly. "Tell me everything that's in it, what type of box it is, what it looked like, everything."

Whitcomb looked up at Dean. "Why? So you'll know if I really saw it before?" Dean didn't answer and Whitcomb continued to slowly excavate the small hole as he spoke.

"It was a tin box with flowers on it, probably used for candy or cookies. It was small, about eight or ten inches long, six inches wide, a couple of inches deep. The lid was rounded and hinged. I didn't see everything Sarah put in it but I did recognize a few coins, mostly pennies, and two or three buttons. One of the buttons was large and dark-colored around the edges and light in the middle, with a cameo-like image in the center. Oh, and there were two or three collar studs. There may have been more stuff, I don't remember. She wrapped the animal in a white cloth and placed it on top of the trinkets."

The hole was slightly less than a foot deep when the shovel struck a hard surface; not metal but rock.

"Looks like you hit bottom," Dean offered, bending down to see.

"No. She covered the box with a flat stone," Whitcomb answered, with increased anticipation creeping into his voice as he scraped away the dirt, exposing the top of the rock. He delicately reached his fingers around the sides of the stone and removed it.

Later, when Dean was reassessing his feelings about what occurred next, he remembered the tremor of excitement he felt. His heart raced, one part of him knowing it couldn't be happening as appearances showed and another part seeing the impossible come true before his eyes, the magician sawing the woman in two, the body floating, the card where it never should have been. But this was different. It was somehow real.

Henry Whitcomb, ever so carefully reached down into the hole, worked the tin box loose from the bonds of the earth and set it, like some precious relic, on the ground between them. It was 1922 and he was Howard Carter, entering the tomb of Tutankhamen. Neither man said a word.

The size of the container matched the general measurements Whitcomb had suggested although any design on the outside had long sense given way to the elements. But the surface of the tin was unbroken; stained and darkened but unbroken. Whitcomb stared at the box for several minutes before turning to Dean.

"Ready?" he asked, as if needing permission to open the treasure to which he had unerringly traveled.

Dean nodded and Whitcomb began working to free the lid. He inserted a knife along the edge and gently pried at the top until he was able to lift it open.

A white cloth, yellowed now from age, a shroud for a long forgotten pet, was all that was first visible. Henry Whitcomb carefully unfolded the linen, exposing a stained interior, black dust and small white skeleton with tiny bits of fur.

"Meet Cinnamon Sam," Whitcomb said solemnly, his voice no more than a whisper.

He removed the linen and its contents, carefully placing them aside and examined the rest of the box. Dean could see several coins and buttons, exactly as Whitcomb had described. David Dean was speechless.

And then a very strange thing occurred. Dean, kneeling inches away from Whitcomb, saw large tears slowly seep down the cheeks of the hardened millionaire.

"I'm sorry," Whitcomb said after a few moments when he noticed

Dean staring at him in wonder. "You can't possibly understand but this is a very emotional experience."

While it was true there was a world of things David Dean did not understand, it was nevertheless infinitely apparent the discovery was producing a profound effect on Henry Whitcomb.

The reverie of the occasion was quickly broken by a sound totally alien to the location; an automobile. Although the two were hundreds of feet above the valley road below, sound, in the near-soundless vacuum of the lonely mountains, carried with incredible clarity. Both jumped to their feet and hurried back to the edge of the site, with Whitcomb carefully carrying the tin box.

Far below, the front of a car became visible at the turn of the road entering the ghost town of Sneffels. It was a blue Ford. A man alighted and stood, looking up in their direction and holding what appeared to be a camera.

"What in God's name does he think he's doing?" Whitcomb yelled. "Who is he?"

They both moved back from the edge, out of view.

"Give me your binoculars and I think I can answer both questions," Dean answered. "He surely isn't a tourist photographing the mountains."

Whitcomb scrambled to his knapsack and handed Dean his binoculars. As Dean adjusted the focus he could clearly see enough of the car to confirm the make and model from the motel parking lot. Mr. Griffin was out for a ride, a photographic jaunt.

"He calls himself Griffin but there's reason to believe that's not his real name. He claims he's from New York and he's been asking around town about me. He's not sightseeing. He's concentrating on us."

"You son-of-a-bitch. If you've told anyone about Byrd's Song, I'll ruin you!"

"Take it easy. I've never even spoken to Griffin. If he knows why we're up here he didn't hear it from me." He declined to add that he knew exactly from whom Griffin had obtained his information. It was Hays Crawford. "I'll say one thing. He must be intent as hell about something if he drove his car up that road!"

"I can't be seen here! I'll not subject myself to publicity over this!" Whitcomb snarled.

"My guess is Mr. Griffin, or whatever his name is, feels just the opposite. He could probably trace the jeep to you without any trouble and there's only one path down and one road out of here."

"I'll fix the bastard!" Whitcomb reached in the knapsack again and pulled out his cellular telephone, punched in a number and crawled away from the edge, out of earshot.

Dean continued to watch Griffin. It looked at first as if he might try to climb up the trail but changed his mind. He wore a black suit and necktie, and Dean had to chuckle at the incongruity of his attire. He simply waited by the car, scanning the site above him with binoculars, a camera resting on the hood of the automobile. Dean remained crouched behind a large rock watching him, hopefully out of sight.

Whitcomb was apparently having difficulty picking up reception on what was certainly the first telephone call from Byrd's Song. Finally, scooting along on all fours, he joined Dean.

"I fixed the s.o.b.," he said with a growl. " I called Neil Archer and gave him a choice; either come up here and personally beat the shit out of the jerk or call the police and tell them someone's breaking into our car. Some choice, huh? Neil would rather cut off his dick than come back up that road. And he couldn't beat up his mother if she didn't have arms. Now we can sit back and wait for the cops."

"I don't suppose the police will be sending you an invite to the next policeman's ball but it might work. Griffin doesn't strike me as the type of guy who gets along well with the men in blue. But as for sticking around and watching, no dice. We've got a hell of a hike down and the weather could get iffy any time. You might think going downhill is a breeze but your legs will feel like rubber after the first hundred yards."

Whitcomb started to object but one look at the advancing clouds and lowering sun convinced him otherwise. He repacked the gear and carefully placed the tin, wrapped in a sweater, in the bottom of his knapsack.

Dean was right on the mark. While their stay at Byrd Song provide a respite to tired muscles, once they were back on the trail all the aches and pains resurfaced with renewed vigor. Any thought of Griffin was forgotten. He was out of sight once they were back from the cliff and they gingerly made their way down. Neither man was used to this much activity and the steepness of the trail together with mud remaining from the earlier rain combined to make the return trip pure torture. They slipped and slid, banging elbows and knees until both began to carefully sidestep their way, grabbing at any nearby tree or rock for support. While the return trip didn't take them quite as long as the assent, dusk was closing in when they reached the jeep. There had been no sound from any automobiles above the sound of their noisy descent but the road was empty of either Griffin or the police as the two collapsed into the seats of the red vehicle.

Dean had all he could do to stretch his legs to the pedals for the ride home. The two exhausted climbers spoke little during the short ride. But in spite of their tired bodies and aching muscles, there was a personal satisfaction neither man admitted; they had made it, and Byrd's Song was real.

Chapter XI

Dean successfully insisted to Whitcomb that he consent to a detailed examination of the tin box to authenticate the age. Whitcomb passed it off as a pointless exercise, grumbling he didn't care one way or another about the results. He was more than satisfied simply finding the box. He knew its age, had seen it buried. Period. While Dean didn't expect an inspection to reveal anything of substance, he was unwilling to concede any opportunity to test Whitcomb's story or any aspect of it.

The entire group, absent Dorrie Briscoe who was still among the missing, was waiting at the door when the two adventurers returned. But the homecoming party for the weary climbers was an anticlimax, due principally to Henry Whitcomb who brusquely answered "Yes" he'd found what he was looking for and promptly retreated behind a closed bedroom door.

While the others looked to Dean to fill them in, he disappointed them as well by following Henry Whitcomb's example. The group was left to pace the living room floor and wonder what they were missing. Dean allowed Fred to follow him and the two closed themselves in the den and examined the tin coffin and its contents while Dean related in detail the tales of the day.

Part way through the discourse Fred suggested fixing his stepson some supper. As soon as Dean was left alone, he made the mistake of laying his head back and fell into a sleep that would make Rip Van Winkle look like an insomniac. He didn't awaken until Fred returned forty-five minutes later with a large pizza and a six-pack of beer.

"Sorry I took so long. There weren't nothing in the house so Brown and me went into town. She wanted to get something for Henry, too. Maybe it'll coax him into coming down and filling everyone in. There's a bunch of folks out there wondering if modern science has been turned on its ear. The only one who doesn't give a hoot is little Nattie. She's in her room, most likely dreaming about her cowboy lover. Neil Archer looks like a ghost and Hays Crawford is as nervous as a November turkey. I guess the police routed his buddy Griffin and, if I were to bet, I'd say he's ready to bolt."

"I didn't tell Whitcomb I saw Crawford and Griffin together," Dean yawned, rubbing his eyes as he picked up a slice of cooling pizza. "I keep trying to stay ahead of Henry by knowing something he doesn't but so far, he's leading by a mile."

He took a bite. "That was really quite a happening up on the mountain today."

"Sounds like it. What do you make of your audience, Mr. Griffin?" Fred opened one of the beers.

"I'm sure it was Crawford who sicced him on us and I'll bet there's money involved somewhere. Hays Crawford would sell out his mother for a buck. And if he got a chance to screw Henry, he'd do it in a minute." There was an impatient knock at the door.

"Hey, how about it? Let me in!" It was Neil Archer's shrill voice.

Dean made a move to hide the tin box but Fred O'Connor reached for it before he had a chance. "I'll just take this someplace cozy and check it out." He covered the container with a towel, grabbed a couple of slices of pizza, opened the door to Neil Archer, nodded at the anxious visitor and was gone, all before Dean could protest. Neil looked like a scarecrow on a bender. He held a fifth of whiskey by the neck and his clothes looked like he had spent the night in a Goodwill drop-off bin.

"I'm heartsick, Dave, I'm heartsick. I can't take all this shit, I'm not a well man." He plopped down on the bed. "Mentally, I'm like...unstable. Dr. Angus Brawn in Scotland wrote a paper on it, people like me, super intelligent. I'm not bragging. I mean, we're different. We react differently to stress."

"You certainly are sick, Neil. I couldn't agree with you more," Dean said with a sigh. "You don't suppose a fifth of whiskey a day is contributing, do you?"

"It's stress, pure and simple. I can't take the intellectual pressure of all this shit. My mind needs more room to work. It can't get excited. It, like, short circuits. I mean, what if that damn contraption really works? Have you thought of that? Henry comes back from the mountain smiling like a damned Cheshire cat and nobody says shit. It's like the rest of us don't exist."

He waved his arms and the bottle as he rambled on. "Think of the implications! Think of it! Some invisible creep twenty years from now peeking under your sheets, learning all your secrets, watching you do it for

God's sake! I mean, what would happen if they found out Christ was just a big con job or Honest Abe Lincoln beat his wife or liked little boys? There wouldn't be any such thing as a secret anymore. No history, only someone turning on that damned dunce cap and taking a peek back! The world would be one screwed up mess!"

"It already is. Besides, there's only one helmet...and only one Henry."

"Yes, but if it did work, some asshole scientist would figure out how and get a government loan and make 'em and sell 'em to Sears."

"Even if it did work, it's random, remember? Henry doesn't have the vaguest idea what he'll see." Dean chewed on a piece of pizza and opened his second beer. He still couldn't overcome feeling like a fool just discussing the possibility the ancient wired headpiece held some mystical ability to transverse time and space.

"I don't trust it and I don't trust Henry. He's getting into my head and I don't like it." Archer took a long draw from the bottle and wiped his mouth. "God, I can't even get drunk!"

He looked at Dean for sympathy but found none.

"And on top of this, the first time, the very first time in my life I'm in love and I'm getting beat out by the teenage son-of-Hopalong Cassidy!"

"Neil, you've been in love three times a month for at least twenty-five years."

"No! Not like this! This is real!"

Dean didn't pretend to hide the disgust in his voice. "Did you ever think of seeing a shrink?"

Archer stood up and began to pace. "I've been to eleven of 'em. I even lived with one for four months. They're all a crock, they don't understand me. Listen Dave, you've got to tell me what you found up there!"

"That's Henry's call, not mine."

"Then make him come down!" he squeaked. "I've got to know!" He began pacing.

"Why don't you ask him? You know him a lot better than I do. I'm just the landlord; you're the bosom-buddy."

"He hates me. He'd kick me in the ass and my ego can't take it. I don't do rejection. Besides, I'm a bundle of nerves. That shit with the law today. I thought they were going to toss my ass in jail for God's sake!"

"So what happened?" Dean asked, showing interest for the first time.

"I called them, just like Henry told me to do. They said I had to come down to the courthouse. The bastards had me sitting there while they went up the mountain to haul the guy down. They wanted me to ride up with them! Fat chance of that! They couldn't drag me up that road; I told them I'd puke all over their squad car. So there I sat, scared shitless. I had no idea what to expect. I figured some goon would rush in with a Tommy gun and rip me to pieces!"

"What did you tell the police?"

"It wasn't the police. It was the sheriff, some dude with a big mustache looking like a western movie. I told him what Henry said to tell them, that someone was trying to steal the jeep."

"Did you mention Henry's name?"

"Hell, no! Do you think I'm crazy? I told 'em it was you. They want to see you, by the way, to file a report or press charges or something."

"Shit! Henry can go to hell if he thinks I'm going to file a false police report. So what happened to Griffin? Did they talk to him?"

"Barely. They brought him in and the cop says, 'Is this the man?' Like I was supposed to know! The guy stares at me with daggers and swears he was taking pictures of the mountains and it was all a big mistake. They had to let him go and he hightailed it out of there like a rabbit. But his name isn't Griffin; it's Angelo Faldi."

"I know an Angelo Faldi. I sent him to jail three or four years ago. Actually, I sent him to the hospital first."

Archer waved him away. "Terrific! Just what I wanted to hear! God, I hate violence! Don't tell me about it!"

"I broke his jaw." Dean was seldom quick to anger but Faldi had made a caustic comment about Dean's ancestors and it had not been a good day. "He was resisting arrest." As a result, Faldi had spent the following six weeks with a wired jaw, sipping baby food through a straw.

"I wonder if he's back here to kick my ass or something."

"I told you not to tell me," whined Archer, covering his ears. "He saw me. He knows who I am!"

Dean took a good hard look at Archer and decided the jerk deserved some modicum of consideration. He rose from the bed, picking up the last piece of pizza, and moved toward the door.

"I'll get Whitcomb down here if you ditch that bottle and start acting like a sober human being. And stop drooling after Nattie. I'm in charge of babysitting her and I'll kick the shit out of you if I hear you've gone near her! You'll be having dinner through a straw like Faldi!"

"Dave, you've got it all wrong!" he protested, banging his shin on the bed as he tried to follow Dean.

Dean didn't wait to listen. Instead he climbed the stairs to find Henry Whitcomb sound asleep. Without a pause he rocked the bed until the older man awoke.

"Come on downstairs and tell these people what happened. You owe them that." He turned, flipped the switch on the overhead light and left the room before seeing if his message was heeded. He smiled to himself as he heard the footsteps of Henry Whitcomb shuffle behind him as he descended the stairs to the first floor.

The five were there; Hays Crawford trying to look cool, Neil Archer trying to look sober, Mrs. Brown trying to look efficient, Fred O'Connor looking curious. Nattie Briscoe looked only mildly interested.

Henry rubbed his eyes and gazed back at the group. "You tell them, Dean. You were there." Dean sighed and began to relate the afternoon's events but Henry interrupted.

"Tell them about the tin first, otherwise it doesn't make sense."

Dean continued his story. "When I listened to Henry's summary of his session in Byrd's Song it seemed as if he passed over a portion of the time spent there. His summary wasn't long enough. When I pressed him, he told me what he held back, something that had occurred up there that he'd watched. It was something he felt might confirm what he was seeing in the session had really happened."

Dean described the funeral of the pet in detail and continued with the events of the afternoon, including a step by step description of the unearthing of the tin box. He then had Fred retrieve the hundred-year old container and show it to the group. The effect was varied but striking. Neil Archer and Mrs. Brown looked as if they would faint while Hays Crawford simply smiled. Nattie looked perplexed and Henry was smug.

As Dean spoke he came to realize the impact of what he was saying and the independent credibility he was unwittingly delivering to Henry Whitcomb's adventure. A solid, albeit inadvertent, endorsement of the Klaxton turban.

"Yes," he confirmed, the soil appeared to have been unaltered for decades and, "No," he could think of no logical way anyone could have planted the box. Then, like passing out dessert, he opened his mouth when a rested mind might have thought better to keep it shut.

Mrs. Brown cautiously suggested a Byrd descendent might have said something Whitcomb had heard and subconsciously retained; a description of the site, only to have it later resurface during a "sleep" session. It was then Dean blabbed the news of the deaths of all of the members of the Byrd family. Henry looked truly shocked. So did the others, Hays Crawford and Nattie Briscoe included.

Henry Whitcomb gave Dean hell for holding back information but Dean ignored him. However, the net effect of the pronouncement was to further bolster the reputation of the Klaxton turban and the strange trips back in time the instrument appeared to facilitate. Dean had made Henry's case, at least in the eyes of the crowd standing open-mouthed around the room.

Henry Whitcomb was about to make his triumphant exit when Dean spoke up. "One more thing, Henry. I want to sit in on a session."

Whitcomb looked startled. "There's no need. You've done enough. You earned your money and I have what I wanted."

"That doesn't matter," Dean continued stubbornly. "I want the session and if you remember our agreement, you consented to it. How about tomorrow morning, at eight?"

Whitcomb stared at Dean for what seemed like minutes and Dean was sure he'd refuse. But the request had put him on the spot in front of the others and a refusal would dilute the effect of what had just been related. Whitcomb turned and muttered over his shoulder, "Eight it is," and started to leave the room.

Dean called after him, "What about that police business? The man with the camera, remember?"

"That's been taken care of," he muttered without turning around.

Hays Crawford looked irate. "Hey, what about my opinion? I'm the one who rigs the damn contraption! Don't I get a say? It takes time to do that! Look, tomorrow's out of the question!" No one paid him any attention.

Fred walked Dean back down the hall before turning off at the bathroom. "Why did you ask for a side show?"

"The truth is, I didn't know what else to do. So far it's been all Whitcomb's production and timing. Let's see what happens when he has to perform impromptu."

Just as Dean was about to enter his room, he caught a quick glimpse of Nattie going into the den. She was crying. He retraced his steps and knocked gently.

"May I come in, kid?" She didn't answer but he pushed open the door and entered anyway, closing it behind him. "What's the problem?"

"Go away," she sniffled.

"No dice. Not until you tell me why the tears."

"No one's supposed to see me cry."

He sat on the edge of the bed and just touched her shoulder. "We're friends, aren't we?" She nodded ever so slightly.

"That's what friends are, people you can let see you cry."

The tears came more heavily for a few moments and she pressed her head against his shoulder.

"It's silly," she said in a muffled voice. "You'll think I'm a baby."

"The reason's never silly if it affects you enough for tears. Tell me

132

about it."

It took her a few moments to regain her composure. "It's the little girl, Sarah. See? I told you it was silly. Of course she's dead; it's not like I didn't know it all along. She'd be about a hundred and twenty if she were alive, but it's sad. I mean, she didn't have a chance to do anything."

Dean pulled Nattie to a sitting position but continued to hold onto her. "You know what I did when I found out her father died? I went out to the cemetery, alone. I didn't do anything special, I just stood there like a jerk and thought about him awhile. No one else has done that for a long time. And no one has thought about Sarah Byrd either. Your crying isn't silly at all. I think it's nice."

Mrs. Lincoln wandered into the room, as if to give solace. She purred her way onto Nattie's lap. Maybe she wasn't such an uncaring soul after all.

"Did he have a grave marker?" Nattie asked as she stroked the black cat.

"No."

She pondered the answer. "I'd like to go there, too, sometime."

He got up. "Grab your jacket."

"Now?"

"Yep."

The two drove to the darkened cemetery but a full moon slipped from behind a cloud just as they entered the gate, casting a pale light on the silent stones. He held her hand as they walked along the paths, circling the small graveyard.

"She's here somewhere," Dean said softly, "and I'll bet she's pleased you've come to visit."

"I'm sorry she died so young," Nattie repeated. "And I'm sorry I couldn't know her. I'd have liked to have her for my friend." She sniffed a little. "I don't have...many friends."

When they reached the car she looked up at him. "I'm glad I came. Thanks for bringing me."

He drove her back to the house, with neither speaking until he turned off the engine.

It was dark in the driveway but he could make out her silhouette as she looked straight ahead. Her voice was soft but firm. "Maybe some day I'll have a marker put up. It wouldn't matter if it was the wrong spot. She'd know. Then I could put flowers down, sometime."

Dean smiled as he led her back to her room. "First things first. Right now I want to hear all about the dinner out at the ranch."

She plopped down on the bed and in a short time the old Nattie Briscoe returned. "Well, I'll tell you. It was like nothing that ever happened in Spinnersville, that's for sure. Ron's old man; he's like humongous. He wears this John Wayne hat and has shoulders like a school bus and a waist that makes me look fat. And Ron's mom, what a cook! If I lived there, they'd have to roll me to school! They have a gigantic house with a front yard as big as Arizona, and about a zillion cows, babies and everything, and horses, too! You know what Ron does for kicks? He gets on some of those animals, the really nasty ones that try to toss you to the next county, and he rides 'em! And in the winter, just so he won't get bored, he ice-climbs, up these giant frozen waterfalls! They had pictures! The boy has a death wish, I swear!"

Dean laughed as she continued. "And they wouldn't tell me what I was eating until I was finished; it was elk! God! The night before I was dancing at their hall and the next night I'm eating them!"

"Sounds like true love to me!" Dean said with a grin. "What a whirlwind weekend! It's been a busy few days for all of us."

She looked around to see if anyone was listening. "I'll tell you what, it's time you and me have a little powwow, babysitter man. There's been too much happening; we need catching up. Let's get together with the geezer and talk this business out. There's an ice cream place in Ouray that looks interesting. What do you say we blow this joint and hit the Rocky Road?"

David Dean pried Fred O'Connor away from what was probably the fifth reading of a Nero Wolfe mystery and the three piled into the jeep for the short ride to town.

The ice cream shop was in the death troughs of the tourist season and virtually deserted. But the weather had moderated so the threesome sat outside, watching the near circular moon slowly dance with the clouds above the rim of the rock wall above them, while savoring a variety of butterfat, deliciously disguised.

"Spit it out," Dean finally said as they were scraping the last tasty bits from their containers. "What's on your mind?"

"It looks like you and the tree-maker struck the mother lode up in the hills." She said it carefully, as if waiting for further details.

"No one is going to get rich from four Indian pennies and a few buttons but it certainly made for an interesting day. So what do you think of Byrd's Song and all these goings-on? What do you think of the mysterious tin box?"

"I'll say one thing," she answered. "It's making me rethink the whole caper."

"Really? Are you ready to book passage in the time machine?"

"No way! That stuff's not for me! Why would I want to go back? I'm thirteen years old. I only want to go forward."

"Hooray for you!" Fred exclaimed as he scooped a swab of butterscotch.

"Think of all the great mysteries of the world," Dean chided, borrowing from Neil Archer. "Who really shot JFK? Did Lizzie Borden really do it?"

"A novelty, that's all. Everyone would spend so much time messing with yesterday, tomorrow would go to hell, more than it already has!"

"Don't tell me Nattie Briscoe would be immune from taking a peek back. What about Fort Lauderdale fourteen years ago?"

Fred coughed on his whipped cream, and Dean immediately regretted his presumptiveness.

"You really get to the heart of the matter don't you?"

"Sorry. That question is a little off base."

"Not really. It's nice to see an adult take kids seriously. And to answer your question, I don't want to know anything about Fort Lauderdale."

"Why?" Fred asked as he continued to dig away at the upper goo in quest of the rich chocolate below.

"I been thinking. I been building up in my mind all these years what kind of a saint my old man is, you know, brilliant scientist, handsome dude, tall, dark and gorgeous? And if I were to really meet him, chances are I'd be disappointed. Don't get me wrong. I'm not scared he'd be some ogre or something, just not the Mr. America I'd made him to be. And it doesn't make any difference anyway, does it? I'm what I am, regardless. Knowing him isn't going to change perfect Natalie Briscoe. Maybe some things are best left alone. Sure, I'll never stop wondering about the guy, just like you'll never stop wondering if Lizzie Borden did it or who killed JFK, but when the dust clears, suddenly it's not so all fired important, is it? Do you understand?"

Fred O'Connor set down his dish and applauded.

Dean crossed over to Nattie and gave her a big hug. "Whoever he was, he must have been one hell of a guy to be your father!"

"You weren't in Fort Lauderdale fourteen years ago, were you?"

"No, but I wish I had been! I'd be damn proud to father someone as wonderful as you!"

She was embarrassed. "Cut out the mush, you two. Tell me some secrets. You know more about this stuff than you're letting on. You've been holding out." She suddenly looked sadder. "Like Sarah and her mother being dead."

"Okay, we'll fess up, but you go first," Dean smiled.

"I know where my old lady is."

"Where?"

"Down the road, in Montrose. She didn't want to stay in the same house as the tree-maker so she skipped out in the middle of the night."

"Tell me about it." Dean asked without thinking. It was really none of his business. Fred the gentleman got up and wandered away, ostensibly to dump his trash, but out of politeness not wishing to hear the sordid details of Dorrie Briscoe's love life.

"She pussy-toed up to his room Thursday night. She told me where she was going first; said he'd invited her the night before." Some invite, Dean thought, remembering Henry's command and Dorrie's reaction to it. "Anyway, I guess it didn't go so hot. She never came back down. But I talked to her on the phone after she spoke to you and she's okay. Just confused. She's cooling it in Montrose in a motel."

"And Henry knows about it?"

Nattie looked disgusted. "You guys have a lot to learn about women. My old lady has this like love/hate relationship with the tree-maker. He keeps playing her like a Gilligan's Island rerun and she keeps pulling in the residuals. Don't try and figure it out with common sense."

"So why the big mystery?"

"Beats me. But this game's been going on for years. Your turn. How about a secret?" She spooned the last of her sundae and wiped her mouth.

Dean hesitated but finally told Nattie about Angelo Faldi and his curbside discussion with Hays Crawford. She digested the information slowly and then shook her head. "If Henry finds out, Faldi's dead meat, not to mention the long-haired hippie. What do you figure? Think they're trying to rip off the Mickey Mouse hat?"

Fred returned. "Seems like that would be a mistake. Henry is the only one who's supposed to make the thing work. Without him, it's not worth a pence. Maybe Crawford and Griffin are in cahoots to sell the story. Faldi was up there taking pictures. Seems like a magazine would love a scoop like that."

They all agreed that made more sense.

"Speak of the devil," Dean exclaimed as he glanced up in time to see Faldi's car pull up across the street. Dean abruptly rose to his feet.

"I just spotted an old friend."

He dropped a bill on the table. "Have some dessert with your dessert. I'll be right back." He crossed the street just as Angelo Faldi reached the entrance to a bar.

"My, my! If it isn't Mr. Faldi," Dean said, leaning against the door.

"I remember you," Angelo said with a coldness that would chill a penguin.

"Yum, yum, yum, strained peas," Dean answered, putting on his silliest smile. "Small world and all that horse shit. You didn't come out here to murder me or something as Hollywood as that, did you?"

Angelo continued to stare with a look that said the opposite of the words he spoke. "No. Didn't you get the word? I'm reformed."

"The wonders of our penal system never cease to amaze me. And so quickly! Here I thought you were an incorrigible low-life slime ball and now you're a model citizen. Prison must be a marvelous place. I understand they have courses and everything. You could have gotten a kindergarten equivalence if you were really ambitious."

"Always the smart mouth."

"So how come you left your comfortable cell? It seems like society thought a minimum ten-year vacation was in order."

"The appeal judge agreed with our wisdom that I got shafted. He tossed the whole case out. I never did it. So here I am enjoying your scenery." The sneer coated each word with acid.

"Folks tell me you've been taking pretty pictures of our mountains. Souvenirs to send back to your friends? Pictures are so much nicer than letters, especially when most of your friends can't read. Now, let's cut out the bullshit and get down to business. What do you have cooking with Hays Crawford?"

"Who?" Angelo asked with the innocence of an infant angel.

"The guy you were talking to in your car two days ago. Dressed like a bum? Long hair?" Dean moved close enough for the smell of beer and a greasy supper to nearly knock him over.

"Oh, him. I was just asking about a nice place to dine. Pleasant young fellow."

Dean took a step closer until his chest touched Faldi. "Who are you working for?"

"Me? I'm just on vacation; getting over the trauma of unfair incarceration."

"I'm sure you wouldn't want a return visit, would you?"

"Listen you bastard. I'm clean. No one's looking for me. It's a free country, home of the brave and all that bull shit. If I can make a quick buck out of this dumb-ass business, why should you give a..."

"Mostly because I just don't like you," Dean answered, matching his snarl.

Faldi turned and brushed by him. "Just don't get in my way." Then he turned and smiled.

"'Millionaire visits Fairy Land', read all about it, at your local super market!" He left Dean standing on the curb.

Dean turned slowly and retraced his steps across the street.

Later, after the trio returned to the house and Nattie was off to bed, Dean filled in Fred O'Connor on his conversation with Faldi. Both decided to sleep on it before making a decision about whether or not to inform Henry Whitcomb of the upcoming realization of his worse nightmare – national publicity, of the most embarrassing kind.

Chapter XII

It was a restless night for David Dean. He drifted fitfully in that nether world between insomnia and slumber, juggling facts and theories like a court jester; a tennis player serving pros and cons across a net of common sense. A dream snuck in just before dawn; Sarah Byrd, young and innocent, trying to talk to Nattie and Dorrie about giving life a chance. She was in the graveyard but it was daylight, and she was trying to reach Nattie's outstretched hand. Little Ella was behind the fence, basket in hand, locket on her cotton dress. Finally Dean woke, but he remained in bed, shuffling the facts and theories of the case around in a sleep-filled head.

If the murder of half the Whitcomb family was the bottom line to these strange happenings, and Dean believed it was, then why couldn't Henry have come up with a simpler gambit? If he believed one of the people he dragged to Colorado was guilty, did he want to force a slip-up or confession from one of the reluctant attendees? Was Byrd's Song just an elaborate hoax? So elaborate a hoax just offered more opportunity for error. Surely Henry Whitcomb could have come up with a simpler way of testing his suspects than the time trial the Klaxton turban suggested. No, there was a missing ingredient.

Dean considered himself a better than fair judge of character and a thousand interviews over the years enabled him to judge the difference between a lie and an honest response, at least most of the time. He was willing to bet Henry Whitcomb showed a genuine reaction to both the excavation of the tin box and the news of the death of the Byrd family, without heirs. Yet, no matter how convincing the evidence seemed, Dean certainly could not be convinced Henry Whitcomb, wearing a ridiculous antique helmet, was transversing time and space like a comic book hero.

Morning slowly seeped into the room and with it reality and the same assortment of unresolved questions from the night before. Dean expected to be the first at breakfast but, surprisingly, the gang was there, everyone except Henry Whitcomb. Those staying in town had driven out earlier and the household was up and active; Mrs. Brown frying eggs, Jeremy eating like a lumber jack, Neil dissecting an English muffin, Nattie pumping in cream of wheat and Fred grumbling about the lack of prizes in the cereal packages. Hays, not eating, immediately cornered Dean and tried to convince him again to reconsider the eight o'clock session, which, by the looks of the attendees, had attracted considerable interest.

Hays Crawford continued to grumble while Dean poured coffee and toasted two slices of bread. He explained to the young man the session was no different from the earlier ones and as Henry had agreed to it, Dean had no intention of calling it off. Crawford was not happy but seemed to accept defeat and sulked away. It was unspoken but he realized that once Henry had decided something, it was going to happen.

Dean hadn't reached a decision about Angelo Faldi. While he felt an obligation to tell Henry Whitcomb about his conversation with the man, he still wanted to keep some matters to himself, information for a rainy day. He did, however, plan to confront Hays Crawford about Faldi as soon as the session was over. As he munched his raisin bread he couldn't help but feel anger at what the bearded electrician was apparently doing to Whitcomb. If there was a way to stop the unfair publicity Faldi had alluded to, Dean felt he owed Whitcomb at least that much, in spite of his dislike of the man.

Although there was no mention of the session at the meal it was obvious nerves were tight. Mrs. Brown seemed particularly uneasy. Neil Archer was a wreck. Nerves, hangover or a combination of the two had taken their toll and Jeremy Whitcomb looked only slightly better. Even Fred O'Connor seemed more uneasy than usual. Only Nattie Briscoe displayed any sign of animation, talking away in spite of no one listening to what she was saying. But even her conversation stopped when Henry Whitcomb yelled from the floor above, signaling to get things going. The group tramped obligingly up the stairs.

"I've got a splitting headache. Let's get this damn thing started," he mumbled, as Hays Crawford placed the Klaxton turban on his head and fiddled with the dial.

Dean felt like the Hardy boys at a seance; a bunch of somber faces awaiting a visit from "the other side," two knocks and the ghost shows up. Most were standing about the bedroom as there were insufficient chairs in the room. Dean had trouble telling if he felt more uncomfortable or just stupid putting up with the silly charade. He wasn't alone; the room was awash with twitches and squirms. The only one relaxed was Henry Whitcomb, the guest of honor. His eyes were closed and his breathing slow and easy as he lay atop the sheets, his hands crossed like a fresh corpse. Hays Crawford continued to fumble with the apparatus. Except for the smell of flowers, church music and the ridiculous Klaxton Turban strapped to his head, it was an Irish wake, complete with a body and dutiful mourners.

The scene remained unchanged while the clock ticked away slowly for twenty minutes, with no movement whatsoever on the part of somnolent Henry Whitcomb. Finally Hays Crawford began to fidget in earnest, trying to get a nonverbal conversation going with scowls and eye contact with Archer who ignored him. He was probably afraid he'd piss off the sleeping prophet if he should awake. Dean got in on the act with a what-the-hell's-going-on gesture of his own and a tap on Archer's arm.

Archer drew a pencil and paper from his pocket and wrote in third grade script, "He should be talking by now, telling us where he is."

But Whitcomb didn't speak; nor did he move; or give much indication he was still alive. Only the rapid eye movement behind closed lids indicated what the barber shop magazines listed as dreaming.

He kept this up for one hour and twenty-three minutes. He was off to Oz, or wherever else the Klaxton Turban was supposed to transport him, leaving his bored audience flopped down on the floor, taking turns nodding off.

Dean's bladder was winning an argument about sticking around when the sleeping mummy finally awoke, sat bolt-upright and asked sharply, "Where is the gold watch?"

Neil Archer and Hays Crawford looked shocked, everyone else, bewildered. Finally it was Dean who asked the obvious. "What gold watch?"

Whitcomb himself looked almost as confused as the others. He rubbed his eyes, swallowed a couple of times and turned to Archer.

"Get me a beer. I'm thirsty."

Archer scrambled away to do his bidding like a beagle fetching a newspaper, pounding his way down the stairs as Henry stood up, looking from one to the other, scratching himself and yawning.

"So where did the magic carpet take you?" asked Dean.

Henry Whitcomb's expression gradually turned to an I-know-some-thing-you-don't-know look. "I agreed to let you attend a session. You did. End of agreement."

Hays Crawford continued to look extremely agitated. "We're in this together. That was the deal from the start. We're supposed to know what happened!"

"Bullshit. Maybe that was your agreement, not mine. I'm not even sure I need you anymore. I've seen Byrd's Song. I know the turban works."

He stared at Crawford. "I know where it takes me is real; that's enough."

Whitcomb carefully removed the helmet from his head and began to slowly wind the wires and replace it in the aluminum case. Crawford looked as if he couldn't make up his mind to run or take a swing at the older man just as Archer kicked open the door, four foaming beers pressed to his belly and dripping down his fly.

"Drinks all around!" he called, as Crawford spun on his heels and stormed past him.

"What's his problem?" Archer asked, looking for a place to set the spewing cans.

Whitcomb didn't answer. He reached out and took one of the beers, pouring a long enough draught to dribble a stream of white foam down his chin and chest.

"It looks like your boss has decided to fly solo," Fred O'Connor said.

"What do you mean?" asked Archer, a look of alarm on his face.

Whitcomb answered him. "It's simple. You're all free to go, get lost, take the day off. I know this thing works. No more group experimenting. Maybe I'll try it on my own."

"Great," said Dean disgustedly. "Have a delightful trip. And don't forget to leave a tip for the maid when you clear out of my bedroom!"

"Not you and the old man. I still need you two. I want to know as much about the Byrd family as you can find." Dean was about to respond but Archer cut him off.

"Hey, Henry? What about our deal?" Archer whined but Whitcomb didn't bother answering.

"You can control it, can't you?" Archer continued. "Is that what happened? You can go back to where you want?" There was a shrill panic to his voice.

Whitcomb just gloated, comfortable in their discomfort, neither adding to it nor detracting from it.

The sound of the downstairs phone could be heard above Archer's whining and Dean ambled down the stairs to answer it, leaving the others behind.

"Mr. Dean?" asked a familiar female voice. It took Dean only a second to recognize Alice Adams, Ron's mother.

"It's nice to hear from the best cook in Ouray County," he answered. "Nattie had a ball."

She laughed. "Nattie is a sweet little girl. And I'm not the only one to say so. I think my Ron has put her pretty high on his list, too."

"That's very kind of you to say. And I appreciate your taking time to call."

She hesitated. "That's not the only reason I phoned. I'm down at the motel. Mr. Griffin is gone. I just thought I'd let you know."

"Thank you. And 'good riddance' to Mr. Griffin."

"There's more to it. He left all his belongings. The bed wasn't slept in. Normally I'd wait a day or two in case he just stayed a night with a friend but with all the mystery about him, and the blood... "

"The blood?"

"Mostly in the bathroom. But the room is pretty messed up, too. Do you think I should call the police?"

Dean tried to think. "Why don't you wait awhile? Did he leave any papers? A wallet or anything like that?"

"No. Just a suitcase and some dirty clothes and shaving things. I'm not going to get in trouble over this, am I?"

Dean immediately felt guilty for involving the woman unfairly. "No," he answered quickly. "Perhaps you'd better not wait to call the law. It was unfair of me to ask you to. Why don't you call the police or the sheriff and just explain the situation? I'm sure they'll wait to see if he's reported missing."

She seemed relieved. "I'll call them." She thought a moment. "I don't see any reason to tell them I spoke to you first, do you?"

Bless you, Mrs. Adams, Dean thought. "No, I don't see any reason to complicate matters. But if they ask, don't feel you have to lie on my account; just tell the truth."

"A man called for Mr. Griffin earlier, just after the maid found he hadn't been back. He was very upset." She paused. "You don't suppose someone killed him, do you?"

Dean silently hoped she didn't suspect him as he brushed off the possibility of a murder as highly remote. All he could think of as he hung up was Henry Whitcomb saying he didn't have to worry about Faldi anymore. Billionaires don't wipe out their problems like mafia hit-men, or do they? Dean desperately hoped not, but wasn't sure.

Fred O'Connor stood close enough to eavesdrop Dean's side of the conversation. The others remained upstairs. He filled Fred in on Alice Adams' comments while cautiously looking around to confirm no other ears were listening.

"If someone did kill Faldi, there'd be damn few mourners," Dean said as he finished. "But I don't like the timing or the location, or Henry's blasé attitude last night when I mentioned Faldi."

"Suppose it was Hays Crawford who called for Faldi?" Fred asked.

"I imagine so. I think I'd better have a little talk with our friend Mr. Crawford; I've waited long enough. Where is he?"

"You may have waited too long. He hightailed it out after the seance. I saw him going up the driveway. He had his bag stashed by the garage. I guess he checked out of the hotel before he came over this morning. If he learned Faldi is missing, he may be worried about his own hide."

"If Faldi and Crawford are both gone there isn't a thing we can do to stop the presses if they decide to feature Whitcomb at the checkout counter with the weekend sale of beans and baloney."

Dean retreated to the living room with a fresh cup of coffee, trying to clear his head while Fred sat nearby, filling his ever-present pad with more penciled notes.

Nattie Briscoe and Mrs. Brown came downstairs and kept walking back and forth. Mrs. Brown, in an uncharacteristic flush of domesticity, was taking Nattie to church and the proper dress code seemed in dispute.

After that obstacle was surmounted, Neil Archer, as upset as usual, was enlisted to drive them.

Archer looked at Dean as if to ask if he were allowed to be that close to Nattie but Dean simply shrugged. Brown made a formidable chaperon; Nattie was as safe as in a nunnery.

Jeremy Whitcomb, dressed more for a round of country club golf than Sunday in the mountains, strolled about the grounds, bored or nervous; it was difficult to tell which. Whitcomb senior remained closed in his room until nearly lunchtime.

When he finally came down, Whitcomb was one step ahead of Dean to the bathroom. In a flash he was pissing like a buffalo after a beer bust, not bothering closing the door or concentrate on his aim while Dean waited outside. Whitcomb was in a particularly good mood.

"I suppose you think I'm being a bastard to all these jerks but it's like I said," he called as he splashed the seat of the toilet, "I don't give a sweet shit what anyone thinks. I do what I damn well please."

"Didn't your mother teach you to flush?" Dean grumbled as Whitcomb sauntered out to the hall, zipping his fly. But, as usual, Whitcomb ignored him.

"Faldi's missing," Dean waited but no response was forth coming. "He's the guy with the camera."

"Glad to hear it. I told you not to be concerned about him." He slapped Dean on the back as he passed. "You just earned twenty-five thousand bucks. Smile a little and stop looking like you lost your dog. Just keep digging into the Byrds and you'll make some more money. You're still on the payroll. I want to know as much about them as you can find." He didn't wait for an objection.

After Whitcomb returned to his upstairs domain Dean slumped back to his chair and coffee.

"Looks like the king got what he wanted," Fred said. "He has the troops believing the gizmo works and the competition has suddenly vamoosed."

"I don't buy it for a minute!"

Fred smiled. "I don't know that it matters none. I'd guess you're in the minority as far as believing goes, looking around the room up there. The other folks are the one's he's interested in selling. They either bought it hook, line and anchor or at the least he has them thinking."

"I feel like I'm on a train just going along for the ride with Henry Whitcomb pouring on the coal and acting as engineer. Phase two," said Dean. "He's setting 'em up."

"Just like we said," Fred muttered. "You've got five people, and one of

144

'em Whitcomb is sure killed his wife. With our help he's got them all thinking he can plug in his Rootie-Kazooti hat and hop back a couple of years to August eighteenth and take a peek at the dastardly deed. It doesn't matter that he's full of shit, if he is."

"Do you still have your doubts that it's a con?" Dean asked.

"I just don't like not knowing how things work, that's all. Taking something on faith ought to be reserved for church and marriage, not solving mysteries. Sherlock Holmes and those guys wouldn't put up with it. There's too much that ain't answered."

"I'll add another question to your list. If Henry planned it all, why wasn't everyone involved from the start? Jeremy wasn't, at least until later."

Fred thought a moment. "Maybe Henry didn't suspect Jeremy."

"I can't buy that. Henry seems to suspect everyone. It was Jeremy who discovered the bodies, remember? Jeremy was the closest to all of the Whitcomb family. If Henry was groping for suspects, Jeremy would have to be on the list."

"So what does that tell us?"

"I wish I knew," Dean answered. "But the more I think about it, it doesn't make sense he was faking the sessions in some elaborate hoax to smoke out the killer, at least at the start. The idea may have come to him later. But that begs the question of what the turban business was at the start."

Dean thought back to his private brain session. Premise number one, you can't go back in time. Premise number two, someone, singular or plural, is trying to tell the world number one premise is nonsense. If that someone isn't Henry Whitcomb, then who is it?

"Questions, questions, questions," mumbled Fred. "It kind of numbs the mind, don't it?"

Dean answered with a smile, "The biggest question is what in hell do we do about it?"

A loud knock sounded on the outside door, an occurrence so uncommon it startled Dean. When he opened the door, a smiling sheriff grinned down at him from beneath a wide-brimmed hat, a gold star glittering in the sun on his khaki shirt.

"'Morning, Mr. Dean," he said.

Dean experienced a fleeting fright that, "Damn, these guys are good, they know about Faldi already," before realizing the absurdity of his thought process. Alice Adams hardly had time to call the authorities, much less have them connect Dean to the disappearance. "Come in," he stammered.

The sheriff ducked through the doorway, removing his hat as he entered the living room. He certainly looked the part, down to a handlebar mustache and a holstered canon on his hip. Fred discreetly moved away before introductions were necessary but Dean was sure the old man was close by, his ear primed.

"I expected you might stop by the office and file your complaint against Mr. Faldi. When you didn't show, I thought I'd mosey on up here and save you the trouble." The sheriff spoke slowly, taking in the surroundings with a practiced eye.

"I guess it slipped my mind," Dean answered, unconvincingly.

"Surprising, you being a cop and all."

Dean smiled in spite of himself. "You don't miss much, do you, Sheriff?"

"Ouray's a small county. It doesn't take long for gossip to make the rounds. We might get a little behind in the summer when we're knee deep in tourists but we manage to catch up come September." The big man sauntered over to the sofa and sat.

"What made you think Mr. Faldi was trying to steal your car? It seems like it'd be quite a feat getting two vehicles off the mountain, when he drove up there all by himself."

Dean sighed. "Actually it wasn't me who reported it." He glanced upstairs. "I have this sort-of house guest. He's one of these rich bastards, reclusive-like. The fellow's a bit gun-shy when it comes to publicity. He had Neil Archer use my name when he contacted you. I didn't even know about it until later when Archer told me. Faldi was trying to take the man's picture."

"Is that so? It doesn't seem like much of a crime. I suppose that would be Henry Whitcomb you're talking about, wouldn't it?" He peeked up at Dean to see his reaction. He wasn't disappointed.

"Like I said," he added, "we don't miss a whole lot around here."

"No, you don't."

"This here Mr. Faldi had me puzzled a bit. Seems he spent some time in a government facility, involuntarily, and rumor has it you had something to do with him being sent up." Dean felt the room getting warmer as the sheriff continued. "I had my men stop down at the motel this morning, just to chit-chat further with Mr. Faldi. Seems the gentleman flew the coop. You wouldn't know anything about that, would you?"

"No," said Dean quickly, "nothing, directly."

The sheriff's voice stepped up a notch in seriousness. "If Mr. Faldi came to town to rub your nose in his past and you decided to take exception to it, I wouldn't look kindly on any unilateral action you might take in my jurisdiction. Do we understand each other?"

"You needn't be concerned, sheriff."

"I'm always concerned. We're a small town," the sheriff continued, "with a small jail but I'm told it gets mighty uncomfortable in there. And the heating is unreliable. Winter's coming on, Mr. Dean. Anything else you want to tell

146

me about Mr. Angelo Faldi?"

Dean took a deep breath. "Beside the fact he's a misfit cretin with an attitude which I imagine you've found out on your own, I can't add a whole lot. I spoke to him on Main Street last night. That's the first time I've seen him in years. I didn't even know he was out of prison."

"What time would have that been, last night?" Something in his voice told Dean his answer to the question might be important.

"Before nine o'clock," he answered and added, "We were home by nine. You can verify that with my stepfather and a thirteen-year-old who doesn't miss a trick. We were doing the ice cream bit."

The sheriff still didn't smile. "I might just do that. What did Faldi have to say?"

"He claimed his sentence was flipped on appeal and he was as clean as a virgin. He was in Ouray to look at the scenery."

"Aren't we all?" The sheriff sighed as he rose to leave and then added. "By the way, do you happen to know Mr. Atherton and Mr. Waite?"

"No," answered Dean honestly. "Who are they?"

"I figured you didn't know 'em. They're buddies of Mr. Whitcomb's. He has 'em holed up in a motel in Ridgway, kind of keeping tabs on what goes on, I figure, and probably keeping tabs on you."

Dean wondered why Henry hadn't sent them up the mountain to chase off Faldi.

"By the way," the sheriff added, "I don't suppose you care to tell me just what is going on?"

"It isn't anything illegal or sinister; just sort of wacky. I'm pledged to play stupid, if you know what I mean."

The sheriff smiled his widest grin. "Sounds like you're playing it right to the letter! Anything else you want to add?"

Dean thought a minute. "We may have had a prowler."

"Oh?"

"Last Tuesday night. It was either a prowler or the over eager imagination of one of my wacky guests."

"Archer?"

"Good guess."

"His name comes to mind when the description is 'wacky.'" The sheriff smiled.

Dean described the occurrence. "Archer went out for a smoke and came hightailing in claiming to have seen a man who ran back to his car and left. It was late and no one had any business being in my driveway."

"My guess would be either Faldi or Whitcomb's two sneaks, Atherton and Waite. I'll have to give that some thought."

The sheriff shook hands at the door and added, "I saw your bearded friend down on the highway with his duffel, looking like a hippie and looking like he was off somewhere."

"That would be Hays Crawford. He had a tiff with boss Whitcomb this morning. I guess he's heading back east."

"Crawford isn't heading east in the direction I saw him hoofing. He was hiking south, back toward Ouray. I thought I was back in the '60s when a few hundred hippies camped out in every ghost town they could find to squat in."

"Crawford is sort of a throwback."

"By the way, does the old guy you've got here know how to drive? I spotted him coming into town the other day. He looked a mite unsteady. I would have stopped him but he stuck to back streets and didn't seem to be doing any real harm."

Dean could picture unlicensed Fred O'Connor weaving through town. "He's my stepfather. He doesn't get much driving practice."

"He ought to get a bit more. Is he staying here long?"

Dean didn't answer as quickly as he should have. "I'm supposed to go back in a week or so. He'll return with me."

"Thinking of staying?"

"Dreaming mostly. You have a great area out here."

The sheriff chuckled. "Most people think so. I couldn't tell you how many visitors stop by and want to sell out back home and move here. Instant paradise. In some respects it is, but don't forget to mix reality into the equation. We don't have the answers to most of the problems folks bring with them and we have a few of our own to boot."

After the sheriff left, Dean continued to think about Hays Crawford hiking toward Ouray. Not north toward Montrose and the airport and ultimately the East Coast. Strange. There was nothing south of Ouray for seventy-five miles, just three mountain passes and the old mining town of Silverton, a tiny isolated community, the terminus of a summertime tourist railroad from Durango. Was Crawford meeting someone in Ouray? Maybe the bloodied Faldi was giving him a lift out of town, if he were able. Dean dismissed his thoughts as Fred entered the room, smiling and holding up a check.

Chapter XIII

Sunday afternoon was not unlike Sunday afternoons in the rest of America; a lazy kind of day, stretched between a pot roast dinner at the hands of a newly-reborn Mrs. Brown and Fred O'Connor, displaying heretofore unknown culinary charms, all followed by a quiet cloudless sunset with apple pie and no conversation. And, like Joseph Addison said, "Sunday clears away the rust of the week." Forget Henry Whitcomb locked away in his room; don't give a thought to still-missing Hays Crawford and the rest of the nuts gathered; Sunday afternoon meant peace on earth.

The good sheriff had failed to return with embarrassing questions about Angelo Faldi nor had a body turned up in some embarrassing place like Dean's front hall closet. Brown had shamed Neil Archer into driving to Ridgway for provisions, cooked and even brought Whitcomb his supper in bed, while the rest let out a collective sigh of relief to be free of his nasty presence.

In spite of Whitcomb's pronouncement of the morning that he was finished with the lot of them, no one made a move to leave. If there was further conversation on the subject, Dean didn't know about it. Later, with dishes cleared, Jeremy was off in the den, losing his inheritance to Nattie Briscoe in gin rummy, while Neil was sulking God-knows-where. Neil picked a bit at dinner but said little. His fingernails were down beyond the quick and he looked like hell had sent him a personalized invitation. Dean retired to the porch with only Fred for company, a warm breeze and the whistle of the wings of the end of season humming birds, stocking up calories for their long trip south. Life was truly tolerable. Even after Fred wandered off to tackle some obscure mystery, real or printed, the early evening continued to hold its charm.

Dean spotted the automobile just as he put the rocking chair in gear and opened his first beer of the evening. Only the top of the vehicle was visible above the trees as it slowed to turn into his drive, dragging a cloud of dust and swirl of leaves behind. He recognized the insignia of a Montrose taxi as it pulled atop a rise and descended out of sight before reaching the house. Just what I need, more company he thought. Then with a sinking feeling he wondered if Dorrie Briscoe was returning. Taking one long pull to finish the beer, he rose and walked slowly toward the drive to meet the visitor. He turned the corner with the enthusiasm of a truant to the principal's office just as the vehicle pulled to a stop at the rear of the house.

Validating speculation, Dorrie Briscoe stepped from the cab at the same time as the driver, planting a kiss on his cheek.

"That's an extra tip, hon," he heard her call as she turned and waved and started toward him. Almost at once, the opposite door opened and standing there hesitantly was Cynthia Byrne. You could have knocked Dean flat with a stiff breeze.

God, said Dean to himself. Here together is the woman I slept with and wished I didn't and the one I haven't and wish I had!

"I'll bet you're surprised," Dorrie smirked as she rustled past him, sporting a grin that spoke volumes. "We both called for a cab at the same time. Wasn't that lucky?"

Luck wasn't what Dean would have called it.

"Where's Nattie?" Dorrie added over her shoulder as she proceeded toward the house.

"In the den, playing gin rummy, if anyone has any money left," Dean mumbled as he walked toward Cynthia. The cab driver was handing her a small overnight bag as Dean reached the car and he reached for it.

She turned and faced him, a touch of a smile on her lips. "Before you yell at me, I did telephone. You weren't home and Fred told me to come anyway and surprise you. I flew from Las Vegas to Denver and then to Montrose."

"You did surprise me," he smiled in return. "No doubt about that." He bent to kiss her. It lasted surprisingly long. He couldn't tell if Dorrie had stopped to gawk at the scene on the way to the house but he didn't give a damn. This was Cynthia Byrne and everything else paled to her presence.

She was dressed in a pink suit, as out of place in the Colorado mountains as a coonskin cap in Cleveland but it didn't matter a lick. She was beautiful; a tiny thing barely over five feet with short dark hair, blue eyes and a smile that made his heart stop. What a damned fool he'd been. At that moment if Dorrie Briscoe together with the entire Dallas Cowboys' cheerleader squad had jumped his bones in their birthday suits, he wouldn't have moved a blink from gazing at Cynthia.

It had been a little over six months since Dean had met Cynthia Byrne. The first three were spent searching for her missing husband while a feeling between them warmed and the last three were spent letting her adjust to widowhood and him to a bullet in the ass. God, it was good to hold her.

"I was unfair running off to Vegas and not telling you." She was against his shoulder and he couldn't tell if she was crying or happy. He gently pushed her to arms-length and smiled.

"You're here. That's what's important." They walked arm in arm toward the house with Dean still carrying the small overnight bag.

"It's beautiful here, like a National Geographic centerfold." she said, gazing at the towering mountains surrounding them. "It's so peaceful."

"It is beautiful and it used to be peaceful," he grumbled.

Cynthia laughed; tiny bells, just as he'd remembered. "Are the rest of your houseguests as...interesting as Doctor Briscoe? She nearly propositioned the cabby!"

He cringed. "Dorrie is in a league by herself, believe me, but the entire crew needs intense psychiatric help." He opened the door just enough to set her suitcase inside but when she moved to enter he put his hand on her shoulder and turned her around.

"We're going to town, just the two of us." He guided her back down the walk to his car.

"Do you have a bevy of bimbos in there you're hiding from me?" she teased.

"You're my one and only bimbo. We're going to buy a bottle of the most expensive wine we can find and order from the top of the menu, and thumb our noses at the rest of the world."

"Can't I at least say 'Hello' to Mr. O'Connor?"

"Let the conniving old goat suffer. You belong to me. Besides, I'm saving you from Neil Archer. You're wearing a skirt so he'd be all over you clawing and whimpering."

"I suppose, if you insist," she smiled. "But won't you be missed?"

"Dorrie will spread the news, believe me."

They dined in Ouray, in a new, less intimate restaurant than he would have liked but tonight the two would have been alone at a rock concert. The wine was perfect and so was Cynthia.

"I want to stare at your face until my eyelids flop," he said over their second glass of cabernet. "God, I've missed you."

"You say such nice things, sir," she answered, the candles making pinpoints of stars in her eyes. "Tell me more." And he did.

It was dessert before anything as mundane as the present became a topic but they lingered over coffee and finally brought each other up to date. She had been in Vegas at the convention for three days but felt guilty being only half their usual distance apart and not even telling him. On a whim she had booked airline passage, the back end of a gambler's special to Denver and on to Montrose. "Thank God for plastic," she laughed. He had a sense there was more to her quick departure than she let on and visions of the suave but lecherous doctor who accompanied her filled his mind.

"Did the doctor's Jag run out of gas?" he asked and immediately regretted bringing up the subject. He had ghosts of his own that best remain closeted.

She looked down at her food and said nothing for a few moments. "Part of me wants to know if you slept with her and part of me doesn't. Part of me wants to talk about Dr. MacNaught but most of me doesn't." She looked up. "Let's both forget yesterdays and pay more attention to tomorrow." Then she added, "And tonight."

Later, he couldn't recall what they had eaten, only feeling a level of utter contentment as he sat across from her, contentment he hadn't experienced in weeks. Hours later they looked up and laughed to notice they were alone in the restaurant, the other tables cleared. They left hand in hand and he reluctantly began the drive back from town.

Dean pointed out various buildings in Ouray as they circled the block on a side street to reverse their direction. "Isn't that a cute Bed and Breakfast?" she said in her most refreshing tone, pointing out a newly redecorated building. "Wouldn't it be fun to stay there...sometime?"

He looked at her with surprise. "I do believe I'm being seduced!" At the same time he jerked the wheel in a skidding U-turn and pulled up in front of the pleasantly refurbished Victorian building.

She looked at him with raised eyebrows. "Sir, we don't even have any luggage!"

"This isn't the fifties. I'll bet they'll take our money anyway."

"Now I'll really feel like a bimbo," she said as he led her up the walk.

"Are you scared?"

"Petrified," she answered, and her voice confirmed it.

"Me, too."

A gracious young woman in a full length calico dress registered them, with only a hint of a smile and a comment, when he truthfully listed his address but five miles away, that most of their guests traveled further. She led them down a long corridor to a room that was of a different time and a different world. An oak dresser and commode, complete with pitcher and bowl, stood on either wall. Lace curtains filtered the light from a nearly-full moon just beginning to rise over the hills and blended it with the warm glow from an oil lamp on a corner table. The bed was a four-poster, complete with a canopy and a quilt of a thousand different pieces and as many colors. Their host discreetly departed, dispensing with the usual list of rules and services, leaving them standing hand in hand, alone, the door closed to the rest of the world. They stood there for a few moments, each as nervous as the other, before either moved.

"Let's not say anything," Cynthia said before Dean could think of an appropriate comment. She kissed him lightly and went into the attached bath.

Cynthia Byrne had confided, when Dean was investigating her missing husband, that Jeffery Byrne was the only man she had ever known. She had married at a young age and both had been faithful. She kidded about it, a very un-nineties background she'd said, but he knew that her being here with him was a major step in her life and in their relationship. He would treat the night with the tenderness and dignity it deserved.

She emerged, clothed in a terry cloth bathrobe the house had thoughtfully provided, crossed to the bed, and without looking over at him, pulled down the covers. She slid into the bed and covered herself, before disrobing. He waited a moment, blew out the oil lamp, crossed the room, sat on the edge of the mammoth mattress and began to undress.

He slid under the covers and when he was beside her and felt her warmth, time stopped. He could hear and feel the rapid beat of her heart and he was sure she could feel his as well.

"I was just thinking," she said nervously, as if trying to somehow lighten the intensity, "I ought to be in mourning, wearing black or purple instead of sleeping with someone between lavender sheets." It didn't call for an answer. She'd already answered by coming with him to this quiet room.

A legion of women flashed by his mind; Suzy with the wide hips and willing arms, Ann and Mary and Bev and little Amy Jackson. He saw Jane and Brooke and Peg and a score of almond-eyed ladies of the night. Monica Cutler passed by and Ethel Rosewater and Betty from Boise and even Dorrie Briscoe. He knew he'd slept with each and every one of them, some scores of times but he couldn't recall a thing about any of the encounters. It was as if he were with a woman for the very first time. And it was beyond description.

Later, when all his dreams were realized and all his fears put to rest he lay there, watching the moonlight glisten on her dark hair, little ribbons of silver along the lines of the waves.

"The answer to every question you want to ask but won't is exactly what you'd want to hear, if I could form the words to say them the way I feel."

"Thank, you," she said, words muffled in the pillow. "That's so sweet, so nice." And then she turned to him and pressed herself against him again, the length of their bodies one, arms around his neck; face against his chest. "Be there for me, please?"

"Always," he murmured, and meant it. Then he added, "But I've been a no commitment-type guy for a long, long time; you're taking a chance."

"I'm a commitment-type gal and you can't live without me, so you're stuck!"

She spent the night in his arms, making love and taking turns listening to and telling a hundred little stories. He knew she had to be exhausted by three days in Vegas, the double flight and layover but neither slept a wink. Near dawn, he began to tell her in detail about the Klaxton turban, the murder of Whitcomb's family and everything that had transpired the past week.

"I don't think I'd like being able to go back in time," she said.

"You ought to meet a thirteen-year-old I know. That's what she says, too."

"I wouldn't want to be able to see Jeffery and me when we were first married, happy and having fun. Or have you spy on us either. It's all over, gone forever and there's no good to bringing it back. I don't want to see your past; that's yours to do with what you please and so is mine."

He had no quarrel and told her so. They agreed, not just on a personal basis but for the broader picture as well, that the past best rest. "It's like the Loch Ness Monster. People have been chasing it for a thousand years but if they found it, what would happen? There would be a flurry of excitement for a couple of weeks and then nothing. The interest is in the search, not necessarily the result. Not that the past can't teach us, but it should never take precedence over the future," Dean explained.

She was fascinated with Byrd's Song and cried a little when he spoke of the deaths of Sarah and her mother and the widowed father alone for another year, dying without family, and probably without friends. She was moved by Nattie's reaction, so out of character to how Dean had described the girl. She, too, wanted to visit their graves.

"No one in the world knew they existed until a few weeks ago," he told her.

"That's so sad, to not be remembered. Such a short and tragic life."

"Not all tragic," he said. "They had their few months together in the mountains, as difficult as the time must have been. Lord knows what they left behind before they came west but here they at least had dreams and hope."

"Byrd's Song sounds like a beautiful place, like an eagle's nest, above the world. Perhaps we can hike up sometime, if I ever come back, and maybe plant some flowers."

"It's a tough climb," he said, pulling her closer.

"I'd leave you in the dust," she kidded, tickling him unmercifully. "And now the bad news. I have to be back at the airport at seven."

"A.M.? Tomorrow morning? This morning?" He could feel her nod.

"The convention is over and my return trip from Las Vegas back to Pennsylvania leaves tomorrow afternoon. Will you drive me to the Montrose airport?"

"I'll do anything for you."

"How much more time do we have?" she purred.

They made love again and afterwards noticed that the room was beginning to fill with the first light of the new day.

"It's so peaceful here. It must be heaven, owning a warm and cozy place like this where you can give your guests a little break from the world. I love it."

"I'd like to stay. Here."

"In Colorado?" She sat up in the bed, pulling the covers around her.

It was his turn to nod. "If I could figure out a way of pulling it off. It's so much cleaner, more natural than the east. I feel as if I belong and I've just gotten here. Ouray is more like a neighborhood than a town, everyone knows each other and the countryside is like no place else in the world."

"Does your gunshot wound have something to do with it?" she asked cautiously.

"No. Not directly, at least. Yes, I suppose, in a way. Part of me feels guilty about turning my back on the ills of the city and part of me can't wait to dump all the problems on someone else. They're not of my making; let the next guy pick up the load. I'm nearly forty years old and I need a change."

"Is that unfair? It's not as if you haven't contributed. You spent fifteen years putting your life on the line locking up scum. You deserve a break." She turned and looked up at him.

"What about the winters here? They must have a dozen feet of snow."

"The winters couldn't be any worse than the sleet and slush I've been used to. The locals all say it's sunny and dry most days, even though the snowfall is massive. I guess I'd just have to try it."

"What would you do?"

"Maybe something like this. Run a little Bed and Breakfast or small inn. Take some of the guests up to the high country by jeep in the summer. No big plans, just a quiet life, smelling the pine needles, I guess. But anything like that is a long way off." He reiterated his conversation with Lieutenant Anderson and his promise to return to work in a few days.

"It doesn't hurt to dream. Sometimes they even come true. Want a partner?" She said it cautiously, with eyes cast downward.

"You know I do. But you have a son just starting college, a new career and my income prospects are zip."

"You just made twenty-five thousand dollars in a week! You can do whatever you set your mind to! I haven't earned that much money in my whole life!"

"You've always been a housewife until you became a widow. Give it time. And twenty-five grand wouldn't be a down payment on Ouray real estate in this market. My only chance would come from a peck of luck and freeing up some of my police pension money. I don't have any savings."

"I have a contract on the house," she said.

"That's great!"

"Yes...but the realtor won't make any guesses about the buyer's finances and the price is a lot less than we asked. The market is the pits in the east. But it's the first real bite and I'll come out of it with some money so I'm keeping my fingers crossed."

All of their further conversation concerned David Dean or Cynthia Byrne, individually, as if neither dared to talk about David Dean and Cynthia Byrne together. While no plans or promises were made, what was left unsaid told both of them only the details were lacking. Each knew the future included the other, somehow. The fit was simply too perfect to sunder.

Their talk became more subdued after they showered and began the thirty-five-mile drive to the Montrose airport. She stayed in the car when he stopped at his house for her luggage. The case sat where he'd left it and no one had risen at that early hour. They stopped for a quick breakfast in town, a roll and coffee with only the most general comments on weather and travel. Both had immediate demands facing them before the future could even be discussed.

After Cynthia left there was a void unlike any he'd felt before. They'd clung to each other as the flight was announced like a World War Two movie; two lovers facing an unknown future while each promised to call soon and often and that their absence would be of short duration. There wasn't near enough time to say all the things he wanted to say, or hear all the things he wanted to hear.

The drive back by himself was the loneliest he ever remembered. He'd become used to his own company, but that was in the void of not having someone with whom he desperately wanted to share his life.

When he returned, the others except for Henry Whitcomb, were awake, gathered around the table and living room. It was as if they all wanted to talk to him but he waved them away, even Fred O'Connor, and closeted himself in his room. After stripping off his two-day clothes he flopped into bed and slept like a three-day drunk.

Chapter XIV

The rest of the world was finished with lunch by the time Dean rolled out of bed and showered the last sweet scent of Cynthia Byrne from his body. He was searching for a pair of jockey shorts without holes when there was a knock on his door. He pulled on the first pair he found, followed by jeans and a tee shirt and opened the door to Mrs. Brown. She was attired in her usual business garb but wore an apron over her suit and carried a tray with two covered dishes. At first he thought she was delivering room service but she held onto the food.

"May I ask you a question?" she asked, glancing over her shoulder to see if anyone else was watching. "Do you think the turban really works?"

Dean was startled not only by the question but by Mrs. Brown's presence. He'd not spoken a dozen words to the woman since she'd arrived.

"All I know is everything Henry says he saw apparently really happened. But even Henry himself said no one could ever prove he actually traveled back in time and what he saw was real."

She seemed to ponder his answer as he ran a comb through his hair. "So you're saying no one really knows?"

He nodded and she sat on the edge of the bed, clinging onto the food tray in her lap, as if he might steal it.

"I know this much for sure," she continued. "Henry Whitcomb isn't lying when he says he thinks he was really there. He's telling the truth."

"Why do you say that?"

"I've worked for Mr. Whitcomb for nearly twenty-five years. That should tell you something."

Dean chuckled. "You're saying you've seen him lie enough times to know when he's speaking truthfully?"

She looked at him sternly. "Young man, I take my pay check from Mr. Whitcomb every two weeks. For that he is entitled to four things; honesty, dependability, efficiency and loyalty. Do you understand?"

He nodded, feeling like a third-grade pupil being chastised for forgetting his multiplication tables.

She continued, "I don't have to like everything Henry Whitcomb does or approve of all his actions but I'm not being paid to make judgments about him either. God knows there are few secretaries nowadays who operate under any code of honor but that's how I was taught and that's how I'll conduct my affairs." She pointed a finger at his chest, "But I do know Mr. Whitcomb, even better than his mousy wife did, and he isn't lying about Byrd's Song!"

Dean opened his mouth to respond but Mrs. Brown wasn't finished.

"I'll just add this. That Klaxton machine is evil. No good will come of poking into the past. It's against the order of things and it should stop."

"That's a decision for your boss, not me. You should speak to Henry," Dean answered.

"I have, but he's up there as we speak with that contraption strapped on his head, doing God knows what. He hardly wants to eat." She started to leave but turned back to him.

"The change from the groceries? You haven't seen it have you?" she asked.

"You mean the money in the bowl on the kitchen counter?"

"Yes, that's where it has been, at least in the past."

"I haven't noticed. Did you ask the others?" He wondered if his voice sounded defensive, even though there was certainly no reason.

"No one's seen it. The bowl is empty."

"There must have been a hundred and fifty dollars in there the last time I looked." Over the past few days the money supply ebbed and flowed as different people picked up groceries and left receipts. Henry Whitcomb's wallet, via Mrs. Brown, miraculously replenished the kitty periodically.

"One hundred and seventy-two dollars and fifty-three cents," she answered. "I wasn't accusing you, just confirming my own suspicions."

"And what are those?"

"I'm sure it was that awful young man, Hays Crawford, who stole it. Now he's run off. Sorry to bother you about it. I've replenished the funds. By the way, we're out of milk and bread and I need a few other things. I left you a list."

She turned on her heels and was gone, leaving Dean standing there looking after her retreating form, and the trailing smell of toasted cheese beneath the cloth on her tray. The lady led a life governed by rules that were unalterably fixed in her mind, no doubt about it. And she certainly had an opinion which she readily displayed on those few occasions when circumstances warranted her expressing it.

Dean wondered if the primary purpose for her visit was the turban or the missing money. Personally, he was more interested in her unbending position on the Klaxton turban and it's purported access to the past. Did Henry now have the ticket to fly solo? He wondered. Brown wasn't helping him, that's for sure. A strange woman, he thought as he strolled out to the kitchen at the eager urging of his stomach. He wondered if anyone ever took time to get to know the Mrs. Browns of the world. Surely there was more to them than first visible. Or did the Mrs. Browns keep their doors closed too tightly for anyone to venture close enough to smile?

Dorrie Briscoe was cracking a pair of eggs in a bowl and burying them in salt and pepper while a black skillet heated on the stove. He reached over her head for a coffee cup.

"Hi, lover!" she said over her shoulder.

"Hi, yourself," he answered, pouring a cup of coffee and sitting at the kitchen table.

"Just kidding. Don't go and get surly on me."

"You're in a chipper mood. Your little vacation in Montrose must have done you a world of good."

"I'm a new person. By the way, your lady friend is a really sweet girl."

"I won't give you any argument on that point."

"I hope you two are serious."

"We are."

She dropped a half stick of butter in the frying pan and jumped back as the fat sizzled and splattered her.

"Damn!" She turned toward him amid the smoke. "If it's true love, I'm sorry I made you fuck me."

"That's history. Cynthia and I are going to have a happily-ever-after life."

"Good for you!"

"What have I missed around this place?" he asked as he popped two pieces of toast in the toaster.

"You slept through the big exodus, for one thing."

"Don't tell me everyone has finally left?"

"No such luck. I meant Nattie's visit to school. That child! I told her to just be quiet and observe, but that's not Nattie! I know they're going to have a handful with her. And, by the way, thanks for the babysitting while I was gone."

"No problem." He chose his next words carefully. "Nattie is not as secure a person as she makes out. She needs a lot of tender loving care and I'm not sure she's getting enough of it."

"Ouch! That hurts!"

He didn't answer for a few minutes.

"Much as thirteen-year olds would like to run their own lives, I'm not sure they're equipped to do it."

She dumped the eggs on a piece of white bread. "I guess I'm a piss-poor mother. I'm not setting a very good example, am I?"

"If we're still playing honest injun, I'd have to say no."

"God, you're blunt!" She ate a few bites. "Maybe that's what I need, but I'm sorry to drag you into all this shit. My head's a little mixed up just now."

"So is the rest of your body." Then he bit his tongue.

She laughed. "Touché! I deserved that! And you're right. That part of my body always has been a little bit flaky. But really, with Henry and me, it's not the sex-bit. God knows he isn't any good at it."

Dean was surprised. He'd assumed the king was terrific at everything he did, screwing included.

"He's a sick man," Dorrie continued. "Half the time we're together we don't even do it."

"Look, I really don't want to get involved in your personal life. That's between you and Henry. My opinion doesn't count a lick."

"I know, but it's just when he asked me to sleep with him the other night... "

"'Told you,' not 'asked you;' he demanded it."

"Okay, and I was really hurt; it was the way he said it. I mean, it had been ages since we were together. Then I began thinking about it. Maybe he really needed me. So I sort of went to see him, the next night, Thursday."

Dean could still hear the soft shuffle of her slippers in the hall. She waited for him to respond, but he didn't. She stirred around her eggs, dripping the yellow yoke over the edge of the plate.

"You don't choose who you fall in love with, it just happens. Sure he's an ass, don't you think I know it, for God's sake? But the other night he was really nice."

She looked up at him. "You know what? He asked me to move in with him."

Dean raised one of his eyebrows.

"Isn't that a hoot, after all this time? That's why I scrammed to Montrose. I needed to think about it, away from him."

"And?"

"There's Nattie to consider. She could have everything she wants."

"Not everything," Dean murmured. "There's also Dorrie to consider." He wondered if Dorrie had slept with Whitcomb the night before, when he was with Cynthia Byrne.

"Henry isn't a shit all the time. I think he really needs me. He had to put up with his wife all these years. He deserves some happiness." A tiny tear wandered down her cheek and dropped with a little splash on the table. "Oh, I don't know!" She laughed as she wiped it up with her elbow.

"See? I'm just as screwed up as ever." She ran her sleeve across her face and continued eating, in silence.

Finally Dean changed the subject. "Hays Crawford is gone."

"So I hear. Lucky Hays Crawford."

"Brown thinks he stole the food kitty."

"He probably had to. He didn't have a pot to piss in. I loaned him money for a hamburger in Chicago on the way out here when we stopped to refuel. He was dead broke." She mopped up the last of the egg with a crust of bread.

"I thought Henry was paying all you folks a king's ransom for this gig."

"He is, but not until after he's finished; then the money goes in an account. That way he keeps us on a tight chain while he needs us."

This is the guy you want to live with, Dean thought disgustedly. Then he asked, "Where do you think Crawford went?"

"Me? I wouldn't have the foggiest. Probably back east. That's all he knows. Henry doesn't have you chasing him for the lunch money, does he?"

"Not exactly. Call it personal interest."

"Maybe Hays is upset now that Henry's proved the Klaxton turban really works. It's exciting, isn't it?"

"So now you're a confirmed believer?"

"How could anyone not be? Henry told me all about it." She got up and began running water over her dishes.

"What's his next stop on the train to dream land? August, two years ago?"

She took her hands from the water and bowed her head. "God, I hope not."

"He's up there now, with the turban on his head. Don't you think that's what he has in mind?"

"I don't know but I wish he'd leave it alone, the whole murder thing. It's driving him crazy."

"A lot of people would like to see him forget it." He rose from the table and dropped his dish in her water and poured another cup of coffee. She didn't answer and he wandered into the living room just as Neil Archer came in from the deck, a glass of amber liquid in his shaking hand. When he saw Dean, he bounced over to him, spilling his drink. Grabbing Dean by the arm, he led him off toward Dean's bedroom.

"I've got to talk to you," he rasped in a harsh whisper, sounding like the heavy in a forties "B" movie. "I've got a problem, a big problem."

"Like that's a novelty?" Dean allowed himself to be led into his room where Archer closed the door behind them.

"If that damn machine works, Henry will kill me! No doubt about it."

"What did you do?" Archer didn't answer but began biting his nails, already chewed bloody.

Finally he muttered, "It's about his wife."

"What did you do, sleep with Phyllis Whitcomb?" For some reason, Dean wasn't even surprised.

"God, no!" Archer yelled, jumping from the edge of the bed. "Henry would have cut off my balls if he ever caught us!"

"So what are you worrying about?"

He shuffled around and began to pace. "God help me. Having this inquiring intellect, I'm always wanting to experiment... reach for new plateaus..."

"Sure."

Archer paused, searching for the right words. "I did something Henry Whitcomb might not interpret the right way."

"Like what?"

"I talked his wife into meeting me at a motel. She thought Henry was going to be there, too. I had a bottle of really great French wine, a terrific year, and we had a few drinks, just while we were waiting. She was getting super mellow, you know, laughing at everything I said? But she...wouldn't...do anything else. Honest, I swear, we never did it!"

"Not because you didn't set it up! The poor woman was practically a mental case from what I hear! What kind of creep are you?"

"See? See? See how Henry would misinterpret it?"

"How else could he interpret it? You tried to bang his mentally incompetent wife only you struck out!"

"What a crude way of saying it! Besides, Phyllis was practically normal, most of the time. She just went through these spells every once in awhile."

"If I were you, Neil, I'd hang onto my balls. If that machine works, Henry's going to get 'em, and deservedly so!"

Neil rose from the bed. "I've got to go. Jeremy is flying back east for the day, some business shit, and I'm going to tag along. I've got to get out of here for a while."

"Henry is upstairs now. Do you know what he's doing? He's wearing the hat. You're probably on borrowed time!"

"God, don't say that! Tell Henry I'm gone, will you?"

"Tell him yourself. Besides, didn't Henry fire all of you?"

"I don't know. I haven't seen him since and I don't think I want to. God, my brain is in a whirl!" He staggered out of the room as Dean heard a car in the drive; Jeremy arrived to pick up his hapless fellow traveler.

When Dean returned to the living room, Fred O'Connor had just come inside. He wore one of his ear-to-ear smiles.

"Nice day for a walk. Autumn air gets the blood a-flowing. Time for a talk?"

"Look," Dean said before Fred could open his mouth further, "I don't want to talk about it. I don't want any questions, and I sure as hell don't want any cute remarks about Cynthia and me."

Fred raised a defensive hand. "Business, only business. First day of the work week and we ought to do something about Whitcomb's twenty-five thousand dollar check." He held it out to Dean.

Dean looked at it, reread it and then kissed it before folding the paper and carefully putting it in his wallet. "I feel like a whore but twenty-five grand is twenty-five grand. As soon as I figure which side is up we'll drive down to the bank. We have some other errands to run as well."

Fred O'Connor projected a broad smile. "Getting to the bank is at the top of the list. He might change his mind!"

Dean took Fred's elbow and propelled him back to their room. "We need some privacy. Who's still in the house?"

Fred ran down the list. Jeremy and Neil Archer were gone until tomorrow, Dorrie was in her room, doing Lord knows what and Brown was locked away with Henry, standing by as he tripped to the past, in spite of another headache. No word had been heard from Hays Crawford.

Dean sat on the bed. "First off, what about the box?" Fred unlocked his cardboard suitcase and retrieved the metal container.

"I can't find a thing to dispute it ain't what it's supposed to be," he said, placing the contents on the bedspread. "The dust and bones are years old and nothing looks disturbed."

There were four coins, three pennies and a two-cent piece, a coin Dean had never seen before the box was opened. It was copper colored, like the pennies, only larger, the size of a nickel. "They only made 'em for a few years," Fred explained. "I guess they were like the two-dollar bill, never popular." The date on the coin was 1864, and it was worn but still legible.

Two of the pennies were Indian heads, one dated 1889 and except for being tarnished, looked uncirculated. The second, showing some signs of wear, was dated 1887.

The fourth coin, also a penny, was dated 1858 and Fred explained it was a "Flying Eagle," the predecessor to the Indian head. The coin was heavily worn.

"How do you know so much about this stuff?" Dean probed, but cut Fred off halfway through the explanation of a certain lady friend in years gone by who dabbled in numismatics.

"One has to wonder why a poor little mountain gal would go and bury five cents which might have bought a heap of candy down at that Porter's store."

Dean thought about it. "I guess we'll never know. Maybe she thought they no longer belonged to her. They were Cinnamon Sam's." He began to sort through the other items.

Two gold collar buttons were unmarked but a round button with a metal loop protruding from the back bore a name, "W. Twigg & Co. Birmingham." It contained a raised cannon and a crown on its face and appeared to have come from a military uniform.

"That's the only piece we might be able to trace, but chances are it's old. Folks collect buttons and maybe the library has a book on 'em."

"We'll check when we go to town," Dean said as he examined and put down two plain white shirt buttons and picked up two pen-points, the traces of ink still visible on them. "The little rat was a selective cuss, wasn't he?"

"Them pen-points kind of stumped me," Fred said. "I guess I didn't think of those folks doing a lot of writing."

"Why not? Even if the parents might have been illiterate Sarah was in school. The pens probably belonged to her."

Dean gathered up the items and replaced them in Fred's suitcase before they left for Ouray. On the trip in, Dean filled in his stepfather on the missing food money and Mrs. Brown's suspicion. They both agreed it was worth the time to check with some of the stores in the small town to try to learn whether Hays Crawford had made any purchases before leaving.

"That shouldn't be a difficult chore," Dean said. "Unless he's buying a tee shirt, art, or a tourist gift there aren't many choices."

Also discussed was the future assignment Henry had hired them to perform, further research on the Byrd family.

"That stuff is easy. I'll give Gloria a call. She was the lady who does all the genealogy business. Between immigration records, census, ship's passenger lists and all that, we should be able to give Henry a pretty good history."

They agreed there was no hurry to begin phase two; phase one was more important.

The first stop was the bank where Dean opened a new account in both of their names. They could always transfer the money back to a Pennsylvania account after the check cleared, Dean explained. Or leave it here as a nest egg he thought to himself. Outside the financial institution they planned their next step.

"You take one side of the street, I'll take the other," Fred stated, and then added, "Too bad we don't have a picture of Crawford."

"Once you describe him, if anyone's seen him, they'll remember."

They agreed to meet in a coffee shop in thirty minutes to compare notes. Fred moved down the east side of the main street, painted in the afternoon sun, and was quickly lost in the few late season tourists. Dean crossed to the other side and began his shop by shop inquiries, with no success. It was Fred who finally hit pay dirt after three foul balls, and it was a grand-slam.

The owner of a shop specializing in mountain bikes and camping gear remembered the bearded young man immediately. Hays Crawford had looked at a mountain bike and asked about the price. He had settled on an inexpensive sleeping bag, cooking utensils and a cheap stove. The bill came to a little over one hundred and twenty dollars. It had been a good week for the shop keeper; Henry Whitcomb had stocked up in the same store a few days before. As Fred told it later, he almost missed the big news. The shopkeeper added he remembered Hays, not only because of his beard and attire, but because the young man had been there before.

When Fred excitedly pressed him, the shopkeeper explained that Crawford was in the shop weeks earlier, but try as he could, he had no point of reference by which to pinpoint the date any closer. He was positive it was Crawford; he prided himself on remembering faces. But, no, he hadn't mentioned to Crawford that he remembered him. As far as the man could recall, the sole earlier purchase was a map.

"When was the Byrd's Song session?" Dean asked quickly. Fred extracted a notebook and began thumbing the pages.

"August twenty-third. About four weeks ago. But it's funny if Crawford hightailed it out here to check the place out for Henry, no one said beans about the trip. And that's a best case scenario. Maybe he hightailed it out here to bury a box."

"We're missing something. The pieces don't fit. I still say that box was in the ground a hundred years. But locating Mr. Hays Crawford is becoming increasingly more important. He has some explaining to do."

They discussed trying to find out where Hays stayed in town during his first visit but recognized the difficulty in doing so. While the shopping in Ouray was limited, the places to stay were not, nor were they so close together. Hotels, motels, bed-and-breakfasts, dude ranches and campgrounds made the chore a major one, especially as the trail was a month old.

"Lets give it a little thought," Dean said, "and in the meantime, follow a warmer trail. Where is he now? His purchases don't make it look like he's traveling with Faldi, do they?"

"From the way you describe Faldi, I wouldn't think he is the camping type. Likely Crawford is hitch-hiking and the sleeping bag is in case he gets caught someplace out of doors."

Dean just grumbled in response; somehow the facts didn't seem to point in that direction.

"Well, he has about fifty bucks. What would he do?"

"That's easy," Fred answered, "He'd buy some grub. Let's try the grocery store."

Luck was with them a second time. Hays Crawford had purchased thirty-five dollars worth of non-perishables.

"You're on foot, you've got about twenty bucks left and four or five days' food. What do you do?"

"You stick out your thumb and pray. You know someone kicked the business out of your pal Faldi, or killed him, and maybe you're next. You can't get away fast enough." Fred answered smugly.

"Maybe. But why do you come back to Ouray instead of heading north? There's shopping in Ridgway, too. If you're trying to make time hightailing it out of here, that's the direction to go. No need to double back, unless you're staying in the area."

"Could be he's still around but I can't fathom the reason why. Whatever he's doing, there must be a couple million acres around here for him to do it in."

While Fred finished a second cup of coffee and a piece of pie, Dean went to the phone and made a credit card call to the Parkside Police Department. After asking the appropriate questions about office gossip and happenings, Dean sweet-talked Rita Angeltoni into digging into Angelo Faldi and his present connections. He then tried to call Harry Hammond at the Spinnersville station but the officer was out. He wanted to call Cynthia Byrne as well, but she would either still be traveling or resting after the trip.

After Dean was able to pry Fred away from an animated conversation with a middle-aged waitress, the two drove to the library. Dean made no effort to get out of the car.

"Aren't you coming?" Fred asked.

"I'm going into Ridgway and chase down Mr. Waite and Mr. Atherton. I'll come back for you."

"This here button business won't take but a few minutes. Hang around and I'll give you some company."

"Look," said Dean over the rolled-down window, "we have no idea what these two are like. You and I have an agreement. I'll handle it if it looks like it could get hot."

Fred wasn't happy. "This may take you a spell and I'll be stuck here. What do you say I drive you over to Ridgway and come back. Then I can pick you up."

Dean let out an exasperated sigh. "Two reasons. First, it's getting late and the library would close before you got back. And secondly, you don't have a driver's license and I'm not even sure you can drive! Didn't you hear the sheriff when you were eavesdropping? It's a wonder he didn't toss your ass in jail!"

"No need to get excited, I just figured on giving you a hand," Fred said, backing off. "No problem. I'll stick around here. Don't worry about it getting too cold after the library closes. I'll find some place."

Dean wasn't buying the sympathy bit for a minute. "While you're in there, look up the coins. The library must have a book that tells what they're worth."

"Why?" Fred asked as Dean began to pull away.

"I don't know why. I don't know why I'm doing anything on this stupid business."

The fifteen minute ride to Ridgway was uneventful, but it allowed Dean to ponder the implications of Hays Crawford making an earlier visit to Ouray, perhaps before the session where Whitcomb allegedly mentioned Byrd's Song for the first time. While that tidbit of information seemed, on the surface, to simply confuse the facts, in Dean's mind it did the opposite. For the first time there was something, however minuscule, that pointed toward Byrd's Song and the Klaxton turban being a scam, a feeling Dean had harbored all along. While he recognized the fallacy in over-reacting to so small an item, it nevertheless felt good, a hint of progress.

The only motel in Ridgway was a new structure, located at the crossroads of the route leading west forty-some miles to the ski resort of Telluride, home of the rich and famous, and the route south over which Dean had just traveled, from Ouray and the mountains beyond. Dean, always the detective, considered trying to develop a plan of action but instead simply entered the building and asked the clerk for the room numbers of Waite and Atherton. Simplicity has its rewards. A smiling young girl, looking like a high school cheerleader, told him Waite had checked out but gave him the number of Mr. Atherton's room, first floor, rear.

A knock at the door brought a response, a surprising one for Dean.

"Hi, Phil Atherton. You're David Dean. Nice of you to stop by." He was a big man, almost jovial, with a smile that looked like it was frequently used. He wore jeans, no shoes or socks, and a red tee shirt advertising a ten-kilometer race seven years past. His greeting left Dean at a momentary lapse for a response. He needn't have worried. Atherton held the door open while retreating into the room and carrying on a steady stream of conversation.

"Sorry about the snoop-bit. That was Henry's idea. He's an asshole, isn't he? Me and Walt...that's Walt Waite, we've been doing this kind of shit for Henry off and on for years, body guard from across the fence. Same shit, secret, secret, secret; the jerk is paranoid. The guy's a loony! If he wasn't so fucking rich, I'd have dumped him years ago. By the way, if you're looking for Walt, he's already gone back east. Seems Henry is getting ready to move on.

What's the gig, anyway? He doesn't tell us shit."

Dean dropped into a chair, trying to catch his breath. He found himself sounding like Atherton. "Loony is the key word, believe me. Cross my heart. All that shit-sorry, I can't blab. But if Henry is ready to move on, that's the best news I've heard in days!"

Atherton nodded. Then with a shake of his head, he said, "That's Henry! No problem with the sealed lips bit. I know the shithead. It's like that most of the time. What can I help you with?"

"Crawford?"

"Yeah, the hippie." He opened two beers, handing one to Dean without asking.

"Looks like he vamoosed. We don't have him, but I can tell you, if I did, he'd have some questions to answer. Apparently he sold out the boss to some sleazy magazine that sent Faldi out here to snoop. We put the buzz on Faldi and sent him running. I think we queered his magazine deal but I can't be sure without Crawford, the little shit. You don't know where he is, do you?"

"No," Dean answered honestly, "but I've got a few questions of my own." He added, "You didn't kill Faldi or anything like that, did you?"

Atherton laughed. "No, we just kicked the shit out of him and put him on a plane. I've got his car out back though. The plane was ready to leave and he wasn't in any condition to drive so we had to take him. Any ideas how I can dump it? I get the feeling the local sheriff isn't exactly stupid and I don't want to do ninety days here for assault if I can help it."

When Atherton slowed his rat-tat-tat conversation Dean learned he was an ex-cop from Chicago who had gone private with some buddies seven years ago. While his methods were primitive, Dean couldn't help but like his open, no nonsense attitude. He was the type of guy who got the job done and looked up the rules afterwards.

Dean finally swung the conversation around to the murder two years ago. Atherton became very subdued.

"I was sorry as shit about that. I'd met Phyllis, a wimp but a nice broad when she was with it. But she needed to see a shrink. Henry treated her like shit, when he even noticed her; you know he was fiddling that English teacher? Still is, I guess. We asked him if we should watch his wife, like we watch him. He swore by his fucking alarm system and wouldn't hire us to do it, the cheap bastard. I can tell you, if we'd been around, somebody else would be dead, instead of Phyllis and the asshole son."

"Asshole?" Dean asked.

"Michael wasn't all he was cracked up to be. 'Nuf said. No need to bring up all that shit, the kid's dead. Henry lights candles on his grave, so what? It's his kid, let him think he was a saint. Meanwhile, the old man shits all over Jeremy who could buy and sell his brother in the nice-guy club any day of the week."

Dean elicited further information that Waite was the prowler outside the house on Tuesday night. He "ran" just to scare the shit out of Neil Archer who, according to Atherton, both pegged as a first-class asshole. As for Dorrie, Atherton dismissed her as an oversexed head-case with a daughter who deserved a better home life. He had done some background checking on Dorrie, more for his own benefit than at Whitcomb's direction.

"I won't bore you with details," he said, "but the lady fucks like a rabbit. I bugged her phone for a while. She plays these games, like she needs companionship and all that crap, while what she really wants is a frantic lay, as often as she can get it."

"Do tell" mused Dean. "You don't have my house bugged, too, do you?"

Atherton smiled. "No, but perhaps we should have. It might have given us a line on Crawford."

Dean considered telling Atherton about Hays Crawford's purchases but decided against it. Atherton's prime responsibility seemed to be protecting Whitcomb and Crawford didn't appear to present a threat.

Dean shook Atherton's hand as he left with the ex-Chicago detective saying he expected to be leaving town the next day. He was keeping his fingers crossed.

Fred was still in the library although it was past closing, deep in conversation with the librarian who seemed to hang on his every word.

"It was getting a bit nippy outside and this kindly lady agreed to let me wait," he said, rising from a comfortable armchair as Dean entered.

The woman smiled coyly, "They say the temperature is going down in the teens tonight."

Dean smiled but made no effort to advance the conversation as he took Fred's arm and led him out to the car. Bringing Fred up to speed on his visit to the motel didn't take long nor did Fred's research on the coins and button, unfortunately.

"The button is English, at least a hundred years old. It came off an army uniform. It ain't worth anything unless you have the uniform and are missing a button. The coins weren't anymore helpful. The library's coin book was four years old but there was a magazine that listed the selling prices, if you want to buy 'em. The two Indian heads would cost you about a buck each, depending how you grade them, the two-cent piece, between five and ten dollars. That leaves the flying eagle penny; you'd need ten to twenty dollars to buy it. They only made 'em for a couple of years."

"So the whole box doesn't have thirty-five dollars in it a hundred years later."

"That's about it. I don't know what you were expecting, but no surprises. There ain't no reason that stuff couldn't have been there as long as it was supposed to be. You got to give us an 'A' for thorough," Fred mused. "What's the next step?"

"Well," Dean answered with a sigh, "the day wasn't a complete loss. We found out where Mr. Faldi went and that Hays Crawford probably visited these gorgeous mountains earlier than he let on. Let's see if we can pin down that little topic."

Fred grunted. "First off, there's the topic of my belly. How about a couple of rich guys like us springing for some western ribs?"

By the time they finished a large order of succulent pork ribs, washed down with a pitcher of beer, night had fallen. The town was warmed by the bright lights of a score of vacancy signs and closed shop windows as they drove back to the house. It was decidedly colder. Steam rose in blankets from the hot springs pool and continued up the highway. A few miles later, Dean turned left and climbed up the road to the house. He could see someone had lighted the wood burning stove as gray smoke drifted down the valley.

Nattie was poised on the sofa, her ubiquitous notebook in her lap and a quizzical look on her face. The TV picture was on without sound; Monday night football.

"Hi, punk! How's school," he greeted her. "Did they make you beat the erasers or sit in the dunce corner?"

Fred smiled, retreating to a corner chair closer to the silent television.

"It's really pretty cool," Nattie answered. "They do all kinds of stuff with a TV satellite and the classes are tiny! There's no place to hide! They let me observe, but I didn't have to do any of the stuff. I'm putting down some impressions." She began to write as Dorrie came into the room, holding a head of wet hair in a large towel.

"Have you been out detecting?" she smiled. She was wearing a loose bathrobe that provided little protection from eyes or the elements.

"Look," he said, leading her down the hall, "will you give me a straight answer on something?"

"Sure," she answered.

"Hays Crawford."

"What about him? Have you found him yet?"

"No. But someone in town said he'd been out here before."

"When?" They were in the shadow of the hall and she stood far too close.

"A few weeks ago," he answered.

"No way!"

"Don't just say that. This is important." He said it more sharply than he'd intended and she was irritated.

"I'm not! Look, since we started doing these sessions in earnest, when Henry put us on the payroll, back in June or July, all of us have been together, almost constantly, working our asses off, talking about it, going over the tapes. You just read about the sessions that worked; there were scores of ones that didn't. We'd sit around on our asses and wait and then, nothing. It was as boring as daytime TV. I've been staring at Hays and Neil and Henry every day, for weeks and weeks! There's no way Hays could have come out here. God, it took an entire day for us to make the trip one way in a private plane! Going commercial from Spinnersville would take him at least two days, plus getting down and back from the airport. No, he hasn't been here. Someone is mistaken."

She was unshakable and there wasn't any reason not to believe her. Even small town shopkeepers weren't infallible. Dorrie wasn't finished.

"Just because Hays got pissed and left doesn't mean he's some kind of a fraud and the Klaxton turban doesn't work! Stop being so damned cynical all the time and believe a little bit!"

She turned on her heels and closed the den door in his face.

As he turned to leave, Nattie was standing there.

"That's my mom!" she said with a smile.

"Isn't it about time for bed?" he asked, leading her back to the living room.

"Are you kidding? The Cowboys are down by three and struggling! Besides, I've got a question. You're a cop, right? Have you got a gun?"

"Not here. I have one back in Pennsylvania. Why?"

"'Cause the tree-maker has one and if he gets his Flash Gordon hat to work so it tells him who wasted his family, he may come out blasting!"

"You've been watching too much television! Besides, how do you know he has a gun? How could he get it here? The airlines frown on that stuff."

"He flew out on a private plane, Sherlock! Remember? Dorrie told me about the gun. He keeps it under his pillow and we all know she has firsthand knowledge of his bed covers."

Romantic as hell, Dean thought. Just then, Emmitt Smith scored a touchdown for Dallas and Nattie dashed back to the TV.

Dean took the opportunity of relative quiet in the house to use the kitchen phone, noticing the room looked particularly clean and neat. The absence of Neil Archer and Hays Crawford was already telling. Although the hour was late in the east, he dialed Cynthia Byrne's telephone number. She answered on the first ring.

"I knew it was you. I miss you already," she said with a purr.

There was not much news. He brought her up to speed on his day's activities and she described her trip home. Dr. McNaught had decided to remain in Vegas a few days longer; something about a chorus girl. As the conversation lapsed into quiet small talk, the reverie was harshly broken. Mrs. Brown let out a blood-curdling scream from the second floor.

"What was that?" asked a startled Cynthia Byrne from two thousand miles away.

"Don't-know-gotta-go!" yelled Dean as he dropped the phone and raced up the stairs, just ahead of equally startled Nattie Briscoe and Fred O'Connor.

Chapter XV

Mrs. Brown stood there in a scarlet bathrobe, looking like an Indian widow at a funeral pyre, and let out with a second banshee scream that echoed around the room like breaking glass. As Dean rushed in, she met him at the door and grabbed his arm, "He's dead! He's dead! Do something!" She was hysterical, clawing at him and dragging him to the bed where Henry Whitcomb lay, unmoving. She began shaking, first the bed, then Henry Whitcomb, yelling, "Mr. Whitcomb, Mr. Whitcomb, wake up!"

Dorrie Briscoe charged in, adding to the melee with a scream equal to or exceeding Mrs. Brown's. Fred O'Connor grabbed Brown, held her sobbing frame tightly, and none too gently pulled her away. Nattie, who hadn't said a word picked up the phone, dialed 9-1-1 and handed the instrument to Dean, who looked shocked at her poise while trying to find a pulse on Whitcomb.

"They taught us in school," she said, quickly taking her mother's arm and pulling her away from the bed.

Dean told the professional voice that answered the call it was a medical emergency and gave the address, explaining only the victim was unconscious from unknown causes.

"He's been poisoned!" screamed Mrs. Brown, still being restrained in the hall by Fred O'Connor.

The door slammed and Dean was left alone with Henry Whitcomb in immobile repose. He was clothed in a maroon bathrobe and propped up slightly on two pillows, his feet covered with the edge of a blanket. His limp hand held a spoon and a half-finished plastic container of pudding spilled on his lap. His lips were blue but when Dean continued to search for a pulse, he found a slight movement. He immediately began mouth to mouth resuscitation, amid continued frenzied crying and sobbing from the hall. His rhythmic deep breaths produced no noticeable reaction but Dean paused only when he felt a presence behind and looked up to see Nattie.

"Tell them he's alive, barely," he muttered breathlessly, and added, "and keep them the hell out of the room!" He caught his breath and resumed his task. Nattie dashed out, leaving him to the taste of butterscotch, and, he hoped, not strychnine or some equally potent killer.

Time passed with inexorable slowness until the sound of a siren could be heard, and a few moments later, the rumble of voices, stomping feet and a roomful of people better equipped to resurrect Henry Whitcomb than David Dean.

"He may have ingested something," Dean mumbled as the team relieved him.

Dean was used to mayhem; fifteen years of maimed accident victims, botched suicides, shootings, stabbings and death in a variety of forms and locations had become familiar occurrences. But familiarity did not breed a blasé acceptance or anything close to it, only a continued and intensified hatred of the whole business of pain and disaster. But the exposure bred the ability for him to handle situations professionally, if not with detachment, and he knew he had done all in his power for Henry Whitcomb.

Dean felt completely drained as he left the room to the medics and retreated to the hall, and the peppering of a hundred questions by those anxiously awaiting news. He relayed what he knew, which was almost nothing, except that Henry Whitcomb still had a pulse. He suggested Dorrie and Mrs. Brown dress if they were going to the hospital and then quickly ducked into the bathroom where he spit, brushed his teeth, and repeated the process a couple more times. He sat on the toilet a few minutes to catch his breath, noting the spilled water on floor and seat, a final legacy perhaps, of Whitcomb's inconsiderate sloppiness. Finally, after splashing water on his face and taking a few deep breaths, he went downstairs.

Neither Fred nor Nattie said anything but the three could hear the continued sobbing of the women as they changed. Dorrie was the first to finish and when she entered the room she and Nattie sat on the sofa while Nattie put an arm around her shoulders. Mrs. Brown made a more dramatic entrance.

"He was poisoned," she choked, wiping her eyes and biting her lip. She began to wail anew, albeit at a lower volume than her earlier sobs. "The police should be here!"

Dean took her by the shoulders. "What makes you keep saying Henry was poisoned?"

"Because it's so," she blubbered, "and it's my fault. I shouldn't have left. I knew I should have remained by him! I didn't give him that pudding! Someone else did!"

Dean turned around to a chorus of "no's" and "not-me's." No one had served the pudding or remembered seeing it in the house. He looked directly at Mrs. Brown who was still trembling.

"Talk." He said it as sternly as he dared and the tone of his voice seemed to calm her slightly. She had spent two hours of the late afternoon having her hair done in Ridgway and returned about five o'clock. The house was empty except for Whitcomb. Dorrie had picked Nattie up from school and taken her out for dinner. Mrs. Brown, immediately upon returning, knocked on Mr. Whitcomb's door but there was no response. She seemed embarrassed to admit she peeked in only to find what she supposed was him sleeping. Later, after her shower, she became concerned and repeated the process, this time noticing the spilled pudding. When she started to clean it up, she saw how still he was and on closer observation, she was certain he was dead.

"He's been murdered," she moaned. "Someone, one of you, killed Mr. Whitcomb!" She turned in time to see the medics struggling down the angled staircase with the inert body of her boss and she began to sob uncontrollably.

Dean crossed to the phone and telephoned the sheriff who, fortunately, was still in the office. He identified himself and got right to the point.

"Sheriff, we have a situation out here." He explained what was happening. Whitcomb was on the way to the Montrose hospital but Dean would remain in the house until the sheriff arrived, and, no, he wouldn't touch anything. Fred O'Connor looked as if he'd die to remain, too, but the still distraught Mrs. Brown needed someone stable. That wasn't Dorrie Briscoe as she was in worse shape than Brown so Fred and the ladies followed the ambulance. Dean didn't dare ask who was driving. Nattie went, too, guiding her mother along and feeding her Kleenex by the fistful.

Dean was left alone, for a few minutes at least, with the receding sound of the ambulance siren ringing in his ears. He returned to the upstairs bedroom and stood looking pensively at the now-empty bed, the covers tossed aside from the medics removal of the lifeless form of Henry Whitcomb. The pudding container was upside down on the floor where it had fallen, the lid on the night table. Papers were scattered on a second table, usually in a corner, now pulled next to the far side of the bed. The only missing item was the Klaxton turban, nowhere in evidence. The aluminum case was on the floor, open but empty.

Dean's pulse picked up its pace. The damned contraption was at the heart of everything going on and it was missing. He quickly checked under the bed, in the closet and in Mrs. Brown's room but the doorbell rang before he could conduct an extensive search.

He hurried to the front door to greet the sheriff who was accompanied by an other officer whose mumbled name sounded like Cummings. The mood of the sheriff was much different from the previous day. He was all business as Dean led him to the bedroom and explained the circumstances of Henry Whitcomb's condition.

"I have no reason to believe Whitcomb's problem is other than a heart attack or something natural except for his secretary's accusation that he was poisoned. She was hysterical but very insistent so I figured I'd better call you before someone messes up the scene, just in case there's something to it." He pointed out the pudding container and explained how everyone in the household had denied serving it to Whitcomb.

"Couldn't he have gotten it himself?" asked the sheriff logically as his assistant deposited both cup and lid in separate evidence bags.

"Yes, if it were in the refrigerator, but no one's seen it in the house. Plus, I've never seen Whitcomb downstairs in his pajamas. He's always yelling for someone to wait on him."

"But no one was home."

"True," thought Dean, feeling sillier by the minute. In response to the sheriff's question he ran down a brief description of the household guests, those present, temporarily absent and Hays Crawford, missing in action.

"Anyone have an interest in killing him?"

Only anyone who's ever met him, thought Dean but answered with a shrug.

"Is anything missing?" The question caught Dean off guard. The last possible item he wanted to try and explain was the Klaxton turban. He crossed his fingers before answering.

"I haven't taken time to search thoroughly, but Mrs. Brown would know more about Henry's things."

"What about fingerprints?" asked Cummings as he began snapping flash photographs of the room.

"Just seal the room until we find out what's cooking at the hospital. No point in jumping the gun, but as Mr. Dean here says, better to be safe than sorry." The sheriff turned to Dean. "What about next of kin?"

Damned! thought Dean. He'd forgotten completely about Jeremy.

"There's only his son, Jeremy. I'm not sure how to contact him, but maybe Atherton, Henry's man in Ridgway, has a phone number."

"Let's get down to the hospital and see what the doc says. We'll stop in Ridgway on the way to Montrose," the sheriff continued. "I've been wanting to see Atherton anyway, since he and his buddy chased Faldi out of town."

He told Cummings to hold down the fort and he and Dean started to leave.

The phone rang as Dean passed it; it was a concerned Cynthia Byrne. He briefly brought her up to date and she understood enough of the situation to hold off for a longer explanation later.

"Do you want to follow?" asked the sheriff as they reached his car, their breath making puffs of white in the plummeting temperature.

"I'd rather ride along with you if you don't mind." Dean harbored visions of Fred O'Connor weaving down the road. "My car's already at the hospital and it might be better if I drive it back."

It was eleven-thirty by the time Dean and the sheriff reached the Ridgway motel and Atherton was counting sheep. When he opened the door to the gleaming badge of the local law, he woke up immediately.

Dean didn't waste words. "Henry's in a coma in the Montrose hospital. Do you have a number where we can reach Jeremy?"

Atherton turned abruptly and reached for his phone. He dialed a number and barked instructions for the party on the other end to locate Jeremy and have him call back immediately. He turned to Dean and the sheriff. "What happened?"

The sheriff let Dean explain. He down-played the poison possibility but not Henry Whitcomb's condition. "He wasn't dead but he didn't seem far from it."

"Damn!" Atherton pounded his fist on the night stand. "I'm supposed to be guarding the asshole and now he's practically stiff."

To Dean he seemed more concerned with his professional standing than the health of his employer. It was understandable. Henry Whitcomb's life style wasn't designed to make many friends, just influence people.

"He's been in pretty poor health by the looks of things," Dean added. "Those headaches were nearly constant."

"Been here by yourself all evening, Mr. Atherton?" asked the sheriff, moving the conversation from chit-chat to more serious business.

"Yeah, why? You think there's something to this poison shit?"

"Too early to tell. Just covering bases. I understand you're acquainted with Mr. Faldi."

Atherton rolled his eyes and sighed. "Look, he was scum. I did the county a favor. I'm sorry it was so...abrupt, but at least he's out of our hair."

"Not necessarily. Faldi didn't make it back east. He never got on the plane out of Denver for the second leg of his flight. For all we know he rented a car, drove back here, and is getting ready to blow your ass off."

"Shit!" was Atherton's sole response. The sheriff let the subject drop but had made his point.

The two left Atherton, sitting in his boxer shorts, awaiting a phone call from Jeremy and continued the trip on to Montrose. Atherton would follow as soon as he heard from Henry's son. The journey took twenty minutes with flashing lights but no siren and little conversation except some further discussion of Atherton and his methods of business.

The hospital was a bevy of white clad figures amid the signature smells of ether and anxiety. The waiting room scene was only a slight improvement over the earlier frenzied vigil at the house. Henry was in the hands of the doctors and no word had emerged from behind the swinging doors. Dorrie was pacing the waiting room like a cat and Mrs. Brown, with Fred close by, wrung her hands nervously. The sheriff spoke to Mrs. Brown and Fred moved away out of courtesy over to Dean's side.

"Here we have a full fledged 'who-dun-it' and I end up nursemaid to an hysterical woman," he grumbled in a low voice.

"But you do it so well," Dean replied with a smile. "No news?"

"No. They wheeled Henry directly in and we ain't heard beans since. I can tell you, he don't look good. I suppose they're pumping his stomach to get the poison out."

Dean looked at him. "You're buying the poison bit pretty quickly, aren't you? All I tasted was butterscotch."

Fred scoffed. "I keep telling you, you don't read enough. There's all kinds of exotic poison you can't smell or taste. How about that South American stuff the natives put on their blow guns? And there's poison frogs in Costa Rica that'll kill you in seconds!"

"I guess we can discount the poison frogs," Dean said with a chuckle. "Henry's still alive. Besides, hiding a frog in a little plastic cup of butterscotch pudding would be quite a feat!"

"Laugh all you want," Fred said with a grunt, "but we got a potential killer around here. Besides, whatever the stuff was, it was pretty damned fast. He didn't even get to finish the pudding! I sure hope the sheriff has his crime lab boys on the scene and they know what they're doing."

"Just like 'Allstate.' We're in good hands. But don't you think butterscotch pudding is a rather strange vehicle to poison someone?"

"Butterscotch pudding, elderberry wine. What's the difference? Didn't you ever read 'Arsenic and Old Lace?'"

"We've got a bigger mystery than that. The damn turban is missing!" Fred didn't have a chance to reply.

Dorrie Briscoe came up and grabbed Dean's arm. "He's dead, I just know it!"

"You don't know that," Dean answered. "You just have to wait."

"Butterscotch pudding was his favorite, too." She flopped down in a plastic chair.

"How many of the others knew that, besides you?" Dean asked the question more conversationally than because he believed it pertinent but Fred pulled out his notebook, eager to record the answer. Dean quickly added, "Not that I really think he was poisoned..."

"Nattie knew, and surely Jeremy..."

"Hays and Archer?" Dean asked.

"I don't know! God, you sound like a cop!"

"I am a cop, and everyone but me seems convinced there's been an attempted murder in my house! Look, we're all upset. Let's... " Just then a doctor emerged through swinging doors and stood looking at the waiting crowd.

"Is one of you next of kin?" he asked and Dorrie burst into tears.

It was Fred O'Connor who answered him. "We're all more or less on equal standing here, Doc. How is he?"

The doctor was obviously not used to providing medical updates to so large a crowd but no one argued Fred's pronouncement. "I won't kid you. Mr. Whitcomb is in serious condition. He's still unconscious and we won't know the extent of permanent damage, if any, until we're able to wake him."

"Did you get all the poison out?" Mrs. Brown asked meekly.

"We could find no evidence or symptoms of poison but in view of what was said, we'll be analyzing his stomach contents."

David Dean's frivolous side strained to ask if they'd found the frog as the doctor continued.

"Mr. Whitcomb has suffered a massive stroke."

The women sobbed and everyone else remained silent, except a voice from the back of the room that no one recognized.

"Excuse me, it's Henry Whitcomb you're talking about, isn't it? The 'Henry Whitcomb?'"

"Yes," answered the doctor, as the young man rushed from the room.

"Jake Horowitz, from the newspaper," the sheriff muttered. "He'll have it on the wire before you can say fourth estate. I have an idea this place is going to be buzzing!"

Mrs. Brown took a deep breath and as if the reporter somehow shocked her back to her professional status, made a pronouncement to no one in particular. "I'd best contact the board of directors," she said and marched to the corner phone.

Dorrie, wiping her eyes on her sleeve, also rose and went to the drinking fountain where she soaked an already damp paper towel and bathed her face. Nattie came over to Dean.

"Hi," she said, looking drained.

"Hi, yourself," he answered, giving her a hug and holding her. "I'm proud as punch of you. You were a real pro."

"Yeah, well, maybe so far. But I don't do the death-bit very well. I haven't had any experience except Sarah Byrd, and that didn't go so hot." She looked up at him. "Henry was just laying there, like he was hypnotized or something. I don't care a whole lot about the tree-maker, but the idea of his checking out kind of scares me, and Ma will be a basket case."

"Hang close, kid. You're doing a hundred and ten percent. Remember what I said about tears and stuff? You're entitled to act your age. Now, let's get you a place to lie down. You don't want to miss chapter two of your observations of rural education tomorrow!"

Dean found a helpful nurse who remembered him from physical therapy. She located a small room with a cot and blanket where Nattie was placed, safe from the growing turbulence of the waiting room. As the night progressed, reporters bred like rabbits, flying in first from Grand Junction, and later Denver and both coasts. "The man" was down, and although Dean realized Henry Whitcomb was a national figure, he too was overwhelmed by the level of interest in the financier's critical condition. Atherton arrived around one a.m., Jeremy two hours later along with a bevy of vice presidents, board members, hangers-on, and a personal doctor, all efficiently greeted by Mrs. Brown who was rapidly moving into her element. Montrose airport was experiencing a traffic volume of charted flights previously unseen.

The sheriff left by three-thirty, after hearing the latest of the half hour medical updates; no change. No one questioned his presence and no mention was made of poison. The waiting room talk revolved around suggestions of moving Henry by helicopter to a bigger city (vetoed) and just who should be the official spokesman of his condition. And, guessed Dean from the whispered conversation, who would be his replacement after they buried him.

Jeremy, looking understandably concerned and nervous, seemed to be handling himself surprisingly well in view of the circumstances. Archer was nowhere in sight and if he had accompanied Henry's son back from the east, he had elected to stay away from the hospital. Dorrie, apparently not a favorite with Henry's co-executives, had wandered off, presumably to join Nattie or perhaps she'd found a similar nap room. Fred stayed near Dean but in the chaotic confusion of the waiting room neither had a chance to carry on much of a conversation. Dean had managed to let Fred know the details of his discovery that the turban might be missing. Henry might have disposed of it somehow or Mrs. Brown might know it's whereabouts. Dean longed to ask her but even a word with the corporate mother-hen was out of the question.

Everyone wondered what Henry was doing in Colorado and speculation was rampant. A mountain holiday was collectively discounted with the general agreement that "H.W. never takes vacation."

"It must be the teacher," was the whispered consensus. "He's out here bopping her for a few days."

"Think the kid's Henry's?" asked a particularly pompous fat man in a double-breasted suit.

"No," was the reply. "Henry burns his bridges. He doesn't stick around with the same broad for fifteen years."

"He was a saint," someone else said from across the room, loud enough to be widely heard, and hopefully quoted. He was answered by nodding heads and not too hushed stories of financial gifts and charity.

"He was a self-centered, obsessive bastard who never thought of anyone but himself!" Dean grumbled to only Fred O'Connor's ears.

"Listen to them," Fred added. " Here's a guy who was as pleasant as a bucket of swill and now they can't say enough good about him just because he's bending over his grave. I can't understand how a guy who was giving nasty lessons to the world can be held in such adulation as soon as they think he's a corpse."

"There must be a lesson there about human nature but it's beyond my weak brain to grasp it," Dean said disgustedly. "Let's get out of here.

It's nearly five o'clock."

Fred hesitated. "I think I'll hang around. Mrs. Brown looks like a vision of efficiency but she's running on borrowed gas. She may need a hand a little later. I can hook a ride with somebody."

He's a good man, Dean thought to himself as he stepped out to the cold night air. A crotchety, old, opinionated pain in the ass on occasion but a good man. He scraped the heavy frost from his windshield and began the thirty-five-mile ride home, just as the first glint of Tuesday rose above the mountains. One week since this crowd arrived. What a week.

Chapter XVI

It was the second of October and the elk were migrating down from the high country. Dean first saw them grazing in the meadow on the east side of the highway as he passed the cemetery and neared the turnoff to his house. Two other cars had pulled to the side of the road to observe the large animals as they slowly grazed in the early sun. They would stay the winter, so he was told, chased from the upper elevations by increasing snow and plummeting temperatures, following some age-old instinct that called them down to their wintering grounds. Wapiti, the Indians had called them. They moved slowly, cows ambling along, spring calves playfully tagging behind. Then off to the side stood the bull elks, undisputed leaders of the group, some weighing a thousand pounds or more.

Dean stepped out of his car and watched them. The herd numbered about thirty and the social order was apparent at a glance, the bulls standing aloof, overseeing their harem of more docile cows, and chasing away, with ducking head and quick movement, the younger bulls who dared venture too near. The king of the herd, a massive bull with a broad spread of antlers, displayed a level of confidence Dean envied. The vanquished would sulk away, biding time until they too might lead a herd of their own.

A neighbor explained to Dean that small herds wintered in the meadows of the Uncompahgre Valley but it surprised him to be able to observe them so close to the house where he was staying. As he watched, the sun rose higher and the elk began to wander away, slowly retreating to the tree line at the eastern base of the escarpment.

When he returned to his car with a yawn, his body reminded him of his lack of sleep and he realized just how tired he felt. While not a stranger to all night police work, the strain of the past week, coupled with a sleepless Sunday night in Cynthia Byrne's arms, left him exhausted. He longed for the soft comfort of a few hours' sleep as he pulled up to his temporary home.

It was not to be. A frantic Neil Archer met him at the door.

"Is he dead yet?"

"No," Dean answered as he pushed by him.

"Oh." He almost sounded disappointed. "Why in hell is there a cop blocking Henry's bedroom? What's going on? She won't tell me shit!"

"It's not Henry's bedroom, it's mine. And he or she or whoever the police officer is, is guarding a potential murder scene." There went Dean's chance to search further for the Klaxton turban.

"Look, Neil," he said. "I've been up all night. I need some sleep."

"Whose murder? Henry's? God, it was Faldi, wasn't it? He was looking for me!" The phone began to ring. "That damned thing! It hasn't stopped since I got here!"

Dean picked up the instrument. It was Rita Angeltoni.

"Faldi was working for a freelance magazine writer who specializes in dirt and big names. The word is out someone paid off the sleaze and killed the idea Faldi was working on. He's history. No one has seen him in a few days and no one's looking." She had also spoken to the Spinnersville police department but nothing was new on the two-year-old murder of Henry Whitcomb's wife and son. Rita was aware of Whitcomb's illness via the radio and was hungry for details, few of which Dean could give her. As he hung up, the phone rang again. It was the sheriff.

"No word on the poison. The doctors all seem to think it's crap. They couldn't find anything sinister in Whitcomb's stomach but it will take awhile to analyze the contents of the pudding container." The sheriff was anxious to have Mrs. Brown check the room to see if any of Whitcomb's things were disturbed and was disappointed when Dean told him she was still at the hospital. A call had been put out to locate Hays Crawford, just for the hell of it, so said the sheriff.

After the sheriff hung up, Dean dialed Cynthia Byrne's office number in Pennsylvania for the dual purpose of shutting up the phone and talking to her. He told Neil to get lost, it was a personal call, and spent a pleasant thirty minutes in a different world. Her boss, the playboy doctor was still away and the office was dead, so the conversation occupied the most peaceful half hour since she'd boarded the plane to leave him in Montrose.

After reluctantly hanging up with Cynthia, Mrs. Lincoln was next to demand his attention. While he was stirring something disgusting into her bowl, the phone rang yet again. This time it was Mrs. Adams, Ron's mother.

The Adams' had heard the news about Henry Whitcomb and Ron immediately drove to the hospital to see Nattie. It was then agreed between Mrs. Adams and Dorrie that Nattie would spend the next couple of days at the Adams' house, away from the anticipated confusion that was sure to reign at Dean's place. Dean thanked her for her continued consideration and volunteered to have a reluctant Neil Archer pack Nattie's things and drive them over.

By the time he put down the phone, the others were trooping and stomping back to the house. A silver-haired man Dean didn't know delivered Fred O'Connor and Mrs. Brown and made no effort to leave. Close behind was Jeremy, with two more men no one introduced, followed by a bewildered Dorrie Briscoe.

No, there wasn't any change in Henry's condition, but they'd reluctantly left the hospital. Everyone had to maintain their strength, so said the silver-haired chauffeur. One of the two who came with Jeremy carried a brown bag that he opened to three bottles of liquor. It looked like the wake was beginning early.

Dean pulled Mrs. Brown aside and asked her to come upstairs, pulling her along before she could answer. Fred followed as Dean explained that the sheriff wanted a check of the room where Henry was staying to see if any of his things were missing. He didn't admit to knowledge that the Klaxton turban was not there. Fred caught the cue and was the silent observer.

Dean introduced Mrs. Brown to the deputy, a young lady who had relieved Cummings. Mrs. Brown methodically looked over the papers and files before turning to Dean, with a surprised look.

"Why the Klaxton turban is gone!"

Dean was waiting for the discovery in order to read Mrs. Brown's reaction; faked or true. But he was disappointed; he couldn't tell. She poked a bit further and then gave her pronouncement that the turban was the only thing unaccounted for.

"Mr. Whitcomb will be very upset!"

"When did you see it last?" Dean asked.

"Before I left. He was...using it." She began to look nervous.

"What's a 'Klaxton turban?'" asked the deputy after being told how to spell it. The three looked at each other until Dean offered an answer.

"It's an antique apparatus used to cure headaches."

"What's it worth?" The deputy continued writing.

The others looked at Dean. What a question. Ten bucks to priceless, if it really worked, which he still didn't believe for a minute it did.

"Maybe ten bucks," he answered. "Henry might have done something with it before he...passed out," he added, causing Brown to upturn an eyebrow as if she'd object but thought better of it.

"Why would anyone steal a headache hot-pad or whatever the thing is?" The deputy asked logically. "This guy Whitcomb is a millionaire, right? Couldn't a thief find something a bit more valuable?"

They shuffled their feet. Finally Fred answered. "Maybe someone thought it was more valuable than it is?" The deputy looked far from satisfied but waved them away.

"I'll call this in to the sheriff and see if he wants to open the room. Better stay clear until he gives his okay," she added as she held the door for them to leave.

Mrs. Brown sputtered something to the officer about the importance of certain papers in the room as Fred held back to talk to Dean.

"She's as nervous as a fish on Friday."

"You're dating yourself, old man." Dean replied.

"Think it's really missing?"

"It looks that way. Who's your guess as the swiper?"

"I'd have to think on that one. It would help to know if the perpetrator just stole the turban or if he or she poisoned people, too."

"Forget the poison. My guess for the turban is Hays Crawford. He's the only one besides Whitcomb who knows anything about it. I think he's still in the area. But," he said with a yawn. "I know this much. It might be easier to figure it out with a little sleep. We're like the walking dead around here. I'll see you in a few hours."

Dean paused in the kitchen only long enough to elbow past two drinkers and grab a sweet roll and glass of milk and wave his excuses. He passed Dorrie in the hall, with his mouth full, on the way to his bedroom. She looked like hell but smiled a weak smile. "You've heard Nattie's staying at the Adams' house?"

"Yes. It's a good idea," he munched. "They're nice people."

She sighed. "It makes me feel like I'm a shitty mother and can't even care for my own child when things get...out of control."

Dean patted her shoulder. "Just take care of yourself and everything else will fall in line. Good night." He left her standing there and went into his room, closing the door tightly. He collapsed in bed without even finishing the milk.

It was four-thirty in the afternoon when Dean was startled awake by the sound of a siren in his driveway. Before he was fully conscious, Fred was in the room with a concerned look on his face. The sheriff and he wanted to see Dean outside. Dean paused long enough to splash water on his face before going out to his drive where the sheriff stood, hand on gun, beneath flashing lights.

"Get in," he said as he climbed into the driver's seat.

"Front or back?"

"Front."

"Am I under arrest?"

"I'm not sure you shouldn't be." He pulled out of the drive in a spray of pebbles, but extinguished the flashers and drove at a moderate pace. "I want some answers."

Dean relaxed somewhat and rubbed the remaining sleep from his eyes.

"Why the siren and lights?"

"I wanted to get your attention."

"You did."

"Look," the sheriff said, turning toward him, "I've cut you a lot of slack but I want to know about this turban shit! You might snow my deputy, but not me! I'll toss your ass in jail!"

Dean sighed. "A week ago today this bunch of kooks dropped out of the sky on my doorstep. Whitcomb swore me to secrecy and gave me some dough to check out some stuff for him. It's nothing illegal, believe me. I told you that before."

"Sorry, not good enough. I don't like being conned."

"I promised Whitcomb..."

"Whitcomb's two steps from dead and I've got a maybe poisoning and a maybe theft of something I'm supposed to believe isn't worth stealing and you're playing crossed-my-heart! You've got about ten seconds..."

Dean sighed. It was against his nature to betray confidences but the sheriff hadn't given him an option. "How about this?" he said. " I'll tell you what I know but unless it's pertinent it stays between us girls, okay? You're going to think I'm pulling your leg anyway."

"Deal." He pulled off the road in a swirl of dust and turned off the ignition.

Dean reluctantly began the tale as it happened, trying to supply as much detail as easily came to mind. He explained how he'd been kept in the dark until he forced the issue and how incredulous he'd been and still was. The trip to Byrd's Song was included but Dean omitted any mention of the tin box, or the two-year-old murders. He portrayed Henry as naively believing in something that obviously couldn't work and the others as going along with Henry mostly for the money Henry was paying them.

The sheriff tried to wipe a smile from his lips. "You're telling me Henry Whitcomb, filthy rich, big man on campus, Henry Whitcomb thinks this contraption will take him back in time?"

"You got it! That's exactly what he thinks." Dean sported his best I-told-you-so look before he continued. "But Henry's scared shitless the world will find out and he'll be a laughing-stock. That's apparently what Crawford and Faldi had in mind before Atherton chased Faldi out of town."

"You surely weren't kidding when you said you had a bunch of wackos up here." He paused, thinking it over. "But this turban thing that's missing, maybe it is a piece of junk and not worth anything but chances are, from what you say, Henry would pay through the nose to get it back. Am I right?"

"I guess so," answered Dean.

"That kind of kicks it up from petty larceny, wouldn't you say? It makes it worth about as much as the Mona Lisa, right?"

"If someone took it. We haven't even proved that. Henry isn't talking."

"You say for sure it isn't in the house?" The sheriff chewed on something, opened the window and spit.

"I haven't had a chance to really look. I haven't even asked if the others have seen it. I've been asleep."

"If it is missing, who do you think took it?" Dean started to protest but the sheriff held up his hand. "Not an accusation, just an opinion."

"Hays Crawford. I'm not sure he's left the area and he's already shown he would sell out someone for a quick buck. Maybe with Faldi's help. You said Faldi is still lose."

"There's an update on that. Faldi is in jail in Denver. Seems he stole a camera in the Denver airport and got caught. That's why he missed his connection." The sheriff started the car. "Let's have you check out the house really well and ask around about the hat, or whatever it is. I'll be in touch. Yes, sir, I'll definitely be in touch."

Dean returned to the warmth of the wood stove and the smell of beans and franks. After a prolonged shower and change of clothes, he wandered to the kitchen where he found Fred O'Connor at the stove alone. A half-full liquor bottle, two empties and a dozen glasses crowded the counter but the merrymakers were nowhere in sight.

"The mucky-mucks went to town for dinner with Jeremy and Mrs. Brown, and Dorrie is visiting Nattie and the Adams. Neil's logged out on Brown's bed. She'd kill him if she knew. So you and me are stuck with poor man's food. I thought you'd be in jail," he kidded. "What was all that about?"

Dean repeated his conversation with the sheriff including Faldi's arrest. "I guess that lets Faldi off the hook as the notorious poison frog killer," he jibed but Fred ignored the comment. Dean then admitted breaking Henry Whitcomb's confidence on the subject of the turban.

"I didn't have a choice. But let's keep it between ourselves." Fred agreed and then suggested after they ate might be a good time to search the house thoroughly.

"Didn't you sleep?" Dean asked as he sat and scooped a plate of food.

" 'fraid I'd miss something, and I had to catch up on my notes. But I'm off to dreamland as soon as I've had some grub and we're finished searching."

"So what didn't you miss besides sleep? I don't suppose there's any change in Henry?"

"Status quo. The gang is off to the hospital after dinner."

"I suppose everyone knows the turban is missing."

"You bettcha'. And I'm not sure there isn't more relief than anything else.

Jeremy doesn't seem to care about it unless the person who took it did something to his father in the process. By the way, the sheriff has sent Miss Tom Mix home. The bedroom is officially open."

When Dean was satiated, the two began a methodical search of the entire house, beginning in the main bedroom where the turban was last seen and ending in Mrs. Brown's room where they made no effort not to wake up Neil Archer.

"Get your ass out of bed, Neil. Faldi's downstairs and wants to talk to you!" Dean said, lifting the mattress.

"Shit!" he yelled, stumbling up, a look of panic on his face. When he realized they were kidding, he sat on the floor and rubbed his eyes as they opened bureau drawers and poked about the room.

"Is it true someone stole the Klaxton turban?"

"No, it's just true it's gone," Dean answered as he stooped to search beneath the bed. "Maybe Henry did something with it."

"We ought to call out the National Guard. It's a loss to mankind." He said it with a yawn, as if it was expected.

"A damn shame," Dean replied. "Now you'll never know if Booth really did it."

"You can kid all you want, but we saw history made. Right here."

"And you almost lost your balls in the process. You've got a short memory, Neil. You didn't swipe it, did you?" They had finished with the room and were starting downstairs, Neil tagging behind.

"Hell, no! It could have been the greatest aid to history mankind has ever seen! Hey, there's something I want to talk to you about. Now that it looks like Henry's about dead, do you think we still have to keep quiet about the turban? I mean the world should know what you found, what the potential was, maybe still is."

Dean turned and faced Archer. "Look, Neil, my deal was with Henry and Henry alone. I'm not getting involved in the business a second longer than I have to. The turban is missing and I say good riddance, but it's Henry's hat, not mine, so I'll look for it. If you want to make a fool of yourself and go public, don't look to me for help or confirmation. Remember, if Henry does come out of this, you're a dead man!" He continued down to the living room.

Neil plodded along after him, a lost dog look on his face. "I don't know why you're always pissed off at me, Davey. We always got along so well. I'm going back to town. Maybe I'll just pack up and leave. Nobody wants me around here anyway."

Neither Dean nor Fred said a word as Neil left. Dean held his breath until he heard a car start and drive away. He gave a silent cheer.

"Think he's gone for good?" Fred asked with a smile.

"No such luck," Dean answered.

"Well, he pouted off in the last vehicle. He took Henry's jeep and Dorrie borrowed your car."

"I'm not going anywhere, anyhow," Dean answered as he gazed out the living room window.

The day was ebbing away and Dean could just make out a cluster of elk beginning to gather in the meadow on the east side of the highway, where he'd seen them this morning. The animals, now a hundred or more feet below and three quarters of a mile away from his living room, were indistinct blurs but after his morning observation he knew they were elk and could even pick out the larger shapes, the bulls.

"Well, the turban isn't in the house. We made sure of that. You still think Hays Crawford came back and took it?" Fred settled down on the sofa, his eyes nearly closed.

"Crawford could have taken it. He was the only one who worked it...except Henry. If Henry himself didn't do something with it, he's still my best bet."

"Crawford is gone. We don't know where, but he doesn't have transportation."

"He could have snuck back on foot. We think he's still in the area, somewhere."

"Like we said, there's a million acres out there. Lots of room to camp." Fred let out a big yawn.

"Not necessarily. He bought a sleeping bag, not a tent. All he needs is shelter."

"Meaning?"

Dean was staring out the window, looking at the remains of the bunkhouse on the far side of the valley, the bunkhouse in which Hays had expressed so much interest. He went to the closet for his binoculars. They weren't there. Hays had used them last. He turned to say something to Fred but the old man was asleep.

If Hays Crawford had climbed to the ruined building, he would be positioned to see the house, albeit from perhaps a mile or more away, as the crow flies. At least he could follow the vehicles as they left, knowing when Henry Whitcomb would be alone. He was anxious to have a conversation with Mr. Crawford. There were far too many unanswered questions that circled around the free-spirited electrician.

But with darkness closing in Dean would have to wait until morning. While the sight line to the bunkhouse was about a mile, the closest access by road was three or four miles, at least. Dean was without a vehicle and it was not a hike to be taken in the dark. Climbing up to the bunkhouse, while not near the ordeal of the climb to Byrd's Song, was still a difficult under-taking. By the looks of the snoring Fred O'Connor, he had an evening to himself to contemplate the trip.

First things, first. He called the sheriff to inform him the search of the house failed to locate the Klaxton turban. While the phone was in his hand, he called the hospital for an update on Henry; no change, but his vital signs were strong and the doctors were encouraged. While he was talking, Fred rose from the sofa and struggled off to bed with a wave. Alone, Dean turned on Vivaldi. He nodded off before the orchestra finished warming up.

Dean woke, several hours later, to the sound of Dorrie Briscoe opening the front door. The music had run its cycle and it was dark in the room. When Dorrie switched on the light, his presence startled her. She was red-eyed and sobbing. As he rose slowly, still half asleep, she rushed to him, flinging her arms around him like a war bride at embarkation.

He let her cry, saying nothing, until she finally pulled back. "I'm sorry. I didn't know you were here. I had to let it out. All night I was Miss Proper when I wanted to scream. The Adams are so nice, just what Nattie needs, so different." She began to cry again and turned back to him.

She remained that way for minutes. Finally, in a whisper she asked. "You know what I need, don't you? Please? There's Henry's room. He won't be back...tonight." She tightened her hold.

"No. Yes, I know what you want, but no." He tried to gently push her back.

"It's the girl, isn't it? Cynthia. She wouldn't have to know... it's not the same anyhow. You love her...that's okay, it doesn't matter. I just want...to be held. Oh, shit, I'm being such a selfish bitch." She pulled away herself.

"Don't say anything, please." She ran down the hall to her room.

Dean waited a few minutes before turning out the light and going to his own bed. But it wasn't any good, sleep wouldn't come. His body was adapting to this strange new schedule of up all night, cat-naps during the day and wouldn't respond. The occasional sobs coming from Dorrie Briscoe's bed next door in the den didn't help a bit.

He fought the battle until the bedside clock read one-thirty and he'd had enough of Fred O'Connor's measured breathing and the dancing shadows playing on the wall in the moonlight. He rose, tugged on the clothes of the day before and quietly crept out to his car. With no destination in mind, he headed north, knowing nothing in Ouray would be open at that hour, nor in Ridgway for that matter. He continued north, all the way to Montrose, his eye on the large "E" on his gas gauge. Finally, the lights of an all night gas station and convenience store came into view.

With a full tank and full complement of black coffee Dean was wider awake than before with no place to go. On a whim, he turned his car east and easily found a place to park by the emergency entrance of the Montrose Hospital.

It was an off night for misery and mayhem. The sole person attending was a pretty young blond who looked barely old enough for high school. She peeked up from whatever she was reading and smiled hesitantly, as if wondering if he were a victim or a mugger. He flashed his badge to instill confidence and returned her smile.

"See, I'm not even bleeding! I'm just in the area and wanted to check on someone. He's been here since last night, Henry Whitcomb. Any change?"

"You're not Jeremy Whitcomb, are you?" she said with surprise. "We've been trying to call all night!"

"No," he answered, "has there been a change?" He was braced to hear Henry Whitcomb was dead.

"Mr. Whitcomb is conscious, but I understand he's been giving Dr. Jacobson an awful time. The doctor wants to talk to his son." She smiled again. "Dr. Jacobson isn't used to someone being so obstinate."

"It sounds like Henry is his old self." He confirmed she had the correct hotel for Jeremy but suggested he might be staying with the visitors from the east. "How is Henry doing?" he asked.

She looked down at a chart and scowled. "He's still listed as critical but I guess his being awake is a good sign... Oops, I'm not even supposed to say that. You could speak with the doctor if he's still around."

"Any chance of saying 'hello' to Henry?" He tried his best smile-charm combination.

"Sorry, but I'll try and get the doctor." She dialed a number and spoke to someone on the other end and then shook her head. "No luck, the doctor has left."

"What happened to the private doctor who flew out from the east?"

"He went back earlier. Dr. Jacobson is the only one on the case who's here."

"Too bad," Dean answered. The eastern guy must have figured Henry was a lost cause not worth his time. He stalled. "It might give Mr. Whitcomb a boost if a familiar face poked its head in."

"Oh, no!" she said quickly. "It's really late. All the patients are sleeping. You can give the doctor a call in the morning..."

"Henry's been sleeping since he got here. He was in a coma. He's bound to be rested ...maybe even bored. Please?" He still smiled. He even thought of saying, "pretty-please" but didn't want to overdo it. He couldn't tell if it was the badge or his winning personality, but she looked undecided.

"Let me try Dr. Jacobson at home. He may not have gotten to sleep yet and he wanted to know when we contacted Jeremy." She nibbled on a fingernail. "I hope he doesn't bite my head off again!"

"How about if I speak to him? I'd hate to see him bite a pretty head like yours..." She was dialing the phone and looked up at him with a "that-sounds-like-a-forties-movie" look but handed him the phone.

The doctor sounded like he could give Henry a good couple of rounds in the grumpy category but, after hearing Whitcomb was staying at Dean's house and Jeremy was still unavailable, consented for Dean to make a short visit. The "consent" was washed with frustration. Whatever had transpired between the doctor and his patient left the doctor with no love for Henry Whitcomb. Join the parade.

"Only for a sec," she said in the most professional voice she could muster, "and don't let anyone see you. Everyone will want to visit in the middle of the night." That smile; she'll break a million hearts.

"I'll just peek in, and then sneak out the side door. Thanks bushels."

"And," she added after giving him the room number, "you're really cute but awfully old!"

Oh, well, he thought, maybe "cute" ages like a good wine. He followed the room numbers easily and found the room, passing no one else in the hall.

The private room was larger than most and dark except for the light from the hall that slid by the crack in the door and the reflection from the parking lot lights outside. Until Dean's eyes became used to the semi-darkness, the body on the bed was no more than a silhouette. Slowly, the form of Henry Whitcomb came into focus.

The vision of dynamic Henry Whitcomb held together with tubes and wires was not a pleasant sight. The right side of his face slumped noticeably and in the subdued light he had a deathly pallor. He lay, breathing slowly, not unlike the slumber of a few days past, absent the Klaxton turban. Dean didn't like the man and had never pretended otherwise but to see him like this registered a pang of sympathy.

Once in the room, he wondered why he had followed the whim that brought him here in the middle of the night and caused him to push so hard for the visit. It wasn't a visit but a viewing. There was something voyeuristic about his coming and he regretted making the trip.

Henry gave no sign of being awake and Dean was hesitant to disturb the pathetic figure. His hand was on the knob to leave when he turned to see Henry's eyes flutter open, only to close again. It happened so quickly Dean wasn't sure he'd really seen it. He crossed back to the bed and spoke his name softly.

"Henry?" The eyes opened again, again briefly, and the lips moved, wordlessly.

"I'll get the nurse!" Dean started to leave but a sound, more a croak than a word, interrupted him. He returned to the bed and saw Henry's eyes open again. He moved his head slowly from side to side indicating, "No."

"Is there something I can get you?" Dean asked.

"No." The sound was audible now, somewhat slurred but otherwise clear.

"Not yet. Sit." Dean sat.

"I woke up a few hours ago. I'm not ready for them...yet." The words came slowly and with obvious difficulty, but spoken with the usual firmness that was Henry Whitcomb.

"I don't think I can move," he continued, "but I'm too frightened to try and I don't want them screwing around yet. Isn't that a switch? I'm working my way up to it. I'm going to try a toe first and then..."

"Henry..."

"Don't interrupt. This is my party." It was as if his condition demanded a reverence, not just the usual arrogance of Henry Whitcomb but something else. Dean couldn't guess the state of his overall health but his viable condition was owed an audience if that was what he wanted.

Whitcomb continued. "Where's my son?"

"I'm not sure. He went out to dinner with some of your execs from the east. He didn't come back by the house. They're looking for him." Henry seemed to mull the answer over in his mind.

"I'm that badly off, huh?"

"I won't pull your leg. You were unconscious for over twenty-four hours. You've caused a lot of concern."

He made a sound, a laugh that was more of a cough. "They're just hanging around to cut up the spoils. I don't give a shit, let 'em have it." He was silent for a few minutes and Dean thought he had fallen back to sleep but he reopened his eyes.

"Is there anyone you want me to get? I could try and hunt up Jeremy myself."

He shook his head. "No one. Only Michael and even you can't resurrect him. God, I loved that kid!" He sounded as if he would cry and a slight drool appeared on the right side of his jaw. "I dreamed about him yesterday, or whatever day it was when I was last human. Phyllis was in the dream, too, like years ago before she...started having problems. Funny, she kept saying for me to leave it alone, she was at peace and so was Michael. She was young again looking just the way I remembered her when we first married. It was strange, I'd almost forgotten how wonderful she used to be."

"Were you wearing the Klaxton turban?" Dean asked cautiously.

Whitcomb made the same laugh sound. "I like you, Dean. You don't bullshit. No, this was a real dream, more vivid perhaps than an everyday dream but just a dream." He took a deep breath.

"You and me, we were something together, the two of us, weren't we? Going up that damn mountain, each of us working our asses off to outclass the other! I'm just sorry about one thing; you'll never believe the damned turban works and there isn't anything I can say or do to convince you otherwise. I don't blame you. I wouldn't believe it either if I hadn't been there but I wish you could have seen it, too. You know what? It was the greatest experience in my life, being in Byrd's Song a hundred years ago and seeing those little girls and then finding out it was true. It's hard to explain but that's saying something; I've had a peck of experiences in my life."

He sighed. "Sorry, I'm rambling. I sound like I've had a snout full."

"Get your health back. Maybe they'll be other trips like Byrd's Song." Dean was fishing and he felt guilty about it. Did Whitcomb know the Klaxton turban was missing?

Henry Whitcomb took his time before answering. "I couldn't get the Klaxton turban to work again. That session with you? A zero. I just slept. So then I tried it alone, same result. God knows I tried, but nothing happened. I wouldn't admit it to those fools."

"Hoping they would think you went back to August, two years ago?"

"Can you blame me?"

"No," Dean answered honestly. "The murders had to be a hell of a trauma, doubly so because you don't know who did it, but you can't let it control your life. You had two sons and you only lost one of them. I think Jeremy deserves a better break than you've given him."

He answered carefully. "You figure I don't love Jeremy; I suppose everyone does, Jeremy included. That's wrong. I do love him. But most times love doesn't come out even. One person loves the other more and that smothers it, and I'm no damn good at pretending."

Both men were quiet for minutes. Finally Dean broke the silence. "Mrs. Brown thinks you were poisoned."

He looked up. "Really? Why?"

"The butterscotch pudding. She didn't serve it to you and no one had seen it in the house. It was half-finished when we found you."

This time the laugh was clearer. "I bought it in town and hid it, like a little kid. A treat for good little Henry. Poisoned, huh? That's just like Brown. If it doesn't fit the mold, it must be something bizarre. So who are the cops chasing for my attempted murder? Faldi? Dorrie? God, I hope it's Neil, the asshole!"

"They're just waiting for the lab tests. The doctors have pretty well talked them out of the poison scenario." Dean was beginning to feel guilty. "I've been here much longer than I'm supposed to. How about getting a little sleep?"

"No, stick around. Really, I'm feeling better. I even think I can sense a squiggle in my right foot. There's plenty of time for the doctors and all their shit. Just talk to me."

"Faldi is in jail." Dean figured he might as well bring Whitcomb up to date on the news.

"Good. I figured he'd be in his grave after Atherton and Waite got hold of him. How is Dorrie? Are you back sleeping with her now that I'm laid up?"

"No," Dean answered. The question didn't even peeve him the way it should have.

"Dorrie is pretty messed up," and he added, "I'm not sure either of us helped the situation."

"I like Dorrie, but I can't fix her. Neither can you, nor the thousand other guys she's had. All we can do is give her a night or two of peace." He dismissed her as a subject as quickly as she'd been put aside in person.

"What happened to Crawford?"

"I don't know," then Dean added, "for sure."

"You'll find him."

Then he asked, out of the blue, "Are you going back to Pennsylvania and be a cop?"

"I'm not sure."

"Stay out here. It's your kind of country." And he was asleep.

Dean remained at the bedside another half hour. No one came by to toss him out nor did Henry Whitcomb wake up again. His measured breathing was a metronome to Dean's thoughts in the darkened room. Henry believed in the Klaxton turban; it wasn't a sham, at least of his doing. But it made seeing Hays Crawford rise in importance.

By the time David Dean left the hospital and drove the thirty-five miles back home, the light of a new day was beginning. While he didn't know it at the time, the sun no longer rose for Henry Whitcomb.

CHAPTER XVII

In spite of spending his third sleepless night in a row, Dean had the crazy notion if he stopped for a full breakfast of eggs, sausage and toast it might convince his body the day was beginning normally. He was determined to spend it awake and revert to his usual pattern, sleep at night, activities during the daylight. He was certainly hungry, but a roast beef dinner followed by a couple of beers would have been preferred in his topsy-turvy world. He took his time over the meal, in no hurry to return to what he was sure would be renewed turmoil at his previously peaceful house. Consequently, by the time he reached home, word of Henry Whitcomb's death preceded him.

A nurse on her seven o'clock round discovered the body. Death was assumed to have resulted from a second, more massive stroke, although an autopsy was scheduled for confirmation. Jeremy had called the hospital only moments earlier to check on his father's condition so they had his phone number and were able to advise him as soon as the death was discovered. Jeremy and the entire retinue from the east had established headquarters in a new motel in Montrose.

Word of the sudden death came to Dean's household from Jeremy calling Mrs. Brown and Dorrie Briscoe, both of whom had already left for the hospital by the time Dean returned home. It was Neil Archer who informed Dean. He'd spent the night in Dean's bedroom, recently vacated by Whitcomb, much to Dean's chagrin.

"So, I checked out of the hotel," Archer wined. "With Henry in the hospital, I couldn't be sure he was still going to pick up the tab. I can't believe he's dead," he said, almost as an afterthought.

Neither could Dean. Death must have come less than an hour after Dean left his bedside. It seemed the others were unaware of his visit, at least so far.

"I don't know why you're surprised he's dead, you practically had him buried yesterday," Dean grumbled. "Look, why don't you go to Montrose, too? They need you," he added.

"I don't have a car. Besides..."

Dean didn't wait for the "besides." He called a cab for Archer, reminded him not to forget his suitcase, and stayed behind a closed bedroom door, away from the obnoxious professor until the transportation arrived.

Fred was out for an early morning walk, unaware of the news. Just as the cab left, he returned and Dean brought him up to date.

"Has the check cleared?" was Fred's immediate response.

"That's kind of callous, isn't it?"

Fred let out a deep sigh. "Maybe you're right, but that's my first thought, not a sob and a tear for the guy. He was a bastard when he was alive. I don't see how that's changed now that he's answering to the angels. We got to look out for ourselves. Besides, maybe now it's all for the better. His son Jeremy and Dorrie Briscoe, and a few thousand other people can have a little peace."

Dean only partially agreed. Henry Whitcomb was more than what the casual observer ever saw. No, Dean thought, he hadn't changed his basic opinion of Whitcomb. He was a bastard but something human neared the surface in the hospital room, as fleeting as it was. He detailed to Fred the substance of his visit.

Fred commented, "I suppose lots of folks would be looking behind the words for some significance and maybe it's so. When you get a little bit older, like me, the grim reaper ain't as indistinct as when you're a pup. You're not as fearful of him neither. Don't get me wrong. I'm not looking for him to come calling anytime soon, but when he comes, I'll be ready. From what you said, Henry was ready. He just wanted to chat a bit before he took the trip and you happened to be a handy ear."

"Are you saying he willed his death?"

"I ain't saying anything that makes sense. Nothing about this case makes a lot of sense either, especially Henry Whitcomb. Most of his actions didn't speak of a man of his position and supposed intelligence, not by a long shot. But maybe when you're peeking over the edge of a six-foot hole things lose a bit of perspective and you don't see life as clearly as when you're tip-top. Whatever the reason, it sounds like Henry Whitcomb went to his grave believing the Klaxton turban is the real McCoy, and we ain't a lick closer to knowing what's going on."

All the more reason to locate Hays Crawford. The young electrician had to be the key. Dean stared out the window at the derelict building across the valley, barely a speck to the naked eye, and wondered if Crawford was meeting his gaze. Without his missing binoculars it was impossible to tell but suddenly Dean remembered Henry Whitcomb had carried a similar pair to Byrd's Song. He located them without difficulty, tossed in a corner with the dead man's hiking gear.

Focusing the lenses on the building brought out the details of the structure; old boards helter-skelter, defined windows, leaning walls. Though he had studied the bunkhouse in the past, he was now looking not so much at the building's structure but for any movement that might hint Hays Crawford was hiding there.

"You think he's up there?" Fred asked.

"I think it's a good bet. It would provide cover, plus give him a chance to keep tabs on the house."

"He sure had a fascination with the place," Fred said, picking up the glasses Dean had set down. "Think he can see us?"

The sun was still low to the east making it difficult to study the building as clearly as late afternoon. "I don't think he could see in the windows but he could spot cars coming and going, and maybe how many people in them, and if there were lights on in the house at night."

"So he'd know when Henry was alone, like Monday evening. Are we going over and check it out?"

"I'm going over and check it out. That's no walk in the park. It isn't very high but it looks steep as hell." He picked up the binoculars again and tried to figure out the path he would have to take.

The trip would be totally unlike the climb to Byrd's Song; it was at most a couple of hundred feet from the closest point where the road passed below the building and the elevation was not much higher than Dean's place. But that didn't mean it was an easy stroll. The hillside was thickly covered in scrub oak, brown and bronze now in the fall air, and no trail was readily apparent. And it was steep. A tailings dump spilled down the slope to the north of the building, a remnant from an abandoned mine the bunkhouse served in days gone by. More loose rock was probably hidden in the brush. Dean knew from poking around in similar places, climbing the tailings resembled walking on marbles, one step for-ward, two back. He would have to pick a site in the oak, south of the tailings, and fight his way straight up the slope.

While he could see the building from his house across the valley, he knew once he was on the escarpment on the east side, he would lose sight of the structure. The slope was simply too steep and too tangled for any visibility at close range. .

Fred followed Dean into the bedroom and sat on the edge of the bed while Dean changed to old jeans and a ragged sweater. Dean was surprised Fred didn't push to accompany him but the old man did look concerned.

"You know, if Hays is up there, and Hays did swipe the turban, and Hays maybe set up Henry, just maybe Hays has some firsthand knowledge of the murder."

Dean didn't disagree. He was no closer to knowing how the facts fitted together than earlier, but what he did know pointed a crooked finger at Mr. Crawford.

"Hays Crawford might not take kindly to your coming by for a visit, did you think of that?"

Dean had thought of that and for the first time since arriving in Colorado was sorry his gun was back in Pennsylvania. Then he remembered; Nattie said Whitcomb had a gun. He went upstairs with Fred close on his heels and began to search the bedroom. He had not seen it when searching earlier for the Klaxton turban but that required a larger hiding place. When he couldn't find the gun quickly, he thought Hays Crawford might have picked it up along with the turban, but Fred finally located it beneath Whitcomb's underwear in an opened suitcase. Dean supposed the sheriff might have something to say if he knew Dean was armed with a gun not registered to him, about to track down a man the sheriff himself was looking for. But it was only a passing thought.

Thus armed, he went out to his car, the only remaining vehicle. Fred followed and stepped into the seat beside him, commenting that it was as cold as Maggie's heart.

"Look," Dean said, "we went over this. I'm going alone."

Fred held up his hand. "No argument. I'm just along for the ride. I'll stay down on the road in the car. If you're not back in an hour or two, I'll assume Crawford killed you and get the sheriff." It sounded like a hell of an idea to Dean; he wouldn't want the coyotes to eat his body.

While the bunkhouse was probably no more than a mile across the valley, getting to it required a much longer trip. Dean drove a mile from his house to the highway, two and a half miles south toward Ouray, and then reversed his direction on a dirt road that ascended the eastern escarpment to the north. For the first mile and a half there were scattered houses but once they were past the entrance to National Forest land there were no further buildings. The road wound slowly upward with occasional steep drop-offs to the left, but basically it was wide enough for two vehicles to pass and had no more ruts and bumps than Dean's road. While the jeep would have been more appropriate, the Honda had little trouble making the climb.

When the tailings slide came into view Dean knew he was approximately below the building even though he couldn't see it above him. Pulling the car as close to the left edge of the road as he dared, he shut off the engine.

Fred looked around. "Sure looks different from across the valley. Them little trees ain't so little." He looked up. "Think Crawford can see us?"

"No. Once we left the driveway, he'd lose us in the trees. Unless he could see our dust on the road, he wouldn't know anyone is down here."

Fred stared up the steep slope. "Are you sure that's the easiest way up there? Seems like the miners must have had a better route than straight up."

"Maybe they did a hundred years ago, but they're all dead and can't show me. If there was a road above it, it's closed now. Off I go." He climbed out of the car with a wave.

Fred stepped out of his side and as Dean entered the scrub oak, he turned around to see Fred wandering up the road. He hoped the old man didn't do anything silly.

There appeared at first to be something of a trail but it quickly disappeared in the underbrush that formed a canopy over Dean's head. The oak branches were relentless in their attack of his arms and body and he was thankful he had sense to wear long sleeves as he picked his way first right and then left, following the clearest way. He had not gone far before he began to climb sharply and moving out of the brush, found he was further to the north, at the edge of the tailings. The going was easier there, at least at first, until the steepness became so acute he was forced to sidestep, and even then with every step scattered stones downward in a bouncing trail behind him.

So much for stealth and all that crap, he thought, sitting on a large rock to dump a shoe full of gravel and catch his breath. In spite of the chilly temperature, annoying rivulets of sweat were soaking his flannel shirt, and a series of red scratches made a road map of his hands. He looked up but still could not see the structure. Heaving a sigh, he continued to scramble upward.

Stones of all sizes continued to roll and frolic their way downward behind him and he was forced to all fours to keep from sliding backward and joining them. Although his plan for the trip was sketchy at best, he assumed he would approach his destination undetected and at least have the opportunity to study the site. That was a laugh. With the noise he was making he'd frighten a deaf man.

By the time he did see the structure, he was slightly above it, to the left. It seemed much larger now that he was close, perhaps fifty feet long and half as wide. He quickly stooped down and watched, but saw or heard nothing. It was obvious he would not surprise Hays Crawford if he were there so he rose and began to cautiously inspect the area.

Eight large windows faced back across the valley and as Dean peeked in, he could see that the building had been divided into at least four large rooms on the first floor. Ever since seeing the building from his living room, Dean had referred to it as a bunk house but in reality it was more of a boarding house with a large fireplace in one of the four main rooms. At the south end, the remains of the kitchen laid in ruin, the crumpled stove pipe and rusting stove now exposed to the elements. The building was originally two stories but the roof and upper floor had collapsed, their debris now tenuously supported by the buckled ceiling of the first floor. Dean peeked in each of the eight large windows, carefully stepping over loose boards, rusty nails and broken glass. He did not enter the structure but there was little need. The remains of the building was wide open with no hiding places. Not only was it empty but Dean saw no evidence of Hays Crawford having been there.

Stepping around to the back, he commenced a closer search of the grounds when he heard a movement behind him. He whirled around to see Crawford standing in a small copse of pine about twenty feet away.

"Welcome to Crawford Castle," he said. "What took you so long?"

"Things have been a little busy back at the ranch," Dean answered cautiously. He felt the comfort of the gun in his side pocket.

"I figured it was you, once I discounted a herd of buffalo clawing their way up that slope. You'd make a rotten Indian."

"I thought you'd figure it was Faldi coming up here to get your scalp."

"That fat slob couldn't climb a flight of stairs. Besides, a couple of Henry's goons beat the shit out of him and chased his ass out of town."

"So I hear. Is that what chased you up here?" Dean asked. Crawford didn't appear in any way threatening as he sauntered toward Dean and sat on a rock a few feet away. He carried a small knapsack over one arm and Dean could see his sleeping bag and gear back in the trees.

Hays was quiet for a moment before answering. "Naw, I just wanted to breathe your mountain air before going back to the polluted east."

"Sorry, no sale," said Dean.

Hays raised an eyebrow. "Really? You don't believe me? Have you been detecting overtime?"

"Just looking for some answers," Dean replied.

"I'm not sure I've got any you need, but if I do, you made it just in time. I'm all packed up and ready to move out; too damn cold. And that building isn't as secure as it looked from your place. Did the old man send you up here to fetch me?"

"Henry Whitcomb is dead."

"No shit? So that's the reason for all the lights and sirens. What killed him? Or, should I say 'who' killed him?"

"I thought you might volunteer." Dean remained standing but leaned against the edge of the building.

"Me? I'm up here playing King of the Mountain, communing with nature, not bothering a soul."

"That doesn't stop you from bopping back down for a little mischief."

Crawford just laughed. "Not this guy. One climb up here is enough! By the way, congratulations. That's a tough climb, a bullet in your ass and all."

"Byrd's Song whipped me into shape."

"Ah, yes! Byrd's Song!" He said it with a theatrical flair. "At least that shit is all finished. But tell me about the King. I'm sorry I missed his death, it must have been a real happening. Did someone really do him in?"

"Mrs. Brown thinks he was poisoned." Dean tossed it out more for effect than anything else.

Hays scoffed. "But he wasn't, was he?"

"It doesn't seem likely. Probably a massive stroke."

"I should be sorry but I'm not." He stood up and pulled the binoculars from a knapsack and focused them on the house across the valley. "It looks pretty quiet." Then he handed them to Dean. "Sorry, these are yours. I borrowed them."

"Along with the food kitty?"

"That was just an advance on what Henry owed me." And then added, "I suppose all the vultures are down there partying."

"If they are, I wasn't invited," Dean answered.

"Me neither, that's for sure."

"I think it's time we talk. All this chit-chat is terrific but I need some answers and Fred's down below waiting for me."

"Are you still working for Henry?"

"Henry's dead. I'm just a curious guy by nature, and I don't give up easily."

"I suppose you want to know about the marvelous Klaxton turban."

"Among other things."

"What made you think I did anything? It could have been Neil Archer. After all, the Klaxton turban was his gadget. I was just the electrician."

"Neil's a history prof. Civil war is his specialty. He'd have plunked Henry back at Bull Run, hanging onto Stonewall Jackson's pant leg like a camp dog. Besides, Neil's too stupid to pull it off. That and a list of other reasons."

"I'll take that as a compliment. What are the other reasons?"

"You bitched too much about the impromptu session."

Crawford first smiled and then his expression turned serious. "Look, before I spill my lunch, I want you to give me some assurances."

"There aren't any assurances about the murders of Phyllis and Michael Whitcomb," Dean said firmly.

Crawford threw his hands in the air. "Shit! I suppose Henry pegged me with that! It would be just like him! What, did the turban tell him so?" Dean didn't answer. The young man tossed his knapsack on the ground in disgust.

"Look," he said in an angry tone, "I'm going to take a chance on you." Dean remained silent. "You'd better sit. This may take a while. It's a hell of a story."

"The story of the Klaxton turban?" Dean asked as he took a seat against the building.

"I hope they buried the damn thing with Henry."

"It's missing. Happen to know where it is?"

"You think I took it?" he asked incredulously.

"You're the logical one."

"Bullshit! I know what it's worth! Why would I take it? Look, just let me tell this at my own pace, will you?"

"I'm a captive audience."

Hays Crawford slumped down against a tree and began. "I did the Klaxton turban on Henry the first time at his house, not the session you read about. I'd come over to see Jeremy but he wasn't home. The old man was having a bitch of a headache and I had the turban in the car. Mommy was dead and buried, so we were alone. Jeremy had told him about the turban and what it could do and he was ready to try anything. He was really a pussy cat. I had him lay down on the sofa and plugged him in. He fell asleep like a rock but that wasn't the half of it. I made a noise, bumped my shin or something and was sure I woke him up but he didn't stir. So, just for the hell of it, I said something out loud. Same thing; nothing. Finally, I spoke really loud, something snippy like what the hell was I supposed to do next, with him sleeping there and damned if he didn't answer me! That was when I realized he wasn't just sleeping but sort of hypnotized. We'd screwed around with hypnotism during my whacked-out stage, you know, trying it with drugs and shit, so I knew a bit about it.

"I tried a couple of silly things with Henry, just for kicks, and he responded. It was bitching! Here I was, a futz, with this billionaire who'd always treated me like yesterday's garbage, getting him to make doggie noises and shit like that! I couldn't believe it!

"It was a power thing, I guess. I'm not proud of it. It was like getting into a girl's pants when she's drunk, but I got to tell you, it was a kick!

"Then I got kind of scared he'd wake up and toss my ass in jail or something so I tried this post hypnotic suggestion for him to not even remember I'd been there. Damned if it didn't work! I took off the turban, had him count to a hundred before he woke up, and scooted out the door. When I came back later after Jeremy was home, the old man didn't bat an eye! It was like he hadn't seen me in months!

"It must have been three or four weeks before I did it again. Same scenario, no one else there. The house was empty as a tomb. Only this time I fooled around more; he was a perfect patient! I had him back in time, like Bridie Murphy and all kinds of shit. I even gave him a post-suggestion if I said a key word he'd travel back to the same place, Brigham, Ohio. There was a picture of a house and I showed it to him and had him 'walk' on the street. I was in Brigham when I was a kid, my aunt lived there a couple of years.

"Then things got serious. Jeremy kept pushing for me to try the turban out on his old man, not knowing I already had! He and Archer finally set up a get-together. That's the so-called first session. I tossed in the key word and presto, Uncle Henry was back in Brigham! Only this time I didn't have him forget! It shook the socks off him!

"I laughed my ass off, to myself. That was really the start; we went on like that. I'd do a private session when his wife and Jeremy weren't around and then a public one and he was on the road to wonderland. The more he believed the more I poured it on. It was tough getting him alone. That's why there were so many sessions that were flat tires; I hadn't had time to prompt him."

He turned to Dean. "Did you figure it out? Be honest, now."

"Not really. I knew you had to be the one pulling it off. You were the only one beside Henry who had any degree of control over the sessions. I never believed it actually worked, not for a minute."

"Maybe if you'd taken a trip you would have. Henry sure bought it."

"Byrd's Song, it was a diary, wasn't it? A notebook, just like the one Nattie writes in every day."

"You're good! I'll give you credit for that! Byrd's Song was the big finale. This girl I knew years ago moved out on me and left all her junk, trunks and stuff from when her family died. I don't know where in hell she got it and I don't think she had ever even looked at it. There was a box that hadn't been opened in years. It had a dozen pictures, Sneffels, Byrd's Song, the girls and Sarah's mother. And there was the diary, a really detailed diary covering three years. It's beautiful! The kid had real talent. She talks about everything and describes it all in incredible detail! It was perfect! I did three private gigs with Henry and he could have told you the number of buttons on any one of the dresses. I copied the pictures of the girls and isolated them, had them blown up so he froze them in his mind. I'd get him to memorize the pictures and hear the words from the diary, over and over again. The buildings and some of the stuff I made up and his imagination filled in the cracks."

"Why?" Dean asked. "What would ever possess you to go to that much trouble?"

"You know, I've asked myself the same question. I don't know the answer. At first it was a toot. Then he hired us so there was some dough in it. That helped, but mostly it was just too perfect to stop! It was like this major theater production with me as producer, author, director!"

"Weren't you worried when he decided to come out here?"

"Why? The worst thing that could happen was there would be no sign of the place, or he wouldn't find it. But I figured there must be more copies of those pictures around and he would piss his pants when he saw one. Neil was such a shithead about finding anything I thought it was a dead issue. It was like I was laying out this perfect trail of cheese and Neil the mouse was too stupid to do anything but chase his tail. Then you and the old guy came on the scene and things started moving. You two were a hell of a help.

"You came out to Ouray County earlier, didn't you?" It was only a half-guess by Dean. He had figured out the trip must have been earlier, when Crawford was planning the "official" session on Byrd's Song, not later when everybody was so busy and Dorrie so positive he couldn't have gotten away.

"You really impress me! Yeah, I came out in June to check the place over. I didn't climb up to Byrd's Song but I took a few pictures of the mountains around there to salt Henry's memory. Mountains don't change much in a hundred years."

"Did you know the tin was still buried up there?"

"No, but there wasn't any reason it shouldn't be. The kid Sarah drew a treasure map step by step and described the stuff in the box in detail. She might have gone back and dug it up, but you don't do that with dead pets, and besides, the diary stopped not long after that. I figured she moved. I never realized the poor kid died. But even if the box wasn't there, I did know Byrd's Song existed and that was all Henry cared about. He'd 'seen' it, or at least he thought he had."

"How could you be so sure he wouldn't wake up one day and remember you had conned him?"

Hays thought about the question. "The truthful answer is I couldn't. It's just that the longer it went on, the more secure I became. They say you can't make someone do something under hypnosis against their will, something they wouldn't do while they were awake. I didn't make Henry do anything sinister and I think he wanted to believe so hard he did. It was a happy experience for him."

"The whole thing went without a hitch, huh?"

"He really faked me out when he didn't come clean about Sarah's tin box after the Byrd's Song session when we were interviewing him. I thought he didn't remember it and the box was the key, then I realized he was just holding out. That made it all the better! Here he thought he knew something no one else in the world knew! It was perfect!"

"When did you decide to make contact to sell out Henry and make some real dough?"

Crawford squirmed. "I feel really shitty about doing that. A guy I know worked for a sleazy magazine and knew I was close to Henry Whitcomb. These guys are like piranhas. Anyone who has a name is fair game for them to chase. He wanted me to get some dirt on Henry and the timing was right. I didn't go looking for it, that's the God's own truth. I just went along enough to keep the deal on the back burner, just in case. It was only a week before we came out here. I figured the whole business was getting out of hand anyway and if something popped I was dead meat. I needed security. I figured if Henry got nasty I might need some dough, quick. Then they sent out this fish Faldi and the whole thing started going to hell."

"Is that why you skipped up here?"

"Hell, no! When you made Henry do a session on short notice, I knew he wouldn't 'go back.' The way he looked at me when he came out of it! That's why I beat it the hell out of there!"

"And the gold watch?"

"I nearly shit! In one session in his house I used a watch when he wouldn't 'sleep' quickly. When he woke up at your place and asked me about it, I panicked. But I guess it left his mind almost at once. Thank God, he forgot it! But then he intimated he had 'gone back'. I didn't know what to think! If he figured out what I'd been doing, I'd be looking at some serious problems. The cops might even have a warrant out on me, and I didn't have any dough so I decided to take a few days up here and cool it. I kept an eye on the house to try and figure out what was happening. If I let a little time slide by I might have a better chance of hitching a ride back east, especially if everyone thought I'd already left."

"What did this have to do with the killing of Michael Whitcomb and his mother?"

"Nothing! Not a damned thing!"

"So the Klaxton turban doesn't have anything to do with the murders?"

"No, but it scared the shit out of me when Henry started thinking in that direction. I knew the turban bit was a sham but I was afraid he'd 'read' something that never happened, accuse the wrong person."

"Do you think he ever caught on that you were pulling the snow job of the century?"

Hays Crawford thought about the question. "I sure thought so when he decided to do the sessions solo. But after I thought about it a little longer, I don't think he did. He was just bullshitting everyone into thinking he could control the time of the turban to smoke out whoever was involved in Phyllis and Michael's murder."

"But that didn't work, did it?"

"No." He looked Dean in the eye. "We still don't know who did it, do we? But I'll tell you this, it wasn't me."

Dean returned his stare. "I'd like to believe that but the jury is still out." And then he asked, as he got to his feet, "What are you going to do now?"

"I guess it depends on you. Are you going to squeal?"

"Not unless you lied or I need to use the information for some other reason. The way you tell it, it was a stupid prank. But there's still a lot of unanswered questions, like where the turban is now – not to mention who killed Henry's wife and son?"

Hays gathered up his gear. "You know, it's kind of funny. I thought I was pulling Henry's chain so hard it would choke him and instead I gave him the only wink of happiness he had in his whole sorry life. I did it with all the wrong motives, and it came out just the opposite. It was all bullshit but Henry ended up buying it, lock, stock and barrel, to the day he died. He died believing he really visited Byrd's Song, was there with Ella and Sarah and her mother, a hundred years ago. That's kind of cool, isn't it?"

In a strange way Dean had to agree as he rose and started down the slope with Hays Crawford following. The trail downward took less time and exertion with Crawford leading the way over a path he had apparently scouted. It followed a spill of rusted cans and other debris, not adding to the footing but the trees were spaced sufficiently close so Dean could grab from branch to branch and maintain a stumbling balance.

Fred O'Connor never said a word about the long wait he endured as he stood patiently by the car but Dean noticed a telltale streak of dirt on the leg of his usually immaculate trousers and scratches on his hands. Damned if the old goat hadn't tried to follow Dean up the slope! Dean was secretly pleased his stepfather had the sense to give up the climb before he killed himself.

Fred nodded to Hays but otherwise it was a silent trip down the dirt road to the highway. Hays Crawford asked to be let out when they reached the pavement, murmuring that he would hitch a ride into Montrose. Without slowing the car Dean suggested he return to the house; most of the guests had moved on to other quarters and temporary space was no longer a problem. It wasn't an act of pure charity. Dean wanted Crawford close by until he could sort out the facts he'd been told.

Dean's mood was decidedly pleasant, the best in days. Never mind Henry Whitcomb was dead. Never mind Dean had no clear idea who had killed Henry's wife and son. He was getting closer; he could sense it. They drove home, the sun beginning to dip low behind the western ridge, searing the amber cottonwoods that lined the river like sentinels, guarding the precious Colorado water from the lust of the California golf courses. He began to whistle a cheery tune.

CHAPTER XVIII

Hays Crawford was assigned to Dean's old digs in the downstairs bedroom while Dean assumed territorial rights to the sanctity of his own bed upstairs. Even though Henry Whitcomb had spent his last conscious night in it, wrapped around Dorrie Briscoe, Dean knew it was still the most comfortable room in the house. A quick change of sheets remedied any lingering hint of subdued passion that might have permeated the percale. Fred would occupy the other second floor room, previously Mrs. Brown's quarters.

Before Hays crept off to his first night indoors in three, he pulled Dean aside.

"I guess I owe you thanks for keeping my ass out of trouble, or maybe out of jail."

"You can even the slate if you want to. Just bundle up the diary and pictures and send them to me," Dean answered.

"Why? What are you going to do with them?" Hays asked cautiously.

"Don't worry. Forget about them. They'll be in good hands."

Crawford thought about it a minute. "Okay, I'll trust you. You've been straight so far. Deal."

As he left for his room, the phone rang and Dean answered; a reporter who was abruptly dismissed. By the time he hung up the instrument, the light beneath Crawford's door was already out. So much for the thrill of sleeping in the great outdoors.

Dean wandered to the kitchen where Fred O'Connor was opening a large can of beef stew. He filled Fred in, detail by detail, as they sloshed the last of the bread in the brown mixture. Just as they were finishing, the phone rang, for the second time. It was another reporter.

This time, the excited voice wanted to know if Dean could confirm that Henry Whitcomb was involved in a cult that believed in reincarnation. He again dismissed the caller with a quick denial, trying to make the suggestion sound ludicrous.

When Dean sat back down, he noticed Fred was looking a bit

melancholy. Finally it dawned on him the reason.

"You're disappointed the turban isn't for real, aren't you?"

He smiled. "Oh, I guess deep down I realized that stuff doesn't happen. I suppose everyone did, except maybe Henry Whitcomb. But you've got to let yourself dream once in a while."

Dean just shrugged. "If you say so, but as far as I'm concerned, I'm glad of it."

Fred spoke in a quiet voice. "When I was just a little shaver, six or eight years old, I remember sitting in our big old kitchen. It was winter time. The windows would all be painted with frost in squiggles and icy feathers, shapes of every kind your imagination could play games with. My Ma, she was an old lady by the time I came around, she'd be cooking on this big old black stove, with a smile on her face and a tune on her lips. She was always humming or singing, not songs you'd recognize but always something cheery. That's not to say my growing up was all sweet-cakes and roses either, but we made do. Stella Dallas would be pouring out her soul on the radio and Ma would be singing away.

"She'd bake this pie, cutting them big red apples as careful as could be, making the crust from scratch, laughing at the little clouds of flour that would puff up when she'd wipe her hands on her apron. Those sweet smells! Sugar and spices and apples and fresh made dough! I tell you, I can't recall happier times.

"Nowadays there's a bakery three steps from your door and they'll sell you a pie all sealed up in plastic so's you can't smell it. They swear it is better in a dozen different ways than homemade, but you can't convince me. I'm not saying I want time to stand still and no one's hankering to swap their modern stove that does everything but serve the meal for one of those black monsters stuffed with wood or kerosene. But that still don't mean I don't miss it once in a while and taking a peek back sure would be pleasurable. Maybe you'll think likewise when a few more years pass."

Memory is a marvelous thing, Dean thought. The great winnowing process, unlike reality, as selective as it wants to be. Forget the bad and leave the perfect, and fit it together in a pleasant picture that with time becomes the truth. Stella Dallas didn't start on the radio until Fred was in high school or older but she still whined away in the radio of Fred's mind. No one could have convinced him otherwise, even if anyone was cruel enough to try. Today is always harsher than the yesterday of our memories. He sighed. But that didn't mean David Dean didn't have frost patterns of his own and memories of the smell of winter apple pie. And other memories.

"Maybe in thirty or forty years you'll hanker for a peek back at last Sunday night!" Fred said it with a wink. It gave Dean pause for thought but only briefly; the phone rang again.

Same story, same answer. Only this time Dean left the phone off the hook. As he returned to the table, Fred was opening the refrigerator and with a big grin produced dessert, two containers of butterscotch pudding. "They were behind some stale celery in the vegetable drawer," he said.

"Save mine for Mrs. Brown," Dean muttered.

"It seems to me," said Fred O'Connor in his most learned voice, "even if the Klaxton turban was a fraud, it's still the key. If Hays Crawford didn't take it, who did?" He answered his own question smugly. "It has to be the killer who took it."

"Why?" Dean answered with a yawn.

"So Henry Whitcomb wouldn't 'go back' and learn the truth." He dumped the dishes in a sink of soapy water as Dean got up from the table.

"Then you're talking about a true believer. If you didn't think the contraption worked you wouldn't have a reason to swipe it, would you?"

"Half the crew here were 'true believers' according to what they said; Neil, Dorrie, maybe Mrs. Brown." The two went into the living room with Fred wiping his hands on a dish towel as he added, "I'll vote for Archer."

"Not liking Archer doesn't make him a killer. Besides, even though Henry thought one of the group killed his wife and son doesn't mean it's a fact. There's something I'm missing but my brain is too tired to sort it out."

The day had finally caught up with him. Much as he wanted to digest the new facts and discuss them further with Fred, his body and mind were too tired to do the subject justice. With a wave, he was off to his room and the first night's sleep in three days.

Overnight the snow came. The storm raced up the valley in the early morning hours, huffing and puffing with a wind that woke Dean before the light, scattering the last of the fall leaves before it and thrashing pine boughs against his window. He turned back to the warmth of the pillow and burrowed deeper beneath the covers, but try as he might, he couldn't return to sleep.

His mind, more anxious to begin the day than his body, commenced a systematic recap of all that had been said and done over the past ten days. Perhaps a mind, absent the duties of functioning a wakened body is able to process facts and thoughts more accurately. Whatever the reason, little items began making sense to David Dean, things that previously had been part of a tangle of confusion. When he finally stepped out of bed and showered, he was ready to attack the day and attempt confirmation of his new suspicions.

Dean was surprised to see Jeremy Whitcomb seated at the kitchen table when he stepped downstairs. He hadn't heard the car, its tires muffled in the three inches of autumn snow.

"There's fresh coffee in the pot," Jeremy said, "and oatmeal. As a kid we always had oatmeal in the middle of the winter, and it sure looks like January out there today."

"Thanks and good morning," Dean said as he poured a cup and added all the appropriate words of condolence before he sat. "What brings you back here?"

Jeremy hesitated. "I'm taking my father's body back east for the funeral, if the weather clears and we can fly the plane out, but I wanted to talk to you before I left." Dean waited for Jeremy to continue.

"I wanted to thank you for what you did for the old man upstairs. It was quick thinking. The doctor thinks he would have died then if you hadn't given him oxygen. It was above and beyond the call."

Dean dismissed the thanks. "I'm a cop. I do that stuff for a living."

"Dr. Jacobson finally told me late last night that you spoke to my father. Everyone thought he'd died before regaining consciousness."

Dean chose his words carefully. "I couldn't sleep and drove into Montrose. The hospital was trying to get hold of you after your dad woke up. I just happened to be there. He was certainly lucid." He told Jeremy of his father's fear he might be paralyzed and his reluctance to try and move. "He may have found out he didn't have any feeling after I left and the shock was too much."

"I guess the first stroke was a beauty, according to the doctor. He wouldn't have had much function if he'd lived."

"I suppose you know the poison bit was a mistake," Dean said. "Your father told me he'd bought the pudding himself."

"Yes. The doctor confirmed that there was nothing in it."

Dean looked directly at Jeremy. "He talked about you."

"Really?"

"He might have had a shitty way of showing it, but he really loved you. He even said the words."

Jeremy rose and turned his face away. He took a deep breath. "Well, it's all over now. We don't have to disappoint one another any longer."

"What are you going to do now that you own your father's empire?" Dean asked.

"I haven't had much time to think about it. Somehow, it isn't as important to me as it is to a flock of other people."

"I'm no expert but you handled yourself pretty well back there at the hospital the other night with all the mucky-mucks."

Jeremy laughed. "If you do anything long enough you get pretty good at it. But that doesn't mean you like it."

"You're in a position to do anything you want. There's nobody left to tell you otherwise."

Jeremy looked up. "That's a sobering thought, isn't it? By the way, speaking of sobering, I swore off booze. After I tied one on the other night with you, I decided the damned stuff didn't work. After all, did you ever look closely at Neil Archer?"

Dean laughed as he gazed outside. The snow had begun to abate and the wind quieted down. "It looks like you may be able to fly out of here after all," he commented as he poured cream over a bowl of oatmeal. "Are the others going back with you?"

"Dorrie is picking up Nattie at the Adams' and Mrs. Brown is supposed to stop by here to pick up my father's papers. Neil's coming, too, and then we're taking off, hopefully. I suppose you'll be glad to get us out of your hair."

"It has been interesting," Dean said tactfully. "They're quite a group of people. 'Missing them' might be a touch too strong, except for Nattie. I'll definitely miss her. She's quite a young lady. I just wish her home life were a bit more stable."

"I'll look out for her and Dorrie. The rest are on their own as far as I'm concerned."

"By the way, the press is starting to ask questions about the reason your father was out here. If you have any influence over the group you may want to tell them to keep their mouths shut tight."

Jeremy scoffed. "I have the same influence as my father, money. I told them I'd pay what dad had promised and then some. The whole business should be dead and buried now that my father is gone." He paused before asking the next question. "Did my father destroy the Klaxton turban?"

"I suppose that's possible," Dean answered untruthfully. "He had enough time. He was all alone for the afternoon."

"That's what Archer thinks. He says my father was too damn selfish to leave it for mankind."

Dean laughed. "That only holds true if you buy the concept that it worked."

"My father didn't really go back to Byrd's Song, did he?"

Dean thought about his answer. "He did in his mind. He never stopped believing. He told me that in the hospital."

"Did he go...anywhere else?"

"If you mean did he discover who killed your mother and your brother, the answer is no. That matter is still an open issue."

"No, it isn't. The only one pushing for a resolution to the murders was my father and he's dead. Leave it alone!"

Jeremy's intensity startled Dean but before he could reply, Hays Crawford descended the stairs. When he saw Dean speaking with Jeremy, he stopped, mouth agape.

Jeremy stood up with a smile. "Hays! Good to see you! I thought you'd taken off back east!"

Hays muttered condolences and apologies and said something mundane about needing a little space and getting away for a couple of days. Jeremy put his arm around his shoulder and led him aside.

"I just wanted you to know I realize my father promised you some money for your work this summer," he said, as he walked Crawford down the hall. Dean didn't listen to the rest. He was content to devote his attention to the mush of the oatmeal.

Before he finished, a car pulled in the drive and Nattie Briscoe burst in the door, snow trailing behind her.

Dean stood up and gave her a hug. "Skipping school again, huh?"

"Big doings. It's back to the soot and grime." She stood aside, more nervous than her usual self.

"I'll miss you." He said it without a smile and he was sorry because it made her cry and that embarrassed her.

"Cut that out. You'll get me started and I'll get all red-faced and make a fool of myself." He held on to her until she bit a lip and stopped.

"Where's the old lady?"

"She's staying out in the rent-a-rod. She doesn't do the 'goodbye' scene very well. Neither do I, I guess."

"You're just excited about the plush plane ride and seeing your friends back home."

"I got to tell you, this getting-there-is-half-the-fun is a crock. I'm not that pleased about doing the bird-bit in the first place but the tree-maker laid out in baggage gives me the creeps! And mommy dearest is still doing a box of tissues an hour."

"You'll do fine!" he laughed. "Take care of her, she needs it."

Nattie gave a serious look. "I think I'll work on the Dorrie-Jeremy connection. He's a bit of a wimp but you've got to admit he is as stable as they come. There's a time in your life when security is important. I'm not always going to be around to look out for Dorrie

214

and this bed-hopping business is getting stale."

"You've got a few hours on the plane with a captive audience. They're as good as married!"

"Then I can come visit you when they're on their honeymoon!"

"You don't need any excuses to come and see me. The door is always open. Besides, there's a lady I want you to meet."

Nattie smiled a little but was still not herself.

Dean added, "I've got a present lined up for you, something really special, just between you and me. You'll understand when you get it but you're to keep it to yourself. Don't even show it to your mother. Okay?" Maybe Sarah Byrd could become a closer friend to Nattie Briscoe through her diary. Dean was willing to take the chance.

"Sure thing, cop-guy. I love a mystery!" Her mood had picked up a step or two. She told him Mr. and Mrs. Adams had invited her out for vacation and she and Ron agreed to write weekly.

"Can you imagine that? I sound like 'Anne of Green Gables!'" She asked about Fred who was still sleeping and was tickled to be able to go upstairs and wake him.

Dean was not going to let Dorrie skip without saying a word. He went out to the car, a Lincoln, no less. She was turned the other way in the seat and didn't see him until he knocked on the steamy window.

"Cool wheels," he said. She looked embarrassed, in addition to red-eyed and drawn.

"I'm sorry. I just couldn't face you this morning. I've been such a bitch. Pretend I never came out here. God, pretend none of us did!" She looked as if she'd start crying.

He opened the car door. "If you start bawling, I'll tickle you until you stop. And don't be a drudz. Come on inside, it's cold out here."

She laughed in spite of herself. "What in hell is a 'drudz?'"

"I just made it up but it fits, don't you think?" He took her arm and walked back toward the house just as Mrs. Brown and Neil Archer drove up. Dean waved at them over his shoulder but didn't stop to talk.

When the two caught up to him inside, Mrs. Brown grunted a minimal greeting to Dean and went directly upstairs. Jeremy was sitting on the sofa talking to Fred O'Connor while Hays Crawford stood nervously by the window. Neil started to say something to Dean who ignored him and he sauntered down the hall toward the bathroom and den. Fred was talking about the merits of the Klaxton turban if the contraption had worked while Jeremy listened politely. Dorrie, surprised to see Hays, moved to talk with him. Dean went to the kitchen for a cup of coffee.

It wasn't long before Mrs. Brown came downstairs, her arms loaded with files and papers which Dean had set aside. Jeremy rose and took them from her. Fred also stood up, his usual action when a lady entered the room. Mrs. Brown walked up to him, put her arms around his neck, and to the shock of the others, planted a big kiss on his lips. It was one of the few times Dean remembered seeing Fred O'Connor blush.

"That's for being so kind and considerate to me during these recent trying times." She nodded, as if to say, "now that's done," and strolled out the door.

"Tell Mr. Archer I'm ready to go," she called over her shoulder as she left.

Dean couldn't help smiling but as he had no appropriate comment to contribute to the scene he moseyed down the hall to see what Neil Archer was up to. The den door was closed but he could hear Archer's voice speaking in hushed tones. Little bells and alarms sounded in his brain. He pulled open the door to see the professor sitting with his arm around the shoulder of Nattie Briscoe, saying sweet somethings in her ear.

Neil jumped up, a shocked look on his face. Dean motioned with a crooked finger and unsmiling face for him to come out in the hall and Archer quickly obliged. It was a short, right chop to the jaw, not quite hard enough to put Archer on pabulum but enough to drop him on his ass in the middle of the hall, where he sat with a startled look on his face and blood running from his lip.

"I..." was all he could muster.

"Don't bother saying it. Just get the hell out of my house."

Dean grabbed him by the collar and half-dragged, half-pulled Archer to the door where he unceremoniously tossed him across the deck onto the snow-covered lawn. He turned to the others.

"Too bad. He ran into a door." He then returned to the den where Nattie stood smiling.

"My hero," she said.

David Dean wasn't smiling as he took hold of her shoulders. "Look, lay off playing Lolita to these low-life characters or you're going to get yourself in a peck of trouble. Do you understand?" She nodded in startled agreement and let him lead her to the living room and her mother.

Looking duly chastised she muttered, "I had my other hand on a bookend. If he'd tried anything, I'd have knocked the shit out of him."

Fred met Dean as he entered the room and pulled him aside. "Look," he said out of earshot of the others, "are you going to just let them fly out of here? There's a killer to be found!"

Dean smiled. According to Fred, Dean should sit the group in a circle and in cold logic announce the murderer of Phyllis and Michael Whitcomb, just as the police jump out from behind the drapes and tackle the accused. Instead, he lined up by the door to say his 'good-byes.'

Nattie left with a hug. Further conversation seemed inappropriate. Dorrie put her arms around Dean's neck and whispered, "I should have chased away that girl friend of yours and kept you for myself!" Hays simply shook hands. Only Jeremy Whitcomb hesitated, waiting behind as the others made their way to the car.

Henry Whitcomb's son looked at Dean and spoke in a low voice, but enough for Fred to hear as well. "You're not going to let this alone, are you."

"No," was all Dean responded.

He sighed. "Even if you thought you had the answer, chances are you'd be wrong and you'd never be able to prove anything anyway."

"Maybe not, but I could make a hell of a stink."

"Why?"

"Because it's right and a lot of people will be able to get a decent night's sleep when the truth comes out, that's why."

"Do you really know or are you just bullshitting?"

"Try me. I may be off on the details but I have a pretty good idea."

"You first," Jeremy responded, like a kid playing "secrets."

Dean sat on the sofa. He might as well be comfortable, this might take awhile. "The only person who didn't want to see the murders investigated was you," he began. "I had to ask myself, why? Because you were the murderer? Because you knew who the killer was? It didn't make sense if the killer was some transient. It had to be you or someone very close to you.

"Killing is a terrible, violent, gut-wrenching act, born out of passion and feelings so strong no alternative seems to remain. Who had those feelings? Who had the strongest emotional ties? Neil? Mrs. Brown? Hays? Dorrie? None of them had unbreakable alibis and perhaps a motive if you stretched it, but none of them seemed to have the passion. It had to be family. Your mother had become, at best a recluse, at worse someone with a serious mental problem. That left Michael. He had to be the key."

Jeremy began to pace as if Dean had hit on a sensitive note. Dean continued. "Tell me about Michael."

"Big brother? What do you want to know? Was I so jealous of him I killed him?"

Dean ignored the question and asked another. "Michael wasn't the saint your parents believed, was he? You don't have to deny it, Atherton said as much."

"Michael had problems, serious problems."

"Tell me about them."

"Look," Jeremy said angrily, "Michael's dead. Leave him alone!"

"So is everyone else that matters. It's time for it to come out."

Jeremy let out his breath. "Michael was a hell of an actor. King Arthur in Camelot, Billy Bigelow, he did them all, and not just on stage. He had the world fooled, too. Even the girls."

"He didn't like 'the girls?'"

Jeremy answered only with a shake of his head as he crossed to the window.

"Who knew about it?" Dean pressed.

"No one, except me. No one who knew the 'pretend' Michael. It was as if he led two lives, one down in the city chasing little boys and the other around Spinnersville, big man on campus. I don't want to talk about what he did; there's no undoing it. My mother found out. She'd have periods when she was as perceptive as anyone and other times when she was out of it. God knows how she found out but I guess she confronted him. Crazy, wasn't it? Her big concern was how the old man would take it, nothing about the victims."

"She was going to tell?"

"You'd have to know my mother. Her sense of right and wrong wouldn't have allowed her not to, if she remembered during one of her lucid stages. There wouldn't have been a question."

"What would have Michael's reaction been?"

"He'd have gone bonkers. She wouldn't have understood but he couldn't have lived with it. No way. His reputation, his image, they were everything to him. They were his life."

Fred spoke for the first time. "So she killed him?"

Dean answered, "No. There wasn't any murder, was there?"

It was along time before Jeremy answered, a burden long carried in silence staring him down. Finally he told them.

"Michael killed himself, with his own gun, after she confronted him. It must have shocked her nearly to death; she wouldn't have been capable of understanding his reaction to what she told him she knew. I guess she sat there with his body for an hour or more, trying to figure out what to do, how to save the old man the pain and embarrassment of what his own son was, and what he had done. So she dumped the whole business on me."

They waited for him to continue. "She somehow knew I'd be the first one home. My father was supposed to be off on a business trip. Instead he was probably out balling Miss Dorrie, but Ma was too far gone to even guess that."

Dean spoke softly, asking the question that had to be asked. "She put the second bullet in her son's head?"

Jeremy nodded. "And then she shot herself."

"God," Fred said with a sigh. "What a scene to find."

"Where did Michael get the gun?"

"It was his. He used to cruise some pretty scary parts of Philly looking for fresh young meat. I knew he kept it in a shoe box in the bedroom but nobody else knew it existed."

"What did you do with it... after?"

"Hid it in my car, and later dumped it in the Susquehanna. Pretty risky, I guess. If the cops found it I'd have had a lot of explaining to do."

"Not much chance. You weren't a suspect and they didn't have a search warrant." Dean thought a moment and then asked, "Why did you go along with the whole thing?"

"I never really had time to think about it. I was just doing what I'd been told."

"Who told you?"

"She did."

"Your mother?"

"She laid it all out in a letter, just before she put the gun to her head. She was very specific. It was as if she was as sane as the pope. Make it look like a burglary, hide the gun. Destroy her note," he was nearly in tears, "and shoot her a second time."

"Why would you agree?"

"I was just doing what I was told. I always have, maybe always will."

"There's nobody left to tell you what to do now."

"There's nothing left, period." He let a weak smile cross his face. "God, that makes me sound like some sympathy-begging fool! Look, I did it and that's that. Whitcombs always clean up their own messes. No excuses."

"It sounds like three people treated you like shit and you went the full measure for all of them." Dean didn't know what to add. It was Fred who picked up the conversation.

"Sounds to me like it's time you took a deep breath and looked at the rest of the world and started thinking for yourself."

He laughed. "Oh, I'll manage to find some domineering broad who'll lead me around like a pig to market, loving it every minute, I suppose. Some of us are just born to be led."

219

"I'm surprised you can still keep your sense of humor," Dean answered.

"Maybe that's my escape," Jeremy answered. "What are you going to do now that you know the whole story?"

Dean wasn't sure he could answer. Perhaps he'd feed enough to Hammond, the Spinnersville Police Chief to enable him to close his file and have a little peace of mind. A little bit, not enough to jeopardize Jeremy's future. God knows, the man had suffered enough. After some thought he said, "Don't worry. I won't sell you out."

"Did I do wrong?" In some ways he was still the little boy, looking for the approval he'd never received.

"You were foolish, perhaps naive, certainly more accommodating than anyone should have to be, but wrong? I don't know. I'm not sure I wouldn't have done the same thing, given the circumstances. Love drives a hard bargain."

CHAPTER XIX

After Jeremy Whitcomb left, the house held an aura of silence unknown for the past ten days. Even Fred O'Connor was unusually quiet. Dean expected him to be busting out like a kid in last year's pants with questions and opinions on all that had taken place. Instead, he went to the kitchen and made another pot of coffee without saying a word. Finally the silence got to Dean.

"No questions?"

"Lots. But I'm just digesting a few things, like how much love it must have taken for Jeremy to do what he did. And doing it for a family totally undeserving. Imagine putting a bullet in the head of your dead mother! It makes you wonder."

"Henry, his wife Phyllis, son Michael, what a dysfunctional crew!"

"How did you know," Fred asked as the coffee pot began to bubble, "or were you just fishing?"

"The time sequence didn't fit. If Mrs. Whitcomb was home, and she was supposed to be most of the time, what was she doing for an hour while her son was getting shot? Even if she was out of it often, a gunshot would wake up most people. There was no sign she was restrained in any way and no sign of a struggle. The suggestion any of the others came into the house, put a gun to the heads of two defenseless people and killed them in cold blood somehow didn't fly. The killing was no act of passion; it was too damn cold-blooded. Nor was it a robbery gone bad. What robber couldn't find something of value if he had two hours to search? Besides, the alarm system went a long way toward negating the hold up theory, too.

"The rumor that Hays Crawford might be gay made me wonder if Michael was, too, and somehow that got him in trouble. Remember Atherton's aside that Michael was no angel? That made me think Michael might be the key. I played around with the crime being a vendetta against some nefarious act saintly Michael might have pulled off but that didn't answer the time problem or the mother's death. That left me with suicide or murder-suicide. But there wasn't a gun, and both victims were shot twice. Then I asked myself, who was first on the scene? Son Jeremy. That meant he was either a part of the killing or swept up the scene afterward." Dean smiled with satisfaction.

"Do you think Hays is gay?" Fred asked.

"I don't know. I doubt it. But it really doesn't matter, does it? It's none of our business. End of case."

"Not quite," Fred answered. "Where is the Klaxton turban?"

"Gone. Destroyed would be my guess."

"By who?"

"'Whom'," corrected Dean. "Figure it out. Archer and Jeremy weren't here at the time we learned it was missing; they had gone back east for the day. Hays was off in the hills and in spite of what we originally thought, I doubt he came back to the house. Dorrie might have taken it but she was a big fan of the gizmo. Besides, Henry was going to move her in with him, or so he said. Nattie? That would be a stretch. It's just not her style."

"Mrs. Brown? How?"

"It's only a theory but I think she snuck in the bedroom and took it."

"Where could she have hidden it? We searched the place."

"When I went in the bathroom, the floor was all wet. I assumed it was Henry, pissing and splashing as usual. But it was fresh water, and he'd been unconscious, probably for hours. My guess is Mrs. Brown thought he was asleep and pinched it, and then panicked when she later found him unconscious. The back of the toilet was a quick hiding place. She probably smuggled it out later."

"Damned! That's where they stash the goods in half the detective books I've read! And I didn't even think to look there!"

"Give us credit. We weren't figuring on someone sinking it under water where it might be destroyed. We were looking for safe hiding places. She didn't care if a tank full of water ruined it or not, she just wanted to get rid of the damned thing. She may have even flushed parts of it down the toilet."

Fred looked pensive. "She was the most outspoken about not liking the turban, scared to death someone might take a peek at her past. She seems like a nice enough woman, once you get to know her. I wonder what she's hiding?"

"Probably something you or I would laugh at but Mrs. Brown lives in a very structured world that revolves around appearances. If something should disrupt how the rest of the world sees her she'd be devastated."

"You never were much of a fan of the Klaxton Turban or what it was supposed to do, were you?"

Dean laughed. "No. Nor in tea leaves or fortune-telling, even if they did work. The future's going to come in its own time and on its own terms and the past is dead and gone. It's fine to remember yesterday but there's no benefit in bringing it back. That's one point on which we agree to disagree, I guess."

Fred O'Connor chuckled as he picked up the latest thriller he was reading and absentmindedly flipped the pages. "I'll tell you, son, a part of me wanted the contraption to work. Maybe a bigger part than I'd care to admit. It's a little like Santa Claus. You're hoping and believing but deep down you know the truth. It doesn't stop you from dreaming."

"So how else would you use it, beside smelling home-cooked apple pie? Search out all the great unsolved mysteries of time?"

"Nothing like that," Fred answered. "There's a lot about my life I've never confided to you, son."

"You can say that again! I've never pushed but you've never volunteered either!"

"And never will! Maybe there's a little Mrs. Brown in me on that count. I'd have taken that there Klaxton Turban in my room, locked the door, and taken a little jaunt down memory lane. There's a woman I miss, every day of my life. I can't think of anything more pleasant than sitting back and watching her a spell, seeing her smile again. I didn't have near enough time the first go-around."

"My mother?" Dean asked quietly.

"Let's not get into any mush-mush. We got business to do and plans to make, now that you and me have solved a double killing and have twenty-five-thousand in the bank. What's next?"

What's next? Dean wondered, too. Ten days ago the autumn leaves were bright with color and now the vivid hues were fading, pushed along by the early season snow. Dean's time in Colorado, at least the present stay, was fading also. He rose from the sofa and stretched just as his cat turned the corner, looked at him with soft and curious eyes, and meowed, as if asking the same question.

"Pack your catnip mouse, Mrs. Lincoln," he said reluctantly. "It's time we thought about heading back to Pennsylvania."